THE WIZARD'S MUTT

WereHuman book 4

Gwendolyn Druyor

A Wyrdos Universe Novel

Get your Bonus Wyrdos Book!

Want to know more about the Wyrdos world? Visit my website below and subscribe to get your complimentary copy of *Doug vs. The Boogeyman* and catch a sneak peek of the Wyrdos web series teaser!

Wyrdos.net

Enjoy!
Gwendolyn

CHAPTER 1

I *will find my family.*

Nine-year-old Daniella Corwin stretched her fingers over the keys of the spinet in the front room of Corwin House. One more growth spurt and she'd be able to play an octave. Instead, she tripped through a few scales as she declared her intention for the day. It was the same intention she set every day, the same intention she'd set every morning since her daddy left.

I will find my family.

The notes echoed through the sparsely furnished front room as she turned from the instrument to gather her carrysack from the coat rack. A stool built by some great-grand father or uncle helped her reach Grandmother Misty's sun hat, which lived on top of the pile. The clothes draping the coat rack represented all the generations of Corwins who had lived in this house since it was built in 1675. She was the last.

Speaking the third iteration aloud and pouring all her power into the words, Corwin said, "I will find my family."

A cry sounded outside. Close. Corwin cracked the front door to see what had made it. She had to tug on the door to get it to open.

The Corwins had been Puritans by every outward sign. The house reflected their austerity, down to the cement slab they had where the neighbors had porches. Whichever ancestor had installed it hadn't even bothered to craft a bridge between the cement and the wooden threshold. The cold slab—gray, like everything else—was separated from Corwin House by an inch-wide gap where beetles swam in the rainy season. A deep-blue basket of woven seagrass sat on this stoop. It looked like the sort of basket a family might store firewood in if they didn't have a fireplace with eternal flames.

Edges of a fluffy, baby-blue blanket stuck out of the basket. Deep in the middle of the blanket, she found a dog with his head thrown back and mouth open in a tiny wail. Corwin frowned. She stepped outside and peered around. The neighborhood was as quiet as she would expect at five in the morning. She sighed and crouched beside the basket. The little, fawn-colored fellow crawled over the edge and tumbled into the hammock created by her skirt. Corwin grabbed him up before he fell from her skirt onto the cement.

The dog was a puppy. It clamped its useless gums on Corwin's finger. Despite herself, Corwin smiled.

"Bad dog." She said the words and instantly regretted them. It wasn't nice. The dog was just being a puppy. He didn't know better. "Don't bite. Okay?"

He released her finger and she ran it along the splash of white on one side of his nose and then over his velvety ears with tufts of fur spraying from them like her daddy's crazy eyebrows. He sniffed the scars on her palm as she tried to examine the blue collar that dangled loosely around the three-pound animal's neck. Corwin struggled to avoid the little guy's kisses as she read the heart-shaped tag bumping his chest. *Milo.* No address. No phone number. No rabies tag or city license.

"Who does he belong to?" she asked out loud.

The puppy licked her nose and fell over in her lap. While his topside showed a respectable short, blond coat, Milo's undercarriage was a fluffy mess of multicolored fur. Before she could be seduced by feelings, Corwin set the puppy back in his basket and dragged it inside.

The thing wasn't heavy. It was just too unwieldy for her to lift. Though she grew out of her clothes super quickly and was constantly having to find new ones in the empty bedrooms and crowded basement, Corwin was still only tall enough to reach the middle shelves in the house library and it felt like most of that was legs. She wasn't the most graceful child, as Mr. Dal, the gym teacher said, often. She didn't want to drop the dog, so she dragged the basket, hefted it over the beetle moat and into the house, and then shoved it in the corner by the coat rack.

The dog cried out a silly attempt at a howl when she turned away to rescue Grandmother Misty's hat from where she'd dropped it. She ran a hand over the thick, black braid she'd twisted into a bun at the base of her skull and pulled the hat firmly on her head.

"Let's go, dog." She held her hands out.

The puppy attempted to leap to her. The result was pitiful, thanks to the inadequate launch pad and his utter lack of coordination. She scooped him up instead and headed for the door. "It's okay," she told him. "Grace isn't everything."

Milo snuggled into Corwin's arms as she locked the door and walked down the hard-packed path to the sidewalk. She never saw the blue envelope tucked in the folds of the blanket.

The sun was still low, painting the bay with morning fire, when Corwin reached the Salem Animal Shelter on Hobbomock Street. It was closed. There was a gorilla-sized cage in the front with a sign saying you could leave found strays there. But the cage was in the shade and it was chilly this early in the morning, even in July. Corwin sighed and carried the dog with her as she headed off into the woods.

She filled her sack with the bark and herbs she needed for a particular charm she wanted to perform later as the dog tripped over the busy forest floor in her wake. Corwin liked the forest. She could relax among the trees. There was no risk of running into adults who would ask where her parents were. Occasionally, she would run into other gatherers, but she usually heard them in plenty of time to hide until they had passed by.

Corwin was ten feet up the trunk of a maple when she heard the dog call out a frightened yip. A quick glance showed her nothing but quiet forest. Corwin maneuvered her way back down the tree. Another yip had her scrambling too fast for safety. She called out, "Milo?"

A sudden commotion broke out several yards from her tree. Corwin ran toward the rustling bushes, picking up speed when she heard a bone-jarring roar off in the deeper woods. She burst through a thicket to find a bear cub crouched on its hind legs, clawing between two young maple trees growing close together. The tiny puppy shivered in the clearing beyond, just out of reach.

"Shoo." Corwin stopped the instant she saw the little black bear cub. She did not want to be too close when Mother arrived; and based on the quickly increasing volume of roars, that wouldn't be too long. "Don't you hear your mother calling?"

The cub turned to her so sharply that Corwin tripped backwards and fell on her butt. She cried out. Her voice startled the cub, but not enough to make it run off. Tears sprang to Corwin's eyes. She fought them and the tightness in her chest. Her mother did not approve of tears. It didn't matter that she was hurt and scared.

"Your. . . your mother is coming. If that were my mother, I'd run to her." The thought of her mother wasn't helping with Corwin's tears. She yelled at herself, "You're a Corwin, girl. Behave like it."

She sucked in a stuttering breath and flipped through the pages of her ancestors' spell books in her mind. She'd always focused on how to find things, how to find people. Now, she had to find a way to save herself and the dog before this bear cub's mother found them.

Milo howled.

The cub turned back to him.

Corwin scrambled to her feet, howling louder. She growled and jumped up and down, waving branches in both hands. "Don't you look at him. You look at me. I'm bigger food. I'll keep you full longer."

Food. She had to find food for the cub. There was a lake just north of them. It would be filled with fish. Smelly fish. Corwin glanced down at the branches she'd grabbed off the ground. She picked the one that almost had two handles and a pointer. One of the 'handles' was really just a twig, it even had leaves growing from it, but it was the closest thing she had to a divining rod. She focused her power through the branch and chanted, haltingly, "Water, wet and fishy, too, show me now the way to you."

The wood twitched. Corwin raised her hands and felt the rod pulling north. She couldn't lead the cub to the water. First, she didn't have the time. Second, why would it follow her when it had a tasty, helpless puppy right there?

She focused her intention and muttered a slightly altered line from one of her favorite musical scores, *Into the Woods*. "Go to the fish!"

The malformed rod flew from her hands. It tore through the air in a straight line until a tree loomed in its way. The branch swerved erratically and continued on.

The bear cub perked up and tore after the divining rod, making enough noise to wake the dead, a dangerous prospect in Salem, Massachusetts.

I won, she thought. Her magic had saved them. Corwin dropped to her knees and buried her face in her hands. The danger was gone, but she was shaking. She stared at her hands. They were trembling. The puppy attempted to howl again and his cry twisted at the end in a strange note. Corwin looked up.

And up.

There, not five yards away, stood a nine-foot-tall bear. Its fur was a gorgeous, fluffy mix of deep browns. The dark tufts around its face flared out like the fan thingies on the scary dinosaurs in that movie daddy liked. It had two puffballs for ears and white claws that could rip her throat out in one swipe.

Corwin sucked in a breath but her mind had frozen. She couldn't think of one spell to get her out of this. The only thing that came out of her mouth was a hopeless cry for help. "Daddy!"

CHAPTER 2

Mother and Daddy were gone. They couldn't save her. She had to get herself out of these woods. Only, she couldn't even breathe. Corwin's heart had leapt into her throat and was trying to strangle her. The puppy had no such problem. It wailed, the sound echoing through the forest, calling all predators.

The pitiful sound called to Corwin. She was just a kid, too. She wanted to wail. But her parents were counting on her. It was up to Corwin to find the family's lost power and deliver it to her daddy so that he could find her mother and they could all be together again like a real family.

Step one, she had to survive this bear.

A frog or a toad, she didn't know the difference, hopped out of the leaves onto the big brown bear's foot. The bear looked away from Milo and down at the amphibian. Corwin's head filled with a song her daddy used to mumble to himself, way back when he still sang.

El grillo. El grillo è buon cantore.

With the song came courage. Corwin took advantage of the bear's momentary distraction. She raced around the pair of young maples to scoop up the puppy, stuck him in the front pocket of her collection bag, and ran. Her breathing deafened her. All she could hear was the racket she was making. She peeked back as she approached a tree that she could climb to see if she needed to climb it, but the bear was not chasing her. She didn't see the huge brown bear anywhere.

The mama bear was still calling for her cub but her cries were fading. Still, Corwin allowed herself only a moment to catch her breath and then she kept going, trekking as fast as she could to the nearest edge of the woods. When she emerged behind Goody Talmadge's Bed and Breakfast, she turned and peered back into the forest, looking and listening as best she could, despite the wash of exhaustion blurring her vision and the sound of her heart pounding in her ears.

When it was pretty clear that no bears were on her tail, she dropped to her knees and pulled Milo from her bag. She struggled to catch her breath. The puppy licked her face and hands while Corwin turned it over and over, looking for any injuries. She didn't find any and hugged the little thing, crying with relief.

The instant a tear fell on the puppy's head, Corwin's stomach twisted in disgust. She was crying. Over a dog. A dog that had distracted her when she should have been focused on collecting the ingredients she needed to follow her daddy's orders. Her face was wet and probably red. Anyone looking out the windows of the bed and breakfast would see her and wonder about the sad little girl all alone at the edge of the woods. Mr. Talmadge might call the police. The police would demand to speak with Corwin's parents. And then Corwin would be thrown into foster care and she'd never become a great wizard and get her family back together. All because of a stupid dog.

Corwin ducked back into the cover of the woods. She stayed in the forest's shade as long as she could and then hurried through the streets back to the Salem Animal Shelter. The sun was up. It should be open, and if it wasn't, she would just leave the dog in the cage out front.

Corwin hurried to Hobbomock street. She held her breath as she passed Drakes Woods Cemetery. When she was a gullible little girl, her daddy had told her if she didn't hold her breath, the dead of Salem would steal her magic. When she was older and knew more, she'd asked how the dead could steal her magic if all the Corwin magic had been hidden. He'd tickled her instead of answering.

Corwin approached the center of the three buildings that made up the shelter. She pulled on the door. It was locked. She turned to the bear cage and shivered. She had thought it was enormous, but now she knew it would barely contain the brown bear she'd just escaped. She didn't like the thought of leaving a tiny puppy in that cage.

A tall, broad-shouldered man approached from the path that wrapped around the buildings. His massive chest heaved as if he, too, had been running. It made the tutu-ed rhinoceros on his shirt dance. His dyed-blond hair and dark brown beard flared in the wind as he waved at her. "*Dobry den.*"

Corwin kept her eyes down. "Hi. This dog—"

The man held out his hand as he reached her. Corwin shook it, because that was what you did with older people who didn't know how to fist bump. She looked down at his hand in shock. It felt oddly rough and looked furry for a moment. It was too blurry to be sure. Corwin let her Sight take over but didn't see the glitter of any magic. She must have been confused.

"I am Jack Jaga," the man said, in a gruff, but not unkind, voice. He had an accent, which explained his strange greeting. She was glad he spoke English. "And you are?"

Corwin paused for a moment. She was always careful about giving her name. The people of Salem didn't like her name. They didn't like her family. Most of them were either mean or dismissive. There was something friendly about Jack Jaga and Corwin didn't want that to go away. She wanted him to like her.

Which was something Coogans wanted, not Corwins. The Coogans were the popular coven. They sucked up to people and pretended to be charming. They wanted people to like them. Her mother would be ashamed of her for thinking like a Coogan. She held the puppy out in front of her. "I'm Corwin. This dog was left on my porch."

The man looked away from unlocking the door to give her a once-over, but his smile didn't fade. He stuck one finger under the tag on the dog's too-big collar and said, "Come on in, Corwin. Let's see if Milo has a chip to go with this very nice collar."

"Do I have to?" Corwin asked, automatically walking into the building at his gesture. "Can't you just take him?"

"Well, if he doesn't have a chip, you could keep him." The door jangled shut. Jack Jaga hustled behind the wide counter.

Corwin followed. "I don't have time for a dog. I'm starting fifth grade next month."

He grinned at that. "Fifth grade does take a lot of work. But that makes you, what, ten years old?"

He disappeared around a wall and returned holding a silver instrument with a circle at one end which he set on the counter. He leaned beside it, raising a wildly bushy eyebrow at her.

Corwin nodded as she lifted Milo up onto the counter. She had just turned nine on the fourth. There were fireworks.

"An important age. And you are a Corwin, so you'll have lessons this fellow can help with." He leaned over the dog to say quietly, "It is healthy for a *Skilled* kid to have a pet."

Corwin's heart beat faster. He'd used the secret lingo of Salem's witches. He meant a magical kid should have a familiar. This stranger had pegged her as a witch. She glanced toward the door, wanting to run. It wasn't a stretch. Most people in Salem would be familiar with the Corwin name, if only because of Great-great-great-great-grandfather Jonathan. She tried to keep her voice level. "My family doesn't keep pets."

"Oh, I am aware, young Corwin. But the reality is, in this world, you should gleefully accept any offering of true love, no matter who your family is." He sighed and finally waved the strange instrument over Milo. "This is my microchip scanner. It will help us find this little boy's family. You can think of it as my wand." Jack Jaga winked and then waved the wand over Milo again. "*Dziwaczny*. How strange."

He held the scanner out so that she could see as he read, "Milo Hu. But there is no code, no contact information." He turned the face of the wand to the dog, who tapped it with his nose. "I will make some calls. If you leave your number, I'll call you if I don't find his family."

Corwin shook her head. "We don't have a phone."

"You can put your name down, come back with your parents later."

Of course, she couldn't do that. "No, thank you."

She shot one last glance at the puppy. The little thing nearly disappeared in Jack Jaga's massive hand. His black eyes stared at her. She imagined his tiny puppy voice in her head saying, *Take me home.* Silliness.

She had just reached the door when Jack Jaga said, "You know..."

She turned to find him leaning against the counter, the puppy cuddled against his "Save the Fat Unicorns" t-shirt. "...Kat Coogan refused to take a pet in her day. Very Corwin of her, everyone said."

The name pricked Corwin's hackles. The last person she wanted to be compared to was Katherine Coogan. She drew herself up and pushed out of the door without another word. She had things to do, spells to learn. It was getting late, and she still needed wolf skull bones.

———

CORWIN WAS TOO small and not nearly powerful enough to hunt on her own. She had to buy the fauna elements of her potions and spells. Salem being the village it was, the butcher stocked items which would be considered unusual anywhere else and he was a particularly discreet man. As was the bookseller the tourists rarely found, and the candlemaker who used energy captured from tourists in her various waxes and so encouraged their patronage. Corwin made her own candles and rarely needed books that weren't already in the extensive library in her 350-year-old home. But she knew Kali the butcher pretty well.

Kali only had one other customer. Mr. York, whose son Levi was in her grade at school, was picking through items on the shelf along one side of the shop. Corwin looked between him and Kali uncertainly.

"What can I do for you, young Corwin?"

Kali had never once called her Daniella since she had told him she'd like to be called Corwin. He never questioned her or tried to convince her Daniella was a pretty name, like the teachers at school. Kali was nice.

Even though the Yorks were a Skilled family, Corwin still kept her voice quiet as she asked for the wolf skull powder. When Kali brought it out from the back, she asked for a cut of whitefish for dinner, too. He gave her enough for three. It was okay. She was used to having the same meal several days in a row.

"On your father's tab?" Kali asked, more loudly than necessary.

"Yes, sir." She wondered why he was asking. She always put it on the tab. "If that's okay?"

"Of course it is. Thank your father for paying his tab like a responsible citizen," Kali said, in a voice intended to carry through the small shop.

Corwin glanced over her shoulder as Mr. York snorted. He kept his eyes down on the box of Panko.

Kali went on. "Not everyone is so conscientious. I always say: Corwins may be different, but their money comes on time."

Mr. York set the breadcrumbs back on the shelf and shot Corwin a tight smile as he headed for the door.

Corwin looked back to Kali as the bells over the door jangled. "Thank you. I'll tell my father."

"And you, my dear, you are a good girl for helping out your busy parents." He flipped the shop-padd around so she could sign the tab with her finger.

"Yes, sir."

"But your puppy is a bad dog. He'll bring the health inspector down on me."

Corwin turned to see Milo sitting in the middle of the shop, his tail thumping on the slick floor. "That's not my dog."

"No?" Kali looked around as if there were anyone else but the two of them in the place. "Oh dear, well, I can't leave the shop unattended. Here." He opened a lacquered wooden box on the counter and fished out a small packet of black powder. "Powdered owl beak, for natural wisdom. I assume that's what your mother is using the wolf skull for. I'll give you this if you'll take that over to Jack Jaga."

Corwin sighed. Powdered owl beak was rare and she would never have spent the money it cost.

"Your mother will appreciate this."

Corwin nodded. "She will. Thank you." She put the packet away in the pocket that had held Milo on their race out of the forest and then scooped her purchases from the counter.

She piled the dog on top of the carefully wrapped packages as Kali came out from behind the counter to open the door for her. As she made her way through town, Milo licked her face. Folks laughed at him and looked her over. Corwin felt an unfamiliar tingle in her gut at the kisses. But ice ran down her spine at the looks. She dropped the dog off with Jack and held her purchases close, keeping her head down. Nobody looked at her without Milo. She safely watched the groups of people out together, laughing and sharing the beauty of the afternoon. Everyone seemed happy. She turned her eyes to the sidewalk, watching her feet kick weeds with her mother's too-big boots.

Chapter 3

"Want a ride?" Morgan Coogan hopscotched up the walkway beside the middle school band room. Her violin case bounced against her back in sync with her uneven braids. It crushed the poofy sleeve of her Dorothy costume.

Corwin wasn't wearing a costume, though that hadn't stopped teachers from complimenting her on wearing a costume respecting the town's history. She got so many comments she eventually put her daddy's old gray-and-scarlet sweatshirt on to hide at least the top half of the dress she'd pulled from some dusty closet.

Kids were roughhousing and chattering with each other like jaybirds fighting over a mourning dove's nest as their parents inched along the circular drive to pick them up. Morgan was twelve, a year older than Corwin, even though they were in the same grade. She was also a Coogan. Corwin shook her head. She hitched the strap of her oboe case higher on her shoulder, tucking it under her backpack strap, even though it never stayed there.

"Okay." Morgan chewed on her lip and looked over at the line of cars before she peeked at Corwin again from under her long lashes. Her green eyes sparkled against the color that rose in her dark cheeks. "You're

really good, you know. I sound like a screeching cat most of the time."
She laughed.

Corwin felt her own pale cheeks glowing with heat. She offered a
little shrug. What was she supposed to do? She looked away in the direction she'd been heading. She had a long walk home. The sun was already
going down. She shouldn't have been wasting time performing in the
Halloween concert. Daddy would be mad if he tried to call and she
wasn't home.

She looked back. Morgan was still standing there.

Corwin felt her cheeks flex in a smile. She stopped it and said, "I
have to go." She hurried away around the side of the building. Even
those few words felt like a betrayal of her family. She'd smiled at a
Coogan.

"Happy Samhain!" Morgan called after her. Corwin pretended she
hadn't heard.

The chatter of the other kids faded as Corwin crossed the athletic
field. Their covens would be getting together for Samhain feasts after
trick-or-treating. School was canceled tomorrow, since most kids would
be too tired to pay attention anyway. It meant she could study all night.
Her family had always celebrated privately. She wasn't missing out on
anything.

Corwin kept her eyes on the artificial turf beneath her boots and
stepped over the white-painted bits as if they were cracks. Didn't want
to break her mother's back. Not that she would know if her mother's
back broke. She was no closer to finding her mother than she had been
the day her father ordered her to. Playing in the band wasn't getting her
any closer. She should be home, studying. Although, music came so
easily, it wasn't like she had to waste much time practicing. And making
up little tunes helped her memorize the long lists of herbs and what they
were used for, as well as all the other arcane knowledge she had to learn
before she could even begin to understand the finding charms, spells,
potions, and curses.

A flash of magic pulled her from her excuses. She looked around,
unsure where it had come from. Nobody was supposed to do magic so
openly, even on Samhain. Black sparkles glittered between the benches

of the opposing team's bleachers. Corwin picked up speed and detoured in that direction.

Nobody practiced such crude magic in public. Not that most people would be able to see if they did. Corwin had always been able to see the sparkle of magic. Her daddy said it was her gift. As a baby, she'd tried to grab on to the sparkles the way other infants chased bubbles.

Another spray of magic, dirty yellow this time, filtered out through the seats along with young voices. There was more than one person attempting magic under the bleachers. It was weak, but that didn't mean it was harmless. Corwin dropped her bookbag on the bleachers, making them rattle and shake noisily, hoping that would scare the kids off. She set her oboe more carefully beside it, using the action to subtly peer between the benches.

A trio of bullies stood in a semi-circle, holding wands they were definitely not old enough to have. Corwin recognized the kids from school. They were all in the upper grades but there was no way any of them had been confirmed by the Council yet. They must have stolen the wands. Like most of the kids in her small school, these three were from Skilled families and thought they were Skilled. But they hadn't been practicing every free minute since they turned five, like Corwin had. The wands were sparking back at them with each weak curse of pain they tried to shoot at whatever they were facing.

Corwin slid her oboe aside to see what they were trying to hurt. Goosebumps rose on her skin when she saw the tiny, fawn-colored dog facing down the bullies. His tail stood stiff and straight behind him, the culmination of the raised hackles that started at the nape of his neck and ran down his entire spine. With all four paws planted solidly in the dirt, Milo was growling and not giving an inch. The kids were bullying an eight-pound puppy.

Jack Jaga had gotten Milo adopted very quickly after Corwin returned him from the butcher's shop two years ago. He'd gotten him adopted again after that family returned the dog. There wasn't anything wrong with Milo. He was a good dog. He just had a habit of running away and showing up on Corwin's doorstep or outside the Music Shoppe or at the edge of the forest. His tail wagged joyously whenever he saw her. His tail wagged even when she called him a bad dog and hauled him back to the animal shelter. Milo's tail wagged no matter what she said to him.

It wasn't wagging now.

"Stop it, Davy." A blond girl in a Sailor Moon costume held a hand to her face, hiding it from Milo. "We're gonna get caught."

Davy wore a clown costume with blood painted onto a corner of his mouth. "I just want to know who's riding the mutt, Colleen."

"By hurting the dog?"

Corwin couldn't see this boy. His voice was distorted as if he were wearing a retainer.

"Who cares about the dog? I want to send a message to whoever's riding it." Davy shot another spray of weak magic at Milo.

"Yeah, that's how we'll get caught." Colleen rolled her eyes.

"Chill, Colleen." The retainer kid tried to shoot magic out of his wand. When nothing happened, he flung yellow magic at Milo using his hand.

Milo yelped. The kid ignored him. "They've already seen us and they're not doing anything. It's got to be a kid."

"Yeah," Davy added. "No real witch would have a puppy for a familiar."

They knew he was a puppy and they were still trying to hurt him. Corwin growled, deep in her throat. She looked at Milo. He stood solid, refusing to back down or run away, as if he was deliberately defying them. He looked intelligent, like a possessed familiar would. But, thanks to her gift, Corwin could see the dog had no tell-tale glow around him as he would if he were being ridden.

She sighed and pulled the hood of her father's old school sweatshirt up over her head. She trudged around the side of the bleachers, chanting, "Fire burn and cauldron bubble" to focus her power as she reached into the past. Bonfires had been set on this land back during the Witch Trials. She pulled sparks from those fires and sent them flying over Milo's head at the bullies who, lacking her Sight, could not see the danger they were in. The power of ancient witches hit them. They didn't catch fire. They didn't burn. The sparks Corwin sent at them hurt them psychically, attacking the source of their Skill as the burning witches had attacked their accusers, according to her ancestors' journals.

Colleen was the first to go. She backed away, half-laughing as she hid the stolen wand behind her. "I gotta go. Can't be late for dinner."

A boy in a drooping skeleton costume strolled after her. He twirled his wand at Corwin, but it didn't even dribble magic. He tugged at the third kid's sleeve. "Come on, Davy. Let the baby wizard have her mutt."

"She doesn't scare me."

Colleen called back, "Don't mess with her. The Corwins are evil. It's probably her crazy mother riding that mutt."

A look of fear loosened the muscles of Davy's sneer. He flicked the wand at Corwin. Black sparkles streamed out of the tip. They might have reached Milo if Corwin hadn't raised her voice and pulled another spark from the past. The ancient flame seared Davy's magic and followed it upstream to the wand, through the wand, and into his arm. The boy's mouth dropped open. He felt her spell that time. The wand dropped from his hand tip-first, so it buried into the soft dirt and stuck up at an angle, vibrating with the pounding of Davy's feet as he ran after his friends.

Corwin looked down at her chest. "CORWIN Class of '94" was printed across the front of the sweatshirt. She waited until she was sure the bullies wouldn't circle back before she bent to check on Milo. The dog's tail wasn't wagging. He still stood as solid as a statue. She removed the hood so he could see her face, but the dog did not relax. She rubbed a hand along his hackles to settle them. The hair on her arm stood up and an angry energy shot through her entire body. She snatched her hand away and turned to face another attack of weak magic. But Davy, Colleen, and their friend were long gone, racing across the far parking lot.

Milo barked. She looked down to find her skirts in his teeth.

"What is it?"

The dog released her and ran away toward the field, stopping at the edge of the bleacher frame to see if she was following. She was. As soon as she cleared the framework, she saw them.

A wave of rotting spirits surged over the athletic field. They were so strong, they smudged the carefully painted white lines in their wake. Spirits weren't corporeal. She shouldn't have had to cover her nose with her sleeve to block the horrid stench. Spirits shouldn't rot, either.

Corpses rotted. Spirits retained their form at death or the image they had of themself when they didn't look in a mirror. These spirits appeared as zombies risen from the grave — flesh dripping off bones, eyes sunken in skeletal faces.

Corwin froze. She flexed her left hand as her old scars pulsed with unexpected pain.

These spirits were unhappy ghosts, ghosts who were punishing themselves, who had, from the style of their clothes, been punishing themselves for a very long time. They were heading straight for the spot on the bleachers where she'd dropped her backpack and Aunt Nell's oboe.

Milo barked. Corwin followed him away from the mob of angry ectoplasm, scanning the area for any place of refuge.

Milo dashed around a wide Red Maple tree with roots pushing out of the earth and a thick canopy of leaves stretching overhead. Corwin followed and turned sideways to hide her whole body.

It didn't work. The spirits detoured from her belongings to waft like a dark fog directly at Corwin. There was nowhere else for her to go. Corwin laid her hands on the trunk. She reached out with her senses and felt the power of the ancient tree, which had likely stood here when these spirits had lived.

Her improvised words fell into the rhythm of a song the band had just played in the concert and she found herself singing the spell. "This is Halloween. Please shield Milo and me. Shield us from the dead that come, with life you store inside your leaves."

A faint glow, tinged amber and yellow, arced from the leaves overhead to those already fallen. The first of the spirits hit this shield and stopped. Up close, Corwin could see the spirits were mostly working men. They wore the clothes of their trades, though those clothes were tattered and burned. Many had twigs and sticks piercing their bodies. Others' skulls had been caved in. These people had died violently. They had all been killed.

And they all wanted to kill Corwin.

A living figure followed the fog of dead. Corwin struggled to look through the filmy ghosts. What human would want her dead? She only had one enemy and Kat Coogan hadn't been seen in Salem in seven years. The delicate woman brushed a lock of her dirty blond hair out of her eyes as she hurried across the athletic field, avoiding those spots where the ghosts had disturbed the AstroTurf. She wore what Corwin's Daddy would call hippie hiker gear, though that felt wrong to Corwin. Everything about the woman seemed wrong. Corwin's vision went blurry in a way that couldn't be explained by the ghosts, and her head ached. She leaned around the tree as if two inches closer would help her see the stranger better. The ghosts launched themselves at the barrier. Blood flew from their wounds and splatted against the protection in a way that shouldn't be possible with ghostly manifestations. Whoever the woman was, she was strong and she knew how to use her magic. Corwin ducked back behind the tree. She should use her own magic. There was nobody else around. And, if anyone saw, it was a tit-for-tat situation.

She took a breath and peered out again. The ghosts went ballistic, but Corwin focused her attention on the approaching witch and unfocused her rational gaze. She looked with her Sight and she saw.

The woman was wearing a glamour. She had used magic to change her appearance. The stranger was not blond, not wearing hiking boots, not delicate, and not a stranger. The witch driving the ghosts to kill her stood tall, with broad shoulders, longish black curls, and freckles. The woman was Kat Coogan.

A memory stabbed through Corwin so hard she lost her balance. Her head slammed against the tree as she fell to her knees.

CHAPTER 4

The hardwood floor echoed beneath Corwin's head as she banged it along the floorboards under the spinet. Mother had tucked her under the instrument after returning home and changing out of her muddy, messy clothes. Mother had never been muddy before. Corwin loved mud. Daddy took her with him when he wandered the forest and let her crawl through mud after the white flowers that grew in the swampy parts of the woods. Mother had left her at home and Daddy was at work, so Corwin had been lonely. Now, Mother was home and smelled like the lavender soap Daddy made just for her and Corwin got to play in the same room where Mother was working.

The toddler lay spread-eagle, feeling her limbs grow cold one by one as Mother draped each window with the heavy fabric that would isolate Corwin House from Salem's Samhain traditions.

"There will be no testing of my powers," she'd told Corwin as she brushed her long hair. "We don't require any council's approval." She'd grinned at Corwin as she lifted the little girl and her blankie out of the rocker and carried her downstairs to set her under the spinet. "Not that we'll have to worry about the Coogans anymore, in any case."

Then she'd set to work, muttering spells as she hung the holy day curtains.

Corwin bounced her head from the remaining patch of sunlight across the hollow spot to the darkness and back again, giggling at the drum built into their front room floor. A harsh knock at the door echoed the thumping of Corwin's head.

Mother didn't notice. She was standing on an old ladder-back chair by the far window when the door flew open and smashed gashes in the gray brocade wallpaper.

Corwin sat up.

A tall woman filled the doorway with her broad shoulders, freckles intermingled with blood and soot on her face; black curls lay matted against her skull. Her clothes were muddy and Corwin would have been yelled at for how torn they were. Great swaths of burns covered her exposed skin. Her chest heaved with the effort of breathing and her aura pulsed deep into the house, casting everything in a golden light that Corwin knew was magical even though it didn't sparkle.

Mother stepped down from her chair. She let the curtain slump to the floor, her voice thick and low like when she was mad at Daddy. "You were dead."

"Two things you should know, Sita." The woman paused to wipe away the blood that was about to drip into her eye. "You can't burn a witch in our coven. Also, a Corwin can't kill a Coogan."

"So, you're here to kill me, Katherine?" Mother laughed, but it was short and sent shivers up Corwin's spine.

Katherine didn't reply immediately. She was watching something over her shoulder, outside. She didn't bother looking at Corwin's mother when she said, "A Coogan can't kill a Corwin, either. You should do more homework before you pick a mark, Sita."

"I did my homework, Kat. Your brother was the one tasked with protecting the Corwins. He can't do that now, can he?" Mother smiled at Corwin and moved toward her, though she turned her gaze back to Kat Coogan in the doorway. "Can't blame me, though. You just said a Corwin can't kill a Coogan, right?"

Sita froze when the burned woman turned her attention away from the street. Kat spoke through gritted teeth. "The cancer killed Archie. The cancer you gave him."

Kat checked over her shoulder again and Sita rushed to the spinet.

Corwin stood and raised her arms to be picked up. Tears poured down her cheeks at the fearful image and smell of Kat Coogan and the scary conversation.

Her mother hissed, "Don't cry."

The bloody, burnt, scary Coogan woman's gaze shot back to Sita. "Don't touch her."

Mother stopped.

"The vow is written thus," Kat Coogan hissed. "The eldest of each generation shall watch over the eldest of the next. Since Archie is gone, I am now the eldest and you will not—"

Mother reached for Corwin. Before Corwin could leap into her arms, Kat Coogan flew over the protected threshold and slammed into Mother. The two rolled across the floor until they hit the daybed in the center of the front room. The green-gray couch toppled. Sita scrambled over it and spun to spread her fingers wide, one palm aimed at Kat Coogan, the other at Corwin.

Corwin felt a tug in her chest. She toddled a few steps towards the women until a warm, tingly shower of golden sparkles fell over her, separating her from her mother.

Kat Coogan turned away and flicked a few fingers in Mother's direction. The golden magic wrapped Sita's wrists and drew them together for just an instant before red burned the gold into mist.

Mother leapt over the toppled daybed and physically shoved Kat. A wash of red kept the witch sliding backwards into the ladder-back chair. Magical ropes slithered out of the wood like vines, not just encircling Kat's limbs and neck, but piercing them.

Then Kat knelt forward and the chair flew through the air after Sita, who was making a break for the kitchen.

With a wave, Mother sent the chair and its flailing red vines soaring back into Kat's face.

The Coogan witch hit the threshold of the open door as though it were a cement wall. She rebounded forward, barely missing the spinet and Corwin. With a groan, she hauled herself to her knees and then to her feet.

Corwin followed as Kat dragged the chair through the front room and off into the kitchen. Ceramic plates and iron skillets that had hung on the kitchen walls for Corwin's entire life flew through the open doorway with blasts of red and gold magic. Corwin ducked down, covering her head with her blankie. Her mouth hung open in a sob she refused to give voice to. Her mother had told her not to cry. Soon, she found her courage and toddled through the doorway to help her mother against this Coogan witch.

The kitchen was destroyed. The pantry door had been torn from its hinges. Food and flatware and dishes littered the floor and counters. The pile of pillows Corwin sat on at the table had been shredded. Fluff filled the air like a dandelion field in summer. Mother hovered near the sink, which dripped red with blood. Her feet floated off the ground, supported by nothing other than an aura glowing red and extending out from her body in a nearly physical bubble. At her gestures, knives leapt from the drawer and flew at Kat Coogan, who only managed to avoid about half of the blades. She had knives sticking out of one shoulder, both thighs, and her chest.

Suddenly, the pump handle spun from the sink, dropping into the belly of the kitchen table, which had been flipped over. Water arced upwards and drenched Mother, pressuring her back to the floor and then down onto her back. Corwin ran to help her up as Kat Coogan swept the ladder-back chair into the air.

"Do you yield?" Kat Coogan glowed with rage.

The ancient iron grate that kept sparks from the fire from leaping out onto the wooden floor pivoted out and blocked Corwin's path. She tried to move around it, but the iron curled and gently pushed her back, away from the battling witches, preventing her from helping her mother. Corwin dropped her blankie. She wrapped her tiny fingers around the metal and yelled out words like Daddy did when they got stuck in a bramble and he wanted the plants to move out of the way. The grate didn't budge.

"Do you yield?" Kat Coogan cried again.

Sita Corwin rolled to her side, unable to sit up against the force of the water. She coughed and then vomited blood into the pool rising around her. "Never, Coogan." She spat the words with more blood and then grinned up at the other witch. "I've already won."

She slid under the stream and leapt over the iron grate to kneel beside Corwin on the hot stones of the hearth. Her mother held her close and Corwin felt safe again.

The stranger, Kat Coogan, froze. Gold glittered prettily from her fingers, held still in the air. Her voice was distorted by missing teeth and a broken jaw, as well as the bruises around her neck. "Sita, don't."

The grate stood in front of them, protecting Corwin and her mother from the witch. But the fire behind them licked at Corwin's back. It was very warm. She clung to her mother as Sita lifted her off her feet. The vibrations of her mother's soothing voice cuddled Corwin and calmed her.

In a blink, Corwin was on the stones as Kat Coogan dragged Sita back over the grate with magic alone. Then the pretty golden sparkles sputtered out and Mother fell to her knees. Kat grabbed the rod-backed chair that had sat by the front door for centuries.

Mother snagged a knife that had been standing with the blade buried in the pantry door. She dove for Kat's back.

Impossibly, the stranger witch spun around and smashed their antique rod-backed chair down on Mother's head, knocking her unconscious.

Corwin cried out now that Mother couldn't hear her. She shouted in her mind, but she was too scared to find words. She let tears pour down her face and shook the bars of her little prison as she cradled her left hand against her heart.

But the Coogan wasn't done. The knives that had stuck in the floor and the walls and the broken furniture began soaring up to the ceiling. They rained down, stabbing into the floor around her mother. The knives buried in Kat Coogan's body yanked themselves out, making the woman cry aloud, and they, too, joined the blades outlining Mother's body.

Corwin's vision, practical and magical, washed away in a flood of white as she screamed and cried for her mother. When it cleared, Kat Coogan was picking her way around Corwin's trapped mother. She peered through the iron grating that would not let her get closer to Corwin. Breathing as though she'd forgotten how, the witch held onto the grate to keep from falling over. Her eyes glowed golden out of a bloody, misshapen face.

Corwin backed away from the monster as far as she could go. She huddled against the now-cold stone of the hearth.

Red flooded Kat Coogan's pupils as she turned away, crawling to kneel at the edge of the knife circle.

"Go, Sita Corwin," she said, sucking in air like she didn't have enough room in her throat. "You are banished from Salem."

Without waiting for any response, Kat Coogan dragged herself to the kitchen door and stumbled out.

Corwin had watched as her mother had reached for the open door and pulled energy from the young elms Daddy had planted along the kitchen path. Mother healed herself and rose from the floor. She collected some of the antique decorations from where they lay strewn about, then left the kitchen, returning later carrying a pair of stuffed bags. She crouched at the iron grating.

Corwin held out her burned hand, but Mother didn't touch her.

"Mother has to go now, little Corwin. Never forget I made you a Corwin. You don't belong here. But, if you work very hard and search every inch of this house — if you find the heart of their power, you might yet become a powerful witch and a worthy daughter." She ran her fingers through the lush hair that Corwin longed to touch and picked her way through the mess of the kitchen. She opened the door and then turned back, letting her eyes rest on Corwin for a moment. "Kat Coogan wants to kill you. Survive, find the heart, and I will come back to you."

That was the last time Corwin had seen her mother.

"Ahwoooo!"

Milo's howl dragged Corwin out of the past. He alternated between his vastly improved howling and licking her face until she opened her eyes. Dry leaves drifted over them from quaking branches. She pushed herself upright, one hand going to the bloody lump on her forehead. Despite her pain and confusion, the magical barrier she had begged from the tree held. She pushed a thought of thank you against the tree with her scarred palm and turned to face the dozen ghosts whose trailing black auras made them look like an army. The barrier sparked each time one of them threw themselves at it. The tree shook from their efforts and more leaves fell, the new death a contrast to the ancient death confronting her.

Corwin picked one up. Her head spun and she leaned against the trunk as she stood with a brilliant red leaf in her hand. Did the leaf mind that it had died? Would it be missed? She looked up as the shadow of a young man in dockworker clothes punched the barrier. Corwin barely kept herself from cringing at the sight of his face. Kat Coogan's sloughing cheeks and red eyes flashed into her memory again. This man had been burned, too. Corwin kept her eyes on him. In her peripheral vision, she could see Kat Coogan standing on the bleachers, watching, waiting for Corwin to fail and be destroyed at long last.

A woman in the back of the crowd flung something at the barrier. The carving knife sailed through the shimmering wall and sank into the maple. Corwin had to do something or she and the dog would die. Her mother would be shamed if Corwin let Kat Coogan win.

She was a Corwin. Her mother had made her a Corwin.

She dove out from behind the trunk before her courage failed her.

"I'm Corwin," she said to the dead man who had punched at her. "What's your name?"

The dockworker had pulled his foot back to aim a kick at the barrier. He stopped. His face dropped its snarl and his eyes locked on hers. "Henry."

She heard his voice more in her head than in her ears. It scraped against her nerves but she kept her tone even. "Hi, Henry. Did I wake you up?"

"I just came to see the witch burn. You're the witch, right?" The dockworker tilted his head and, instead of swaying, the dangling bits of flensed skin healed.

Another ghost slammed a palm against the barrier and leaned in to scoff at Henry. "She's not the witch we tried to burn. She's just a kid."

Corwin stumbled back and searched for a response. "I'm eleven. The Council doesn't call us witches until we pass their tests. But I'm a Corwin," she added. "So, I'd be called a wizard."

"Why?" The dockworker laughed. His body and clothes had healed, as well. He was a handsome young man.

She shook her head again and shrugged. "I don't know."

The ghost leaning on the barrier sneered. "That's so Jonathan Corwin doesn't feel so bad hanging witches."

"What's your name?" Corwin asked the new guy. She couldn't keep her eyes on his destroyed face. Her gaze kept slipping to the horror of the burning stick piercing his neck. Instead, she placed her small hand against his on the barrier. "I'm Corwin."

The man's gaze shot from Henry to her hand and she felt her scars burning, but then the sensation disappeared and his expression softened.

"I know the Corwins," he said. "A real mixed bag, you lot. I'm Samuel." He took his hand away and flexed it, watching the burns heal and the skin firm up. His clothes straightened and she could see that he was wearing an apron with carpentry gear sticking out of the pockets.

"Hey, Samuel, I have to lift my door to get it to close," she said. "I want to shave some of the door away so it'll fit in the frame again. How do I do that?"

"Are you touched, girl? Tighten the hinges. Peter, what does she do if the hinges are coming out of the frame?" He grabbed a young boy out of the crowd by the back of his collar.

Corwin smiled at the boy's startled face. This ghost wasn't burnt. He'd hit his head pretty hard on something. Or, she realized, something had hit his head pretty hard. "Hi, Peter."

Corwin talked with the ghosts. She learned how to fix her door and that Samuel had built the stake and bonfire to keep his wife off of them. He felt badly about it, all the same. She learned most of the ghosts had just come for the entertainment. They never imagined the judge would go through with the sentence. They really never imagined the witch would turn the fire around on them. Corwin didn't get all of their names. Some of the ghosts dissipated as the mob anger subsided, some as the sun went down. Most of them just wanted to yell at her for killing them even though they'd just come to watch.

The woman who had thrown the knife screamed over and over, "I didn't set the fire!" She pounded on the barrier with a sharp, hooked tool. It slipped through and Corwin plastered her back to the tree to avoid being hit.

"I'm sorry," Corwin apologized. It wasn't her fault. She couldn't blame the witch who had been tied at the stake, but she said she was sorry until she meant it. The witch might have been condemned by Corwin's great-great-great-great-grandfather Jonathan, after all. She took her family's responsibility on herself and sincerely asked the ghost's forgiveness.

The ghost did not give her any. She screamed and railed and stabbed at Corwin until her semi-corporeal form burned up and floated away as ash.

"I'm really sorry." She turned to the ones who had named themselves and found them blowing away on the wind.

Young Peter yelled, "Bye, Corwin!" And then they were gone.

Corwin collapsed. The barrier collapsed with her. She'd sacrificed every bit of her energy to hear the ghosts. She had left herself nothing. She wasn't powerful enough to be her mother's daughter and deserved whatever revenge Kat Coogan delivered.

But the witch never came. Corwin lay in the darkness, half her face in the cold grass, half her face wet with dog saliva. A little voice in her head urged her to get up, but she couldn't. Not for a long time. Snow began to fall, melting on her hot skin and piling up on the fallen leaves. The dog should have run away. Any creature with intelligence would have realized they needed shelter. But Milo stayed. He licked her face until Corwin recovered enough to push him away.

She struggled to her knees and blinked her eyes clear. The field was empty. Nothing was on the bleachers except her bag and Aunt Nell's oboe. Kat Coogan was gone.

Corwin stumbled over to her things and sat, sharing an apple and some water with the dog before she walked him through the Halloween celebrations to the animal shelter.

Jack Jaga's reaction told her everything she needed to know about how bad she looked.

He invited her in.

She refused, wondering to herself why he wasn't at a Samhain feast. She lifted Milo into his arms and walked down the path to Hobbomock street. The dog's howling cries followed her for blocks.

CHAPTER 5

The canopy of her White Oak kept Corwin House in shade even on the hottest summer days. Corwin walked along the sidewalk toward her house, watching as a doe leapt the fence around Ms. Chever's yard. Her two fawns followed a little less gracefully. The doe herded them out of sight. Corwin was sure they were going to visit the deer feeder that hung from the lower branches of the White Oak. She'd have to check the water barrel outside the kitchen. When it didn't rain, she had to fill it from the kitchen pump. Thinking of the chore made her screw up her face. She turned twelve in two weeks. She should really have a better system for watering the deer, the White Oak, and the garden by now.

Corwin's head was full of these thoughts, her arms were full of books, and her back was bowed under the weight of her backpack when she found a man knocking on her front door. Her fingers clutched reflexively around the handle of the cornet case and she took a step back.

Twin braids reached nearly all the way to the pockets of his cycling jersey. One leg of his loose trousers had been cinched tight against his leg with a reflective band. Corwin's eyes darted to the black pedal bike leaning on its kickstand in the street beside her. Her heart stuttered.

That was Pops Coogan on her threshold.

She considered turning around and fleeing. Pops was the most powerful practitioner in Salem. Her father had avoided him at all costs when they saw him on the streets. Not to mention, he was Kat Coogan's father. Even though it was well known that Kat had fled Salem, and Corwin hadn't seen the witch in over a year, she couldn't be sure Pops wasn't here to kill her in his daughter's stead.

Pops spotted her before she could run. To her shock, he greeted her by name with an infectious grin glowing from his eyes.

"Daniella Corwin, you played beautifully in the graduation concert." His long beard bounced as he spoke. The gray sides had been braided from his ears down to join the black mass at a point just a few inches below his chin. He stroked the beard and she realized she had been staring. "I've been playing with French braids," he remarked, running a hand along one plait. "You have quite a bit of hair. Do you ever braid it differently?"

Corwin had to think to remember if she'd braided it or worn it down, which was ridiculous because if she'd worn it down, her backpack would be pulling on it. She shook her head. She didn't have time for fancy braids. The single, thick plait was how Mother had always done her hair.

Pops didn't frown or tell her that she should or suggest she'd be prettier if she cut it. He just tilted his head in answer and said, "I am looking for your father. Is your namesake at home?"

His question threw her for a moment. She felt her brows squeeze together and tried to relax them. Teachers got upset when her face did its thinking thing. Her father wasn't her namesake. She was named for him. The whole turnaround distracted her from the fear she should have been fighting. Even if he wasn't there at Kat's behest, she was going to have to lie to him now. He would be able to tell. You couldn't lie to the head of the Council. He might even be the high priest.

But she didn't really need to lie. She could tell him the truth. He had asked a specific question.

She shook her head. Her father was not at home.

Pops smiled.

Corwin felt her heart lighten. He hadn't caught her. She'd kept the secret. Then Pops gestured with an envelope he was holding and her eyes caught on the glitter flying off of it. The envelope was held shut with a raised circle of wax that blinded her with multi-colored magic.

"Ah, well," he said. "I suppose I will have to return at another time."

Corwin took a step forward, searching for her courage. After gaping like a tuba player ahead of the beat, she managed to say, "I can give your letter to my dad."

Pop's white eyebrows shot up. "You can see this, can you? Well, I suppose there's no point in hiding it from you, then." He started walking towards her, holding the letter out.

Corwin itched to know what was inside.

His voice dragged her eyes away from it. "My granddaughter danced home from school today. Why on Earth are you hauling so many books on the last day of classes, Mistress Daniella?"

Just before he reached her, the ten-pound bundle of blond fur and trouble trotted past the pair of them and right up to Corwin's front stoop. Jack Jaga had placed Milo in half a dozen homes in the year and a half since she saved him from the bullies under the bleachers. Each time, he'd run away just to show up on her doorstep or at band practice or to find her in town and follow her around. He was driving her nuts. The dog pawed at the door.

"So sorry, young sir, but nobody is home at present." Pops and the letter turned toward the house and out of Corwin's reach. "The mistress of the house is here."

Corwin blushed. She hissed at the pest. "Go away, Milo. I don't have time for a pet."

Milo's perky ears drooped. He lay down and let his long muzzle hang off the edge of the cement stoop.

Corwin sighed.

Pops tucked her father's envelope away in a pocket of his jacket. He scooped Milo off the stoop and considered the little dog's pitiful face, running a finger along the white markings that dripped off one side of his muzzle. "I think you could be a stellar companion for my Morgan. I believe she has time and love enough for a little thing like you." He strolled down the walkway with his eyes on Milo. He passed Corwin without a word and settled Milo in the wicker basket on the front of his bicycle.

"Sir?" Corwin screwed up all her courage to ask, "The letter?"

"Hmm?" Pops looked at her as though he'd forgotten all about her. "Ah, yes. I believe the letter will have to go elsewhere. For now."

Corwin wanted to ask him why. She wanted to tell him to say hi to Morgan for her. She didn't say anything as he strapped on his helmet. Instead, she dropped her eyes to her books and turned to head up the path to her door. A glow sputtered through the cross-hatched windows. Corwin looked up. The front windows were barely visible behind the overgrown shrubs but the glow wasn't bothered by them. It lit up her front yard like the glow from Ms. Chever's television lit up her trees. Corwin didn't have a television. There was only one thing that made a glow like that. Forgetting Pops Coogan, she raced to her door and burst inside, running straight to the kitchen, through the hearth, and into the secret lab on the other side of the fire.

"Where are you, baby girl?" Her father's voice filled the little room.

Corwin sighed. The lab was her favorite room in the house. She never felt lonely in the lab. The fire crackled and spat in all seasons, echoing off the stone walls and floor. She could imagine it as the voice of the house, talking back to her as she mumbled her way through the magical knowledge in the family spell books, grimoires, and journals.

She tried to keep the lab neat and clean like Daddy had taught her and she was successful with the shelves that circled the room above her head, built of disparate materials as each generation ran out of room. They held herbs and crystals and chemicals and animal bones and a wide variety of items that might be needed for a spell or potion. She kept each item in its place, clean and neatly labeled. But the worktable courted chaos. The wide, wooden table stood in the middle of the room, heavy and indestructible. Its many scars and stains were hidden by the pestles, flasks, tokens, scrolls, crucibles, tongs, beakers, pencils, strings, rags, and notebooks strewn on its surface.

The very first thing she'd ever sewn was a giant beanbag that sat against the back wall by the water pump. The back wall had been cut and rebuilt as the White Oak grew larger so Corwin could slump in her beanbag and lean against the tree in any weather, reading her ancestor's words or writing in her journal. And all the most secretive books lived in a cubby hidden under a cobblestone that could only be removed by one with power.

Best of all was the old standing mirror carved from branches of the White Oak and charmed by her great-great-grandaunt Judith to allow the family to communicate even when they moved far away. It hadn't been able to overcome the family curse. The branches of the family that moved away eventually stopped calling until, by the time her father had gone away to college, the Corwin family had been only him and his parents.

And then his parents died and Daniel was alone, until he found Sita.

Corwin dumped her books on the stool and dropped her bag on the stones. She carefully set the black plastic cornet case on the only clear space on the worktable. She placed it to hide the little kalimba-like hand piano she had designed and built herself. He would consider it a waste of her time. "I'm here, Daddy."

Her father's face didn't quite fill the mirror as it usually did. He must have set his compact mirror on something and backed away. He sat on the foot of a twin-size bed. Behind him, the daisies on the browning wallpaper clashed with the gold-framed painting of bright pansies in a cracked pot. Corwin wondered if he'd used the bed. The blue work-man's coveralls he wore were wrinkled, but he still had shadows under his hazel eyes.

The relief that flashed on his pale face for an instant was at odds with his scolding tone. "I have been calling for you for ten minutes."

Corwin caught her breath. She needed to pay better attention to her surroundings. She hadn't seen Pops or his bicycle until she'd been right on them, and then she hadn't noticed the glow of her father's call even though she'd been facing the house while she talked to Pops.

She dropped her head to hide her blush. "I'm sorry, Daddy. Mrs. Hammersmith kept me after to give me summer school work and then Mr. Frazer gave me his old coronet so I can learn brass—" She was about to tell him about Pops and the letter he'd walked away with, but her father interrupted her.

"School doesn't matter, Daniella." He shook his head as he rolled down the sleeves of his deep-blue coveralls. "You need to focus on learning magic."

"Yes, Daddy." Corwin covered her mouth with both hands. Her father only called a couple times a year. It cost too much energy to reach out more often. She shouldn't waste his time with her silly thoughts. Although, she wondered if Pops' letter was silly or a serious matter. If her father didn't respond, would Pops come back? Would he discover she was living alone?

"I have found out who took in your mother."

Her father's declaration dragged Corwin from her circling thoughts. She stepped forward, closer to the mirror, probably too close for his tiny compact. She stepped back again. "Who?"

Her father ran a hand through his scraggly hair. He'd been shaved bald when she'd spoken with him last fall. Now, his unruly curls were tickling his face again. She grinned. She loved his curls. If she could change herself, she'd want those curls instead of her boring, straight, black hair. She'd ask for his freckles, too, a spray of them across her nose, like his. Her own complexion was growing pastier every year.

"This is nothing to grin about. It's serious, Daniella."

Corwin schooled her expression. She grabbed a notebook and pen from the worktable and moved her books to perch on the tall stool. "Yes, sir."

"Your mother was taken by a group called the Consortium." He whispered the last word, looking to one side of the room before he dared say the name.

Corwin wrote it down. "Where are they?"

"They operate all over the world. It is more important than ever that you master magic and recover our family's power."

Corwin looked to the side now, at the fading wooden sign over the hearth. *Whosoever holds the heart of the house holds the power.*

"Baby girl!" Her father's harsh words drew her eyes back to the mirror. "I will keep tracking her. But you must find the heart. It is your mother's only hope."

"Yes, Daddy. I will work harder." She peeked up from scribbling notes to ask, "Are you getting any sleep?"

"I will sleep when your mother is safe in my arms again." He stood and his body filled the shot.

She couldn't see his face, only the name embroidered on his breast pocket, *Sam*. Then the image tilted. His eyes flashed with power.

"If you were as dedicated to finding her as I am, you'd have already brought us all back together, I wouldn't be exhausted, and I wouldn't have to remind you to stop wasting your time on music. Focus, Daniella. Your mother is all that matters."

"I study all the time, Daddy." She did, and she wanted to talk to him about what she'd learned, but he was moving, getting ready to leave, the image swooping behind him as he carried the compact. "I've read nearly every book in the library." The Corwin House library held over two hundred volumes. She'd had to read some of them with the dictionary open beside her, and that didn't help her with the witchy words.

"Do not talk back to me, young lady."

"I'm sorry, Daddy." She sucked in a wet breath and pushed on, trying to make him stay. "I have questions. Can you—"

"You are not a dud." He said this without much conviction.

The image brightened for a moment, as if he had pushed a curtain aside. Then it went dark again and Corwin leaned forward to get closer to her father.

He slapped a tattered ball cap on his curls, not even looking at her as he said, "I wouldn't have left if I didn't have faith in you. And yet, where is your Council mark? I had been tested three times by the time I was your age." He glared at her then, his eyes fierce. "Work harder."

"Yes, Daddy. Daddy, Pops Coogan—" she began, but the mirror went blank and all she could see was her own plain face: red nose, flushed cheeks, and all.

She turned away as if she could hide her tears from herself. It had been almost five years since she'd hugged her daddy, nearly a decade since he'd smiled. His smile had lit up her world. It scrunched his freckles and brightened his eyes till they were nearly green. She'd thought his smile was magic. But there were no smiles in the magic he had taught her. Day after day, from the moment she got home from school till she fell asleep on the worktable, he'd shown her how to access power and how to focus it into spells and potions and charms and curses. But he never showed her the magic of his smile. Not after her mother left.

Corwin tried. She kept studying every day after homework until she couldn't keep her eyes open. But she was a failure.

She slid off the stool and stole over to her beanbag, behind the pump, on the far side of the worktable, hidden from the mirror. She curled up and squeezed her eyes against the tears.

Her father was mad. He was angry and a little bit crazy. And it was all her fault.

CHAPTER 6

Three-year-old Corwin was scrubbing at the blood on the kitchen floor when her Daddy came home. She'd covered the broken ladder-back chair with her scorched blankie. The once-peach fabric had sucked up much of the blood and water. The bar of soap had gotten smaller as she scrubbed it against the wooden floor. Bubbles floated up and popped in her face. Her eyes stung. Her hand burned. Her arms ached. Her heart cried. But Corwin didn't.

"What are you doing, baby girl?" Her father had crouched at her side and pulled her from the pink, soapy flood on the floor. He tickled her and smiled his magical smile at her. "Where's Mommy, Daniella?"

Corwin didn't smile back. "Mother gone." She didn't want to be tickled. She had to clean up the mess. She had to make everything right so her mother would come back.

"Why are you covered in soot? What happened to your clothes?" Her father's voice went flat as he looked around the destroyed kitchen. "What made this mess, Daniella?"

"Mother gone." She wriggled out of his arms and returned to her scrubbing.

Her daddy left her then. He searched the house, calling Sita's name.

Corwin focused on the shushing sound of her soap on the floor as his voice grew more and more desperate.

When he returned to the kitchen, he'd lost his smile. He asked her again, "Where's Mommy?"

Corwin had to tell him again, "Mother gone."

"Where?" He gripped the first aid kit from the downstairs bathroom in white fingers. "Where did Mommy go?"

Corwin pointed at the kitchen door. He'd closed it when he came in. He didn't close it when he left. Laughter from neighbors gathering outside for Halloween floated in with cold air. Corwin didn't shut the door. She didn't wrap her blankie around her. She scrubbed.

She kept scrubbing as her daddy searched the town for Sita. He returned home with food, comforted her, and wrapped her hand in cool gauze, letting her sleep on his lap as he called people all night. The next day, he fixed the damage from Kat and Sita's fight with a wave of his hand, all the damage except the burns on her hand and the stains where she had tried to scrub up her mother's blood. He brought a rug up from the crowded cellar and laid it out in the kitchen, declaring that day a memory to be forgotten. As if that were a thing that was possible.

He didn't see the stains on the ladder-back chair.

Slowly, from that productive day on, her father had descended deeper and deeper into his search. He called out Sita's name in his sleep so loudly that Corwin could hear it in her attic bedroom. She tried to go to him once, scooching down the stairs on her butt and then knocking on their door.

He'd screamed at her.

Too scared to manage crawling back up the stairs to her little room, Corwin had gone down instead and slept under the spinet with the blanket from the daybed Sita had bought to make the house more modern.

In the morning, Corwin woke to Daniel calling her name, an edge of panic in his voice. She kept quiet, fearing he would scream at her again. When he found her, shaking under the blanket, under the spinet, he gathered her into his lap and apologized, crying into her matted hair. "I'm so sorry, my baby girl. We've both lost her."

Her daddy had called in sick to work that day and kept her home from daycare. He brushed her hair like Mother used to and took her to the forest, showing her how to recognize the different herbs they used for potions. They stopped at the butcher shop to get a whole fish. Back at home, he taught her the words that would let her walk through the fire and took her into the lab for the very first time. He set her on the tall stool and let her watch as he mixed a salve from the herbs they'd gathered, along with oil from the fish. He massaged it into the bruises she'd gotten from sleeping on the wooden floor.

"Why didn't you sleep on the daybed?" he'd asked.

She answered honestly, "It makes me think of Mother."

The lovely day had ended then. Her daddy went cold. He cooked the fish but made them eat it in the lab while he searched through the family's old books for a spell that would find Sita and bring her back to them.

From then on, every day after work, her Daddy took her into the lab and made her watch him work as he mixed potions and crafted spells and broke mirror after mirror in his search. If she fell asleep, he'd wake her up and make her stand on the stool. She started sleeping at daycare instead of playing with the other kids whose mothers all picked them up. When she was old enough to go to school, she learned to walk there so she wouldn't be late and found places where she could nap during recess.

One morning, she made her own lunch because Daddy was still in the lab when she had to leave for school. He never made her lunch again and instead dragged her into the lab to work the instant she got home. She learned to pack herself a dinner, too, and would sit on the cold cement front stoop to eat it before going inside. That was when she discovered the beetle moat between the stoop and the house.

Eventually, he lost his job because he had stopped going to it. He stopped bathing, stopped shaving. He stopped coming to her attic to rub her back and kiss her goodnight.

Then came the day, nearly five years after her mother had been driven away, that Corwin's father sat her down on the floor of the lab. He showed her how to open the hidden library she'd already learned how to access by watching him. He pulled an old, crumbling, leather-bound volume from the cubby and laid it on the worktable.

Corwin climbed up to sit cross-legged on the tall stool because her legs weren't long enough to reach the foot rests.

"Read that." Her father pointed at the family motto, carved into the stone over the hearth on this side and on the kitchen side.

"Whosoever holds the heart of the house holds the power."

"Now this." He slammed his hand down on the open book.

Corwin leaned in to peer at the swooping cursive handwriting.

It was a journal entry from Jonathan Corwin's sister, Abigail. Corwin knew that Great-great-great-great-grandfather Jonathan had brought shame upon the family with his persecution of so-called witches during the famous trials.

We can no longer hope the plague will pass. Mother is sending George and Bess away. Those of us who remain will strive with every breath to defeat this curse on Jonathan and the village. I fear it is the same curse which made our fellow settlers break faith with the Wampanoag. Mother gave me one chance to break the curse and I have failed.

I tried to honor the wisdom gifted to us by Hobbomock and his tribe. I reminded Jonathan of the debt we owe them to be a light in the world, how our family would have perished if he had not taught us the magic of this land and how to respect it. I entreated him, holding out the totem Hobbomock had made to bless Corwin House and hold our power protected. My brother would not be moved.

While we were at court today, the coven's high priestess hid the totem and ordered Corwin House to keep it safe until the family can again be trusted with such great power as we have amassed. We are weakened now and can only command such power as is available to all. My sisters and I have begun—

Her father flipped the page before she'd finished reading. He pointed to the bottom of the next page, stabbing the words with his finger. "Here. This. Read this."

I fear only a great sacrifice of love will return the power this House once had. I say to you, Jonathan's children, show heart, be kind, be strong for others, grow not in your father's selfish example, for you must open your hearts for the heart to come back to us. Whosoever finds the Heart of the House shall find its power.

"You must find the heart," Daddy had said.

"What does it look like?" she asked.

"You were given the gift of Sight. When you find the heart, you will know it for what it is. You must find it and bring it to me."

Her father had left her then. Just as her mother had.

Corwin had made dinner and waited for him to come home. She lay coldly in her parents' bed that night, fighting tears for as long as she could. She awoke in the morning to the shame of red, swollen eyes and brushed her hair for hours. Then she pulled herself together and began searching for the heart.

CHAPTER 7

Incessant howling cut through Corwin's nightmare. Wind whipped loose hair in her face as she knelt in the Corwin House library at Jonathan Corwin's feet. She was three years old again, but she had the same hair as her fifteen-year-old self. It wrapped around her body like that coat for crazy people. Her knees ached from the wooden floor. Shame burned through her skin at her ancestor's accusations.

Worst of all, Kat Coogan stood nearby with a long Red Maple wand held at Corwin's throat. The wand had been honed to a point sharper than her awl. Kat leaned in.

At first, the bright red drop of blood at her neck sang out, filling her ears and drowning Great-great-great-great-grandfather Jonathan's lecture exhorting her to find the heart. Then the clear, piercing note rested, lifting silence into her dream before it rang out again, transforming into a distant canine howl.

Corwin's fevered brain woke slowly, releasing her from the terror of the torture in her dream to the torture in her entire body. Her head pounded. Her lungs felt as if they were filled with sand. She wanted to close her eyes and return to unconsciousness but her eyes burned when she closed them. And the howling burrowed into her skull. Before anything else, she had to stop the howling.

Corwin dragged herself down the stairs to the second floor and then down the longer, wider second flight to reach the bathroom on the first floor. She tried to remember when she'd gone to bed. Images of the backyard rose in her head. She'd lain down beneath the White Oak. Her sketchy memory conjured the tree tossing a forked branch down on her before something in the present tripped her and she sprawled into the bathroom door. Her stomach churned as if it wanted her to vomit, but there was nothing left to vomit. The flu had drained her dry.

A trail of tools and harp parts connected the bathroom to the sitting room, which Corwin had turned into her instrument workshop. She saw it was the sound box that had tripped her and tried to find the energy to worry if she'd broken it. The half-apron she wore when she was working lay on the tiled floor of the bathroom. It did not smell good. Corwin crawled around it to take care of business.

"Ahwooooooo!"

"Shut up!" In her head it was a yell, but in reality, she didn't even open her lips. She had made a potion. She remembered making a potion. Why did it feel like she was dying?

"Ahwooooooo!"

"Ah, stuff it." She got her lips moving that time and used the success to propel herself out of the bathroom. She hauled herself across the main room, using the walls, and the daybed, and eventually the floor because she wasn't going to lean on a three-hundred-year-old spinet when she was still unsure her stomach wasn't going to find something more to upchuck. Somehow, her burning, aching body reached the front door. The thought of having to stand and address the locks undid her. Corwin laid her face against the door for only an instant before another long, aching howl shattered her delicate skull. In a burst of panic that couldn't really be called energy, she managed the locks and flung the door open to find that tiny, annoying terror, Milo, waiting on the other side of the beetle moat.

The terrier hopped over the moat and the threshold as easily as Kat Coogan had on that day so many eons ago, careless of the wards that were supposed to be impassible by any but family without an invitation. He trotted past her.

A cool September breeze flowed into the stifling house. The sun was high enough that, while it hurt her eyes, it wasn't blinding. Corwin leaned against the door frame that had started her on her woodworking adventures. Her eyes followed a water spider's spinning adventure through the moat, riding water misdirected from Ms. Chever's unregulated sprinklers.

"Woof."

Wake up. She bent over the cement stoop, proving she did still have something to throw up. She spat a thin, nasty, green liquid into the grass, not entirely avoiding the moat. After wiping her mouth on a sleeve covered in sawdust, she fell into the house and wrapped her arms around herself. Where was her blankie? The satin edging of her peach blankie would feel good on her face. It was cooling and soothing, until it got drenched in Mother's blood and burned in the fire.

"Stop it." The words came out slurred. She didn't do anything else to stop Milo, though, as he nipped one of her toes. She felt him adjust his bite and drag her leg aside by the sock. The door shut with an easy click that made her smile. She'd fixed that.

She woke again to find him barking in her face.

"No. Get out. I don't want you here," she mumbled into the floor.

The dog licked her nose. And then he licked her eyelids.

She dragged a hand up to shove him away and knocked something over. The object rolled along the floor until it hit her. She opened her eyes.

A blue plastic water bottle lay on its side in front of her, a little pinkish liquid dribbling from the nearly sealed pop top. She'd made the medicinal potion but forgotten to drink it.

Milo nosed it. He barked.

"Yeah, okay." Corwin put a hand over her ear and then scratched her scalp. Her fingers came away greasy. She was gross.

Drink it.

Thanks to the pop top, she didn't have to sit up. She sucked in the nasty, chalky concoction until she thought she would choke. She did have the presence of mind to sit the bottle up and push the top closed before she sank back into her misery.

Gray light bathed the room when she opened her eyes. Her head was as thick as an overstuffed beanbag chair, but the drum and bugle corps had taken a rest. One hip and shoulder hurt rather than all of her joints screaming at her. A whiff of something ancient woke her completely. She was still lying on the floor in the front room, but her head rested on one of the overstuffed seat cushions from the kitchen and she'd been covered with the musty blanket from the back of the daybed. Corwin hadn't touched it since her father draped it there. A shiver ran through her body. The pillow, the blanket, and all of her clothes were wet. The flu or whatever illness she'd come down with was wringing her dry.

She pushed herself up and paused a moment as a wave of nausea washed over her.

Go slow.

She nodded to herself. It was good advice. Her stomach growled its disagreement. Luckily, her eyes fell on the blue bottle lying on its side nearby. She lifted it with effort and drained the bottle.

"Woof." Milo sat beside the staircase.

Beyond him, the bathroom door sat open invitingly. Corwin dragged herself to her feet and stumbled to the stairs. She used the railings and then the wall to help her reach the bathroom. The t-shirt and long johns she usually wore to bed were piled just beside the door. The last she remembered, she'd left them folded on her pillow upstairs. It didn't matter. Taking off her clothes had never felt so good. Her skin pimpled in the cold air but she rubbed a hand towel over herself before she dove into the fresh clothes. She dumped her toothbrush into the sink and drained two full glasses of water.

"Ahwooo."

The dog bounced in the open doorway to the kitchen. The flicker of the fire and promise of a soft carpet moved her more than his howls. The kitchen was delightfully warm. A pillow and the deep-green blanket from her attic room lay on the plushiest stretch of carpet, under the dining table. A sleeve of saltine crackers lay beside them, against one leg.

Corwin didn't dare reach for the crackers, knowing she wouldn't be able to resist lying down if she got that close. She ignored her insistent stomach and fetched a small bowl from the lowest shelf. Instead of working the hand pump, she leaned out of the kitchen door and dipped the bowl in the rain barrel, standing full from a recent thunderstorm. It would overflow when the gray sky broke and it looked like it was going to break soon. Corwin did not have the energy to check the troughs and pipes she'd installed to deliver overflow to the base of the White Oak and the garden tanks. She did remove a forked stick floating in the water and remembered it leading her there after the White Oak had woken her by dropping the perfect divining rod on her head.

Rest.

She needed to lie down. She didn't worry about locking the door, having already forgotten how the family wards had failed to keep Milo out. Some water spilled out of the bowl as she set it on the floor by the crackers. She wiped a hand through the puddle to thin it out. The fire would dry it.

"For you." She waved Milo over as she crawled under the blanket and ripped open the saltines. Her brain took his drinking and remixed it with the crinkly cracker wrapper and spitting flames into a song that the digital-crazy kids in her composition class would die over.

"I don't want to die," she moaned into her pillow, confused by her own thoughts.

A warm tongue lapped at her forehead and a soothing lullaby floated through the surface of her mind until she fell asleep cuddling the divining rod.

Each time she woke, Milo harassed her into eating and drinking something. Sometimes, he brought her new clothes from the cast offs she'd left on the floor in her room, the library, and the sitting room. Once, she opened her eyes to find herself facing the blue bottle that had held her healing potion. She took the hint and grabbed the remainder of the potion from the ice box.

He couldn't convince her to move to the daybed until after her fever broke and her bony joints' complaints were able to overwhelm the fever soreness. Later that day, or possibly the next day, she was able to get up without the dog's insistence and eat a real meal. She put a matching plate of rice, smoked salmon, and asparagus on the floor. Though she didn't feel like she needed to lie down again right away, she also had zero interest in cleaning the dishes that had piled up in the sink.

She might have been able to convince herself to go outside and check the garden, but it was raining. Still or again, she couldn't say. When she went to rest on the daybed, the spinet called to her. Then her father's voice crawled up her spine, reminding her she'd lost too much time already. She should get back into the lab. But she'd have to walk through the fire to get to the lab and she'd been walking through fire for an eternity. Music was magic to her. Music would heal her more now than bending over incomprehensible ancient texts.

Corwin lifted Milo to the bench seat beside her.

"Any requests?" she asked him.

The dog tilted his head in a gesture she interpreted as a shrug. Her brain was still tired, so she let her fingers make the choices. They started with a classic Bach piece and quickly wandered off into improvisations. Corwin let her power send tendrils out into the room on the sine wave of the notes. The glittering music curled into all the joints of the house that creaked and moaned in wet weather, as well as Corwin's joints, and for good measure, Milo's.

He yawned and reached forward to stretch against the keyboard.

Corwin folded the notes he played into her composition.

He'd cared for her, she thought, and she could use that intention to care for the house which she'd neglected. She thought magic into the kitchen to sand the floor where she'd spilled water and not wiped it up. She thought it into the bathroom, which needed a thorough scrubbing, and onto the stairs where she'd vomited at some point days ago.

A crack of thunder nearly covered the quiet sound of someone knocking on the front door, ignoring the brass knocker as everyone did. Corwin lifted her fingers from the keyboard, irrationally terrified that her father had come home and caught her wasting time. A second series of knocks sounded, louder. Corwin held her breath, hoping they would just go away.

Milo didn't. He sang out a happy, growling howl.

The intruder pounded on the door.

CHAPTER 8

orwin glared at Milo beside her on the spinet bench.

He hopped off and ran to the door, still singing like an idiot.

The someone knocked again.

Corwin realized she would have to answer the door. She only swayed a little as she pushed up from the spinet.

Morgan.

The thought struck her as she looked at Milo standing up against the front door. She hadn't taken him back to the shelter. It would make sense that Morgan would come to Corwin House to fetch her dog. Corwin stumbled to the door, more eager now than scared.

Morgan Coogan indeed stood on the doorstep with her golden skin, shiny hair, and curious green eyes. Her hair was braided into a crown and, for just a moment, Corwin's tired mind thought she was wearing a cape, too. Then the cold air woke her up a bit more and she saw it was a raincoat.

Milo spun around and ran to leap back onto the spinet bench.

The goddess said, "I should have checked here first." Then she looked Corwin in the eyes, ignoring her tangled hair, filthy face, and slept-in clothes. "Was that you playing?"

Corwin nodded. She stepped aside to invite Morgan in. "Sorry about the mess."

She glanced around the room and realized it wasn't a mess. The wood and tools from her triple harp project were strewn along the passage behind the stairs and Milo had been dragging all of her blankets and pillows into the kitchen in between uses. It was like he thought the heat from the fire would sanitize them. The front room was as austere and tidy as ever. Corwin caught Morgan's bemused expression and hurried back to her seat on the spinet bench. She played a dramatic chord. "Time to go home, Milo. "

Milo crawled into her lap.

Morgan tossed her raincoat onto the overfull coat rack, then strolled over and took his seat.

The instant she sat, Milo hopped down and ran to the wicker basket that Corwin hadn't touched since she tucked it behind the coat rack the day he arrived on her stoop. He hopped up to snuggle in the blue blanket, pausing for a moment to look over at Corwin, his expressive eyes huge.

She could almost hear him thinking *I forgot about this blanket.* It was nearly the only blanket in the house he hadn't dragged to Corwin's side.

"So," Morgan said, "You play oboe, coronet, piano, violin, guitar, and spinet? I guess you deserved to skip the rest of high school. Is college fun?"

If she were forced to admit it, Corwin was liking college. A lot. She got to study what she wanted to study. Her father was mad at her for all the time it took, but the only reason she was going was because it had been the easiest way to get out of high school early. There were too many permission slips and events that parents were expected to attend. Teachers had started noticing. Plus, she could take all her college courses online, which actually gave her more time to focus on her magic studies.

Corwin stared at her hands. She didn't need to. It was actually kind of hard to play that way. She realized she'd been quiet too long. "I don't play violin that well."

Morgan's laugh lit up the room like Corwin's magic had earlier.

Corwin blushed.

"I should bring you my grandpa's recordings. He was a musician, too. Corwin?" Morgan said this last gently, as if she were uncertain of what she was about to say.

Corwin was fascinated. She couldn't think why Morgan would ever be uncertain.

"Have you eaten anything recently?" Morgan asked, watching Corwin's hands as they continued to play.

"Yes," Corwin said. "Milo and I had food just before you knocked." She added hurriedly, "Are you hungry?"

"No." Morgan laughed again.

Corwin imitated the sound on the keys, which made Morgan squeal.

Then she spoke so fast her words ran together. "That is supes cool. You need a shower."

Corwin stopped playing.

"I just wanted to make sure you'd eaten. You have color in your face, but maybe I hang out here while you get clean, just in case you need help?"

"I had a fever."

"Yeah." Morgan laughed gently, kindly. "I can tell. I guess Milo could tell, too. He ran away right after we saw you at The Music Shoppe."

Corwin didn't remember going to The Music Shoppe. She had a vague memory of Billy, the owner, telling her they didn't stock raw gut but they could order harp strings. Also, she had tried to tune their grand piano because it hurt her head.

She fled from the bench to bury her face in her ancestors' coats and jackets and scarves. She'd made a scene. Her mother would be ashamed of her.

"It's okay, Corwin." Morgan stood. "Billy thinks you're fabulous, just in a crazy artist kind of way. Want me to help you upstairs?"

"It's down here," Corwin mumbled into the comforting coat rack collection.

"Well, come on then. You can do it." Morgan turned Corwin around and laid a hand to Corwin's forehead.

A cooling calmness flowed from her hand through Corwin's entire body. Her muscles released a tension that had been holding her up and she slumped a bit into Morgan's waiting support. It felt nice.

Milo joined Corwin in the bathroom while she showered. She felt good enough afterwards to haul herself all the way up to her attic room to get fresh clothes. The dog stayed with her. He followed her down to the kitchen then, where Morgan had scrambled eggs and burnt toast.

"Oh, you look so much better." Morgan choked on a laugh and added, "I mean, you're always pretty, you just look . . . clean." She spun to the stove where the eggs were starting to smoke.

Corwin lifted some plates down from the shelves. She didn't need to use the step stool anymore and had stashed it in the library. She never expected Morgan Coogan to be cooking for her. The plates clattered onto the table. There was a Coogan in her kitchen, again. A sudden, sharp pain stabbed into her temple. She looked at the fireplace grate. It didn't swing out to protect her.

"What is music theory?" Morgan set a pair of trivets in the middle of the table, near a pile of books that had melted into a puddle of books.

Corwin hurried over to gather them up and turned away, looking for a place to hide them. They weren't all college textbooks. Family grimoires were family secrets. Corwin shouldn't have left them just lying around. She shouldn't have let a Coogan into the house at all. She shouldn't have let anybody in. She needed to get back to searching for the heart.

Morgan startled her with a touch on her arm. "You should see if they'd let you keep playing in the band. We miss you. It's not healthy to be alone so much, is it? I mean, your parents aren't really around, are they?"

Corwin spun around and searched Morgan's face. Did she know that Corwin's parents weren't around at all? Was she just there because her aunt Kat had sent her?

"You came for Milo," she said, dropping her gaze from that beautiful, deceitful face. "You should go. I'll get your coat." Corwin rushed out. She slipped into the library to set the books on the table in there and then grabbed Morgan's raincoat from the rack. She found Morgan in the doorway when she headed back to the kitchen.

"I made eggs," Morgan protested, even as she took the coat.

"Thank you. But—" She wanted to cry. The tears burned in her nose, filling her head. Corwin schooled her face. She would not shame her mother any more than she already had. "Thank you for the food and for telling me to shower." She walked through the kitchen to the door in a fog, remembering Kat Coogan walking where she was walking, only Kat had to pick her way around blood and knives and Corwin's mother. Then she remembered her mother striding out of that door, leaving it open, leaving Corwin alone. It took everything she had to open the door.

No. Let her stay. You like her.

"Awhrrroooo." Milo mixed a growl into his howl as Morgan scooped him up.

Corwin kept her eyes averted. She wanted to pet him, to thank him for helping her. But if she did, she was sure she wouldn't be able to kick them out. Instead, she stared at the forked divining rod that she had cuddled in her fever. It lay in a puddle of water under the sink.

Morgan paused in the doorway. She rubbed the toe of one Doc Martin against the other. "I'm sorry if I said something wrong."

"It's not you," Corwin mumbled. She didn't want Morgan to ask questions. Because it wasn't her. It was her Aunt Kat. It was her grandfather, Pops. Her whole damn Coogan family was the reason Corwin couldn't like Morgan. And she hated it.

Morgan didn't ask anything. She tucked Milo into her jacket and walked down the kitchen path in the drizzling gloom. Corwin closed the door. It didn't do much to muffle Milo's barking.

Corwin sat. She ate while reading Uncle Samuel's entry on spells to find money. Her eyes read the words but her mind only conjured up the hurt in Morgan Coogan's depthless green eyes and the coldness of her lap where Milo had slept.

CHAPTER 9

Her slip-up with Morgan inspired Corwin to focus, keep alert, and take better care of herself. To keep herself from impulse buying crap food, she set up a regular order with the grocery to be delivered to her kitchen door every two weeks. She practiced spells and potions on the garden to make it thrive with healthy food and keep critters from eating it before she could. On those occasions when she had to leave her house for supplies, she kept to the backroads when she could and made her trips quick. She'd run into Milo a few times in the two years since she'd kicked Morgan out, but slipped away before giving in to the temptation to take him home to Morgan. She didn't even know where the Coogans lived. It wouldn't be too hard to find out, but she didn't want to know. She kept her mind on Corwins, finding the family's heart, and bringing her parents home.

Except, sometimes, a flash of emerald green, like from the leaf designs she'd carved into the triple harp's column, would bring Morgan's laughing eyes to mind. Morgan would be interested in how Corwin had built the harp from scratch. After all, she was the reason that Kali, the butcher, ordered exactly the kind of gut Corwin needed to make the strings. Would it be so bad if Corwin dropped a picture of the harp in an email with a thank you? Morgan still had her Salem High email until June.

"Ow!" One of her hand-spun strings snapped as she wrenched it too tight because her mind was on pretty Morgan Coogan. Blood seeped from a slice cutting across two of her five white scars. It dripped onto the plastic Corwin had laid over the antique rug in the sitting room.

Corwin wrapped a rag around her hand and held pressure on it. She really wanted to finish the harp tonight. Then she would have a few days to get familiar with it before she had to play it for her Fabrication thesis. The wound was her own fault. She should have kept her mind on her work. Just like she needed to learn more focus in the lab. She was sixteen years old. All the coven-bound witch kids she knew from school had tested into their majority nearly two months ago. She'd spent Samhain dodging Kat Coogan when she'd meant to be gathering tourist auras for a mashup of spells based on Uncle Samuel's nonsense grimoire.

Now all of those kids could tap into their family's amassed Skill while Corwin still hadn't the faintest clue where the Coogan high priestess could have hidden the Corwins' heart.

Her eyes flitted over the clean, simple lines of the benches and chairs, painted gray to blend in with the walls. Some relative—Corwin secretly hoped it had been Nell, whose half-empty journal read like she was a rebel—had painted the outline of blue hearts on the back of the chairs. Otherwise, it was the epitome of plain. The only secret it held was the one-way door out of the lab which even she couldn't see. There was nowhere to hide the heart in the sitting room.

A sound drew Corwin off her working stool. She hurried out of the room, releasing the heating spell she'd placed on it. Her father's voice was louder in the kitchen and she could see the shimmer of magic floating through the walls. The fire grate stood aside to let her duck under the mantel and into the lab and yank the painter's tarp from the standing mirror.

"Why did you cover the mirror?" Her father skipped the niceties that Corwin observed when encountering familiar faces on her rare trips into the village.

"I felt like I was being watched."

"Who would watch you?" He asked. His eyes flitted around as

though he were tracking something beyond his mirror. The view shifted when he lowered his compact mirror to swipe at something on his arm. Her father was wearing tech. They hadn't even had a computer in the house until Corwin won one with her full-ride college scholarship, but her dad had an armpadd.

Corwin shrugged in answer to his question. She didn't want to tell him about Kat Coogan stalking her on Samhain. When she had quietly inquired, everyone who would know told her that Katherine Coogan had abandoned Salem and witchcraft for a fancy medical degree. She left town for school two decades ago and never returned. But Corwin knew they all thought she had never returned only because they couldn't see through Kat's glamour. She fortified the house wards and redirected a minuscule stream of water from the water barrel around the house to the little beetle moat. The stream provided running water in front of both doors most of the time. It made leaving the house difficult for her, which was not a huge issue. It was more important that it would make it more difficult for any witch to enter. Witches hated crossing running water.

But she didn't bring up Kat or the fortifications to her daddy. A reminder of Kat, who left for college, would only give him ammunition to scold her for the distraction of her own college studies. Corwin could justify to herself the time it took because music was like magic to her. Daniel Corwin would never see it that way. The only thing he wanted her to study was magic. He expected her to spend all of her time learning magic and searching for the heart.

She'd tried nearly everything in the family spell books. She read every one of the two hundred and thirty-five books in the house, plus the dozen or so useful books she'd found hidden in the stacks at the Salem Public Library. Nothing had worked. She didn't see how mulling over the problem while building and playing instruments was any less helpful than everything she'd done so far. Getting into college had gotten her out of school, which meant less chance of anyone finding out that she was living alone. None of that mattered to her daddy. He only cared about finding the heart and rescuing Sita.

Sure enough, he had called with another idea for the search. "Try digging in the yard. My grandfather used to talk in circles about some old tunnels under Salem being some buried secret. It occurred to me that maybe he meant that we literally buried our secrets like time capsules."

"It's ten degrees outside, Daddy," Corwin pointed out, keeping the sigh out of her voice. "It looks warm where you are."

He was outside, in some kind of stone alcove. He needed a haircut or a ponytail holder. It could have been the sunlight creating shadows, but he looked thinner. His cheekbones were getting to be as sharp as the harp strings. The thought led her to look at her palm. It was still bleeding. She snatched a fresh rag from the bag hanging off a peg on the side of the workbench and pressed it over the bloody one.

"Are you trying blood magic with your own blood? You fool." Her father didn't wait for her answer. "You are the only hope your mother has. Find someone else. Use their blood."

"Daddy, I haven't read Jonathan's grimoire in years. It makes my skin crawl. He's the reason our power is lost."

Her father flipped through a stack of passports in different colors. He turned his attention back to her after selecting one and sticking it in a back pocket. The rest he slid into the lining of his soft-sided briefcase.

Corwin grinned at the brown magic he used to repair the ripped seam. She missed his magic. When she was a toddler, he had tickled her with it. Her grin fled at the scowl he turned to her.

"You must use all of the resources at your disposal. I didn't leave you in that house so you could lounge about in comfort while I search the ends of the Earth."

"I'm trying, Daddy. I really am. I just don't have any Skill at Finding."

"Skill." He spat the word so hard, she stepped back from the mirror. "You're using their words, now? I am ashamed of you. You were born with the *power* of Sight. You are a Corwin. How is it possible you can be such a failure?"

Corwin's breath came in short gasps as if she had been running. There was no answer to his question, so she squeezed her lips together and wrapped her braid around her neck a few times. She rolled the elastic off the end of her hair and onto the rag on her hand. Running her fingers through her hair made her feel close to her mother. She tried to hold her mother in her heart and remember that her father was only being like this because he loved her. She kept her thoughts to herself. She didn't ask why he didn't come help her search the house if the heart was their only hope. She didn't ask why being a Corwin should make her any more powerful, since the family cache of magic had been hidden from them for generations. She didn't tell him she was lonely or that she was frustrated by all the trial and error because she had no teacher to tell her better. She didn't say anything at all.

Once her daddy deigned to pull his attention away from whatever he was watching in the distance, he sighed. "I'm sorry, baby girl. You are not alone. I, too, am a failure. Your mother will be tortured for eternity because we aren't good enough." He paused, looking like he was going to sob, but then a shadow crossed his face and his attention was caught like a magpie chasing the reflection off a watch face.

"Tortured?"

"Shush." Her father cut her off.

Corwin watched him. He never answered when she asked why he thought Mother was being tortured. He never answered most of her questions. There were so many things she wanted to talk with him about but none of it mattered to him, so she sat on the stool and wrapped her arms around her knees.

He grabbed a suitcase and moved close to the mirror. "Keep trying, my baby girl," he said, not even looking at her. "As will I. This may be a dead end, but I will not quit. Dig in the yard."

"There's three feet of snow outside, Daddy."

He didn't hear her outburst. "I've got to catch this guy before he gets on the train. Stop using your own blood. Find some creature in the woods and sacrifice it. You must try everything. We can't let your mother be tortured for eternity because you are weak." The view shifted away from his face to the arched stone overhead.

Corwin hurried to say, "I love you, Daddy. Merry Christmas." But the mirror was black. He'd shut his compact and terminated the casting.

Without thinking, Corwin lifted the tarp over the mirror again. She stained it with her bleeding hand. She stared at the cut for a minute before running her fingers over it. She should try to heal it. Only, she wasn't very good with healing spells. The only doctor in the family had left his tools but taken his spell book when he left. Besides, Mother had said you learn from pain. She needed to learn to focus on what she was doing.

Her mind was already racing to picture the passages from many-greats-grandfather Jonathan's entries on blood magic. It was dangerous and dark. Witches feared blood magic. But Corwins were wizards, he wrote. Corwins could control the darkness and keep it at bay. She'd always found it somewhat ironic that it was Jonathan who had written this when it was Jonathan, of all the Corwins, who had been overcome by the dark curse that conquered Salem in 1692.

But she was a Corwin. Her only goal in life was to find her family and bring them home. It would be foolish not to try every method at her disposal. Even blood magic.

CHAPTER 10

As sometimes happened when she was spell crafting in her head, Corwin's body took over and she found herself bundled up and marching through the drifts outside her door. She needed blood. Kali was sure to have blood. He'd sold her stranger things over the years. The sidewalks were blocked with snow. She walked in the streets, which had been plowed but weren't being used. A gentle snowfall was already piling up again.

Despite her thick layers, Corwin was shivering by the time she reached the butcher's shop. It was closed. She looked for the sun and found it low on the horizon, but still up. He should be open. She stepped back and looked up and down the empty street. Wreaths and baubles shuddered in the rising wind. All the shops and lampposts were decorated, red and green for Christmas, green and gold for Yule. Yesterday, the streets were packed with tourists and tomorrow would be the same. But today, every place was shuttered. Corwin blushed.

It was Christmas Day. Everyone was home with their families. That was why she was able to walk down the middle of the street and hadn't run into a single soul all the way to town. She pulled her hood close and turned into the wind to return to her empty home. A whimper caught her attention. It was so quiet, she wouldn't have heard it if the streets hadn't been empty.

"Hello?" She peered around.

At the sound of her voice, the dog barked and then shook. Snow flew, spattering the butcher shop steps and Corwin's skirts. Milo's floppy ears pattered against his head like a pellet drum with much the same sound. He slunk out from where he'd been sheltering against the wind.

"You fool." Corwin bent and scooped the little dog up. "Come here."

Milo shivered. He was wet. Icicles clung to his tail.

Corwin tucked him into her jacket and held him close as she hurried home. She couldn't leave him in the cage outside the animal shelter. A storm was gathering. And she didn't know where the Coogans lived. There truly was no thought in her head except for getting him somewhere warm. But the walk home gave her a lot of time to think. Images of everyone else in town cuddled up with loved ones, eating cookies by the fire, telling old family stories and laughing assaulted her even as she heard only her Daddy's voice.

"We can't let your mother be tortured for eternity because you are weak."

If she wanted her family back, Corwin was going to have to learn how to be ruthless.

By the time she got home, Corwin had justified her plan to herself. It took two attempts to get the fire grate out of her way so she could carry the terrier through the fire into the lab. She dried him off with one of the many old towels she kept in a nook high in the hearth for cleaning up messes.

The dog tried to kiss her nose as she rubbed at his pale fur.

Corwin turned her head away. She didn't want to see his floppy ears or the white spill down his muzzle. Instead, her eyes landed on the tarp covering the mirror and her blood fading to brown on the white canvas.

She remembered her father calling her a failure. Which she was.

She couldn't bear to hold the dog anymore. She grabbed her reading beanbag from the back wall and set it closer to the fire, tucking him into it with a fresh towel. The storm raged outside, battering branches of the

White Oak against the back of the house. The eternal flame in the hearth twisted and flared as though it were fighting the howling winds. Shadows jerked around the room. The little dog whimpered.

Corwin blocked the omens from her mind. She knelt by the secret book nook and dug Jonathan's leather-bound grimoire from beneath all the others. The rough leather scraped against her dry hands and the clasp struck her palm, opening the harp-string slice. The cover soaked her blood up before she could wipe it off. For the first time, she wondered what kind of flesh had made the binding.

She dropped it and stood to gather her journal and a pen from the worktable. She flipped through her notes, reviewing everything she had learned so far. There was a difference between finding something that was missing, like the tiny three-hole pipe she'd left in the pocket of a jacket she'd grown out of, and finding something that had been hidden, like the heart. Her father had said she would see the magic on the hidden totem and know. But the glow of magic coated most things in the house. One spell she tried revealed the presence of blue-tinged magic built into the very walls of Corwin House.

Step one: Master magic. Step two: Find the heart. Step three: Find her mother.

She knelt and began taking notes on Jonathan's blood magic entries and adjusting the spell that had revealed the magic in Corwin House's bones. The words blurred before her eyes as hours passed. She blinked her vision clear and kept working, revising the spell and considering all of the angles. She had to be as thorough as her father. Her parents were counting on her.

Somewhere around the time late night turned into early morning, the dog climbed out of the beanbag and trotted over to sit between her and the books, practically in her lap. She left him there, sniffing the books and pawing at the pages while she gathered the ingredients she would need. Poppy juice had been the base of her original spell. For this try, she would simply substitute out the base. Before, she'd added all of the ingredients to the poppy juice, but this time she would have to reverse the process so she could add the blood last. As she crushed seeds and ground flowers, she hummed, keeping her mind too full to think of anything but finding what her father needed.

Her concentration broke for a moment when she went to transfer an ember from the fire to her crucible. The flames licked out and bit the back of the hand she had sliced open earlier. It scared her more than it hurt her, until the bandage caught fire and she couldn't get it off. She managed to tamp out the fire with the towels that were still wet from Milo's fur. As she primed the pump far longer than normal to run water over her hand, her eyes locked on Jonathan's grimoire. He was the reason the family power had been hidden. The heart was concealed to weaken him. Was it such a good idea to use Jonathan's methods to find the heart again?

She climbed on a stool to pull the cheesy, plastic first aid kit off the top shelf where her dad had stuck it beside Great-great-granduncle Doctor Deacon's shoe-sized medical bag. Early on, when she'd really needed the first aid kit, she hadn't been able to reach it even with the stool and just learned to do without. But she didn't know much about burns, and she was pretty sure there were care instructions in the box. Sure enough, tucked in a hard plastic pocket on the lid was a First Aid Booklet. Corwin didn't read it. A folded card distracted her. It sat on top of the bandages, tubes, plastic gloves, tape, and antiseptic towelettes. *Daniel* was written on the front in her mother's swooping script. Corwin lifted the card as reverently as if she had found the heart. Her mother had held this. Mother had left this for Daddy. She opened the card.

There is no wound our love can't heal.

A buzz settled in her head. Her skin tingled, aching to hold her mother's hand. She dropped the card back into the kit and pulled out a bandage to wrap around her hand, skipping any burn cream or antiseptic. She climbed the stool with reverence and placed the first aid kit back in the dust exactly as it had been. Then she returned to her work, nothing on her mind but magic.

She read her notes and Jonathan's one last time then lifted the dog onto the worktable.

He whimpered and minced around the edges, looking for how he could get off it.

She ripped the tarp from the standing mirror and carefully returned to the fire. As a nod to the modern understanding of germs, she held her *athamé* in the hearth for a moment, keeping one eye on the dog in case it wandered off the edge of the table.

But the little guy had given up searching for a way down. He watched her with his head tilted, crying, his tail tucked firmly up against his belly as if he knew what she was planning. The feathery tufts of his floppy ears dangled in the mortar, picking up lavender dust and sandalwood oil.

Corwin selected a vial of rosemary-infused rubbing alcohol and poured it over the knife, letting it drip onto the stone hearth. She shuffled off the niggling idea that she might be procrastinating for a good reason and instead filled her mind with her father's demands and the buzz of longing for her lost mother. She had to find their power and then she had to find her father, and together they would rescue her mother.

The words she intoned didn't matter. They were just a physical way to focus her intention. She let the words come without much consideration, all her focus on getting enough temporary power from life's blood to make her spell find the Corwin family power.

"Show me where my heart lies still. Hear my need, obey my will." She repeated the words, almost singing them as a tune rose in her mind.

Every feeling possible filled Corwin's soul. Her aura pulsed with the thrill of ancient power. She let the feelings guide her to earn her father's pride. She slid the mortar over to where the dog shivered at the very edge of the table. Avoiding its gaze, Corwin pulled the tail out from under the dog's body and held it over the mortar. She sliced once, quick and firm, like she was cutting harp strings.

Milo yelped.

Why?

Corwin chanted louder against the fear of that little voice in her head. She leaned into the buzzing that raised the hairs all over her body. She mixed the blood into the other ingredients and then poured the potion onto the burning ember in her crucible. Lilac sparks of magic, visible only to her Sight, shot from the stone vessel she'd carved herself. Quickly, before the magic fled, Corwin dashed the contents at the standing mirror. Instead of charred wood or the crushed remains of seeds mixed with oil, sparkles red as blood and flame flew to coat the mirror and its frame. A glittering image flashed into the glass, replacing the reflection of Corwin and the bleeding dog.

"No! Not now!" A voice cried from the image. Corwin's father stared out of the mirror, his eyes wide in horror. It was a wider image than she saw when her daddy used his compact mirror to reach her. This showed a landscape slowly passing by behind her father. Wind blew his long hair and scarf as if he were hanging onto the side of a train. The view was exactly as if she were looking out a window at him.

"Daddy?"

He focused and squinted. "Baby girl?"

"Daddy, I made a Finding spell that worked!" She didn't mention she'd been trying to find the heart.

"Go away. I've found your mother." His words were whipped away by the increasing wind.

"Where is she?"

Anger flashed in his hazel eyes, followed too quickly by despair and a glassy obsession. "She's with another man."

"Hey!" A deep, rough voice called out.

Corwin flipped around, thinking it was behind her, but the new voice, too, came from the vision she'd called up in the mirror.

"Shit. Sitaaaaaaaaaa!" Her father pushed off the window and fell, flailing, out of sight an instant before the vision was shattered by a gunshot.

CHAPTER 11

As the bullet sped away from her, through the space that a second ago had held her father's face, Corwin spun away from the mirror, crying out her common protection spell and throwing her arms wide to protect Milo from flying glass as well. Only, no protective shield materialized. There was no glass, either. She turned back to find the mirror whole and unaffected, no longer glittering with power. The buzz had fled from her head and from her soul. Howling wind and crackling fire filled the room with chaos, and yet she ached from the silence of the missing buzz. Corwin did a careful turn, slowly returning her attention to the dog, who was glowing faintly blue and bleeding where she had cut him. Her chest caved in with grief.

Milo lay curled up, his tail tucked under his paws where he licked at the slice.

Corwin climbed on the stool, kneeling as she had when she was little. She ran her fingers over the wound, murmuring a healing incantation her father had used. "Flesh of thine, stitch up fine."

Nothing happened. His tail continued to bleed. She snatched a rag from the bag and wrapped it around his tail. Her eyes darted from the pool of blood to the crucible, the mortar and pestle, and all the other tools lying on the bench. Anger rose in her like flames. The living creature shivering under her touch was not a tool for her to use.

She slid him off the table and huddled against the back wall, rocking and holding pressure on the wound. She reached out to the White Oak on the other side of the wall for comfort and felt none. Her eyes fell on Jonathan's grimoire. She kicked out, knocking it back into the secret alcove under the table. Her skin burned with shame. Her father was out there risking his life while she dabbled in music and mocked all of her ancestors who hadn't fallen to an evil curse.

A hot tongue lapped the tears from her cheeks. Milo buried his head against her chest as if she could protect him.

But she was the one who had hurt him. She couldn't save anyone from her own black heart.

"Flesh of thine, stitch up fine. Flesh of thine, stitch up fine." It didn't work. The world wouldn't let her use magic. What if the slice didn't heal and he bled to death? She had to get Milo out of the house before she hurt him worse.

Corwin dragged herself up and left the lab by the sitting room door for fear her magic wouldn't protect them through the fire. She bundled up in all her outdoor gear without setting Milo down.

He tucked his head under her scarf and braid. She felt his warm, wet breath on her neck as some foolish voice in her head murmured, *it's okay it's okay it's okay.*

Nothing was okay.

Outside, the sun was rising on a new day. Red and gold lit up the glittering snow like the magic she couldn't access, torturing Corwin until she focused her gaze on her great-grandfather's boots, trudging through the snow-packed streets. Milo's stomach grumbled and hers responded. She hadn't given him any food or water since she picked him up outside Kali's. Shame tried to pummel her, but it was shut down by that relentless, insistent voice repeating, *it's okay.*

Shops were just opening downtown. Corwin detoured by Witchy Wicks. Ms. Carrier kept a dog bowl in front of the shop and a dish of homemade treats on the counter. The bowl was bone dry. Corwin picked it up and pushed through the door. Instead of bells, Witchy

Wicks' door played a digital version of *Ding Dong, the Witch is Dead*. It startled Corwin.

"Please have a look around." An annoyed voice floated from behind the counter, even though there was nobody standing there. "If you got a gift card for Christmas, congratulations. Welcome to the free store!"

"Ms. Carrier?" Corwin called out as she approached the counter. "The dog bowl is empty."

"Ahwooooo!" Milo sang out a happy noise against her collarbone.

"Oh, really?" Marjorie Betterman and her intimidating bosom popped up from behind the counter. She gestured peremptorily for the bowl while walking away to grab some water. "Kit would not approve. Are you thirsty, puppy?"

Corwin set the bowl and Milo on the counter. She shoved her gloves in one pocket and rubbed her hands together to warm them.

He trotted over to the barren treat jar while Marjorie emptied several bottles of premium water into the silver bowl.

"Want biscuits, do you?" Ms. Betterman scratched along Milo's spine with pointy, bejeweled nails. "Have you even had breakfast yet?"

The glare she turned on Corwin was tinted with curiosity. Corwin stammered, "I found him in the snow. I'm taking him to Jack Jaga."

Milo whined. He tried to gallop to her, but his feet slipped on the smooth glass. His tail smacked the countertop and he yelped. The pain struck Corwin as though she could feel it herself. She scooped him up and held him steady by the water bowl while rewrapping her rag around his tail.

"Kit's Queenie has some food stashed here. We'll hook you up before you head back through that wind to the shelter." Ms. Betterman rooted around under the counter and came up with a measuring cup of kibble.

Kit Carrier's new familiar was a Great Dane puppy named Queen Katarina la Grosse. The kibble bits were as big as grapes.

Milo wriggled happily. He froze when his tail wagged out of the rag and into Corwin's chest.

Ow.

She whimpered for him and attempted to wrap the rag more firmly around the wound while he munched on the single piece of kibble he could fit in his mouth.

"Bloody day for both of you." Marjorie Betterman made the observation an accusation. Her false eyelashes hid her eyes as she stared at the matching rags on Corwin's hand and Milo's tail.

Corwin nodded in response.

The eyelashes finally rose. "Aren't you the Corwin girl?"

Corwin heard the real question. The real question was, "Can't you do magic?"

The door chimed out *ding dong the witch is dead.* Claws pattered across the hardwood floor and, for just a moment, canine musk overwhelmed the heady scent of all the candles. Corwin bundled Milo back into her coat and stuffed a handful of kibble into her pocket. She turned to see Kit Carrier coming in with a giggling little girl wriggling in her arms. The kid wanted to pet the enormous puppy tripping over its own paws.

"Marjorie, do you have the water bowl?" Kit flashed Corwin a smile as they passed.

Queenie let out a snuffling sound and left a white spray of drool on Corwin's grandfather's coat.

Milo returned the greeting through a mouthful of kibble.

Corwin felt Ms. Betterman and Ms. Carrier watching her as she caught the door and rushed out. She hurried along the newly shoveled sidewalk. Cars had reclaimed the streets. The wind had picked up but it wasn't deterring the gathering tourists. Corwin ducked her head and fed Milo one kibble at a time as she hurried through town to Hobbomock Street.

The wind and gentle snowfall had ruffled the pond in Drakes Wood Cemetery. Half-frozen, the water sloshed on the ice and the shore as if some great beast were doing laps beneath the surface. Corwin considered there must be some rough beast trapped in her soul like that. She wondered if greats-grandfather Jonathan had suffered a beast in his soul, too, and the plague that Abigail blamed had merely released the beast from Jonathan's control. Was she evil because she was a Corwin, or was it her own special failing?

Milo wriggled against her chest when she turned up the walkway to the Salem Animal Shelter. He cried out and she felt it in her heart.

You need me.

She did need him. But he was no tool to be forced to serve as a reminder of her black heart. She had to give him back to Morgan, the good witch. Jack Jaga would know how to reach her. Steeling herself, Corwin opened the door.

"Speak of the devil," Jack Jaga sat on the counter with a pile of kittens in his lap, "and she shall appear."

"Corwin!" Morgan Coogan tumbled a black kitten into Jack's pile and dashed across the lobby. Her face glowed around a smile that shot straight to Corwin's grief. "Of course he ran to you. Thanks for taking him in out of the cold. I know how busy you are with college and stuff. You don't look great. Are you sick again?" She reached a hand out to feel Corwin's forehead.

Morgan's flesh felt cool against her skin. But that was all. No soothing, comforting, glittering magic flowed through Corwin.

In fact, Morgan snatched her hand back as if she'd been burned. Her pupils blew wide with fear. "What's wrong, Cor? What happened to your —"

"I found him in town yesterday," Corwin interrupted before she could finish her question. She unwrapped and unbuttoned until she could extract Milo. "He was shivering. I don't know—"

"What the hell is that?" Jack Jaga hopped off the counter and offloaded his armful of squalling kittens into a box. He retrieved the bloody rag that had dropped at Corwin's feet when she pulled Milo out of his cave. "What have you been doing?"

Corwin unwound the scarf from her neck. Half of it was trapped between Milo and Morgan. She piled the rest of it on him and backed away, not looking at either of them. "I'm sorry."

Cold air pushed the door open in a rush. Before she left, Corwin risked a glance up. All joy had fled from Morgan's face. Her nostrils flared. She hugged Milo to her chest, running a hand over the slice on his tail.

Corwin saw the bleeding stop and breathed easier. She didn't see the magic Morgan used.

Beside Morgan, Jack Jaga held a hand to his chest like he'd lost his breath. His eyes were glued to the rag.

Morgan kissed the top of Milo's little head and turned cold eyes up to Corwin. "So, you're one of those Corwins, after all."

She was. Corwin fled before her feelings could spill out all over her face. She ran down to the sidewalk.

"You know," Morgan yelled, following her. "Blood magic doesn't work unless you offer a true sacrifice. You have to hurt someone you truly love. Do you truly love anybody?"

Corwin was already hurting the two people she loved. They were counting on her to save them, and she failed at every turn.

Morgan took a breath as if she were going to say something else, but she didn't. She turned at the sidewalk and walked away from Corwin. Milo scrambled to her shoulder. He howled loud enough to wake the dead in Drakes Wood Cemetery.

"Don't do it!" A voice cried out from the cemetery.

Morgan swung around to face it as Corwin did. A thin, blond woman was running through the snow-drowned grass in bare feet. She wore plaid sweatpants and a purple t-shirt that read *Foothills High School*. There was something familiar about her, but Corwin couldn't place her name. Salem was a small place. Corwin had probably met everyone. That didn't mean she knew their names. Something just tugged at her, saying she should know this woman's name.

There was a shimmer around the woman, but Corwin couldn't see past the glamour. She didn't even realize that the woman wore a glamour.

"Woof!" Milo wriggled out of Morgan's arms and tore past Corwin, dragging her scarf with him. He reached the woman just as she stumbled and fell to her knees in a snowdrift. His healed tail wagged without spraying blood.

Corwin followed him. She shot a glance back to see Jack Jaga watching from the open doorway of the shelter. Morgan kept her gaze down as she trudged after Milo.

Milo had lost the scarf a few feet from where the lady went down. Corwin scooped it up and crouched by the dog and the underdressed woman. Silly as it was, she spoke directly to Milo. "Go. Morgan can heal you and get you warm. I'll help this lady."

Milo barked at her. He turned and barked at the woman laying crumpled over her knees.

Promise you'll help her.

"Yes, I promise," she whispered to herself. "I will help her." Corwin laid an arm over the woman's shoulders and said, "Let's get you up."

The woman leaned on Corwin's arm, but kept her eyes on Milo. "You know how, sometimes, you feel like you're all alone?"

"You're not alone." Corwin got her to her feet and onto the semi-shoveled sidewalk. "I'm Corwin."

The woman shivered. She looked into Corwin's eyes with a grim smile. "They call me Sher." She turned a warmer smile on Milo. "Thank you." She added in a whisper directed at the dog, "Don't trust anyone named Walter."

Walter.

Corwin felt a shiver run down her spine that didn't come from the cold. It was fear.

Milo yipped a tiny noise that drew Corwin right back to the moment she had cut his tail. Her heart clenched in her chest. She wanted to reach out and rub his fur, to settle the hackles that had spread down his spine.

"Walter will hurt you," the woman went on.

Corwin's mind filled with the image of a blinding light and burning pain rushing through her veins. She smelled licorice. Her own voice startled her, "Just call me Walter."

"Ahrrrooooooo." Milo let out a howl as the voice in her head cried, *no.*

The blond stranger looked up at her. Her eyes flashed. "Do you want to be Walter?"

It was only a lifetime of discipline that kept Corwin from bursting into sobs. Instead, she sucked in a tiny breath and shook her head.

You are not a Walter.

She argued against the voice in her head, *I hurt Milo.*

So, prove you're not a Walter. Help this woman.

Milo barked. Warm air washed over Corwin with his breath. She turned to wrap the scarf around the freezing woman. "Let's get you warmed up." She shrugged out of her coat.

Morgan's cold voice came from a few yards away. "Milo, come."

Milo barked another breath of warm air and ended with a questioning little howl.

Corwin nodded at him. "Go. Morgan's a good person." Without waiting to see if he would obey her, she turned to hold her coat out for the woman. "Here. It's a little long for you. We'll find you one that fits at Kady's Resale."

The woman looked at her curiously and Corwin saw a flash of gold in her brown eyes. "Why are you helping me?"

Corwin looked back. Jack Jaga watched from the shelter. Morgan was walking away. Milo peered over her shoulder, his gaze on Corwin, loving her even after she'd tried to steal magic from his life's blood, after she'd betrayed him. She held her sigh in and forced a smile to her lips, if not to her eyes, as she turned to Sher. "Because I don't want to be a Walter." She added in her head, *I just want to get my magic back.*

The woman leaned on Corwin, drawing her close and sharing the warmth of the coat. "I don't want you to be a Walter, either, Corwin."

CHAPTER 12

Nearly a year later, when Corwin's nineteenth Samhain rolled around, she was still fighting the beast in her soul, her personal Walterness. She couldn't ask Milo for forgiveness, or Morgan, but she found a way to offer the universe an apology for Jonathan's beastly behavior and it assuaged her guilt enough to allow her to venture out into the crowded streets.

Halloween was a big deal in Salem. Tourists flocked to the local festivities, ready to be terrified and amazed and more than ready to shell out money for the experience, as well as souvenirs. For the witches, it was a chance to throw off the cloak of secrecy, or at least drape it behind their shoulders for a day.

Before she left, Mother had kept them home throughout All Hallows Eve and Samhain. After she left, Daddy took Corwin to the train station where she could watch the pretty glittering all around while he siphoned strangers' power to use in his attempts to reach through the veil, thinnest at that time of year, to find a trace of her mother's aura. His thoughts were always focused on her mother, as, Corwin knew, her own should be as well.

But, once her father left, she'd had no teacher. Learning magic from books was like learning music from reading it. They said the composer Beethoven was deaf. Corwin often felt like Beethoven as she struggled away in her family's lab, alone. But on Halloween, she could walk out into the streets of her town and watch kids learning from their parents, witches of different covens learning from each other, and untrained tourists discovering magic in themselves. It was an undreamed-of magical symposium for Corwin and the most glorious night of the year.

Until her nineteenth All Hallows Eve.

Kids who had kept their Skill to themselves throughout school felt free to break out of that stifling box. They put on masks and tested their friends and enemies, fairly sure but not entirely certain which of them were also Skilled. Nobody doubted that Corwin, a spinster recluse at nineteen, practiced magic. What was unknown was if she was any good at it.

After hanging rugs over the windows, pouring salt along the thresholds, and scrubbing a mixture of salt, sage, and lavender oil into the runes carved on both sides of the hearth, Corwin stuck her kalimba in her pocket the way a confirmed witch might carry her wand out of the house on a High Holy Day and slipped out the kitchen door, being careful not to break the line of salt in front of the doorway. She made sure to sprinkle good wishes with the salt and spark the wishes with power. The salt rarely lasted long, in any case. Corwin kept a salt lick at the base of the White Oak and covered it in attracting spells, but the deer still preferred the salt at her doors. She thought it was a remnant of the curse on her family, but she liked the deer. The creatures were treated as a nuisance by her neighbors with their neatly trimmed landscaping. Corwin left them the salt and planted shrubs they would enjoy.

A weak sparkling of magic drew her attention away from the yard to the nearest streetlamp. Tourists gathered in droves to see the infamous Jonathan Corwin's house. What curses would Halloween spirits have brought down on the man who burned witches, they wondered? Only, Salem hadn't burned any witches. They'd hung them or let them die in the horrid conditions of the jails. Giles Cory had been pressed for failing to declare himself innocent or guilty. And one young witch had died in Corwin House at Jonathan's hands.

Jonathan's accounting of the event was a passage that Corwin read every year. And every year, she saw something different in the words. This year, reading it with her eyes opened to the evil in her own soul, it had seemed to Corwin that Jonathan had been testing not *if* Martha Smythe was a witch, but how strong she was. He'd expected her to repel his attack easily. What Corwin couldn't tell from his notes was whether Martha had been too weak in Skill, too untrained, or if she had simply chosen not to fight back.

Corwin kept Martha in mind as she put up decorations. Once upon a time, Corwin had hidden from the tourists, leaving her house early on All Hallows morning and not returning until the following day, when the tourists were sleeping it off and locals were gathering for Samhain observances. After she broke her own heart hurting Milo, she'd decided to apologize to Martha.

Months of fear had followed her experiment with blood magic and her encounter with the homeless woman, Sher. She'd bought the woman shoes and a coat and then left her eating at Kelley's Charms Cafe when it occurred to her that she was still being selfish. She wanted the woman's gratitude. She wanted the universe to give back her powers. She wanted Milo to forgive her.

She'd had the strange idea that she'd made a promise to the dog to help Sher, but it was just her own insanity. She'd made a promise to herself, as if helping Sher could make up for what she'd done to Milo and give her powers back. It was all about her, just like cutting Milo had been. She'd gotten halfway home when it occurred to her that leaving was all about herself, too. But, when she got back to the cafe, Sher was gone. Corwin hadn't seen her since.

She returned home, cleaned up the blood, made vows to herself and to Corwin House, and planted Jonathan's grimoire on the center of her worktable, keeping her sin in sight. For months, the universe denied her power. She focused on her music, dreading a call from her father, and certain she would never be forgiven. But then she started planning her Samhain decorations to honor Martha—to apologize for Jonathan's evil—and slowly, smatterings of Skill returned, blessing her research.

The idea to honor Martha with her decorations had occurred to Corwin during one of the long nights she stayed up in the lab, comparing all her other ancestors' spells with Jonathan's and attempting to re-craft them, scrubbed of his influence.

A close reading of Jonathan's grimoire led her to believe that he was also the reason the family didn't take familiars. Corwin considered visiting Jack Jaga, but knew she would sink into the earth with shame when she saw him and she didn't really want an animal in her house if it wasn't Milo. She hadn't seen him since Christmas. It was nearly a year, and the longest time she'd ever gone without having to shoo him away from her doorstep. She found she missed him. There was no way for her to apologize to the dog, so her brain twisted around to find someone else she could apologize to — a dead woman, killed by her greats-grand-father Jonathan.

Corwin built a human-shaped frame on the front lawn to represent Martha with her arms thrown wide and wove it with dahlia, French marigold, nicotiana, evening primrose, thyme, and honeysuckle. Then she stuffed sacks with hay, corncobs, and peanut shells and fashioned them into a kind of reverse scarecrow to represent Jonathan. She scattered unshelled peanuts, cracked corn, and sunflower seeds on and around the scarecrow.

Martha's familiar had been a bat and, by All Hallows Eve, bats would be flocking to the bugs that were attracted to the flowers of her frame. Meanwhile, crows would descend on the giant voodoo doll of Jonathan and, by the end of the night, he would be eaten away.

Corwin kept her head down as she followed the cobblestone path from the kitchen door to the sidewalk beside the house. She knew tourists would assume her layered skirts and thick, black greatcoat were a costume. Her long, straight, black hair, which she left unbraided, added to the image. There was even a pointed hat sitting on the kitchen table. She hadn't been brave enough to wear it. It took enough courage to go out without her scarf pulled up and newsboy pulled down. She wore only a pair of ear muffs decorated with musical notes that she hadn't been able to resist the last time she'd gone for socks at the resale shop near the shelter. She was carrying the ancient straw broom that had leaned against the kitchen door since long before she was born. This felt like bravery to her.

The sparkle of weak magic drew her attention out of her own head.

She turned toward it and spotted some kids she had been in school with. Of course, they weren't kids anymore. But they giggled and crowded together just as they had when they made fun of her on the playground. They didn't see her approaching.

"Try again. The whole yard can't be protected." Levi York poked a molded pine wand into Lisa DeGiulio's waist.

The blond girl giggled and performed a lovely, if intent-less, swish and flick of her more powerful raw birch wand.

A spray of multicolored sparks raced to the boundary of Corwin's yard and then burst into the crowd when it hit the wards. People in the crowd yelped and danced away from the odd sensations. An older woman wearing a Notre Dame scarf wrapped to just below her eyes exclaimed that the burned witches had come for their revenge. Her friends laughed, more at her than at her joke. Corwin hummed a tune that diverted Levi York's next attempt from her house to Notre Dame's companions. The prick of his failed spell wiped the laughter from their faces.

"Oh, felt it that time, did you?" Notre Dame Scarf asked.

"This place is just creepy." A man with a cloud of hair slipped his arm through hers. "Let's go find that haunted house."

As the tourists passed between Corwin and her classmates, Lisa spotted her. She screeched a noise that sent some of flower-Martha's bats fleeing. "She's right there!"

"How long have you been standing there?" Levi asked this as though they hadn't been trying an All Hallows Eve prank on her house.

"Long enough to know my house is safe." Corwin nodded politely and followed the Notre Dame crew towards town.

"Hey! Where are you going?" Levi shouted after her. "It's not like you're invited to any Samhain feasts."

His friends chuckled.

She held up her straw broom and yelled back, "Only time I get to ride this thing around without shielding."

The guffaws grew behind her but she heard some doubts, too. She wondered how she would even straddle the crooked broom in all her skirts.

The downtown streets were filled. Tourists, locals, and visiting witches were all in the spirit. Most of the streetlamps had been transformed to look like gas lamps or even open-flame torches. Corwin hurried toward a lamp at the far end of the block that glittered brightly with orange sparkles that formed the flames into shapes like hearts, circles, a pointed hat, and a cat.

Wade Kelley, a trumpet player from the band, stood with his mother and older sister, Colleen. They had their backs against Witchy Wicks, facing the bewitched streetlamp. The three of them huddled together against the cold, holding hands and singing a tune in close harmony. They were very good. Tourists had gathered and tossed coins into a hat on the ground near their feet as their song came to a close. None of these tourists connected the chanting with the flames behind them.

Wade spotted Corwin and nudged his mother. "Look, it's the last Corwin."

His mother dismissed Corwin with a snort. "Rotten, the lot of them. Show me what you can do, son."

A wicked gleam in his eye, Wade raised an eyebrow and flicked his free hand in her direction.

Corwin saw the orange glimmer of his intention and easily blocked the flame that shot from the streetlamp at her. A thought struck her as she raised her hand to redirect the flame; she didn't want to use her powers selfishly anymore. Hurting Milo and helping Sher had taught her that. Here was a perfect opportunity to put their lessons into practice.

Colleen Kelley was shivering as she sang, holding a shawl tightly around her shoulders. Corwin changed the magical flame. She directed its heat to dissipate and encompass the Kelley family. Wade's sister relaxed and stood taller. She sang out a crisp, clear high note that silenced the crowd. At the same moment, the streetlamp flared, its flame in the shape of a great Phoenix. Corwin clapped and grinned. Then she caught Wade's glare and moved on.

As she strolled through the crowded street, she spotted a tall, dark-skinned, underdressed man looking around as though he had dropped something. She pulled out the spare mittens that lived in her pockets. They had belonged to her grandfather, as had the coat, and were much more likely to fit this stranger than her gloves would.

"Excuse me. Would you like these?" As Corwin handed over the thick, woolen mittens, she pulled heat from the nearest streetlamp and, unintentionally, from the excitement of the crowd around them. She wrapped the heat around the curious stranger with a muttered couplet.

The tall man hummed a harmony to her little song and she repeated herself, louder, to hear his odd tone better. There was something glittering about his entire person and up close, she could see he had red pupils, so deep they could be mistaken for black. A third repetition of their duet was followed by a crack of thunder far over the water and then the smaller crack of a bark close by their feet.

The man folded himself down to let Milo sniff his new mittens. Then he lifted the little dog close enough that he could lean out and lick Corwin's nose. The gesture brought more heat to her cheeks than the flames nearby and she blinked back the heat that leapt to her eyes.

Don't cry.

Her shame intensified when she heard a familiar voice behind her. "There you are! Milo, you were supposed to keep an eye on Pundu. Oh." Morgan Coogan pulled up short when she saw Corwin. She'd freed her hair from its customary braids and it poofed out like a halo around her angelic face. Her smile dropped. "Hey, Corwin."

Like an idiot, Corwin's heart bloomed. But her memory gripped fiercely to the time she cut Morgan's dog's tail for a blood magic disaster. "H... hi, Morgan," she stuttered, chewing on her lip. "Is this your friend?" She wondered if Pundu was a relative on Morgan's mother's side.

"Yes. Don't worry, Pundu doesn't feel the cold." As Morgan said this, the man repositioned Milo so he could hide his mittened hands. Corwin smiled, despite herself.

"It's okay," she assured him. "You can keep the mittens."

"You gave her clothes." Morgan looked from Pundu to Corwin, a look of confusion growing on her face.

"Her?" Corwin asked.

Morgan laughed. "Yes. Pundu says she is a *she*. Who am I to argue?" Morgan pulled a glove off and held out her hand. "That was super cool of you, Corwin, giving Pundu a gift. Thanks."

Corwin pulled off her own glove and slipped her rough hand into

Morgan's soft, warm one. A chill raced through her bones, followed by a shock that drew a cry from her throat. Hairs stood up all over her body and her Sight was suddenly blinded by the glitter shooting through her from Morgan's flesh. She couldn't pull her hand away.

Morgan threw her head back and laughed. "I got you!"

CHAPTER 13

Morgan held on to Corwin's hand until people started looking over, disturbed by Milo's fierce, incessant barking. Corwin stumbled back. As soon as Morgan released her, the literal shock and metaphysical terror at losing control both disappeared. Corwin tried to grin back at Morgan but she couldn't quite manage it.

Pundu offered her a mitten. Milo howled. Corwin shook her head and backed away. She tried chanting to herself, *it's just a prank.* She'd thought it kind of funny when Levi and Lisa and Wade had tried to prank her. It made her feel like one of them, like she wasn't such a weirdo outsider. But she hadn't expected it from Morgan.

You're not a weirdo.

That stupid little voice couldn't be more wrong. A few cold breaths dissipated the shock enough that she was able to drag a grin to her lips. She raised her bare hand and muttered, "Happy Samhain." Then she ran.

She'd go back home, lock herself in her attic bedroom, and watch the festival fires in safety. If she was alone, nobody could hurt her. The house would keep her safe. But the house couldn't protect her from her own black, cowardly heart. Her shame would go home with her. It would curl up on her bed and invade her dreams.

Corwin left the crowds of downtown. She didn't go home. She skulked through the streets, enjoying the decorations and yelling at herself until she found her feet had taken her to Hobbomock Street. Milo deserved the apology, but she could start by facing Jack Jaga.

Midnight struck as she approached the animal shelter. Cries went up from the kennels as the bells of every church in town rang out the cresting of Samhain. A familiar green-eyed woman hidden behind brown eyes and hair the color of Milo's face stood in the courtyard of the three kennel buildings.

Corwin froze. She should have expected Kat Coogan to show up on Samhain. It was when she had banished her mother and when she had tried to kill young Corwin with ghosts. Corwin was a fool to have forgotten. But she wasn't a kid anymore. She couldn't just keep avoiding this stalker, hoping to put her off until she'd found the Corwin family power. She would just have to face Kat Coogan on her own.

The witch smiled. Corwin walked over the grass in her direction. She took a breath, but before she could say anything, Kat Coogan was swallowed up by a thick fog that rolled in off the water as though driven by demons from the Christian Hell. Corwin stopped walking when she found herself surrounded, drenched to the skin with the otherworldly mist. She flexed and gripped her left hand against the sudden burning of her scars.

A crack of thunder followed hard on the heels of a bolt of lightning that struck the earth not ten yards behind Corwin. She spun to see the fog blown back by a pair of powerful, black-and-white wings, eight feet across. As she dragged her wild hair out of her eyes, icy rain suddenly pelted down and the fog closed back in before she could get a good look at the massive, red-headed bird that had flapped those wings. She saw something clutched in its talons, but Corwin couldn't identify it through the inky fog. She knew only that it was wriggling. It was alive.

The enormous wings pushed the fog back just long enough to give Corwin a chance to think. She spun in every direction. She could see barely three feet in front of her. As the fog closed back in, she realized that she couldn't hear the bird. She couldn't hear the animals in the shelter. She could only hear a faint glittering, like the fizzle of certain fireworks. Magic. There was nothing natural about this weather. Kat Coogan was attacking all of Salem.

Corwin ducked her head against the rain and shoved against the wind. She had to get back to the center of town. She wondered why Kat Coogan would attack her own family's home. Corwin had always thought that she and her family were Kat's only enemies. No matter the forces, Corwin had to get to town, to share her power in protecting the tourists and unSkilled natives.

She broke through the crest of the wind and had run three steps when the ground opened beneath her feet. A sinkhole swallowed her down and kept spreading. Corwin dove for a wall to climb out, but the walls retreated faster than she could run. Her boots could get no purchase on the loose dirt. At the rate it was expanding, the hole would reach downtown in minutes and the animal shelter in seconds. Without much thought to the how, Corwin cried out, reaching for the edges of the hole with her power.

"Earth, hold! Stand your ground."

The earth kept moving under her feet and rain tumbled from the sky like someone had primed the pump good. Corwin searched her memory for a spell that would work. She envisioned the loose pages of Great-grandaunt Camillia's treatise on what the family had learned from the Wampanoag about coaxing magic out of nature. She had to ask, not demand.

"Hear my plea and know my sorrow. Grant my neighbors a bright tomorrow."

With her hands spread wide, Corwin pulled at the earth with all the power she was granted. It wasn't much, but the tide turned. The walls of the hole slowed their outward spread. The rain filled the hole instead of wearing at the edges. It was a start.

Corwin stuck a hand in one pocket, searching for any crystals or herbs she might have stashed there. All she found was her kalimba. She plucked a tune that was so drowned out by the rain even she couldn't hear it. She turned in a circle, pulling at the edges of the hole with one hand and desperately trying to remember a spell that would help. As her mind struggled, her fingers tripped over a song that made her giggle.

No music. This was serious and she needed to focus. Now was the moment when all of her hard work and study had to pay off. Hobbomock had taught the family to care for the land. He was the reason they nurtured the creatures that wandered into their yard. Could her kindness to the deer help save Salem?

A red glow illuminated the rain and fog far over her head. At first, Corwin thought it was the glitter of dark magic. The way it flickered, though, and the roar of crackling, popping power told her it was fire. The town was under siege from all the elements. She needed help.

The rain picked up when Corwin pulled her hand from her pocket and tried to climb the wall of the sinkhole. She managed to get purchase and climbed, advancing slowly but steadily towards the surface. Remembering her offerings, she cried to the deer at the top of her lungs, "Salt for nutrients. Water for life. Weaken the force causing my strife."

A bolt of lightning lit up the fog, revealing the lip of the hole twenty feet above her head and receding. The hole, prevented by her from expanding outward, was expanding downward. A second flash of lightning, accompanied by ear-shattering thunder, struck the wall just over Corwin's head. She lost her grip and tumbled through the air. Her mind went blank, only that ridiculous old Carole King song wailing on. Even that went silent when she landed on the fragmented remains of the sidewalk. One leg shattered. The snapping of her bones echoed a double crack of thunder just before her head smacked into the ruined sidewalk of Hobbomock Street, knocking her unconscious.

She woke to feel a greasy magic worming its way around her broken body, reaching into her cells and trying to tear her apart. After a quick, undisciplined scream of terror, Corwin pulled herself together and shouted more than sang, "Hey Jude!"

The greasy invader fled.

It was a cry to her ancestors. Her great-great-grandaunt Judith's journal focused on healing spells. She'd been a funny woman, a feminist, if such a thing had existed back then. If her spells could heal Corwin, then maybe they could heal the land, too. Corwin turned her intention from her own broken leg, bleeding head, and other cuts and bruises to the earth. She dug her fingers into the clods of dirt and grass around her like roots and shot her power up into the flames like the branches of a tree growing out to clean the air.

"Take what is broken and make it whole again." Great-great-grandaunt Judith hadn't gone in for rhyming, but the spell didn't feel right to Corwin. She added, "Take of my power and build what you intend."

The fog dissipated. The walls closed in again. But the hole did not grow any more shallow. Everything she had was focused on fighting the Skill swirling all around her, trying to hurt her town. She had nothing to spare to heal herself or to haul herself out of the hole.

Rain fell hard against her face as she looked up. She tried to feel love for the water that brought nutrients to the earth. Her brain worked through the thought, searching for the answer she knew was in the elements, just like magic. Great Aunt Nell said that the elements were power. That meant the elements were magical and they were raging all around her.

Which meant she could pull from their power.

Corwin sat up. Her head and her body screamed at her. But pain didn't matter. It was a temporary thing. She took the kalimba from her pocket and set it on a flat slab of concrete beside her. She had used earth, air, fire, and water to build it, and now she offered it as a sacrifice. Raindrops struck the rough metal keys. Corwin grimaced. She couldn't get away from music, no matter how much she tried to obey her daddy. The plinks from the little hand piano weren't really a tune. But the elemental music filled her soul with power and expanded her Sight.

And there, curling within the chaos, she found that greasy Skill that had tried to capture her. It pushed at the walls where she pulled them in. It encouraged rain to shatter the land and fire to destroy. She could feel it in every breeze that blew the fog thicker into the hole. That was what she had to fight, not the elements, which were natural and good.

While the grease kept its focus on her, it didn't have the energy to expand its destruction into town. Corwin had to take the grease inside herself and close the hole. Though her physical vision was occluded, she could see clearly with her power and her heart. It would work. If she could trick the greasy Skill into focusing its destructive aims on her, she could destroy it.

The one sacrificed for the many. She'd always been the one. She could make sure Corwin House stood. As long as Corwin House stood, there was hope that her father could find the heart and rescue her mother. If the grease won, Corwin might live, but so many more people would die and her mother would be lost forever. It was an easy choice.

Before she'd realized her decision, Corwin had already refocused her power. She reached into the heavens for the music of the spheres and focused all the power she had and could borrow from the elements on the greasy Skill slinking into town. She poked at it. She threatened it. Then she asked the fog to blow earth back in place, reversing the sinkhole's growth. She suggested the rain cool itself in the flames and urged the fire to feed itself on the tasty, rich, greasy earth of the sinkhole.

It worked.

She gained the greasy Skill's full attention. Corwin threw her head back and fought her own instincts. She let the Skill come to her, let it invade her pores and her Sight and her power.

Once it got a grip on her, Corwin pulled at it, sucking at it where it had crept in like a thief. At the same time, she pulled the walls of the hole tighter and tighter. The edge touched the toes of her broken leg. It squeezed against her back. Corwin rejoiced. She might be the last Corwin. But she wouldn't be the last Salem witch. She reached out into the earth around her, begging the ancestors for just one more rush of power so she could heal the hole in their earth.

Then her plans were shattered worse than her leg.

Far overhead, a bird cried and lightning shattered the gloom. A figure tumbled through the thinning fog.

Corwin raised her arms in an attempt to break the creature's fall. She caught him, but momentum drove the velvety terrier with fur the color of Kat Coogan's glamoured hair down onto her legs.

Her broken bones cried out. The walls expanded at her distraction. She let them. Crushing herself and the greasy invader was fine. She couldn't take Milo with her. Corwin dropped her head and let her spell die. Why had he followed her this time?

Sing!

The walls spread, moving out toward the city and the shelter. Corwin despaired.

Sing! It will work!

Corwin sucked in a raggedy breath and defied her father's orders.

She muttered the words that had been floating under all her efforts to remember spells from her ancestors' writings. "I feel the earth move. . ."

The walls slowed and then stopped as she took a real breath and sang out, filling the old lyrics with power. Not even thinking about it, she reached over and plucked an accompaniment on her kalimba. The raging storm drowned out all sound, but Corwin poured intention into every note.

The annoying little voice in her head offered a harmony that pulled the walls of the hole back from their expansion, *Whenever you're around.*

Corwin felt the music growing in her gut, the held note filling her with a power that came from within rather than from the elements around her. The power struck her hard and made the ground shake. She grabbed out wildly to keep from falling over. Her left hand landed on an arch of tree root. An image flashed through her brain of the White Oak in her backyard.

That voice in her mind hummed a new tune, something she'd never heard before. She plucked an accompaniment on her kalimba and could suddenly hear it as the rain abated. Lyrics came to her lips, the voice in her head again providing the harmony as she sang at the White Oak root buried right beneath her body.

A shoot poked through the cracked cement. Branches shot out from the growing sapling. She found herself being raised by one as the little tree pushed upwards, sucking in the nutrients released by the fire and poured down in the rain. Corwin sang out her pain as her broken leg dangled from the branch. She hugged Milo between her and the trunk, even as the little dog buried himself up under the buttons of her grandfather's coat. The tree grew faster, soaking in the elements Corwin released from her hold. The greasy Skill struggled to encircle the tree but leaves popped out, green and fresh and full of a life that melted the grease, soaking it in and transforming it into energy to help the tree grow faster.

Corwin kept the tree's melody ringing in her head, screaming out the joy and pain of new life. She folded *Hey Jude* in and around the tree's song, sending the healing into her leg, into the leaves absorbing the grease, and into the earth of the sinkhole. The storm calmed. The fire died. The hole continued a slow and steady march inward. Knowing dirt was no impediment to a tree, Corwin sealed the hole the instant her branch breached the surface. With the only energy left in her, she leaned forward to tumble onto the fresh earth, curling around the warm bundle in her coat, protecting him instead of her leg. The broken bones crunched against each other and she screamed, grasping at consciousness. One last push of her Sight showed her no remnants of the greasy power that had tried to bury Salem. A glance with her eyes showed no damage to the shelter or to any of the nearby houses or the mausoleums in the cemetery.

Corwin lay there while the tree grew on its own, sucking in the swirling power released by Corwin and the elements. After a while, it slowed to the not-quite glacial growth rate of non-magical White Oaks. Beyond the lush canopy of impossibly blue and violet glittering leaves, the stars had begun to fade in the brightening light of dawn. Corwin watched them wink out, focusing on them and on little Milo crawling up her chest, rather than on the many pains of her body. She may have slept. She must have. Because only a dream could explain why Kat Coogan hadn't killed her.

She could have.

The woman approached, her black curls effectively hidden behind her blond appearance only because of Corwin's exhaustion. Milo growled quietly, but kept his nose buried against her throat. Kat knelt at Corwin's side and laid a hand on the remnants of bone that were once her right knee. A tingle that grew into an electrical shock ran through Corwin's skeleton and then her flesh. Corwin let a tear fall sideways into her ear without moving to wipe it. If this was the end, she was okay with it. The town was safe. Milo was safe. Corwin was too tired to care about anything else.

"Congratulations." Kat Coogan removed her hand and slipped on a black leather glove. "The Council has accepted you. You are a witch or, per Corwin tradition, a wizard. You are no longer a child. You are a full-fledged practitioner."

Corwin could only blink at her. She had no energy left to respond, no energy to wonder why Kat Coogan was delivering Council messages or why she was delivering the news now.

The woman scoffed, the harsh breath blowing Corwin's hair out of her eyes. "Fair warning, all it really means is that you are in more danger than ever." She laid a hand on Milo's head. "Beware the Consortium." And then she stood. "I'll be seeing you, Wizard Corwin."

The witch left Corwin lying in the dirt. She didn't kill her. She just crossed the road and walked into the pond at the edge of Drakes Wood Cemetery. Corwin watched as the sun rose and her stomach started growling. Kat Coogan never walked out of the pond.

The sun, glittering like all magical objects to some eyes, rose over the Salem Harbor as it had done every day since time was invented. Corwin, who had been uncertain that it would, breathed out a sigh. Her head dropped back into the crook of the root cradling her. Milo settled on her chest. She laid a hand over his exposed head, petting his golden fur with her thumb and marveling that he and she were both alive. She should check on the town. But she was fairly certain she didn't have any more energy than it took to pet Milo's face.

Sleep.

For once, she agreed with the little voice. "Okay."

Milo raised his head and pinned her gaze with his deep hazel eyes. She stared at him, holding him to her heart. Her other hand lay on the ground, grasping one of the White Oak's exposed roots. She wasn't sure if she was doing any good, but the tree had just raised her from darkness and saved Salem; she would make sure it knew it was welcome to any power she had left to give.

When she finally fell asleep, Milo's eyes were still pinned to her face.

CHAPTER 14

Sunlight sparkled on her eyelids. Corwin turned her head into the shadow and felt the rough gnarls of a tree root on her face. Her backside was cold but her front was too warm for the heavy blanket on her chest. That oddity made Corwin blink her eyes open. Once she realized that she was not in her attic bedroom, everything else from the previous night seeped in and she truly woke up.

Milo was the weight on her chest. And in her chest. She didn't want to take him back to Jack Jaga anymore.

He'd saved her life. If he hadn't dropped into her lap, Corwin would have sacrificed herself and then her mother would have been lost forever. He had forced her to find another way. She wasn't a child anymore. If Milo made her a better witch, then she needed to keep him.

Unless he was already Morgan Coogan's familiar.

The sunlight winking through the branches of the unseasonably green White Oak danced across her face. Corwin flexed her hands and then unbuttoned her coat, making sure Milo wouldn't tumble off. He lay splayed across her chest, all four paws sticking out to the sides. Cold drool pooled on her shoulder, soaking through her many layers. He didn't move. That weight in her heart thumped and she felt an uncalled smile on her lips.

It faded as she took an assessment of her injuries, remembering with a wince the sound when she fell back into the sinkhole. Her head felt clear. It occurred to her that she should not have slept with the concussion she must have gotten from hitting her head so hard. But she had no headache. Her limbs were stiff, but she didn't feel pain anywhere, not even in her right leg. She flexed her toes. They worked and didn't send screaming pain through her body. She engaged her abs and tested her knees. Both legs worked the same. She folded them up and straightened them, flexing them like she did her fingers after playing too long.

"Hey, Milo," she murmured at the soft, warm puppy. "I'm gonna sit up now."

He yawned, his little pink tongue rolling impossibly far out of his mouth and then curling back in. He did not open his eyes. She wrapped her hands around his chest and supported him as she sat up and scooted backwards to lean against the tree. He didn't seem to mind being transferred to the crook of her arm. She watched the breeze ruffling the branches high above them. She'd done good. She knew it. Her eyes drifted down to the helpless, and temporarily boneless, creature in her arms.

"Hey, Milo," she whispered to him. "I'm sorry I sliced your tail open and used you for dark magic."

One eye opened and then the other. Milo craned his neck up and licked her on the nose.

It's okay.

And she thought the little voice might be right.

Jack Jaga waved a hand when she finally noticed him in front of the shelter. She waved back. He ran a gaze up the brand new sixty-foot tree and then offered her a little bow. Corwin laughed. He disappeared inside the main building.

Corwin looked down at Milo, knowing what she had to do. "We can get him to call Morgan."

Milo rolled his eyes up at her and then yawned again and sniffed the air. He barked at something and Corwin looked up. She blinked hard, clearing her eyes, but it didn't change the fact that Morgan Coogan herself was turning onto Hobbomock Street at the corner of the cemetery. Her body turned, at least. Her eyes remained glued on the green canopy of the new oak. She stared at it, remarkably not tripping, all the way to the path leading to the shelter doorway.

Corwin thought she should get up or alert Morgan but she didn't really feel ready to stand yet, or to risk losing the little terrier. She watched as Jack pushed out of the shelter's front door holding two dog bowls. Morgan dashed to hold the door and then walked with him towards the new tree. Morgan's eyes slowly worked their way down to see Corwin and Milo snuggled against the base. Her feet stopped working for a moment. Corwin wasn't sure if the shock on her face was approval or fear. Eventually, she started walking again, but she was still in the middle of the street when Jack reached them.

"This doesn't look tasty, I know," he said, setting one of the bowls on the ground and handing the other to Corwin. "But it is full of carbs and proteins and amino acids."

Corwin's stomach growled. Milo lifted his head and sniffed at the bowl in Corwin's hands.

"No, buddy. That's for her." Jack pulled a spoon and a bottle of water from a pocket. He traded off with Corwin, sticking the spoon in the mush and taking Milo from her arms. Milo reached down and starting scarfing his mush before Jack had even set him on the ground. He took a hiking bowl from another pocket and popped it open before pouring some water into it from the bottle.

He handed the bottle to Corwin with a little laugh. "You built a tree, kid. Eat something."

Corwin shook her head but discovered she was just too tired to deny her culpability.

"Here, let me hold that for you." Morgan knelt and took the bottle from Corwin when she was done drinking. She pet Milo with her other hand. "I'm glad they finally tested you. It's my fault—" she began, but Jack Jaga interrupted her.

"The Council's reasons are their own, Ms. Coogan."

Corwin ate, thinking about how Kat Coogan had called her an official wizard. Her mind felt frozen. She couldn't grasp what was going on and so she ate. It tasted marginally better than it looked but she was grateful for the water. They were saying that last night had just been a test.

She took the bottle back and drained it, then asked, "The town wasn't being attacked?"

Their eyes grew wide and they looked at each other before Jack answered, "No."

"The shelter and all the animals," she asked, "they weren't in danger?"

"No." Jack let out a breath that may as well have been a growl and looked away.

"Didn't your dad warn you about Samhain?" Morgan asked, her eyes searching Corwin's face.

"Mother did," she said. "We cover the windows every Samhain and salt the house."

Morgan blinked. "Why?"

"To keep the—" Corwin stuttered and filled her mouth with mush to give herself time to think. She remembered that the blankets had to do with keeping them safe from Coogans or Samhain traditions, but after Mother had left, she and Daddy had gone out every Samhain after covering the windows. So, maybe it was to protect the house. She really didn't know.

Jack Jaga pulled another bottle of water from another pocket. He cracked the lid and handed it to Morgan, taking the empty. "The Council tests kids after their sixteenth Samhain," he began.

She nodded. "Yeah, but I'm a Corwin."

"I have a mind to go over to your house and have a word with your parents," Jack said half under his breath, already pushing to his feet.

"No!" Corwin and Morgan objected at the same time.

Morgan added, "They're very strict. They'll be mad she went out on Samhain. Plus, it's a weekday and they're probably at work already. They work a lot."

Corwin stared at Morgan, dumbfounded.

As did Jack. "It's Samhain," he said, like they were slow. "Who works on Samhain?"

Corwin shrugged. "You."

Jack Jaga threw his head back and laughed. He wiped tears away as he finally said, "A point to the wizard. You're feeling better?"

She licked the spoon clean and dropped it in the empty dog bowl. "I am."

"And you, sir?" he asked Milo.

Milo licked his bowl clean then turned and climbed into Corwin's lap, burying his muzzle under one of her hands as Jack gathered both bowls.

The big man pushed to his feet. His eyes flicked between Morgan and Corwin and finally down to Milo. "I'll leave you to enjoy this beautiful morning. Blessed Samhain."

"Blessed." Morgan waved a hand.

Corwin called after him, "Thank you."

He waved his hand over his shoulder like he was flicking away a fly. Both Corwin and Morgan watched him walk away for far longer than was really necessary. Eventually, Morgan looked out over the water, following the swooping path of a bird catching currents in the distance.

Corwin enjoyed her grin for a little bit before she dropped her eyes to Milo. The worst that could happen, she thought, and then stopped the thought as her heart began pounding in her chest.

"Milo found me again last night," she blurted the words out like it wasn't obvious.

"I figured." Morgan blushed. "I was on my way to your place when —" she cut herself off and blew out a huge breath of air. She continued, her eyes fixed on the tree, "when I heard about your test."

"It was just a test." Saying the words out loud, Corwin felt a blush rising in her cheeks. She felt like a fool. A tiny laugh burst from her. "Nobody was ever in danger."

Morgan's green eyes returned to hers. They glittered. "Not true," she breathed. "You were. And so was he."

"Were you. . ." Corwin struggled to find the right words to ask the question without speaking of magic right out. The whole idea made her laugh. She was leaning against a tree that had grown overnight but she didn't want to say the word *familiar*? "Were you with him?"

"No." Her hair bounced as she shook her head. "Daniella Sita Corwin, he finds you on his own." She sighed and then scooped Milo from Corwin's lap and held him up in the cool air. He growled at her and she growled back, pulling him close to her face and pretending she was going to bite his muzzle. Milo gave a yippy bark and nipped at Morgan's nose. She laughed, "Bad dog."

"No, he isn't." Corwin reached out but didn't go so far as to take him from her. "He's a very, very good dog.

"He is." Morgan adjusted so that she was leaning against the White Oak's trunk, her shoulder pressed up against Corwin's. She held Milo in one arm and used her fingers to comb the spits of fur at the tips of his ears. "He is also a smart dog. And he knows what he wants. Doesn't he?"

Milo licked her nose and then laid his face against her shoulder with his gaze pinned on Corwin. Morgan gazed out at the bird soaring closer and closer to shore.

Corwin couldn't take it anymore. She just asked. Her voice cracked as she did. "Is he your familiar?"

Morgan's laugh shook Corwin. Leaves fel on them from above at the force and length of that laugh. "He's not my... He's not mine, you idiot." She looked at Corwin for that last bit. Then she turned back to the bay and pointed. The bird flew so close, Corwin could see its black-and-white wings and red head. It was the giant bird that had blown back the fog and given her a moment to think at the start of the attack. At the start of the test, she amended. Up close and calm, she could see it was no mere bird.

"That's Pundu. She's my familiar." Affection lit up her face. It entranced Corwin. "She and Milo adore each other."

Corwin blinked as she remembered the person that looked like a man from town. "The Pundu I gave Grandfather's gloves?"

"Yeah. She can make herself look human when she wants."

"What is she?" Corwin asked.

Morgan looked around and lowered her voice. "An impundulu, a lightning bird. My aunt Myrna rescued her egg. My mother knew what she was from old legends our family brought from Africa. But Pundu chose me." Her eyes glittered.

Both women looked out at the lightning bird who had ducked beneath the waves and was sluicing water from her feathers as she soared back up toward the sun.

Corwin grinned. "I guess you don't have to worry about bullies hurting you through her."

Morgan grinned back. "No. I don't."

Corwin's heart thumped, in part at clearly being back in Morgan's good graces, and in part from fear. Corwins didn't keep pets. Her father would definitely be unhappy. But she wasn't a child anymore. The Council had tested her and she had passed. Corwin was a full wizard. She had the right to make this choice.

Say it.

In the distance, the impundulu gave a mighty beat of her wings. Lightning flashed between clouds.

Say it.

"Morgan," Corwin choked on the word.

Morgan pet Milo. She raised a single eyebrow. "You're gonna have to say the words, Cor."

"I want to take Milo home with me." She had more to say, but Milo interrupted her by singing out a howl that would have impressed a wolf. He leapt out of Morgan's arms. Corwin barely caught him. Once she had a safe hold on him, she had to squeeze her eyes and mouth shut for fear he'd lick an eyeball out. A tingle ran through her, lifting the weight from her heart like magic.

Between her heart pounding and Milo singing, Corwin barely heard Morgan whisper, "Finally," as she turned her gaze back on the impundulu.

CHAPTER 15

Corwin took one of a half dozen spray bottles from the lowest shelf in the lab. She had prepared each of the bottles with a neutralizing wash and a few tablespoons of the powdered invisibility mixture she was certain would work if she could only find the right base to make a sprayable solution. She'd tried sprinkling the powder directly on Milo, but it hadn't done anything except make him sneeze. Seeing the collection of small spray bottles at Kady's Resale had given her the idea of liquifying the potion.

While searching for inspiration at The Bookcellar, Corwin had overheard a couple of kids she knew in school, she shouldn't call them kids anymore, talking about a party. Wade Kelley couldn't remember anything. Lisa was filling him in on all of the rude stuff he'd done. Corwin had risked approaching them just to ask what he'd been drinking. Wade had sneered at her. Lisa had told her he was drinking Everclear. She didn't know what that was, but the little voice in her head suggested she ask Jack Jaga.

Jack used the alcohol to clean sap off of dogs after he took them running in the woods. He could not successfully explain to Corwin why Wade, or anybody, would drink the stuff. But he did assure her it was safe to spray on Milo, as long as he kept his eyes shut.

She poured the sample Jack had given her into the spray bottle and swirled until it was dissolved.

"You ready?" She turned to Milo, who sat staring down at Abigail's cramped handwriting in the family grimoire. He looked up. "Come on. I've got a new one."

Same as the old one.

She ignored her doubt and crouched beside Milo. "Shut your eyes."

He did. She sprayed him while focusing on her intention of making him invisible and singing, "Youuuuu are invisible to sight. Your aura blends in with the light."

He didn't disappear. He did roll onto his side and bury his head in the little beanbag to hide from the *Rite of Spring* melody.

Corwin sighed. "Alright. Back to the drawing board."

Milo leapt up and they raced each other out through the fire, across the main room, and into the library.

It had only been half a dozen months since he moved in with her, but life was better with Milo. It was harder, too. She had to follow a schedule for the first time since she left high school. He did not stay up all night. He did not stay up all day, even. He expected meals at regular intervals and insisted on walking first thing in the morning. If she hadn't gone to bed, that was her problem. She tried just opening the kitchen door and letting him out into the yard but he made it very clear that wasn't acceptable, as did the annoying voice in her head, which she was starting to recognize was usually right.

She felt better, saner, when she started going to bed after he took her out for a night walk. She drew the line at letting him sleep with her, though. She gathered some old skirts from the unused closets that were softened from use but too short or wide for her tall, skinny frame and sewed them into a bed for the dog. She set it in the kitchen, near the fire, where she thought she would like to sleep if she were a dog.

He used it. But only when she was in the kitchen with him. Most mornings she woke to find him sleeping in the library. He'd curl up in her beanbag, near the books she lay strewn about. She learned to be careful about opening the attic door after the fourth time she found him acting as a doorstop.

Corwin knew that her Daddy would not approve of Milo. She looked forward to telling him the Council had accepted her but didn't want to have to shove Milo in a cupboard when he called. There were precious few cupboards in the house, since it had been built to Puritan standards. There were none in the lab. So, to avoid the argument, Corwin permitted herself an hour a week for creating the spell she had dreamed up back in school when the bullies had knelt by her desk to make fun of her clothes and her hair and her books and her silence. She worked on an invisibility spell.

She started as she did all magical endeavors. She scoured the family books and the library. She preferred the floor to the old, single drawer desk and chair. She could spread out as many books as she wanted, referencing them without having to search for them again.

Milo remained glued to her side as she gathered books around her on the library floor. The dog followed her around anytime he was awake, unless she left a book or her notes open on the floor. Then he would act as a guardian over them until she returned or he got lonely.

She didn't mind the attention. He was a very good listener. Her music improved simply because his attention made her more aware of the effort she put into it. Her magic improved for the same reason. She found it easier to remember what she was learning when she talked it through to him. She found herself debating with that little voice in her head and it often sent her diving back into the family tomes to verify that what she thought she knew was true.

That voice also started pushing her to listen to her own instincts as much as the books.

Your instincts saved you on Samhain, not your ancestors.

"My instincts come from everything I've learned from my ancestors."

And music.

Corwin hummed the opening of Stravinsky's *Rite of Spring* as she held her place in Great-granduncle Samuel's journal with a finger and made notes in her own. "I think Sammy used house water as a base because he was a little bit agoraphobic."

A little bit?

Milo laid his head down on Abigail's journal and covered his head with his paws. He, much like the very first audience to ever experience *The Rite of Spring*, hated the composition.

Corwin laughed and stopped. The song continued playing in her head. She'd played the entire symphony on the spinet for her Vintage Performance final that morning. She liked the off-putting music. It just felt right for her life. But even she was sick of it after spending the last month perfecting it.

At that thought, her rebellious *voice* projected Debussy's *Prelude to the Afternoon of a Faun* in her head. It was one of her favorites to play on her triple string harp. Milo would curl up so close when she played it that she had to remember to look to avoid crushing him. It felt like what she wanted her life to be. It felt like running through the forest as the sun came up, a breeze rustling her hair and the leaves.

The feeling made her think that nature had to be able to provide a more useful base for an invisibility potion than house water.

"Where's Cam's paper?" She scanned the splay of open books around her, searching for Great-grandaunt Camillia's flowery script.

Milo lifted his head and flipped Abigail's journal closed with his nose.

"Milo! I wanted that open for. . . oh, there's Cam's paper." Corwin leaned over and slipped the thin book out from under Abigail's worn journal. "Hey, don't crush yourself."

Milo's paw was trapped in the pages of Abigail's book. Corwin flipped it open again to free him. He returned to sniffing every square centimeter of the old paper while she scanned nature-loving Cam's notes.

"Yeah," she murmured. "Yeah, she says here that dew collected on the new moon is good for helping to ease memory. Forgetting might support invisibility. Forgetting to see."

Collect dew from the White Oak. It was planted for protection by Hobbomock.

"When is the next new moon?" Corwin yawned.

Milo rolled over the books to present his belly to Corwin.

She laughed, "You're gonna break all the spines."

Already broken.

"You're getting fur everywhere." Fur, in fact, floated into the air as his tail thumped against the open pages of the almanac.

"Ha! Here we go." She grabbed up the almanac and flipped through the pages to find a calendar of the phases of the moon. They had just passed the full moon so she wouldn't be able to collect dew for nearly two weeks. She lay back in the beanbag and closed her eyes as she reviewed her schedule. She had two more finals and then she had to write an essay for her master's application, not forgetting she needed to make a better plan for how to find the heart of Corwin House. She'd had a good idea about washing everything in the house like she'd washed the mirror so that it would visually sparkle when her father called. Objects that were naturally magical didn't glitter to her Sight. If they did, she would probably go mad living in Salem. The wash had overcome that—she didn't know what to call it—that safety feature. Maybe if she used a powder base instead of...

The thoughts of her frantic mind fell silent. The rich, musky scent of old books and her handsewn beanbag chair faded away, replaced with cold steel, alcohol, detergent, and licorice. Chattering filled her head. It could have been a flock of chickens or animals slithering through the forest, but Corwin knew the noise was voices and more than just voices, full surround-smell thoughts. Some of the many lab techs thought in images. One only thought in music. At all times, he had heavy metal music pounding in his head. He responded to orders in English but the only words he ever spoke —Yes, sir — took up no space in his mind.

She didn't understand most of the words thought or spoken in the lab. There were a lot of words. She was a young boy. Yes, a boy, she realized. She was starting to recognize many of the words but she didn't know their meanings yet. She knew the word needle. Needles were a concept she was very familiar with. She heard the word in Walter's head in his crisp, cold, British accent just before he jammed the cold sharpness into her leg. It didn't have to hurt so much. The needles didn't hurt when Mama put them in. She let the alcohol dry and then slipped it in on an exhale, filling her mind with love.

Not Walter. She screamed as he stabbed her veins. She screamed when he jabbed the shocker stick into her flesh. She screamed when he brought the Eye down to illuminate his work, not caring that it blinded her and her siblings. Whichever one of them was on the table, she would experience Walter bending over, chewing violently on a stick of Black Jack gum, his hands drenched with the sandalwood lotion he slathered on his hands and arms every single time he washed. He never tried to bribe her with liver, like he did the others. She never stopped crying long enough for him to bribe her with anything.

She didn't scream at the thoughts in Walter's head of how he would tear her apart until he figured out her secret. She screamed because of the thoughts of how he would tear apart her brothers and sister. She screamed because, as he took pictures and pumped chemicals through her little body and cut samples from her flesh, he thought about his other experiments. Screaming, whimpering, crying, wailing; none of it could drive away the images of her father grafting salamander DNA into a woman's spinal cord while the salamander and the woman both lay conscious on his tables.

Listen to me. See what I see. *The chant floated over the feeling of glee Walter experienced, remembering how he removed a boy's heart and swapped it with a baboon's, giving the baboon the boy's heart. Love, longing, joy in a sea breeze washed over her as she sent her attention away from Walter and focused on her mama's mind. Instead of a bloody operating room that looked just like the room she lived in, she saw a woman lounging on a beach. The crash of waves on the shore drowned out the other voices in her head. Trees secluded the little patch of sand and there was nobody else there but her mama and her mama's mom. Mama called her mama Mom.*

I call my *mother* Mom, *her mama corrected.*

She absorbed the new word. Mama imagined the letters in her head. She spelled the word mother in clouds across the blue sky over the waves. Mama's Mom's face was painted white. All of her golden skin was painted white. It shimmered as the sun came from behind a cloud and the woman turned to call Mama over. Riding along in Mama's head, she squirmed at the slimy goo Mom—Mama's mother—spread across her skin. Sand grated her flesh as it was caught up in the sunscreen. Mama painted the new word in the sky even as she complained about it on the beach. As soon as her mom let go of her, Mama ran down to the water.

"Don't you dare wash that off, Rhea!"

She turned with her Mama to face her teenaged Mom and laughed.

Then she spun in the wind and the spray and released herself into the world until she felt the wet sand squish through the pads on her paws and the fur that protected her from the sun rather than slimy white goop. She howled at a flock of seagulls and chased them along the shoreline.

Corwin lost herself in the joy of running with the salty wind whipping through her fur. She ran until the needle was yanked from her leg and she was yanked from the shiny table and tossed back into the cage with her littermates. She crawled over them, trying to cover all four with her little body. It didn't work. It never worked. Walter's horrible smelling hand shoved her aside and grabbed Laylea, the only girl in the litter. Rhemy bit her foot as if he could keep Walter from taking her. It didn't work. Rhemy fell back, landing on Corwin as Walter strapped Laylea down on the cold table. Corwin's mind filled with Laylea's fear.

Corwin sat up, still shivering from the nightmare. She sometimes dreamed of being on stage in front of all of Salem with her parents in the wings and no score on the music stand. But this dream had been far worse than that. It was visceral. She struggled out of the beanbag, sitting up to rub at her ankle where she'd felt the needle being jammed in.

Milo lay sprawled over the books. Great Uncle Sammy's massive journal had fallen closed from where she'd propped it open against a few other books. About fifty pages of Corwin knowledge lay on Milo's head. She lifted the front cover and scooped Milo into her lap.

"Daddy would approve of you immersing yourself in the texts." She sighed, not able to ignore the truth behind her joke. "Maybe I'll just hollow out one of these books and you can hide in that if he ever calls."

Milo sang out a bark.

She laughed. "Come on. Let's go get some fresh air before bed. I need to get this dream out of my head."

And like that, the dream was forgotten as her musical mind started flitting through lyrics, unfortunately applying them to the opening phrases of *Rite of Spring*.

"Can't get this dream out of my head. Fill it with midnight air, instead."

The voice in her head giggled.

CHAPTER 16

"The music of the spheres posits that there is harmony in everything. Vibration causes all sound. I can See that magic vibrates. People's auras vibrate. Your aura vibrates." Corwin stepped over a spruce that had fallen in the last big storm and waited while Milo hopped up onto it. "His aura vibrates."

She didn't indicate the nine-foot-tall bear they were trying to leave far behind them. She had discovered over the years that it was best to just ignore the bear with poof-ball ears. He never bothered her and, if she spotted him, she simply called it a day and made her way out of the woods as calmly and quickly as possible. The quick part was relative.

Milo had alerted her to his presence as they were leaving the woods and they'd had to turn around and head deeper in to stay out of his way. They were working their way towards the ocean where they could follow the shoreline back to civilization.

Corwin laid her palm on the trunk of a giant sequoia. "The trees vibrate."

It just makes sense to use music to make magic.

"So, how do I use the vibrations to find the heart?" she asked Milo as he walked along the fallen trunk beside her.

Harmonics.

Corwin had found that her little voice was speaking to her more. It spoke more when she listened. She spoke more because Milo seemed to listen. Her magic and her music had been improving by leaps and bounds since she started talking to Milo.

"I pluck a string —on my harp, the spinet, a guitar, wherever— I pluck a string and all the other strings respond."

A flock of birds exploded into the sky over where they'd left the bear climbing a tree. Their wings cut the air with whistling noises she'd once thought was their song. Everything was music.

Echolocation! The voice exclaimed as Milo gave up trying to navigate around a branch and leapt into her arms. She tucked him into a pocket of Great-great-grandaunt Judith's collecting coat and got down on all fours to crawl under the downed spruce's needles.

"I don't know if echolocation could help find the heart."

Could it help us get out of the woods?

Once she got beyond the branch, Corwin stood again. She looked around. The sky couldn't help with directions because she couldn't see it. She smelled the ocean but didn't have a sensitive enough nose to be able to locate its direction.

Should have brought your divining rod.

Milo stuck his head out of her pocket and sniffed.

She asked, "Can you smell the ocean?" She sniffed, herself.

There's too much pine.

Corwin laughed and brushed the needles off of her jacket and out of her hair. She should have put her hat back on before crawling around. "Echolocation is it, then? Okay. Here we go." She sang out a low note, since low frequencies traveled farther, and then she listened. "I can't hear anything."

Wimpy ears.

"I aced my ear training classes. I have highly educated hearing. But, yes, perhaps they aren't made for this." She tried again, loading her mind with magical intention and singing on a pedal tone, "Show this note so that like a bat, I might figure out where we're at."

Violet sparkles soared through the forest; where they hit trees, they rebounded back to her. She watched until the air was clear and then turned and sang again, "Show this note so that like a bat, I might figure out where we're at."

The voice in her head sang along, weaving a melody around her pedal tone. Some of the resulting harmonies were not good.

Not as bad as the Rite of Spring, the voice commented as Corwin watched the sparkling music floating beyond the trees, some bouncing back, but not much.

She turned and aimed in that direction, singing new words with a new intention. "Echo back if you find water so we can make Milo swim like an otter."

"Ahrooooooo!" Milo struggled in her pocket until she lifted him down to the ground again. She looked up to see violet sparkles racing the wind through the trees toward her. Instinct made her duck, but she had told the magic to echo back and it echoed right back into her face.

Laughing, she pushed off the cold ground and chased Milo through a hall of conifers to find a freshwater koi pond sparkling violet with her magic. Corwin followed Milo around the pond and through the rich people's backyards until they reached Goody Talmadge's Bed and Breakfast. Gregory Talmadge had installed a brick path that led from the front yard into the woods.

Milo led the way down this path even though Gregory and his husband, Irwin, were transferring bulbs from pots into their flower clock. Corwin ducked her head, planning to hurry by, but Milo raced over to the men and circled them twice before dashing back to the path and out to the street.

Gregory Talmade shouted, "Milo, you keep out of the flowers!"

His husband quietly admonished him, saying, "He did."

Gregory sighed and then glared at Corwin. "Does no one in your family respect private property?"

"Dear, we're a public bed and breakfast in Salem, Massachusetts. It is not bad for business to have a witch slinking through the yard." Irwin waved at Corwin. "Apologies, dear heart. You go on and try to catch up to Milo."

Everyone in town knew Milo. Even the people who ignored Corwin on the basis of her family's reputation greeted Milo. It made her wonder why, with so many willing, he'd chosen her.

She caught up with him halfway down the street where he'd stopped to bury his head in some old lady's rosebush. There weren't even any blooms. The lady knelt on a pad on the far side of the bush, picking off yellowish leaves.

"I'm sorry about him."

"Oh, I don't mind Milo. It's not healthy to hold grudges."

Corwin didn't know how to address that. She tilted her head, feeling very much like she'd learned the move from the dog.

The old lady understood her question. She wiped her gloved hands on her apron and sat back on a little stool. "I adopted Milo. Thought he'd be a nice companion to have around. He ran away. Came back a few times. But he didn't want to be my dog." She gave Corwin a second look. "Are you Daniella?"

Corwin nodded.

The woman snorted. "Well, I see Jack Jaga was right again. Can't argue with Milo in any case, but I suppose he knew where he was needed. You used to come here for daycare, you know."

Corwin shook her head. She glanced up at the house but didn't remember it.

"Well, you did. Until your father lost his blooming mind. Poor dear. The roses weren't as lush then. I'm not much of a green thumb. Your father kept them healthy for me until Sita came. I never really got them back until Milo's brief visit." She said this last to Milo, who had circled the bushes to stand up on the lady's knees. He licked her nose and then trotted down the street, looking back at Corwin as if expecting her to follow.

Corwin raised a tentative hand to the woman. "Nice to meet you again."

"Go. Go." The lady waved her away. Then she contradicted herself. "You're very welcome to come by anytime."

Corwin nodded and turned to see Milo burying his head in another bush. Blue sparkles ran along the trimmed stems and out into the yellowing leaves, which perked up and turned green. Of course, her daycare had been run by a witch. She knelt and slipped the open loop of his leash over Milo's head.

Stupid leash laws.

The voice wasn't wrong, but it didn't change facts. Sometimes, Corwin appreciated the range-of-motion exercises he forced her shoulders to go through as he dashed to smell flowers or other dogs or to greet people. They got stiff from playing.

When they got close to town, Milo turned down Hobbomock Street. Corwin followed. He liked to visit Jack Jaga. She hadn't been able to get the supplies she needed for the potion she had in mind, so the day's plan was up in smoke anyway.

They were just passing the pond in Drakes Wood Cemetery when a rental car pulled up to the curb in front of the animal shelter. It parked and a strange pair climbed out and made their way up the walk. Parking wasn't allowed on Hobbomock Street. People considered the cemetery and the little park across the street where Corwin had grown the White Oak as one expanse of green, despite the sidewalks and cobbles between them. No local ever drove down Hobbomock street if they weren't part of a funeral procession. The parking lot between the cemetery and the animal shelter had a Hobbomock entrance, but most people drove in from Smythe Avenue like Jack Jaga's little Smart Car was doing right then.

Milo had stopped to stare off into the cemetery.

Corwin watched as the two, a woman in high heels and a pencil skirt clutching the collar of a short fur coat and a much more casual man wearing jeans and a tweed coat, approached the glass doors of the shelter. There was something odd in the pairing. The woman's tight bun versus the man's messy ponytail made Corwin think she was the boss, but the woman deferred to the man. She knocked on the door after he found the knob locked, but then the man knocked, as well, as if her knock wasn't done right.

Jack strolled from the parking lot, his eyes down as he straightened his clothes. A breeze ruffled his spiky, white-blond hair and his head snapped up. He froze in his tracks for a moment and then increased his speed until he nearly ran around the corner, cutting through the grass to reach the couple at the front door.

The wind shifted again, blowing a smell past Corwin that turned her stomach. It scared her, too. She couldn't say why. A stiffening of the leash drew her attention down to Milo.

He'd stopped staring out at the pond. He faced the animal shelter, his tail sticking straight out behind him. A strip of hair stood on end from his neck all the way back to his stiff tail. Corwin had never seen him look so tense.

Who is that?

She looked back up as Jack stood aside to let the strangers proceed him through the door. Corwin let her gaze go blurry, looking at the pair with her Sight. She saw no sparkles. Neither one was magical. She was so focused on looking for magic she almost missed the slimy quality of the man's aura. It oozed tightly around him like it was too heavy to expand as most auras did when encountering other auras, as Jack's red-tinged aura was doing.

Milo lunged to the end of his leash as the man's dirty-blond ponytail disappeared into the shelter. Jack saw him. His eyes shot up to Corwin's and he gave a sharp shake of his head, mouthing something that could have been "no" or "go." Either way, Corwin agreed. She did not want to get any closer to those two.

"Let's get out of here." She tugged Milo's leash, turning to cross the street.

He did not follow. Corwin had never pulled on his leash as she saw other dog owners do. There was no need. He was easygoing on walks and she didn't mind following his lead if they didn't have a destination. If they did have a destination, he was happy to follow.

"Milo, come." She gave the leash two gentle jerks and stepped into the street. The dog held firm, his gaze fixed on the front door of the shelter.

The door was closed. Jack had gone inside. He was alone with them.

Someone needs to help him.

"There are a lot of animals in there." Corwin tried to reassure herself. Her little voice was not on board.

They're locked in cages.

Corwin thought of the binoculars in her bag. They helped her search for seeds and leaves before climbing up a tree to find it didn't hold what she needed. "There's a better line of sight from the oak."

The words were barely out of her mouth when Milo gave up his stance and dashed into the street. He ran with her until they were safely on the far side. It wasn't a long distance but her breath hitched and she struggled to slow her heart in the face of the panic crawling up her spine.

Flashes from her recent dreams sent spikes of adrenaline through her veins. Needles. The bright eye light. Slashing cuts to her flesh. She slid down the trunk of the tree until she found herself sitting on the ground, holding Milo tight against her chest. He was shivering as hard as Corwin was.

Walter. Walter. Don't hurt them, Walter.

Corwin took a deep breath. She had taken care of herself without any help since she was eight years old. She was not going to huddle, terrified, behind a tree just because someone smelled wrong. Her imagination had just run away with her. The homeless woman, Sher, had planted the name Walter in her head and the stress dreams had plucked it out and made the name her boogeyman. There was no Walter. Just a creepy couple in the animal shelter with her friend, Jack.

She set Milo down in the grass. "Stay here."

Binoculars.

She ignored the little voice. Why should she hide and peer through the doors when she could just walk over and judge them in person?

If he's British, run.

The Walter in her dreams had a British accent. Corwin had tried to parse that out, but the only British person she knew was Marjorie Betterman at Witchy Wicks, and she wasn't afraid of Marjorie Betterman. An image of Marjorie in a lab coat that wouldn't button closed over her enormous chest distracted Corwin from her fear long enough for her to reach the front door. Opening it was just the next logical step.

Going inside became much more difficult when she was assaulted with the sound of a familiar British accent.

"You see, Laylea was a very special dog. And she is sick. My wife is endangering her life, taking her from me. I'm sure you understand." The guy with the ponytail leaned on the counter.

Jack Jaga stood behind the counter with his hands at his sides. He held himself as though he was ready to run.

The woman balanced evenly on her heels a few feet away. Her accent was blandly midwestern. "Ex-wife. As an animal caretaker, you must have heard of Dr. Bowman. He is a renowned therianthologist."

Impossibly, Jack Jaga stood even straighter. Nothing changed in his face, but she saw his aura harden and darken, protecting him. He sucked in a quick breath to respond. "Strays don't come to us with names, Dr. Bowman. Why do you think she might be here?"

"My ex-wife grew up here. Perhaps you knew her? Katherine Coogan?"

Corwin's head spun. She stepped inside just to draw the strangers' attention from Jack for a moment as the big man had gone paler than she thought possible in a man that white.

"H-hey, Jack," she stuttered. "I just came to see if you had any job openings."

His voice was remarkably steady and disturbingly cold. "No, Danny. No jobs. Go home. You say Katherine Coogan was your wife, sir?"

"Yes."

"Katherine Coogan is a well-known name around Salem. Partially because of all her educational successes, and partly because she died rather dramatically in a terrorist bombing twenty years ago."

Corwin felt the blood drain from her face. If Kat was dead, who had been attacking her?

Jack's eyes flicked her way for an instant before returning to the strangers. "So that would make this Laylea a very remarkable dog."

"Oh, she is," was the man's smooth reply.

Someone opened the door at Corwin's back. She tripped forward to keep from falling backwards. Morgan caught her arm to steady her. She read the tension in the room and shot a quizzical glance at Corwin.

Jack's shoulders relaxed just a bit when he spotted Morgan, but he kept his focus on the pair in front of him. "I don't know what games you're playing, Dr. Bowman, but I—"

"Oh, please," the Brit interrupted. "Call me Walter."

Ice formed in Corwin's gut so suddenly she thought she would throw up right there in front of the most beautiful girl in Salem. The little voice became not so little, deafening her with a horrified cry of *Walter.*

"Jack." A new voice called out from behind Corwin. She hadn't heard that voice since she left school.

Morgan's mother pushed on her daughter's shoulder as she rushed past. "Jack, there's a situation out at the Novaks' place. The police need your help with a rabid dog."

"Come on," Morgan whispered in Corwin's ear as she pulled her out the door.

Her mother kept her voice loud as she inserted herself between the counter and Walter. "You folks have to leave so Jack can lock up. Let's go. Jack, I'll meet you there."

Corwin was so stunned she let Morgan drag her out of the shelter, but when Morgan started down Hobbomock Street, she pulled away and rushed across the street to the White Oak. Milo ran from behind the tree. Corwin's heart leapt in relief at seeing him until she heard the crisp, slimy tones of Walter Bowman, arguing elegantly with Morgan and her mom. She spun around and panic rushed blood into her ears until she couldn't hear anything but an E-flat pulsing inside her head.

When Milo reached her, she realized that he wasn't running at her but at Walter. On instinct, she grabbed him by the scruff of his neck and hummed the E-flat out loud, pulsing her hum just as her blood was pulsing the note inside her head. The waveforms, real and imagined, surrounded Milo and suddenly she couldn't see the dog or her hand. She could feel the ground beneath her knees but couldn't see her body. She inched forward and lifted Milo into her arms, despite his struggling. His growl vibrated against her chest.

Across the street, the stiff woman was getting into the rental. Walter was not. He crossed the street, heading directly for Corwin. She could tell from his searching eyes that he couldn't see them, but that wouldn't matter if he could hear Milo.

Please, please be quiet, she begged Milo in her head, wishing Telepathy had been her gift rather than Sight. *Please. He's scary. We can't let him find us.*

She was reeling from discovering that Walter and his licorice breath weren't just a figment of her imagination and that Kat Coogan was supposedly dead.

The growl continued to vibrate against her chest just as her E-flat vibrated in her throat, but both of them faded away until she couldn't hear the sounds any more than she could see their bodies.

Walter was almost on them. Morgan raced across the grass, her mother following slowly behind.

"Walter!" Morgan panted the name. She took a deep breath and reached out to take Dr. Bowman's hand. Then she repeated the name in an unusually low tone. "Walter. You know nothing."

Green sparkles worked their way from Morgan's hand around the creep's entire body. They moved faster and spun wildly when they reached his head.

Morgan held his gaze and repeated, "You know nothing. It's time for you to go."

Walter nodded gently. "I know nothing."

Morgan's mother reached them as Walter started striding back to the street. She turned to walk with him, holding Morgan close.

"So sorry," he said to her in a voice intended to charm but with none of the actual charm Morgan's voice had carried when she told him to go, "It's time for me to go."

They reached the rental car in moments. He got in and drove away.

Morgan scanned the little park. Her eyes never found Corwin and Milo.

CHAPTER 17

Leaves dusted the sidewalks and lawns of Corwin's neighborhood. She shivered as she trailed at the end of Milo's leash, wishing she'd grabbed a coat. A deep yawn brought tears to her eyes. Sleep hadn't been a major priority since she discovered Kat Coogan had died the same year Corwin was born. Kat hadn't visited since that discovery. Neither had Walter. Her father hadn't called, either. It had been two and a half years since she'd startled her father on the train and she was starting to lose hope.

A month into her musicology master's program, Corwin tried to drop out. Her guidance counselor told her she'd have to repay the scholarships that had funded all of her college classes thus far. She had never worried about money before. Everything she needed came from stores her father had already set up accounts with. She knew those bills were paid monthly from an account with First Bank of Salem. She was pretty sure she wouldn't be able to access that account without her dad's permission and, even if she could, her scholarships had covered thousands upon thousands of dollars.

So, she stayed in school, even though she knew that all of her time and energy should be focused on finding the lost heart that held her family's true power and lifting the curse. The voice in her head insisted that the increased protections she created for the house, herself, and Milo were absolutely not the waste of time they felt like. She couldn't save her mother if Kat or Walter got to her first. Milo's walks became an opportunity to work through plans in her head, to reconsider potions and spells and charms she'd already tried and to think up new ways to search for the heart. She stopped greeting her neighbors, or even seeing them. Her focus was entirely on the inside of her head.

Only Milo's bark kept her from running into the sharply dressed man waiting on the sidewalk in front of her house. He was attractive and well-groomed in a way Corwin would imitate if she ever spent money on that sort of thing. She instinctively brushed down the flyaways at her temples and shoved her messy braid over her shoulder. She hadn't trimmed the split ends in ages.

"Ms. Daniella Corwin?" The man asked as if he'd already said her name many times.

"Yes." She tore her eyes from the cleft of his chin and blinked herself awake. "Yes, I'm...that's me." There was no need to tell him she preferred to be called Corwin. He was holding out a business card. She didn't think you offered your preferred name to someone with a business card. She didn't take it.

He pulled his hand back in, unsure what to do with the card. "I'm Conner Drakeson. I work with Smythe, Touche, and DeSantos."

He paused as if that explained everything. Corwin raised her eyebrows at him.

"Your father entrusted us with your, ha ha, trust." His uncomfortable laugh brought out dimples in his cheeks. "Now that you are of age, we need to complete the paperwork to transfer the trust to your control."

"Okay." Corwin's father had never told her about any trust. Her hackles suddenly rose as she saw the man's cute mannerisms and face as a trap. She muttered, "May your nose grow long if there are lies in your song."

"Lies?" It was the only word Mr. Drakeson caught. "No. Has your father not told you? I promise you, we're a legitimate firm and we have taken good care of your money. All our fees were paid up front. We just need to get Mr. Daniel Samuel Corwin III's signature to transfer the accounts from our care to yours." He held the card out again. "You can check us out, if you like."

"Oh." Corwin watched Drakeson's nose intently. It flared a little but it did not grow any bigger. "I can get his signature and return the papers to you." She looked at the card belatedly and realized returning the papers in person would require a trip to Boston. "Would it be okay to scan them?"

"You're welcome to mail them, but we would need the originals back." Mr. Drakeson jogged two steps to set the briefcase on the hood of his car. He opened it and took out a legal-sized folder. "He'll need to have his signature notarized."

Corwin took the proffered folder and the card. She could forge her father's signature. She'd done it hundreds of times. "Would he have to sign it in front of the notarizer?"

"Uh, yes." The lawyer blinked at her. "Yes. The notary is there to verify that it is him and not somebody else signing the papers."

"Oh." Corwin had gotten along fine without her own money so f,ar. She'd be okay. She started up the walk to her door. Then it occurred to her that Mr. Conner Drakeson might come back. She turned to tell him, "My father travels a lot. It may be a while."

"Well, let him know that we emailed him a secure link to the documents. He can print them out and have them notarized wherever he is." He leaned in and lowered his voice. "Is he out of contact a lot? We've been trying to reach him for over a year."

"He'll sign them when he gets home." Corwin tried out a reassuring smile, enjoyed his baffled dimples for a moment, and then fled into the house.

Milo wriggled out of his cinch-leash and dragged the thing over to its home under the coat rack. Corwin watched him, her mind distracted from spell-casting for a moment. The two of them took the folder into the kitchen. Milo hopped onto the table and tapped her deskpadd awake while Corwin filled his bowl and refreshed his water. She grabbed a muffin and sat in front of the padd. First, she searched the law firm and discovered it was an old firm with offices in cities around the world. There were hints in their marketing and in the locations of their offices that they were familiar with Skilled clients; in other words, they knew about witches. If that were so, she probably couldn't get away with a magical solution to the notarization problem.

For the first time, she wondered about the accounts that paid the grocery and utility bills, as well as the various tabs she kept in her father's name around town. While Milo chowed, she pulled down the junk drawer that sat on top of the refrigerator. She was about to begin digging through it when she noticed a brush and realized she'd never checked here for her mother's DNA. She jogged to the parlor and grabbed a pair of the manuscript gloves she used when applying stain to new instruments. The caution paid off when she found a mint tin filled with hair ties. She set them aside and kept digging until she found the First Bank of Salem debit card flat on the bottom.

It took her two tries to guess her father's password. It was Sita100913. Her mother's name and their anniversary.

Milo hopped up onto the table and sang out a small cry as she scrolled to the balance on the account. It was low. In addition to the regular household purchases, her father had been drawing on the account for his travels. He had transferred money in a few years before, but there were no regular deposits.

Corwin sat back in the chair, stunned. She was going to have to find a way to make money. A way that wouldn't distract too much from her search for the heart.

"Guys," she said to Milo and the house. "I need a job."

"Arooo." Milo leapt from the table and ran out. He returned with his leash and went straight to the kitchen door.

"We just walked."

Milo turned, sat, and gave her a look that could have wilted flowers if they kept any inside. Corwin sighed. She logged out of the bank site and powered down the padd. She picked up her end of the leash and helped Milo into his end.

"Back in a bit." She locked the door behind her.

Milo beelined for the sidewalk. He didn't stop to sniff or water anything. He led Corwin out of the neighborhood, into town, and straight to the door of the Music Shoppe. They'd sold some instruments for her before in barter for supplies she hadn't learned to make herself. But they didn't have a lot of customers willing to pay enough to make the work worthwhile. Still, she opened the door. Milo did not lead her to the sales counter in the back of the store. He took her to the corkboard beside the front window where people posted flyers offering services or looking for used instruments.

"Milo." To her shock, Jack Jaga strolled over with a packet of picks and a roll of strings in his hands. "Have you got Corwin trained up, yet?"

Milo dropped to his belly and rolled over so Jack could scratch his chest. Corwin watched as the big man sat down on the floor and massaged each of the dog's legs. She didn't know Milo liked that.

When Jack stood, he said, "Nice to see you. You aren't on your way to the shelter to return Milo again, are you?"

Corwin shook her head and searched for something to say. It was polite to speak to people. She looked at his purchases. "Do you play guitar?"

"Not yet." He grinned. "I was just at the Haunted Grove neighborhood yard sale and this acoustic beauty called to me. I play the radio for the animals to calm them. Thought they wouldn't mind too much if I learned to play music myself." He gestured at the flyers for used instruments. "You can't be looking for a new instrument. Morgan says you play everything."

Corwin's heart skipped a beat at the idea of Morgan Coogan talking about her.

Jack answered the question on her face. "She works at the shelter now. She's a natural with animals. But you know that, don't you, Milo?" He looked down, giving Corwin a moment to compose herself and find words.

Tell him you'll give him lessons.

As usual, the little voice in her head gave Corwin the best advice. Before she could chicken out, she blurted, "I'm thinking of offering lessons."

Jack's gaze shot back to her face. "Really?" His eyes brightened against the flush that reddened his skin. "Would you take a rank beginner?"

Something in her sang like it did whenever she started a new class. She thought she would like teaching someone brand new to music and found herself nodding until words came. "I don't know what to charge."

Jack laughed. "Conveniently, potential teachers have posted their prices right here." He turned to the bulletin board and pointed at the flyer with the highest rate. "How about this?"

The rate made her pulse race. She didn't even know if she was a good teacher. A thought came into her head and she pointed at a lower rate. "How about this, and you keep Milo supplied with dog food?"

"Ahhhh, he told you I make my own, did he?" Jack grinned down at Milo and then stuck out his fist. "It's a deal."

Corwin tapped his fist with her own and felt a thrill race up her spine.

"Now," Jack said, holding up the dulcimer pics and metal strings. "What else do I need?"

The joy Corwin felt at getting a job so quickly was squashed by the fear that she was losing more time and she had no idea where her parents were.

CHAPTER 18

Corwin stopped sleeping at regular hours. Other than Milo's walks, she kept no kind of schedule at all. She taught Jack once a week in the kennels at the shelter and he gathered more students for her who were more than happy to play to the animals. Very few people wanted a Corwin in their home, though they didn't say it in so many words. Most of the parents watched their kid's lessons, watched Corwin. Milo strolled along the cages, exchanging sniffs with the animals waiting for homes.

Since she didn't have a bank account of her own or any ID, Corwin asked for payment in cash or barter. The bartering meant she didn't have to go gathering in the woods as often, which saved a lot of time, even if she did miss the crush of the trees and being surrounded by nature. It also meant she never had to cook. Jack provided Milo's meals while two other parents provided Corwin's. Her bills at the grocery and Kali's butcher shop both went down. The Bookcellar became her own personal library. The owner slipped her books on the magic of music that Corwin would never have been brazen enough to search for.

The books inspired her. Though, while she completed her musicology assignments quickly, she couldn't write the papers she wanted to write. Privately, she still gathered what knowledge she could on the intersection of music and magic and applied it to her search and to their protections.

Music—the lessons she gave and classes she took—sucked up much of her time. The rest was dedicated to magic. She built a model of Corwin House and dusted it with a powder she devised to reveal magic. The result had been a lovely, constantly glowing blue nightlight that sat on the mostly unused desk in the library. She drew blueprints of all the rooms and tried traditional scrying with a variety of different crystals. None of them did anything except spin in her hand. Later, she used the microcosm of the house model to expand the property wards into a magical dome that stretched along their property lines. The first version had hurt a few birds, but she'd been able to heal most of them herself and Jack had found a witch to take the most badly injured of them on as a familiar. The deer had made their displeasure with the dome known until she figured out how to make an exception for them. Overall, it was a work in progress.

She ate when Milo was hungry and slept when she crashed, usually over a stack of books, sometimes halfway up the attic stairs. Milo dragged blankets to her and eventually the house gained some color other than gray as Corwin left the blankets and comforters where he dropped them over her.

Her mind continued working on magical and musical questions in her dreams. When she was particularly frustrated, she dreamt of Walter and the steel-cold lab. She woke from those nightmares desperate to run. But what good would running do when the thing she needed was somewhere in the house? Good naps brought dreams of riding in a car, a woman's voice singing "Jambalaya" or "Lullaby of Birdland" or a hunting melody in what Corwin thought was Chinese.

One morning, the woman in the car finished a song and started talking. "Found Lizzy last night. I was thinking about her while we collected sea sponges. When Mother and Father left to visit Robert and the new baby, I snuck into her room and took her prized sponge. She never let me use it and I, forgive me, held a grudge over that. But I realized that it has her skin on it. Her face was her pride. I thought, with something so special to her, the mirror would surely show her to me. I cut the sponge into many bits and used up nearly all of them before it finally worked. A most impor-

tant factor in my success is that I was thinking about how much I missed her or how angry I was at her leaving us. I truly just wanted to know if she was safe. She is. She is even happy, which I don't think I imagined possible. Here is how I made the potion."

The woman held a paper out to her. The brown paper was blank.

"Breathe on it," the woman said.

As her warm breath drifted over the page, script blossomed like flowers, filling it with her great-great-grandaunt Judith's handwriting.

Corwin woke under the kitchen table, her pillow soaked in drool. She grabbed a banana and rushed into the lab to find Milo curled up in the small beanbag behind the water pump. Corwin had been reading the family grimoire. She remembered leaving to get a snack. Milo had all of his feet and his tail tucked in together. His head rested on a rag doll that he had found in the basement.

She didn't wake him. They could walk and eat breakfast later. She slipped the open grimoire away from the beanbag without disturbing him and propped it on the reading stand on the worktable. It was already open to a section written by Great-great-grandaunt Judith.

She sat on the stool and leaned in, still half asleep.

"Breathe on it," the voice had said.

So, she did.

Green ink surfaced over the familiar black script, listing out the exact technique Great-great-grandaunt Judith had used to find her sister, Lizzy, in the mirror.

Usually, Corwin would mark down the steps of a spell like a recipe, listing the ingredients so she could gather them before beginning. But she was so excited, and nervous that the writing would disappear, that she just started gathering the herbs, bones, oils, flowers, and such, substituting for what she didn't have without much thought. Sometimes, inspiration lay in letting go of her thoughts and letting instinct rule, letting her inner voice tell her what to do. It was one of the hardest techniques for Corwin to learn. Despite her fear that she was losing her mind, that inner voice never steered her wrong. She listened for it through her harried thoughts, but it was silent, for once.

With a last look at Milo, curled up with his rag doll, she left the lab to find an item personal and precious to her mother. After crying on their bed after her father left, Corwin had pretty much left her parents' room be. She dusted and ran the mechanical broom over the carpet, but always put their abandoned knickknacks and boxes and such back afterwards. Her mother had taken everything of hers from their bathroom, but she had left behind a jewelry chest. Corwin went to this and opened it reverently. A short search of the pretty items revealed a pearl inlaid hair comb. There was no convenient strand of rich brown hair woven through the tines. But Corwin took it in hopes there was some DNA left behind. She detoured by the downstairs bathroom and grabbed the hand mirror there.

Back in the lab, Milo stood on the workbench, sniffing at the ingredients in her mortar.

"Good morning, Milo." She scratched his ruff as she leaned the mirror against the book and grabbed a dusting brush to wipe hair remnants from her mother's comb into the mortar with everything else.

"Woof." Milo tapped her arm with his cold nose. He tapped the book, too.

The little voice in her head told her to review the ingredients she'd gathered so far before she went any further. Out loud, she talked through the items, not justifying her substitutions, all the way to *personal item of the subject — not to have been touched by the petitioner.*

Just as Lizzy had never allowed Great-great-grandaunt Judith to touch her facial scrub, Sita had taught Corwin to keep her messy hands out of her hair, making the hair follicles a good personal item to try.

The next step was to crush everything together and wash the mirror with the result. Corwin picked up her pestle and went to work. When she lifted the mortar to pour the mixture over the glass, Milo howled.

She stopped and glared at him. "We'll go out in a minute."

Milo howled again. But Corwin's mind was focused on her work. The voice in her head yelled, *Stop. You're forgetting something.*

Corwin set the mortar down and reviewed the jars and bags and Petri dishes on her table. She tapped every item on the page with the eraser of her pencil as she went. Everything seemed to be there. She lifted the mortar again. Again, Milo howled.

"Fine," she sighed. "Maybe I do need a moment to think." She lifted the dog to the floor and turned to head out through the fire.

Milo barked. She turned to find him leaping back up to the work-table. He tapped his nose against the book.

"Come on. Either we go out or I keep working. Which is it?"

Milo sat. He glanced around the workbench like there might be a stray kibble for him and then walked over to drag his paws through the dust she'd blown from the rarely used mugwort jar. He limped back to the book, holding his right paw up, and then stood on his hind legs to tap at the page.

The book stand collapsed. Corwin dove and caught the hand mirror before it fell and shattered. The book fell back as the stand folded and knocked over the jar of powdered mugwort. Her eyes were drawn to the dusty paw print over a note written in the margins, in script so small and messy she had given up on it before. She grabbed the old box of random tools from the top shelf and rifled through it until she found a magnifying glass.

The notes read, *liquify the mixture with three drops of house water infused with the petitioner's intention. Use a virgin sea sponge for washing.*

Corwin stared at the dog. Reality shifted ever so slightly as certain events over the past years lined up a bit differently than she remembered them. Magic was imaginary to most people. She knew that. She'd been taught so. But it was at the core of her life so how crazy was it to think that Milo was more than he seemed?

She dropped the magnifying glass and grabbed her pencil. Flipping to a blank page in her notebook, she wrote *Can you read?*

Before she was even done writing, she saw Milo nodding his head. When she looked up, he reached out one tiny paw and traced in the spilled mugwort powder.

Y. E. S.

She stared at him for a bit longer than seemed polite. Then something clicked in her brain. She snagged a biscuit from the jar over the crucible and tossed it to him as she headed for the water pump. "Good boy. Let's get us some house water."

She primed the pump to the rhythm of Milo's wagging tail. Once the water started flowing, she chanted, "I seek Sita with this charm, to see that she is safe from harm."

She kept the chant going as she sucked up some water with an eye dropper and added three drops to her mortar. She kept her loneliness and grief at her mother's long absence from her mind and heart. She focused only on the woman as a separate entity whom she loved and wished well, even if that meant Corwin never got her back. She focused on making her intent as selfless as possible.

"I seek Sita with this charm, to see that she is safe from harm."

The voice in her head joined in as Corwin selected a small sample from the jar of sea sponges she'd collected and cured.

We seek Sita with this charm to see that she is safe from harm.

Without any conscious decision, Corwin adjusted her chant to create a round with the voice in her head as she sucked the liquid up and wiped it on the standing mirror. Since she didn't have to pour it, she didn't need to use the hand mirror. She wiped the sponge across the glass from the top all the way to the bottom and then worked it back up in circles, washing away fingerprint smears on the edges and smudges at the very bottom from Milo's nose.

"I can help you with that particular problem, Mr. Charles." Her mother's voice echoed off the stone of the small lab.

Corwin fell back on her rear. She dropped the sponge and sucked in short breaths to keep the burning tears from escaping. Her heart pounded as if it would explode. Milo ran forward and stopped the mirror from flipping at her sudden push. When it was safe, the dog scuttled back, tripping into her lap.

The mirror no longer showed a reflection. Instead, they could see Sita standing in a small, metallic room. There was just enough space for her and the lanky, fancy-dressed man she watched. The man stared forward as if looking at Corwin. A light flashed at intervals, illuminating their faces with a dim, yellow glow.

Corwin's mother wore a shiny skirt suit and had pulled her hair back into a tight bun. The hairdo accentuated the sharp angles of her face and her wide eyes. Her style reminded Corwin of Walter's companion. A chill ran down her spine. Mother did not look like she was a prisoner at all. She looked beautiful.

The man didn't look at her. His voice was brusque, dismissive. "You have been with the Consortium a very short time, Sita."

"But I have worked my way up quickly because I am a fast learner and I believe in our cause." Sita's perfect, pointy red nails brushed a hair out of the man's face as she purred his name. "Mr. Charles."

Where her fingers touched his temple, red sparkles glittered and then burrowed into his skin.

"You have a lot to learn." He sucked in a breath and turned to look at her as if he couldn't resist. His face cooled to a paler white. "But I have faith in you. I will make you my personal assistant." He glanced away as though at something over Corwin's head.

Frustration crossed her mother's face. It was gone by the time Mr. Charles returned his gaze to her. She held a hand to her chest and murmured, "That is an honor, Mr. Charles. I will not fail you."

"Not so quick, Sita." Mr. Charles wrapped his hand around her wrist to keep her from touching his face again. Mother gasped. Her skin turned white where he gripped her. "You must know the Consortium well enough by now to know that nothing comes for free. You will get your promotion, if you get the Montana Collective to swear allegiance to me."

Sita's smile came off as a grimace. She forced her eyes from her wrist to his face. "It won't be a problem."

"The Consortium does not deal lightly with failures, Sita." He grabbed her other hand, which she had placed at the small of his back. "Or with over-ambitious fools."

Her mother's confidence collapsed. Fear softened the harsh lines of her face and she hid her eyes behind lowered lashes. Her voice shook. "I will not fail you, sir."

Mr. Charles used her wrists to yank Sita close. Spittle hit her face as he hissed, "You had better not."

A sharp ding sounded and the image was washed away in a bright light. Corwin blinked and saw herself, Milo, and the lab reflected in the mirror.

Corwin stared at the glass. She felt the heat of Milo's body in her lap and the heat wafting from the hearth fire, which had grown. Neither reached the ice in her veins.

CHAPTER 19

Milo rested his head on Corwin's foot. She'd been tapping it restlessly, out of rhythm. Her mind was on her mother. It had been nearly a year since they'd seen her and they were still no closer to finding her. A quiet bark made Corwin lean over and peek under the spinet as Naomi Carrier picked her way through the first etude in her new level two workbook. She was doing a great job keeping with the rhythm Corwin was setting with accompanying chords. Milo took a breath and released warm air on her ankle, telling her to calm down and focus.

Milo lay under the spinet whenever Corwin played or taught. She'd laid her well-used Oxford English Dictionary under the spinet to keep him entertained. His tail rested on the dictionary. His body lay on a stuffed panda. His head weighed down her foot.

"Ugh." Naomi grunted her frustration and sat on her hands. "You don't even have to look at the music."

Corwin sat up. "How old are you?"

"Eight and three-quarters. I was eight and one quarter when I started taking lessons. I practice every day, like you say, even though my brothers make fun of me and are never quiet, but I'm still awful. I am never going to be able to play a real song."

Naomi babbled on while Corwin remembered the first time her father had sat her on his lap on this bench. Mother hadn't left yet. She lounged on the settee, running her fingers through her hair. More than anything, Corwin remembered her mother laughing as Daddy showed her how to push the keys to make pretty noises.

She interrupted Naomi's moaning. "I am twenty-two. I started playing when I was three."

Naomi sighed. "Sure, but like, look at this." She flipped her new workbook closed, revealing the score for *The Rite of Spring* behind it. "I will never be able to play that. That's just insane. I'm gonna have nightmares about that."

I'm right there with you. Rite, ha ha, rite there with you. The voice in Corwin's head giggled a little hysterically.

Corwin had the score out because she was studying it for a class. Trying to analyze exactly what it was about the composition that made it hard to forget and difficult to remember. The music played through her nightmares all the time.

Corwin kept all of that to herself. "That's an orchestral score, Naomi. Nobody can play all that on a keyboard."

Naomi muttered, "I bet you can."

Under the spinet, Milo sang out a short howl.

Corwin's long fingers flitted over the keys, playing the opening measures of her senior thesis adaptation of the score.

Naomi groaned. "See!" She leaned forward to peer at the yellowing paper and, without looking at her fingers, accurately played two measures of the piccolo line. "I'm hopeless. What are you grinning about?"

Corwin contained her smile. "You didn't look at the keyboard."

"Ooooh, I'm a genius." Naomi rolled her eyes, but her aura pulsed with blue-tinged joy.

Corwin played one of the more disturbing tuba lines as she explained, "This score has been here for as long as I can remember. I don't even see the notes anymore. But the first time I tried to play it, I had to pick out each individual note, just like you."

"Will I be able to read music like that someday? Or is it your special magic? Skill!"

Corwin ignored her slip. "You will, if you practice. No matter how much your brothers bother you, you have to practice. And one day, very soon, you'll read the music and not the notes."

Milo barked and bounded to the door. The knock that followed his outburst was tentative. Naomi jumped from the bench and gathered her books into her bookbag. Corwin faked a cough and slid to the right of the bench, poising her right hand over the keys. She played a C and held it, a foot on the sustain pedal.

Naomi squealed, "Just a minute, Mom!" She dropped her bag. Milo had to dash out of the way to avoid being crushed. Naomi stood behind the bench and played the bouncing two-handed accompaniment as Corwin played the melody to *Heart and Soul*. After she walked down the final notes of the chorus, she slid to the left of the bench and took over the accompanying while Naomi danced to her right and played the melody.

"Good job today." Corwin held out her fist, but Naomi ignored it and wrapped herself around Corwin like a squid before she raced to open the door, Milo again dashing out of her way to avoid being crushed.

When the door opened, Queenie, the Carrier's Great Dane, bounded inside and skittered on the bare wood floor until she found the object of her search and stopped barely short of bowling into Naomi. After a quick sniffing of her human sister, the enormous canine turned her affection on Milo. Naomi wrapped her arms around Queenie's chest to hold her back.

Corwin took advantage of Milo's distraction to step outside for a word with Naomi's mother. She didn't bother grabbing a jacket, even though the weather had turned bitter. She was surprised to find Pops Coogan standing with Kit. As a Coogan, he wouldn't have been able to get past the shield if she hadn't lowered it for Naomi's lesson. His beard had lost all wisps of black and cuddled his chin like a cloud. He hugged an ancient leather portfolio to his chest. Magic sparkled from each fold of the folio. "Hello, Daniella."

"It's Corwin," she said.

"Is it?" He quirked an eyebrow and looked between her and Kit Carrier. "I'll give you a moment." He stepped away to the door and leaned on the threshold to watch the chaos but did not go inside Corwin house.

Kit handed Corwin an envelope. "I have to pay you in cash this time. Marjorie tried to make the thing you asked for, but it was, please don't tell her, terrifying. We were all having dinner on the waterfront and I saw it so I got a picture and sent it off to a place that specializes in that sort of thing. I gave them your address so it should come directly here. They're a bit backed up, but you let me know when you get it and I'll mark four lessons as paid."

One of the great things about the Carriers was that Corwin never had to talk much. She accepted the envelope, hiding her disappointment. "Naomi is doing great. She gets frustrated, but she's progressing fast."

"I would hope so." Kit leaned in and lowered her voice. She shot a glance at Pops and turned her back to him. "Sara Bareilles, the musician, came into Witchy Wicks over the holidays. She was there for over half an hour. And then I followed her to The Music Shoppe where she played a song from her new musical. I made fourteen candles from her essence. I burn one whenever Naomi sits down at our piano. I'd give you one, but you don't need any inspiration, do you? I'm so glad you found some joy. Goddess knows you Corwins have certainly been lacking."

"Ms. Kit," Pops called over, a laugh in his voice. "I believe Naomi could use some help with Queenie."

Milo could use some help with Queenie.

Kit's gaze went unfocused and her aura took on the telltale sheen of a witch not entirely in her own body. Queenie trotted out of the house and sat sweetly at Kit's side, her sleek blue-gray fur emitting a glow that matched Kit's aura. The glow pulsed and then vanished out of existence so suddenly, Corwin stumbled back a step.

Pops was there to catch her.

His touch, the touch of a Coogan, kicked Corwin out of the domestic bubble she'd been floating in. Music lessons could do that to her. She was never so happy as when her students improved. But that wasn't important. Finding the heart was important. Finding her mother was important. Not getting killed by the Coogans or Walter was important. She pulled herself together and returned to the safety of her house.

Naomi crouched on the floor with Milo in her lap. She kissed his head and hugged him to her while he tried to lick every inch of her face. Corwin didn't interrupt. Milo loved cuddles and it wasn't really her thing. It was helpful that most of her students, including Jack Jaga, loved cuddling the tiny dog.

"Naomi."

Kit's call electrified the eight-year-old. Naomi set Milo down and shot to her feet. She bounced out the door, spinning to shout, "Thanks, Ms. Corwin! I promise I'll practice every single day and ignore my stupid brothers."

A deep silence fell over the house once Naomi, Kit, and Queenie's energy stepped past the protective shield guarding the boundaries of Corwin house.

"Greetings, Milo."

Corwin jumped a bit at the deep calm of Pop's voice.

The dog barked and trotted to the door.

"Morgan sent this for you." Pops bent to hand a stuffed llama to Milo who took it and immediately set to cleaning it.

"Thank you." Corwin avoided staring at the other items in Pops Coogan's gloved hands.

Pops dragged his eyes from the dog and stood. He offered Corwin the leather portfolio held closed with a cord wrapped several times around the outside.

Fascinated at the magic escaping out of every opening, Corwin kept her hands to herself. She couldn't accept a gift from a Coogan.

Then he said, "Morgan sent this for you."

Corwin reached for the folder eagerly and then pulled her hands back and folded them under her arms, thinking, *it's still a gift from a Coogan.*

As if he could read her mind, Pops said, "It is a loan." He turned a sad gaze to the folder. "These charts are my father's work. He focused his Skill on traditional instruments, as you do."

That's why they're leaking magic!

Corwin blinked, wondering if Pops Coogan had used the word *Skill* with the Salem meaning. He looked at her as though he expected a response, so she gave him the simple truth. "Traditional instruments are the only ones I have."

"I hear you build your own." His eyes found the triple harp standing against the wall between the library and the sitting room.

Corwin shrugged, certain her pride was showing in her aura. "I have learned to replicate what I have played."

"Modesty has its place. But I meant that I have seen you playing instruments of your own design." He grinned at her shock. "You don't even know when you pluck that kalimba as you're walking Milo, do you? It comes as naturally to you as power or breathing."

She had no response to his nearly open reference to magic and Pops didn't seem to expect one this time. He held the portfolio out so insistently that Corwin found herself accepting it.

"Learn all you can from Father's charts. We do not expect them returned quickly. This," he held up the final item in his hands, the envelope with a glittering waxen seal that he had brought and not left for her father ten years earlier, "This should also be considered carefully. Do not open it before you are ready."

A grin popped up on Corwin's dour face, despite her instincts. She kept her laugh inside. "How should I know if I'm ready?" she asked.

Pops laid a finger beside his nose. "Ah," he said. "If you don't know, you are not ready." He looked down at Milo. "It was good to see you again, young master. My best to your parents, Corwin."

Pops' long legs took him off her doorstep and down to the bicycle waiting at the curb. He swept his long hair into a bundle and tucked it under a helmet before riding off down the snow-dusted street.

Corwin shut the door and turned to take the leather folder to the spinet. The envelope sat, its wax seal glittering in the sunlight, on the instrument's bench. She froze. Pops had never handed her the letter. Milo dropped the new, well-licked llama into his basket and then trotted over to stand up on the side of the bench. It was one of the first things in the house that Corwin had reupholstered. She still regretted losing the history of all the people in her family who had sat there, willingly or unwillingly learning that instrument. But the seat was much more comfortable now. Milo took the envelope in his teeth without a glance at her. He carried it over behind the coat rack and dropped it into his basket.

She wasn't ready to open it. That much she knew. Milo's collection of prized possessions seemed a perfectly reasonable place to store it, in the meantime.

With the bench clear, Corwin sat down and opened the treasure chest of new music sent to her by the most beautiful girl in the world. Every score glittered with all the colors of magic.

See? Music is magic.

Corwin laid her hands on the keyboard, her fingers finding the keys that matched the notes on the first score as easily as Naomi dreamed of. Her eyes drifted over to the burgeoning coat rack.

Oh no.

The coats, the hats, the scarves, shawls, and ear muffs were all notes. She'd lived with them so long that she no longer saw the individual notes of the house. She could have missed the note that was the heart simply because all she saw was the music of Corwin House.

"I can't search the house. I have to search through the things in the house."

This house is filled with things. Corwins have died and left their things here since time immemorial, the voice moaned, conjuring an image of the crowded basement, ignored rooms, and the lab.

"I just have to dust every individual item in the house with the revealing charm."

The voice in her head groaned in an exact imitation of Naomi and filled her head with an image of the sparkling score sitting on the spinet's music stand. *Maybe just one new song first?*

Corwin glanced over at Milo, who sat with his new llama in his teeth beneath the overladen coat rack. "Maybe just one new song first," she said.

Milo dashed over and leapt onto the bench beside her. He stood up on the keyboard and happened to play a C. Corwin played the rest of the opening of *Heart and Soul* and seamlessly transitioned to the magical new music in front of her. For a few minutes, her mind ran through the list of ingredients and quantities she would need to make enough potion, but eventually the magic took over and she lost herself in Warren Coogan's music.

CHAPTER 20

T he potion Corwin had created to dust the doll-sized Corwin House did not work as she hoped on individual items in the house. But she didn't realize this until she'd used up all of the pre-mixed powder and had to create more. It wasn't so much the ingredients as her intention in combining them.

The idea was that the potion would reveal all the items in the house with inherent magic. Corwin didn't see a glitter off of things or people who were, at their core, magical. It would have made it impossible for her to live in Salem without losing her mind. Although, having a full-blown relationship with the voice in her head might mean she'd lost it long ago. Still, if she could charm a thing like her father's mirror calls to emit visible magic, visible to her, at least, it had to be possible to charm anything that way. To make that which was hidden visible to her. It was how her father had said she would recognize the heart after all.

The intention for the Revealing Charm 1.0 had been generalized, *Find the magic in this house, from the gabled roof to the tiniest mouse.* The intention she used for the Revealing Charm 2.0 had to be more specific.

She made three attempts before the fourth—using rain collected in barrels beneath the White Oak and an intention folded into John Williams' five tones from *Close Encounters of the Third Kind*—worked.

She sprayed the potion into the air over her own head, playing the notes on her kalimba and singing along with the voice in her head, *Power, show yourself.* Where the potion landed on her skin, magic glittered from her in shades of lilac, blue, purple, brown, and red. Where excess potion misted down over Milo, sparkles floated off his fur in gold and blue. Corwin was shocked for a moment before the voice in her head said, quite clearly, *duh.*

Milo kept the list. He was not great at writing, but he couldn't spray the potion or play the kalimba. They started by retesting every item of clothing on the clothes rack. With the new Revealing Charm, Grand-mother Misty's sun hat glowed as though it were the sun. Great-great-grandaunt Judith's mile-long scarf, a cloak from the 1600s, and the woolen jacket that still fit her around the time her father left all revealed themselves as inherently magical. Corwin set the magical items aside and decided to donate most of the non-magical items to Kady's resale. She didn't need outerwear for four generations of family when it was just her in the house. Milo came with his own coat.

They attacked the sitting room next. As barren as it was, it would be a good room to mark off the list. One of the benches glowed and all of Corwin's instruments, but they did not find the heart.

By mutual agreement, Corwin and Milo decided to attack the base-ment next. It scared them the most. As it turned out, they were not wrong to be frightened. Aside from the many items glittering with the black, oozing magic of a curse, they also had to deal with spiders. The spiders themselves were easy enough to move with magical assistance, but the webs stuck to skin and fur like super creepy Velcro.

It took them a month of their free time to get through the base-ment. By the time they'd sprayed everything, the basement glowed so blindingly, Corwin had to wear sunglasses when she went down. She had another "duh" moment when the ancient pail of gray paint that never dried up or ran empty glittered. About a fifth of the "treasures" got set aside to be donated, while the hearth fire cheerfully consumed every cursed object.

Time was impossible for Corwin to track in the basement, but she was exhausted, mentally and physically, after they sprayed a wooden library ladder with wheels that had been rusted still since long before

Corwin was born. The ladder sparkled, each rung a different color. But it wasn't the heart of Corwin House. Milo scratched off *ladr* on his list and dropped the broken pencil out of his mouth.

Corwin slunk to the floor beside him, defeated. "If I didn't know we were cursed for torturing and killing innocent witches, I'd guess my family was cursed for keeping all this stuff that could have helped other people."

Milo huffed a quiet bark of agreement.

"I mean, there has to be some witch-run Habitat for Humanity that would appreciate that horrible gray paint, right?"

That smart little voice in her head suggested, *Maybe that's what we do after we rescue your mother.*

Corwin was so tired she didn't even notice the tears until one was rolling down her cheek. She scratched it from her face, furious at its betrayal of her mother's lessons and her own doubt. The voice in her head had more faith than she did. Quick upon that thought came the long stifled surety that sane people did not have voices in their heads.

Food.

"Shh." Corwin spat the response even as her stomach twisted in agreement with the little voice.

Corwin scrambled to her feet. She grabbed up Milo's journal and pencil and stomped to the stairs. Milo dashed over and ran up ahead of her. He led her to the kitchen, where he drained his water bowl.

Dinner was a somber affair. Corwin sat, as she often did, on the floor. She leaned against the door beside Milo's food bowl and balanced her plate on her knees. Her mind filled with despair and also with the *Rite of Spring*. She hadn't played it in weeks, had given up on her master's thesis, but still, the music was the only thing that could have dragged her out of her black thoughts.

It was just ironic that it was that little voice that offered up the distraction.

A metallic tapping sounded from the front door. Milo nearly choked on his food trying to bark before swallowing. He let some chunks dribble back into his bowl and then galloped to the front door, barking like a guard dog. Corwin didn't know what it could be. The grocer always left her supplies by the kitchen door. For a moment, she feared the lawyer had come back, and found herself straightening her clothes and taking her braid out of her skirt pocket as she walked to the door at a human pace.

Outside, a delivery truck was driving away. Milo ran down the path, barking at the truck, and then raced back up to bound around the cardboard box sitting on the cement stoop. His tail wagged so hard, Corwin envisioned him lifting off and flying away. She gathered the box, brushed it clean, and went back inside to open it.

Milo stuck his nose in the way, not helping at all. She let him sniff until he had determined it was not a surprise delivery of food from Jack. When he wandered off to his pillow under the spinet, she ripped off the tape and pulled a plastic bag from inside. She grinned, her heart leaping out of black despair straight into glee. Kit Carrier had come through.

Somehow, the shop Naomi's mother had ordered from had crocheted exactly what Corwin wanted. She tore into the plastic to hold the very first nonessential thing she'd ever bought with her own hard-earned money. It was a bird with red crown feathers, red eyes, and black-and-white wings—Morgan's Pundu.

"Hey, Milo."

The dog was already pinning her with his beady hazel peepers. He tilted his head. Corwin jerked hers in a *come here* motion. She held the lightning bird doll out to him. "I thought you might like this."

He sniffed the doll carefully and then looked up at her. She grinned and threw it across the room. "Go get it!"

Milo bounded after the toy and ran it back to her. She threw it again. He brought it right back. The third time she threw it, Milo took the bird to his pillow under the spinet and began carefully licking the bird from crest to claws. Corwin watched.

She let her mind go blank, enjoying his happiness and not thinking about her mother or her daddy or magic or the heart. She just existed, at peace with her glittering home and her glittering dog. After a bit, she rubbed the old wood floor and dragged her aching bones to the bench. One of Warren Coogan's scores sat on the music stand, waiting for her. She stretched her neck and her wrists and then she set her fingers to the keys.

The music floated visibly through the front room, glittering from the Revealing Charm. Corwin played for Milo, trying to bring his joy at a new toy into the music. As the notes transposed from those on the page to those from her heart, the glittering in the air turned from golden to hues of lavender. They circled her, tickling her hair, and floated under the keyboard to encase Milo and his impundulu.

The little terrier had curled up on his pillow with the bird between his front paws. He'd fallen asleep still cleaning it. Some fright in a dream made him jerk and the toy tumbled from his pillow. Milo woke at once. He reached for it with his teeth and tumbled himself, hitting the floorboards a bit harder than sounded comfortable.

Corwin abandoned the song to check on him. But Milo was okay. The floor had taken the brunt of the strike. A board had popped out of alignment and the far end had been pushed up like a teeter-totter. Milo, with the impundulu doll in his mouth, sniffed at the space beneath the board. He nudged it and the board rose even further.

Corwin joined him. The board lifted up, revealing a cavity under the floor. Deep magic glittered in the space. It was so dark, Corwin thought at first that it was black and backed away. Fearless Milo sniffed inside the cavity. Between his blue collar and the doll's black wings, Corwin could see that the magic was blue. A richer blue than she had ever seen before, except on high holidays in the leaves of the White Oak. The glittering followed the plain ochre medicine bag Milo pulled out of the floor. Corwin rescued his dropped doll and felt along the hidden space, but the bag was the only thing stashed there.

She fit the loose board back into place and reminded herself to breathe. Milo dropped the bag in her lap and took his impundulu. The bag filled the room with light and power; Corwin could feel the hair on her arms, and even on her head, standing on end. She worried about anyone looking at the house from outside. And then she knew that nobody would see anything different. This blue glow *was* the house. The blue glow blended with everything she'd ever known. It was familiar and comforting and powerful. She rubbed a hand on the floor as she had earlier. The wood hummed.

Corwin unwrapped the leather cords from the neck of the bag and opened it. She tilted it and the remnants of a cornhusk doll slid out into her hand. Just some dust, a deerskin dress, a tiny pair of leather boots, two black gemstone eyes, and a wampum belt of blue and white beads.

Milo inched closer to sniff delicately at the medicine bag. The blue magic wafting off of it flowed over him. It ruffled his fur and Milo shivered. His blue ID tag jangled. His tag matched the beads on the wampum belt.

On an impulse, Corwin took the doll's belt and laid it over Milo's neck. She worked the leather ties through the weave of his collar and secured it at the metal ring holding his tag. Milo shook his head, his ears flapping like a pellet drum, and the wampum belt settled against his fur as though it had always been there.

Corwin gathered the doll pieces together in her skirt and slipped them back into the medicine bag. Milo tracked down one black gemstone that rolled away. She tucked the medicine bag into her vest against her thumping heart, holding it there for a moment as she squeezed her eyes shut and reached back through time in her mind. "Thank you, Hobbomock."

Milo added a wild howl to the prayer.

Corwin stood, turning to feel the waking heartbeat of her house. When she faced the kitchen, the sparking fire grabbed all her attention. Milo bounded to the doorway.

"Right," Corwin said to him, to the house, to her ancestors. "Now, it's *really* time to save my family."

CHAPTER 21

Corwin had the Heart. But she didn't have ingredients. They had used up many of the supplies they needed for Finding in making the Revealing charm. Plus, she had lessons she couldn't cancel on short notice, and school.

It took weeks for her and Milo to find the time to go foraging in the forest and stop at all the shops they needed to visit to gather the makings of Finding spells. They tried to be discreet and spaced their visits out to avoid gossip. As slowly as they made haste, they still garnered enough attention that Kali asked straight out what she was searching for.

They were the only two in the shop. Milo waited outside to appease the health inspector, and also, to get pet by tourists and his friends.

Kali washed his hands in the little sink behind the counter and offered Corwin a fist to bump. "I haven't seen you in so long. Have you grown even taller?" He commented on her height but examined only her face. "There is something different about you, Corwin girl."

Corwin shrugged. She slid her shopping list across the counter to him.

He read it and muttered, "Ha, Marjorie had it all wrong," before he looked up and asked, "What exactly are you searching for?"

Corwin meant to give her usual excuse that the list wasn't hers, but she only managed to stutter the truth, "My mother—"

"There's a White Oak in Drake's Park that says we can dispense with all that foolishness. You are a woman of a certain age and we all have needs, Skilled and simple alike."

He chuckled at her blush and gave her a small bag of powdered Rhino horn "from a special animal reserve run by Skilled folk," as well as the Komodo dragon scales she'd gone there for.

She tucked the bags into her satchel on top of the state maps she'd gathered at the Bookcellar, then laid cash on the counter and hurried out to find Milo on his back. Their grouchy next-door neighbor, Betsy Chever, stopped scratching his belly and started to walk away. She'd only gone a couple of steps before she turned back to peer at Corwin.

She thinks you're pregnant.

Corwin wondered how the voice would know that. The woman was still staring, so Corwin asked, "Why do you think I'm pregnant?"

Ms. Chever straightened and tripped backwards off the curb. Corwin instinctively reached out with her power to keep her from falling. She glanced around a second too late to see if there were any tourists or non-magical locals. She found she could see their Skill in their auras now if she opened her Sight a certain way.

Fear scrunched Ms. Chever's old face. She held her arms out, partially for balance and partially, it seemed, to ward off Corwin. She hissed, "You're glowing." And then she hurried down the street into Witchy Wicks, shooting glances at Corwin the whole way.

It was an odd interaction, but Corwin didn't have time to fret over a mean old lady. She was more surprised to have found her being nice to Milo.

They strolled through the little park, past the White Oak to the animal shelter. She had three kids to teach that day, plus Jack. At first, her mind focused on getting home and spreading the maps out in the lab. But Piggy Betterman strummed the chords for *Love Me Do* in rhythm and without a single flub. He was as shocked as she was and she had to catch his guitar while the kid danced down the alley, telling the animals how amazing he was.

"Yes, you're a rock star. Now, get back here and do it again."

Piggy did. But not before he knelt by the cage Milo had been sitting beside and introduced himself to an iguana. The lizard went home with him.

Both other kids and Jack had equally inspiring lessons. Every correction she made was internalized and demonstrated instantly. Jack successfully riffed his way through a chord chart on the first try.

After Jack's lesson, Corwin and Milo detoured to run a hand along the White Oak's trunk. The bark glittered where her fingers brushed it. She could feel the magical life within it, and when she sent her appreciation and love into the wood, the trunk lit up like the town at Christmas. Multi-colored sparkles ran up into the leaves and down into the roots. Milo howled as if he, too, could feel the life beneath his feet.

Corwin looked down at her suddenly burning hand. Her five scars glowed white with pain. When she looked up, she forgot her old scars.

Kat Coogan stood just across the street without her usual disguise. Black curls tumbled out of a ball cap pulled low over her natural green eyes. Though there was no glitter of glamour, the woman radiated grief so intensely that Corwin could see it as a black shadow on her aura. Jack Jaga, still standing in the doorway of the kennels, stepped back, holding the glass door in front of him as if for protection.

Kat Coogan crossed to Corwin. Corwin did not run away. She stood her ground, ready this time for whatever the witch wanted to throw her way. Even braver, Milo took a few steps towards Corwin's nemesis. When there were only a couple of yards between them, the witch who'd abandoned Salem except to torture Corwin stopped. Her face was unreadable.

"You found it," she said.

Corwin had no response. Her heart had leapt into her throat and choked her silent. How could she know? Milo reacted to her sudden paralysis by barking and pulling on the leash. Corwin followed his lead. She wished the tree a goodbye and started home. Kat Coogan walked with her, though she glanced back at Jack Jaga before pulling the cap of her hat down over her eyes. She grabbed at a black curl and suddenly magic sparked from her fingertips, transforming the hair. Kat Coogan's blond appearance melted down her body. Corwin could feel it happen even more than she could see it. She could feel the strength of Kat's magic. It scared her into walking faster.

Kat hissed, "I can't stay. Do you have any friends?"

Corwin looked up from the toes of her boots as they hurried past Kady's Resale, the butcher's shop, and Witchy Wicks. Locals stopped in their tracks to watch as they passed. Kit Carrier, sweeping her steps, raised a hand in greeting. Concern was writ in the wrinkles around her eyes and the tension in her mouth. Corwin flashed a smile and a nod before she dropped her eyes back to her shoes. And Milo.

City streets gave way to the back alleys of the commercial district. She clutched her hands at her sides, hyper-aware of her desire to pat at the inside pocket of her vest where she kept the medicine bag. Intellectually, she understood that the bag didn't hold the family's power. It had simply been storing it in hiding until she broke the curse by finding it. But emotionally, she felt stronger having it on her. She'd always felt a connection to those who had gone before and left their magic behind. She touched trees to reach into the past. The medicine bag was an intrinsic part of the Corwin past and she liked having it near. She liked having a connection to her family so far back when she had such a weak connection to her family in the now.

Kat Coogan's tension eased as they left the commercial part of town and started down the sidewalks of Corwin's neighborhood. She lifted her head to look at Corwin. "You can't run away from your family's past. You must face it, or their sins will destroy you."

Corwin kept her eyes on Milo. "I will never give you the Corwins' heart."

Kat Coogan laughed. Her cackle rang out through the street. It scared a flock of ravens off a nearby fence. "I only want to keep it from your mother."

Corwin shot a gaze at the witch. "I'm an adult now. You can't hurt her through me anymore."

Kat Coogan snorted. A sad smile added shades to the grief carved into her face. "Kids are always kids to a good mother."

"Why? What do you have against her?" Corwin stopped at the path to her front door. "Do you work for the Consortium?"

Silence fell over all the tiny things that lived in the bushes and trees and houses. Kat Coogan's aura pulsed and fingers of frost washed over it, smoking in the warm spring air. The tightness of the woman's voice screamed her fear. "Does she... does she know about Milo?"

Corwin played three notes on the kalimba in her satchel as she stepped across the line between the Corwin House property and the public sidewalk. The protections pulsed. They shoved Kat Coogan's aura away. The witch stumbled all the way to the curb and off it into the street. She almost fell.

Corwin wanted to run into her house and slam the door. She felt the house reaching out to her and Milo standing at the end of his leash, reaching for the house. But she stood her ground. She planted her boots on the grass that had grown under the feet of her ancestors, feeling the roots of her backyard's White Oak far below, reaching its ancient fingers throughout the city, and she took power from them.

"I will find my mother," she declared. "And I will save her from you and the Consortium and anyone else I find responsible for taking her from me. Blood calls to blood, and if I have broken the curse your people placed on mine, then you know the power I have regained belongs to all Corwins. My blood will lead me to my family and it will give me victory over you."

She could see that she had struck the witch. Tears welled in her false brown eyes as her aura dimmed with failure.

Kat Coogan sucked in a deep breath and Corwin could see magic pulled from the air around her into her soul. Her voice was quiet when she said, "You have been badly mistreated, Corwin. And poorly taught. Blood doesn't make family. Though he is my soul, my love shares no blood with me." She stopped, her voice choked off even as her eyes searched for words.

Corwin backed away, a chill crawling up her spine as magic, unbidden, rose from the ground outside her protections and flowed into Kat Coogan. The woman's continued silence unnerved her. She followed Milo's lead to the door. She'd unlocked and opened it before Kat Coogan spoke again.

"You say 'blood calls to blood.' Consider the bond shared between your parents carefully. They share no blood, yet the loss of her drove him mad." Kat Coogan stepped onto the curb and strode to the very boundary of the Corwin yard. "You are in danger, Corwin. Not Sita." She raised her left hand and laid it on the invisible dome that had protected Corwin House for generations. The dome lit up with gold. "I can only give you this. Trust what you have learned, not what you have been taught. Trust your heart."

The barrier held. It buzzed in a rhythmic pattern that made Kat Coogan snatch her hand away. She tapped at the silver band on her ring finger, looked up at Corwin with defeat in her eyes, and then ran away.

CHAPTER 22

All thoughts of what Kat Coogan could have meant fled from Corwin's brain when she walked inside her house. Blue and brown sparkles like dust motes in a ray of sunshine glittered throughout the front room. Corwin followed Milo to the kitchen and through the hearth fire. An E-flat rang through her head and distantly in her ears and, in her exultation, she'd forgotten all about hiding Milo.

The trail of sparkles led directly to the mirror. Corwin feared her shaking legs would give out before she reached it. It had been six years since she had seen his face. A little traitorous part of her had given him up for dead. She felt shame rushing blood to her face, slowing her. Never once did she consider what she might be facing in the mirror.

Corwin whipped the sheet off, murmuring the Pentatonix chorus that she'd set as the spell to mute the mirror in case her Daddy called while Naomi was there. The sound returned before she'd gotten the sheet out of the way and her blood ran cold at the desperation in her daddy's voice.

"Daniella!"

His voice was raw, broken. And when she saw his face, she understood why. He was barely recognizable, standing so close to the mirror she could see a dozen shades of blue in the swelling that distorted the freckles across his nose. Blood dripped from a cut over one swollen shut eye. He held the end of one sleeve up to staunch the bleeding from his broken nose.

He stared fixedly at something beyond his mirror. His voice lowered to a hopeless whisper, "Daniella, where are you?"

"Daddy?" Corwin choked the word out through her nausea.

Her daddy didn't waste time scolding her and he didn't give her time to ask what had happened to him. "I've found Sita," he panted, his image going blurry as he backed away and looked at something she couldn't see. "But I'm not going to survive to save her. It's up to you now, baby." He paused to suck in air and wipe a drop of blood from one eye.

"Daddy! What happened?" Corwin clutched at the frame. "Where have you been?"

He kept his voice low. She moved closer to the mirror to hear him. "I haven't had any time. I've been chasing your mother."

"It's been six years."

Shouting voices drew his gaze again to the thing beyond the mirror. He dropped his voice to a whisper. "Listen. I'm inside the compound. I've barricaded myself in this room to reach you. They are right behind me. I got away once, but there is something wrong with these people. They're freaks, and I—" A crash sounded and splinters of wood flew into view. Her father flinched as some hit him. He gave up on being quiet and screamed, "It's up to you, Daniella. Come, save your mother!"

Then the mirror was shattered so violently that Corwin ducked as if the shards could hit her. "Daddy!"

Milo barked. Corwin spun around to see he'd already unrolled the map she'd tossed on the worktable days ago. He had the nearly brown scrying garnet in his teeth, its new chain dangling over the map. She glanced back at the mirror in the unrealistic hope that her daddy would still be there. He wasn't. Only the silver shards of his mirror floated between her and her reflection. She turned back to face Milo. Her feet felt like they were nailed to the floor, like she couldn't move.

"How?" she cried at him. "How am I supposed to scry for them? I have no idea where to start."

Hurry, before it dissipates! Corwin had no idea what the voice meant. She shook her head, trying to make it shut up.

Milo howled. The garnet fell onto the map. He leapt from the worktable to the tall stool and then all the way to the floor. He leaped at the mirror and bounced off it to hit her. He was surrounded with silver sparkles. The mirror was whole in its frame. But the glitter of silver magic was what had burst into the lab, making Corwin think the mirror had shattered. She raised one numb hand and coaxed a stream of silver remnants to the worktable. Suddenly, she could move again.

And she moved swiftly, scooping Milo up onto the worktable as she reached for the garnet. The crystal lay with its pointed end touching a dot in Montana labeled *Delcampo*. Corwin gripped the chain in two fingers and let the crystal hang from the end. She directed the silver to surround and invade the stone. Then she dangled the stone over the map, starting from the upper right tail of Maine. It twitched over Boston, Massachusetts but didn't pull her there. It twitched again over Chicago.

Corwin huffed out a breath, careful not to affect the dangling, searching crystal and crooned, "Mother who was stolen from me, where in this whole wide world can you be?"

The crystal spun wildly, leaning back east again. Corwin followed where it led. The point of the crystal pinned itself to the map just west of the dot indicating Richmond, Virginia. When Corwin released the chain, the crystal remained standing on its pointed end, vibrating and glowing, not silver, but with the rich lilac sparkles Corwin had started recognizing as her own magic.

Her mother was in a Consortium compound in Virginia. Her father had been captured. It was up to Corwin now. She looked at Milo, who sat on Wyoming, watching her.

Let's go get them.

"I guess we're going on a trip."

Corwin gathered up Milo's leash, the map, the scrying crystal, her own spellbook, and a smattering of other tools that would fit in Great-great-granduncle Doctor Deacon's black leather Gladstone bag. The medical satchel had lived on the top shelf for as long as she could remember beside the white plastic first aid kit. She had begged to use the Gladstone bag as a lunch pail when she first went to school.

She popped it open and removed the ancient bandages and wax-wrapped poultices. Her divining rod wouldn't fit inside, but she could slip it under the leather straps that held the little medical satchel closed. There were a few full vials already strapped into elastic bands along the insides of the bag. She left them. She stashed the family journals and grimoires back in the hidden vault under the workbench, fetching a couple strays from where Milo had been reading them in the library. As an afterthought, she snatched Warren Coogan's music from the spinet and tucked that in the vault as well. She ran a hand over the secret sitting room door, sealing it against all but her touch.

Then she raced through the fire and up to her parents' room. She took her father's dusty hiking backpack from the top shelf of their closet. Picking what clothes to take was difficult. Her clothes weren't exactly made for travel. She decided to go simple and hope she found places where she could wash. She packed several changes of underwear, an extra bra, and a union suit for cold nights. Daddy's suit pants and vest would get wrinkled, but she could Skill the fabric straight if she needed to look nice. Toiletries went into a dopp kit she found in the backpack. She took all of the cash she'd made from her lessons and Great-great-grandaunt Judith's bone knife out of her nightstand. The money went into the various pockets and pouches hidden on her person. She even put a few hundred into the medicine bag. The knife she tucked into her belt before sealing off her attic room and heading for the kitchen.

There was a half-full bag of kibble from the time before Jack started supplying them with fresh dog food. She shoved that in the backpack with the remainder of the fresh and followed it with all the fruit in the house. She dug the Salem Bank debit card from the junk drawer and tucked it into her bra. After a moment's hesitation, she took the mint tin with her mother's hair ties as well. One last trip into the lab to fill the camel bag and water bottles on the sides of the pack with house water and then she damped the fire for the first time in her life. As the embers died, she sang a promise to the house to rekindle them soon when she brought the whole family back home.

She was about to leave when a gleam of glittering blue on the floor of the hearth caught her eye. Her blood ran so cold she stared at her own arm, wondering. Milo barked. She woke from unreachable memory and stepped gingerly onto the cooling stones, more concerned than she'd ever been walking over them through the flames.

There was no ash to brush out of the way, since the Corwin House hearth never needed to be fed. The clean stones cooled to a gray—of course gray—color except for a metal pentagram set into a smooth triangle of sandstone. The pentagram glowed blue. A sting in her left hand made Corwin stare at the old scars on her palm.

What happened?

The voice shook Corwin out of her trance. "We don't have time for this. Let's go."

She left the kitchen and headed for the front door with Milo at her heels. After changing from her house moccasins into her father's hiking boots with an extra pair of socks, she reached over to pack Milo's impundulu, but he took it from her hand and set it carefully back into his basket. The voice in her head agreed with him. *We don't have time for toys.*

She slipped Milo's leash over his head and stood. She hauled the overstuffed backpack on over Great-grandaunt Dorothy's car coat and clipped the straps around her hips and her chest. As a last thought, she dug into the pockets of Great-grandfather's greatcoat and added the penny whistle she stored there to the kalimba in her greatcoat pocket. As she pulled Grandmother Misty's sun hat over her braid, she stepped out onto the cement slab and took one last look around the front room, taking a mental tour of the entire house. The fire was banked. The windows were all closed and sealed. The books of power were hidden. Each entryway had been salted.

Corwin laid a hand on the doorframe. She sent a surge of power into the wood.

"Alone and empty though you are,
you'll stay with me as I travel far.
Your heart sits in my pocket, true,
yet also it remains with you.
You are my home and I, your Corwin.

When I return, I'll bring you more kin."

Milo barked.

Then Corwin closed the door, locked it, and headed to the train station to leave Salem for the first time in her entire life.

She didn't notice Morgan Coogan following her.

CHAPTER 23

For all the years she'd visited the train station to watch the magic glittering off people coming from far away and heading to far away on adventures, Corwin had never been on a train before she bought her ticket to Richmond, Virginia. Her odd clothing became odder and odder the farther they traveled from home. Surrounded by people, Corwin felt trapped. Her heart ached. She was on the move and yet sitting still.

Her father's shoes fit loosely on her large feet. The line of his five-button vest didn't lay right over her breasts and his pants weren't long enough for her legs and too loose for her waist. She'd never cared before how her clothes fit. She didn't care much now, except that everyone else on the train stared at her. She would put Great-grandaunt Dorothy's long linen car coat back on, but it was even older and odder and more out of fashion. She wanted to cast the invisibility spell on herself, but it would probably freak out the people around her if she suddenly blended in with the seat, as the voice in her head vehemently reminded her when she started humming an E-flat. Instead, she pulled down the brim of Grandmother Misty's hat, gripped the Gladstone bag in her hand, and sent silent prayers to the universe to keep her father safe. Even in the safety of her own mind, she couldn't think what her heart knew for certain, that her daddy was dead.

Once on the train out of Boston the next morning, Corwin couldn't keep her eyes open. She had forced herself to stay awake waiting for the early train. Milo would have warned her if anybody had approached, but she couldn't risk anybody knowing she had a dog in her pocket. Dogs weren't allowed on trains. The deep inner pocket of Great-grandaunt Dorothy's coat solved that problem, to an extent.

And it was easy to fall asleep with Milo snoring quietly against her chest. Her body shook with the rhythm of the train, lulling her into her favorite dream where her body vibrated with the rhythm of a car.

"Cuz tonight I'm gonna see my ma cher a-Milo." The lady's voice broke off from the song in a stifled sob. "Nine miles to Salem."

Corwin struggled out of the pile of warm blankets that had been folded over her nose. She was a boy again. She was always a boy in these dreams. It was hard to crawl away from the blankets. They smelled musky, like her sister and brothers, and also like a bicycle. She laid her chin on the edge of the cardboard box. She'd rested her chin there so many times over the past few weeks it had softened and now cradled her as she stared at her mama.

Mama thought about each of the four other stops they'd made since leaving the bike shop. Mama's head was filled with sadness as images flashed through her brain of the fire department, the neighborhood porch, her best friend's husband, and then a flowering garden in the rain where Rhemy stayed while she and Mama drove away alone.

Mama let go of the wheel and buried her fingers in Corwin's fur. Tears rolled down her cheeks.

Corwin pushed thoughts into Mama's head of the smell of sandalwood as Walter's smooth hands snapped the padlock onto Mama's collar, of the stench of licorice as he smacked his gum in her face and promised her that they could leave just as soon as one of her children showed him what they really were. She showed Mama the images that had been in Walter's head then, how he had no intention of ever letting any of them go free.

Mama gasped and the car slowed. It rumbled, jostling Corwin's head on the cardboard. Then the car stopped and Mama held her close to her chest, her breath stuttering as she cried. Corwin didn't cry.

Corwin sniffed at the broken charm that hung around Mama's neck. Mama didn't want to give up her babies, so she cried sometimes. Corwin had always understood that. Her brother Bayard thought crying was weak and kicked her sometimes when Corwin had cried as Walter hurt the others. But crying filled your brain so that you couldn't hear the horrible thoughts, the ones that were worse than anything you could imagine yourself. She let Mama cry out her regrets and practiced reading. F R I E N D S. She knew all of the letters. She didn't know what they spelled.

"It spells 'friends,'" Mama said. "Everyone needs good friends."

Corwin knew that Mama had a good friend other than the Hispanic woman she was thinking of as she took the charm out of Corwin's mouth. She shot her Mama another memory from the night they left Walter's lab.

Corwin lay at the bottom of a pile of her siblings. She liked how it felt when they were all breathing around her, happy in sleep. Only Josh was awake, chewing on Mama's new collar. He didn't know he could never get it off.

Corwin turned as the door clicked and a blond man slipped into the lab with a crowd of people in his head. His body was thicker and lumpier than any other man she'd ever seen. His face was covered in scars where it wasn't covered with face fur. Deep black paintings on his hands made the white of his fingers stand out in the dark.

The voices in his head quieted as they all looked at Mama. His craggy face wrinkled in a smile that cracked muscles he never used. He was proud of himself for keeping his promise to Rhea. It meant he was a good person. Even so, he thought of himself as the killer. *Corwin didn't relay that thought to her Mama. She told Mama the name one of his imaginary friends called him.*

She lifted Corwin up and kissed her on her little black nose. "You're right. Hardknock was a good friend."

"Main Street Station: Downtown Richmond. Take all of your belongings." The announcement blared over the loudspeakers in the car.

Corwin winced as she blinked awake. She hurried to straighten her jacket without dropping Milo out of her inner pocket. He yawned with a squeak that was easily covered by the squealing of the train's brakes.

The announcement repeated, right beside Corwin's head. "Main Street Station: Downtown Richmond. Take all of your belongings."

The world outside of Salem was loud. And dull. Where the little station at home had glittered with Skill, intentional and natural, neither the station in Boston nor the station in Richmond harbored any apparent witches other than her. The crowds were loud and bright and people never stopped moving, talking, scanning their devices. But there was no sparkle of magic.

Corwin lifted Milo out of her coat and let him sniff their way out through the crowds. "Go on. Find us some fresh air."

She kept Milo on a tight leash as he sniffed his way through all the people to a door leading out into sunshine. When they got there, Corwin sucked in a deep breath and coughed. The air wasn't much cleaner outside.

There was a park in the distance. She decided that would be a good place to find some privacy. Corwin stepped away from the doors to dash through the flow of traffic rushing along the sidewalk and ran into a man's backpack. The little girl trailing a couple steps behind him ran into Corwin. The chocolate ice cream from her cone, half of which was smushed on her face, smashed onto Corwin's coat.

The man yelled, "Watch where you're going!"

Milo barked at the man. It wasn't a friendly bark. It wasn't like any noise Corwin had ever heard him make before. She let the dog handle the man while she dropped to catch the cone before it fell to the ground. The tiny child, no older than Corwin had been when her father had started hanging out at the Salem station, had tracks of tears running through her chocolate foundation. She had been crying long before her ice cream melded with Corwin's coat.

Instinctively, Corwin murmured, "Your eyes should be bright. Let's make this right."

She handed the cone back to the girl, chocolate ice cream piled up in a great swirl with violet sparkles only Corwin could see. The girl's eyes brightened. And then they widened as big as cymbals at something over Corwin's shoulder.

Milo stopped barking and backed away, pulling on the leash. Corwin melted back with him. She stood with her back against the station as three large people in uniforms descended on the little girl's companion. They spoke so quickly and angrily that Corwin couldn't understand a word. Once the man was secured, one of them bent to the little girl and gently wiped her hair out of her face. A spark of jealousy shot through Corwin.

"Would you like to go see your daddy?" The uniformed woman asked.

The little girl nodded, bursting into fresh tears and throwing her arms around the woman. Corwin stiffened as the chocolate ice cream transferred to the uniform's neat bun. Her mother would have thrown a fit. If dirty children should keep their hands out of other people's hair, they should certainly keep their ice cream out of it. Ignoring Milo's insistent pulling, Corwin whistled a cleaning tune. The chocolate returned to the swirl before the lady even noticed. Then she gave in and followed Milo's lead into the river of people.

They reached the park, though Corwin couldn't say how. She felt better with earth beneath her feet and let the calm soak up through her body before she noticed that nobody else was walking on the grass. All the slickly dressed people kept to the paved paths. It was weird. But it also meant that she and Milo easily found a space where they could pretend the wash of noise around them was just ocean waves. Corwin laid a hand on the tree that blocked them from view of the street. It was an old tree and its roots reached deep through the joys and horrors that had built the city. Though it had a dark history, it had been loved, too, and was well cared for by a nappy-haired old man who told it stories of his grandchildren while he weeded and watered the park.

Milo watered the tree and did his own research into what other dogs and wild animals visited it.

But the tree couldn't tell them how to find Sita.

Corwin set her backpack aside and dug through the Gladstone bag. She pulled out the mint tin of hair ties from the junk drawer and the divining rod the White Oak had given her. She took a deep breath and quietly sang the song her mother would sing at her mirror. She didn't remember the words, but the tune was firm in her memory. As she sang, she focused her mind on the memory of holding tight to the arms of the old rocker in her parents' bedroom, watching her mother brush her lush, auburn hair. She remembered the smell of her sweet perfume and the lilac sachets under their pillows. With all of this firm in her focus, Corwin took one hairband from the collection and wound it around the handle of the divining rod.

She stood, her eyes half-closed, her consciousness half-lost in memories, and she sent her intention into the rod, singing "Show me in which direction lies, the woman within my mind's eyes."

The wood twitched in her hands. It drew her around the tree. Distantly, she felt Milo keeping close to her heels. After wiggling this way and that, as if it were sniffing the air for Sita's perfume, the rod spun her around and pointed definitively northwest. It pulsed once and then pulled so hard, the wood flew out of Corwin's hands. It flew straight through the air for longer than was possible if it had been obeying physics. Once disconnected from Corwin's intention, the magic faded and the rod dropped. It landed at the very edge of a path, startling the fancy people rushing past. Several people had noticed the stick's odd behavior. A couple shook the impossible vision out of their heads and moved on. Two people headed towards the stick to pick it up.

Milo got there first. He snatched the divining rod up in his teeth and bounded back to drop it at Corwin's feet.

We'd better move on. The thought rushed Corwin back to collect her backpack and satchel, even as she released a tension she hadn't realized she'd been carrying since they left Salem. A part of her—the part of her that wasn't worried about the cost of insanity—had believed that the voice was Salem and worried she wouldn't have its guidance when she left.

"Dogs must be on leash," A middle-aged woman snapped at Corwin. She wore a green uniform similar to the one the tree's friend wore. Hers wasn't as crisp.

Milo grabbed the end of his leash and dropped it at Corwin's feet. She snatched it up. "Yes, ma'am."

Nobody followed as she and Milo left the park, using the paths and heading northwest.

Corwin worried as she walked. It was the only kind of multi-tasking she could do successfully. The branch had wanted her to fly. It wasn't directing her a few blocks northwest or a few miles. Her mother was northwest of them, but far northwest. Had the Consortium moved her in the time it took Corwin to get to Richmond? Maybe they moved her because her father had found her. Whatever the reason, her mother was not in Richmond and it was getting late. Dusk was turning into night and the air had grown chilly. They either had to find someplace to spend the night or find an overnight train heading northwest. Did it make sense to just hop on any train headed in that general direction? How far should they go before trying the divining rod again?

Head back to the station. Use a spell to pick a train.

It was a good thought. But Corwin wasn't ready to give up. The crystal had pointed them definitively to Richmond. Her mother could have been taken and her father left behind. It hurt her heart to think it, but, dead or alive, she needed to know if her father was here before she left. They had to find someplace quiet and private where Corwin could find out for certain if her father was dead.

CHAPTER 24

The morning air was heavy with the promise of a stifling-hot day to come. Sweat already dripped down Corwin's face. The hiking pack pounded against her back like Sisyphus's rock as she ran from the cemetery. Her daddy was dead and buried. He had no headstone, but her spells were clear and the answer clearer. She'd used a strand of her own hair, torn out from the root, to scry for her father. The crystal had pointed unerringly to William Byrd Park on the transit system map near the train station. When they got to the park, the divining rod with her hair wrapped around the handle led them to a small, white mausoleum in a private graveyard across the street from the park.

Corwin had collapsed when they got inside and found two dozen stone squares etched with names and dates. Milo licked her face until she pulled herself together enough to read all of the names. None of them read Daniel Samuel Corwin. But the crystal and the divining rod had been certain. Her daddy was there. And if her daddy was there, then he was dead. She hadn't meant to spend the night in the mausoleum. After singing *Dido's Lament* while plucking the ground bass line on her kalimba, she sank to the floor and wrapped herself around Milo. Sleep crept up between memories.

Dawn had crept up just as stealthily. Waking surrounded by the dead had terrified her. Milo carried his own leash as he stuck to her heels, barking only when she nearly ran into the middle of a busy street. He stayed with her until she was stopped by a railing guarding pedestrians from the river.

"Careful, miss. You don't want to fall in there."

Corwin spun and Milo barked as a pile of blankets rearranged themselves into a wooly man and a more carefully groomed dog that appeared to be a mix between a black lab, a mastiff, and a horse. The dog belly-crawled towards Milo, sniffing. Milo trotted over.

"You don't want to fall at all around this one." The man affectionately slapped the demon dog on its rump. "He'll eat you right up."

"Thanks for the warning." Corwin watched as Milo let the black dog sniff him. He nearly fell when the dog shoved his nose in to get a good whiff of his undercarriage. The dog's head was bigger than Milo.

"He doesn't eat dogs." The man tied his thick, curly hair back with an elastic from his wrist. "I'm Gary."

Corwin saw that the worn, old hair tie was going to snap just before it did. She rolled an elastic from her own wrist and handed it to Gary. "I'm called Corwin."

Gary took the elastic with a grin. "Corwin, the nice lady at Rebel Bagels gave me an extra. Care to join me for breakfast?"

Corwin looked back to where Milo was sniffing inside the big dog's ear. His face was hidden by the flap. "Wouldn't your dog like one of those bagels?"

"Okuri-Inu is a carnivore."

"Oh." Corwin took off her pack and sat. She set Grandmother Misty's sun hat on the pack and leaned back against the railing beside the man, Gary. She rifled through the Gladstone bag and quietly activated a black tourmaline, murmuring a little Peter Gabriel. "Here comes the flood."

When she set it in front of her, the rotting smells that had surrounded the man were sucked into the deep black stone with such force that she could see the air disturbed around his feet. Gary wore graying combat boots held together with duct tape.

"Would you prefer banana nut or cinnamon raisin?" He held a paper bag out to Corwin as he asked.

Milo trotted over and stood on his hind legs to stick his nose in the bag. The man laughed.

"Oh no, Milo." Corwin dug the last of his Jack Jaga food out of the coldsac stuffed into the top pocket of the sack. "This is yours."

Milo picked the container up by one edge and trotted over to set it down by Oku's massive head. The dog sniffed it, gave a surprised, breathy bark, and shoved his face into the food. Milo backed away.

"Looks like you'll be sharing, so here's the banana nut. It's healthier for a dog."

"Thank you." Corwin hid her face with the pack. She needed to offer the man something in return. Her hand brushed a tin as she found the bag of kibble. She pulled both out of her bag. "Would you like some hot chocolate? It has mini-marshmallows in it."

Gary's wrinkled face lit up. "That'd be a treat. You got hot water in that pack?"

"I do." Corwin laid her hand on one of the canteens attached to the outside. She sang, "It's getting hot in here."

"You're weird." Corwin recoiled from the man's words until he added, in a whisper, "I like that in a person."

Corwin mixed the cocoa in a pair of tin mugs Gary set on the ground between them. The man pulled a bottle of hand sanitizer out of the pile of bags hidden under his blankets. He offered some to her and then pushed his sleeves up to thoroughly clean his hands. She washed up and then dumped a handful of kibble out for Milo.

Milo ignored the food. He trotted over and stood up on Gary's knee to sniff the angry rash on his right arm. He barked at it and ran back to tap his nose on the bottle of house water. He didn't notice Uku stand and limp over when he got too close to the man.

Corwin pulled Milo into her lap, just in case. She kept an eye on Oku's limp as the dog lay with his head between her and Gary. Something was hurting his front right paw. She ate a few bites of the bagel and drank her cocoa while it was hot. The man did the same.

After a while, she asked, "Are you hurt?"

Gary offered a piece of his bagel to the giant dog. The dog sniffed at it and then turned his head away. "Oku chased a rabbit into a patch of thorny weeds. I had to help him out."

"And you?" she asked. "Can I clean that rash for you?" Corwin glanced at Oku. "Would he let me?"

The man examined his companion for a long moment before he held out his arm. "I suppose he'd let you do anything that might make me more tasty for him."

She cleaned Gary's arm with house water and a sparkling gel she found in the Gladstone bag. Oku watched her closely. Milo watched Oku.

By the time she'd finished wrapping the man's arm in a clean bandage, Milo had inched his way close enough to the big dog's injured paw that he could lay his head on it. Corwin could hear a low rumble that was less growl and more Tibetan throat chant. Blue glittered around the paw, dripping from the wampum around Milo's neck.

"Careful there," Gary warned Milo when Oku finally noticed him. The mastiff yanked his paw away so suddenly that Milo was tumbled onto his back. Where Oku's paw had been lay a bloody, golden foxtail. The weeds were all over Salem in the dry season. Jack Jaga railed on how insidious they were. Gary scooped Milo out of Oku's reach.

Oku sniffed at the foxtail. Corwin foolishly put her hand out to stop him from getting too close. "You don't want to inhale that."

Oku drew his head back. He touched his right paw down gingerly and then tapped it on the cement. He stood and danced around the blankets and bags, circling back to lick Milo in Gary's arms. The hair on Milo's left side stood up like he'd rolled in a puddle.

It's time to go.

Corwin agreed. She held out the bottle of glittering goo. "I'll trade you."

Gary laughed as he handed Milo over. "It's not a fair trade."

Corwin thought of what Kali said whenever he gave her a little something extra. "Then, I'll sweeten the pot." She set the canteen of heated water in front of Gary.

He eyed the canteen as if it were diamonds.

Corwin packed up her sack and her Gladstone bag. She pulled the divining rod from the side and removed the string of her hair, shoving it into a pocket for safekeeping. She had no item that would help her hone in on the Consortium. Her mother was with them, so she took a hair tie from the mint tin and wrapped it around the pointer.

When she was ready, Grandmother Misty's hat back on her head, she turned to Gary, who had started packing up his little camp. He draped a filthy blanket off of her backpack and then he wrapped his arms around her, whispering, "Heroes wear capes."

It's okay. It's okay. The little voice encouraged her to accept the hug even though she felt trapped.

When he released her, she started to thank him, but he shushed her. "Now," he said, "is when we trade well-wishes." He lifted the divining rod and held his hands over hers on the handles. "May you find whatever you are searching for before it finds you."

Corwin was at a loss until Milo barked, drawing her attention to the duct-taped combat boots. "May you find shoes that will never let you fall."

A glowing smile lit the man's face. Corwin couldn't help but ape him. It made her feel better.

"Bye, Gary."

"Walk steady, Corwin."

Corwin and Milo walked steady for miles. Corwin held the idea of the Consortium in her mind. She thought of her mother and Mr. Charles and of the silver magic from her father's last call. The divining rod pulled her steadily north and a little east, eventually down an alley, past a blue dumpster, to poke at a heavy security door behind a Chinese restaurant.

She tucked the rod into the straps on the Gladstone bag and raised her hand to knock.

Run!

The voice screamed in her head and her feet had no choice but to obey. Milo dashed under the dumpster. She followed, dropping to the ground and covering her body with Gary's cape. Just as it settled over her entirely—larger than she had thought—the door burst open. It slammed against the alley wall.

The weave on the cape was just loose enough that she could see the three people who stormed out. They were silent, but their bearing terrified Corwin more than the automatic weapons they carried over their shoulders or the guns tucked into their belts. She tried to push her body closer to the dumpster and kicked a soda can.

All three people spun. All three drew a weapon. All three aimed directly at her.

Chapter 25

Corwin shivered beneath her cape. She and the voice in her head reverted to the spell she'd chanted in fourth grade. "Don't look at me. Don't see me. I am nothing. Just move on." It wasn't much of a spell, but her intention was strong.

"It's just some fucking homeless person."

"You can't sleep here." The woman kicked her foot.

The third person holstered his gun and marched away down the alley. The other two spat on her and followed him.

Corwin held her breath until they were out of sight. Milo crawled out from under the dumpster and dug under the blanket cape. He huddled in Corwin's lap, shivering in rhythm with her own trembling.

Let's just watch the door for a bit.

A panicky giggle escaped Corwin's lips. The voice, she thought, was a great addition to her homeless disguise. She stayed, holding Milo, missing her daddy, and fearing for her mother for a very long time. Her butt had begun to go numb by the time the door opened again. She sucked in a gasp at the sight of the two men who came out.

One of them was dressed in a crisp, expensive suit that hung awkwardly on his bony frame. He walked with a bounce that kept his heels from touching the ground much. Corwin got the idea that he was trying to appear taller than the other man, even though he actually was.

The other man wasn't particularly tall. Corwin bet she'd top him by a couple of inches. The fabric of his plain suit strained against his muscular form. This man's face looked as worn as the suit. It was covered in scars above his neatly trimmed white-blond beard. His once-black boots were not made to be worn with a suit.

Corwin recognized both of them. She couldn't place where she'd seen the muscle before, but she knew exactly where she'd seen fancy-pants — in the mirror in her lab. That was Mr. Charles, the man who had threatened her mother.

She had found the Consortium.

Mr. Charles held the door open to finish a conversation with someone inside. "I would not have made her a Consortium protégé if I didn't think she could handle it." He rolled his eyes as the other person said something. The scarred man watched Mr. Charles impassively. He stepped away when the man opened the door wider to say, "Yes, yes. You will meet her at the Directors meeting."

Corwin needed the door to stay open. The answers she needed were inside that building. She glanced around for something she could throw to block the doorway. There was a brick, but it was on the other side of the alley beside the door, as if it had been set there for that purpose.

Milo wriggled out from under the cape. He bounded over to the door. He ran full force into the doorstop brick. It moved just a little bit closer to the opening, not close enough. He scrambled over the brick and made a break for the open door. He didn't get past Mr. Charles. Corwin tensed, ready to rescue him.

Stay. The voice was calm, unruffled.

Mr. Charles stopped Milo with a foot hooked under his belly. He dragged the little dog out of the doorway. "Take this, Five-Five-Three. You like dogs, don't you?"

"Yes, Mr. Charles." The rough man bent to pick Milo up with both hands. Milo laid a paw on his beard and tilted his head. An image shot through Corwin's head of that same man holding a different puppy just like that. What could she do if he walked away with Milo?

You follow and we find your mother.

Corwin did not like that plan. It wasn't a good plan. But maybe following Mr. Charles was smarter than rooting through some random Consortium building filled with armed people.

"Get back to it. We'll have our answers in a week." Mr. Charles stepped away from the door. It closed slowly.

Once it shut, she wouldn't have any choice. Corwin didn't dare use her kalimba or whistle to cast a spell. She didn't even have the breath to speak, for fear these men would catch her watching them. She sent an intention quietly, adjusting her frustrated thought into a song.

Telekinesis is not my jam
I can't move the brick from where I am.
Luck be my friend, my partner, my guide,
Hold the door open to let me inside.

Mr. Charles was halfway to the street when he looked up from his armpadd. He turned to see the craggy-faced man still standing by the closing door, examining Milo. "I was kidding, Fivefivethree. Leave it."

The man called Fivefivethree set Milo down. He reached into a pocket with his other hand as he knelt. His rear foot rested on the doorstop brick. He twirled one of Milo's velvety ears around his fingers and dropped a Milkbone in front of him. Then the strange man pushed to his feet to hurry after Mr. Charles. His rear foot kicked the brick an inch farther. He didn't look back to see that the door didn't close.

Corwin took it as a sign. She waited until the two men were long gone from the alley before she tucked the cape around her backpack and satchel and shoved them behind the dumpster with Grandmother Misty's hat. She gave one more furtive look around and then pulled the door open. Afraid it might lock from both sides, she carefully stepped over the brick.

"Milo, come on."

The dog stood staring at the Milkbone as though he'd never seen anything like it. He might not have, she realized. She didn't have any at home. He didn't respond.

"Okay, Milo," she said. "Bark if anyone comes."

He turned to nod at her and then returned his gaze to the mouth of the alley where Mr. Charles and Fivefivethree had disappeared.

Inside, Corwin had a choice. There were stairs leading up and stairs leading down. Mr. Charles had been looking down as he spoke, so she knew there was someone down there. She went up.

The door at the first landing was locked. Corwin continued up. On the fourth floor, the stairwell opened to a small space which had once been shut off by a door. The hinges and frame remained with pieces of the door itself scattered around. Graffiti painted the walls and someone had strewn some garbage. But the place did not smell like the alley. Corwin stepped over the broken door and headed for the thick metal door set in the bare cement wall beyond. She sang a wordless, dancing tune that she sent to weave through the tumblers. Her fingers picked out an accompaniment on her kalimba. She adjusted the tune as she felt the tumblers align. A final trill tripped the lock. Corwin turned the knob and the door opened into a massive space.

She was blinded for a moment by the bright sunshine pouring in though the skylights overhead. When she could see, she wished she had a camera. It would take days just to take in all the maps, papers, pictures, and charts that were pinned up on the walls. She took a breath and tried to listen to her instincts. The first thing she noticed was what she didn't hear. There was no buzz of electronics. This room was entirely offline. Her shoulders relaxed and the little hairs that had been standing up on her arms since she got on the train in Salem rested. The room was so cut off from modern technology that it felt like home.

The second thing that grabbed her attention was the wide table in the center of the room. Ten handles stood out from the long side in a row. As she drew closer, she saw that they were attached to wide, thin drawers. The surface of the table held exactly three neat piles of symphony sized documents.

One was layers of a blueprint for what looked like an enormous office complex built around a garden. A sheet of vellum had been laid atop the stack. The marks on it appeared to be indications of damage and repair suggestions with costs.

The pile on the edge closest to the door was a map of a farm in Indiana. There was a vellum sheet over this one, as well, with damage indications and what might be a body count for each grid section. The lower papers offered details of each grid.

On the far side of the table, the shortest stack was a series of concert posters. There were five versions, all advertising a multi-entertainment festival in Las Vegas, Nevada. In person attendance was highly recommended, although details were given for remote participation. Each of the posters incorporated the phrase, *Come find the solution to what ails us* as well as *No One is Exempt.* The date on the poster was exactly one week away.

Corwin looked up at a distant sound. The hairs stood up on her arms again and the voice in her head barked, *Get out.*

There was no other doorway that she could see. Corwin ran for the door she'd come in and raced through onto the landing. She heard voices. A lot of voices. She also heard Milo barking up a storm outside. A couple of people yelled at him and then the door slammed shut, muffling his voice. Corwin held her breath, chanting in her head with no magical intention whatsoever, *go down, go down, go down, go down.*

They climbed up.

In desperation, she laid one hand on her own chest and pulled the penny whistle from her pocket. Humming an E-flat, she played an E-flat at the same time. She let the vibrations wave into each other, weaving the spell. When she could no longer see the hand holding her whistle to her lips, she let the notes die away. Only then did she creep down the stairs. She'd almost reached the third-floor landing when she saw a young man hustling up. She hadn't heard him under the chatter from farther down. She froze and held her breath. Her heart pounded and she tried to fall into the memory of when she'd first dreamed of invisibility.

Wade Kelley and Levi York tortured her in fourth grade. She'd sit quietly in her seat in the back of the room, reading, not bothering anybody, and slowly their voices would creep into her awareness. They laughed at her clothes and how she was always humming. They wondered, loudly, if she ever got her hair cut. And they made fun of her parents for letting her go to school looking like that. Great-great-grandaunt Judith's journal practically screamed "hate is the most evil thing there is." So, Corwin tried very hard not to hate them. Instead, she dreamed of being invisible and then she worked hard at getting out of school.

She let out a breath as the young man barreled on up to the top floor. Then another person, a dark-skinned young man with delicate features and a striped suit, hopped up the steps to the third-floor landing.

"Jeremy!" The pretty man leaned against a wall, one hand in his pocket, a smirk on his face, waiting for Jeremy to come to him rather than continuing up the stairs.

Jeremy came halfway down. "Yeah?"

"Your boss gonna make it to Vegas?"

Jeremy sighed. He shrugged as he came down a few more steps closer to Corwin. "You know how it is, Carlos. Cedric tried to kill them all three months ago. Does your boss want to go?"

"Mr. Charles is making progress." Carlos waggled an eyebrow. "He's eager to show off Sita and his inroads with the Montana Collective. He'll be there."

Jeremy looked over at Corwin's gasp. She held her breath and focused on the E-flat in her mind.

"Y'okay, Jer-bear?"

"Shh." Jeremy dashed to close the space between himself and Carlos. He hissed, "Not at work." Then he kissed Carlos deeply. An instant later, as though it had never happened, Jeremy ran up the stairs, yelling, "I'll be in Vegas for sure, whether Bulldog shows or not."

Carlos caressed his lips and chuckled, "I can't wait."

Corwin followed Carlos down the stairs. He hopped. She slunk. He opened the door on the first landing by pressing his hand to a plate beside the deadbolt. Corwin peered in, but the door only revealed an entryway with a desk and several chairs. The door closed before Carlos opened the inner door.

She made her way down, decided against checking out the basement and breathed a sigh of relief when the street door opened at her push. She slipped out and crouched behind the dumpster before releasing her invisibility spell. Milo hadn't been fooled. He stood on her thigh before she'd reappeared.

"Good job." She ruffled his fur and then collected their bags. The Milkbone that Milo hadn't eaten lay in the street where the man called Fivefivethree had dropped it. Corwin put it in a pocket of her vest.

"Maybe you'll want it later. Now, we have to get to Vegas. My mother is going to be there."

CHAPTER 26

Corwin bought the train ticket to Vegas with the last of the money on her father's debit card. She didn't have to leave a balance now that he wouldn't be using the account anymore. They spent the night in the Richmond train station. She was rousted out when she tried to curl up in the corner of a washroom. But nobody bothered her when she sat on a chair in the waiting area with a dozen other people. She quietly applied a spell to turn the advertising flyer into official-looking Service Dog papers and then sewed a vest for Milo out of her union suit. Once she put it on him, she ran her hands down the sides, imitating a vest she saw on a German Shepherd standing beside a little boy in a wheelchair. With the vest, Milo wouldn't have to ride around in her coat pocket all the time.

Although, the canine in question didn't seem to mind the pocket at all. While she squirmed in the molded plastic seat, Milo slept so comfortably in the pocket that he started snoring. Corwin couldn't sleep. Her mind wouldn't have let her, even if she could have gotten comfortable.

All her life, she'd been busy hiding from curious adults and learning how to find the Heart and her mother. Now, she was an adult, she had the Heart, and she had a lead on her mother. The successes made room for her to finally consider what was so wrong with her that her mother had to leave. It hadn't taken any of her attention at all for Sita to send the fire grate skittering in front of Corwin to protect her from flying debris in her battle with Kat Coogan. If she could protect her daughter so easily, why couldn't she protect herself? Corwin had defeated Kat Coogan's attacks multiple times and she wasn't even worthy. So, why did her mother leave?

She couldn't find an answer. Though the question harassed her dreams on the train, Las Vegas easily distracted Corwin from her tumbling, hateful self-doubt.

On their first night, after a van ride to a place called The Strip, Corwin asked at forty-three places before she found a hotel room that she and Milo could afford with the cash they had, but the owner wouldn't rent to her without a credit card "for incidentals."

A nice guy who heard her trouble directed her to a place she could crash for cash. He had even offered to drive them there, but Corwin didn't feel comfortable getting into a car with a stranger. Her instincts had been right. But even the little voice in her head hadn't warned her about the cat-house itself.

At first, Corwin had been relieved that the owner had not had any actual cats. Later, she figured out her mistake. She had climbed into the ostentatious bed with all of her clothes on, one hand gripping Grandmother Misty's hat. Milo had slept across the door, not realizing there was a second entrance to the room.

Corwin woke to the owner, naked and screaming on top of her. Milo had clamped onto the man's ankle and didn't let go until Corwin was halfway into the second verse of *Twist and Shout,* and clear of the sheets that had wrapped themselves impossibly around the owner. She grabbed her bag and tried the door, only to find it locked. Milo's sensitive nose led them through the tight, dark hallway they found through the panel in the wall the owner had used to get into her room. He got them to the lobby. Once outside in the cool desert air, Corwin had scooped him into her coat pocket and made for the brightest lights on The Strip.

Corwin stumbled into a casino as the sun rose behind her. The noise and crowd made her feel safe. The smells woke her enough to look around. She could not afford a room. She'd tried several of the bright casinos before realizing that. But there were rows and rows of machines with stools where she could sit just so long as she punched a button every now and then.

She sat at one of these, pulling her hat low on her forehead, and lost herself in the pictures of scenes from *Peter and the Wolf.* The Prokofiev score ran through her head. She didn't own a flute. But she'd considered getting one just because she loved the bird parts of the music. She hadn't even gotten through the first movement before a stranger approached her.

Corwin stood, ready to run.

"Whoa, there. It's okay." A smattering of yellow sparkles floated from the woman's hand.

Corwin blinked. It was hard to tell if the sparkles were magic or just reflections from the thousands of sequins covering the woman's leotard and boy shorts. Her name, Samantha, sparkled on her chest. Her dangling earrings sparkled. Her tights sparkled. Her high-heeled boots sparkled. The feathers in her curly up-do sparkled. Even her impossibly long eyelashes sparkled. Corwin only knew for sure when she felt her muscles relax.

"You're Skilled." Corwin looked around, afraid she'd been too loud.

It took Samantha a moment to decipher Corwin's phrasing. When she did, she let a secretive grin light up her nod. "You, too?"

Corwin nodded.

"Be careful. I grew up here. I know what I can get away with and I'm leaving. Soon."

Something in the way her grin dimmed told Corwin that Samantha had been saying that for a while.

Her little voice concurred. *She needs help.* How did it know?

"Can I help?" she asked.

Samantha sighed. "I wish. But I can help you." She gestured to a slot on one side of the screen. "You need to put a card in the machine."

Corwin sighed so hard Milo twisted in her pocket. "I don't have a credit card."

"Do you have cash?" Samantha leaned back to glance down one of the wider pathways through the casino while Corwin dug into the Gladstone bag. She pulled out her last few twenty-dollar bills.

"Okay. Hold on." The sparkling young witch took the bills and stepped over to a duller machine at the end of the row. She returned with a plastic card and fit it into the slot on Corwin's machine. The three little pictures in the center of the screen started rotating while lights flashed. The words PULL THE HANDLE flashed on the screen in tall red letters.

"This button is the 'handle.' You just have to push that every now and then and you can sit here until you run out of money on that card. If you want to get the money off the card, you take it over to that cage there. If you're super lucky, you might end up with more money than you put on the card."

Corwin held her hand out. Samantha took it. Lilac and blue magic surged down Corwin's arm from her chest and danced around Samantha's bare arm until it wriggled through her aura and disappeared. Corwin murmured, "I wish you bluebirds in the spring." It was a song about love, but also about moving on, and Corwin filled the notes with her wishes for Samantha to be lucky.

Samantha scrunched her nose and giggled. "That tickles." Her eyes lighted on something down the row and she sobered. "Can I get you something to drink? It's free."

"Juice?"

"Orange, apple, cranberry?"

Milo poked his head out of Corwin's pocket and barked. Samantha did a quick scan of the immediate area and pet Milo's head as she pushed him back down out of sight. "I'll get you a glass of water, too."

Corwin lost herself in the spinning pictures. They danced and spun if any of them matched. She wanted to get all of them to match. Seventeen cranberry juices in, she lost her temper and charmed the machine to give her three dancing birds in fur hats. Lights went off over the machine and alarms sounded. Coins rained down the screen, obscuring the birds and all the other pictures. People turned from their own machines to cheer and applaud. Three men in suits appeared at the end of the row and watched her.

They made her uncomfortable. She tried to avoid looking at them as she gathered the pack and Gladstone bag without dropping Milo out of her pocket. She started moving away from the machine when the little voice reminded her to take the card. The men stalked towards her as she struggled to get the card out of the little slot.

A crash of glasses, liquid, chips, and raised voices distracted the goons' attention just long enough for her to get the card and get away from the machine. She ducked right at the end of the row and hurried through the machines, trying to get away before the men could catch up.

Your backpack is neon orange. You're wearing a men's suit from two decades ago and a woman's fashionable car coat from a century ago. Your braid is longer than Rapunzel's. I don't think you're gonna be hard to find again.

None of that mattered unless she could lose them in the first place. Which she couldn't. Each time she looked, one or more of the men were no more than fifteen feet behind her. She searched for a less crowded area where she could move more quickly. A wide aisle wove through a sea of green tables. She headed for it, thinking she could plant herself at a different bank of slot machines on the far side. On the way there, she caught a glimpse of the outside as a gaggle of drunk kids left the casino. The sun was already going down.

She collapsed onto the stool of a machine decorated with buffalo. She'd lost an entire day. That made it two days down and five to go until the Consortium's big meeting. She was out of money, had nowhere to sleep, and no real idea where her mother would be in this big town.

"Hey, kid." Samantha appeared around the end of the row. "No resting, yet. Come on. Follow me."

Corwin felt a magical pull from the young woman who never even looked at her as she hurried by and led her on a dizzying path through banks of slot machines, past gaming tables, and around pillars, melding in and out of crowds like a shell tossed on waves. She didn't stop moving until she and Corwin were alone together in a women's restroom.

Samantha placed both hands on the door and whispered a word Corwin couldn't quite make out. It sounded Latin. Most of Corwin's Latin came from requiems.

Breathe.

Corwin was out of breath and sweating. She looked inside her jacket at Milo. He'd shifted himself so that he was hunkered deep in the pocket. The stitching looked stressed.

"Hi." Samantha reached a hand out to let Milo sniff her.

Blood. She's bruised.

Corwin glanced at the other witch's perfect skin. She didn't see any bruises on her hand or anywhere else.

The voice insisted. *She has a bad boyfriend.*

Samantha's eyes widened as she pet Milo. After a moment, she shook her head. "We've only got a minute. I'm Emily. What's your name?"

Corwin blinked stupidly. "Corwin. Your name tag says—"

"Yeah," Emily scoffed. "I don't need the drunks around here knowing my real name."

Corwin realized that maybe she should have given a false name. Walter might be attending the Directors Meeting. Kat Coogan might even show up.

Emily had to say her name twice to get her attention. "Get out of town, Corwin. They don't know you're a witch. But it doesn't matter. Your face is gonna be shared around and you won't be safe in Vegas for a while."

Corwin asked, "What did I do wrong?"

"The machines are rigged so no one wins a jackpot. You won the jackpot."

"What does that mean?"

"Girl. You have a shit-ton of money on that card. The bosses here are pretty serious about not giving away any money they don't have to."

"The bosses are those guys following me?"

"Nah, those guys are the muscle. That hat does a pretty good job of helping you blend in, but the machine got a picture of your face straight on. You can't—" Magic sparkled yellow in Emily's aura as her eyes went distant. She reached one hand up to touch her earlobe. "You can't walk around with that face anymore."

"I can't leave. My mother is going to be here soon." Corwin held the card up. "If I have a lot of money now, I can check into a room."

Her inner voice shouted, *Not under your name. That would lead Walter and Kat right to us.*

"No," Emily murmured. "Not under your name. But—" The witch suddenly had trouble breathing. Tears welled in her eyes.

Give her the card. The voice flashed images of Emily bringing food to a pair of men. One of them was older, counting a stack of cash. The other stuck his hand up her skirt as she set the food down.

Corwin held the card out. "You need this. It's gonna get me killed. Take it. Please."

Emily shook her head once. Her face went blank, eyes pinned to the slot machine card. Slowly, she began nodding. "You could get a room in my name. I have a credit card."

She's going to run away. If you're her, they'll follow you, instead. She's sad because she has nowhere to go.

Corwin shook her head, trying to focus. She didn't have time to wonder how the voice in her head knew all that. It wasn't Salem. It wasn't Corwin House. It wasn't her. Was the voice one of her ancestors, attached to her from all the time she spent with their books? For the first time, the voice frightened her.

She shoved her roiling thoughts away and forced the card into Emily's hand. "Go to Salem, Massachusetts. Jack Jaga at the animal shelter will help you. Just tell him you're Skilled."

Emily took a slim wallet from a pocket hidden in the sequins of her bodysuit. She put the card into it and took out a driver's license and a credit card. She handed them over to Corwin. "Can you glamour your bags into suitcases?"

Corwin shook her head. "I don't know how to do that."

"Yeah, it's hard. I'll take them. Ask for a room on the thirteenth floor. Nobody ever wants the thirteenth floor. I'll meet you up there."

Corwin handed over her backpack and the Gladstone bag. The backpack looked ridiculous over Emily's sequined, barely-there outfit. "Won't they stop you?"

Emily grinned. "Glamour is my specialty." She set the Gladstone bag on a sink and wrapped both of her hands around the shoulder straps of the pack. She murmured some words in Latin, repeating herself three times. Then she bounced, as if adjusting the weight on her shoulders.

Yellow glittered in her aura and extended around the pack as it melted into a shirt-dress covered with daisies. Emily buttoned it up over her uniform.

"Now, for you." Emily pulled one dangling crystal earring from her ear.

She held it out in her palm. As Corwin reached to take it, the earring transformed into a small gold clip-on earring set with raw labradorite. The metal was hot to her touch and she felt magic sparking from the stone. She looked up to see Emily as much changed as the jewelry.

Her hair was still curly but also wildly frizzy. Her face had softened and old bruises shone green and yellow along her jawline. Her lashes no longer sparkled and the bags under her eyes matched the slump of her shoulders. She looked even more tired than Corwin.

Her eyes darted away from Corwin's searching gaze. "Should I take the dog?"

Corwin's little voice insisted, *We stay together.*

"I'll keep him with me," she said. "Will this earring make me look like you?"

"It can make you look any way you like. But it takes practice. Look at my ID, set your intention firmly in your mind— Oh!" She turned Corwin so that she was facing the stalls and not the mirror. "Now, you say 'transformare imagineum' three times."

Corwin stared at the picture on the ID, where Emily looked younger. She had no bruises and longer hair. Her smile was hopeful. Latin hadn't been a big part of the Corwin family's teaching and the words didn't feel right when she said them. Frank Sinatra seemed entirely right for Vegas so she followed the Latin with the opening of the theme song from *The Americanization of Emily.* "Emily. Emily. Emily."

Yellow sparkles flashed across her eyes, twinkling with her own violet magic. She didn't need to look in the mirror. Emily's eyes told her everything she needed to know.

"You're good," she breathed. Then she turned and released the spell she'd set on the door. "Let's go."

Corwin stepped through the door to find all three goons waiting for her.

CHAPTER 27

Even though she didn't look like herself, one of the goons still followed Corwin on her circuitous journey to find the front desk. He did not follow her up the elevator. Corwin read the room numbers out loud as she looked for 1347. When she reached it, Emily slipped out of the stairwell with her bags looking like her bags again.

See, you were worried for nothing. Her little voice mocked Corwin. She did her best to ignore it.

Emily dropped the bags off in Corwin's room, gave her a hug, and left to cash out the slot machine card before she grabbed the first flight out of Nevada.

She's not going to Salem. Her little voice sounded sad. It confused Corwin.

Alone in a room rented under another witch's face, Corwin risked her sanity to ask, "How do you know?"

The answer came swiftly and did nothing to assuage her fears.

I read her mind.

Corwin wanted to scream, "How? How? How?" But she was too tired. She'd been living with this voice for years. Why was she questioning it now? What had changed?

What had changed in the moment was that she was exhausted. She had been awake for far too long. She set Milo on a corner of the massive queen-sized bed, took off her boots, engaged the deadbolt and chain, charmed the door, and collapsed into sleep as Milo wriggled over to lay his head on her ankle.

She woke at dawn and pulled the curtains. Two hours later, she got up to feed Milo and eat her last apple. She brushed her teeth and Milo's, sitting on the shag rug in the bathroom and decided against a bath before undressing and getting under the covers in the bed. Milo did his circle dance on the other pillow and the two slept until Corwin's belly demanded more food.

Three days down. Four to go. Corwin assumed the Consortium directors would start arriving in Las Vegas before the actual date of the meeting. Each time she scried for her mother using the crystal and map, it insisted Sita was in Richmond. But when she used the divining rod, it sailed across the room until it ran into the northeastern wall.

In the meantime, she played with Emily's *glamearring*, as the loud, incessant little voice called it. She was not very successful at trying to look like anybody specific other than Emily. She came close when she tried to look like Morgan. She had more success changing individual features, like her eye color or the shape of her nose. She couldn't change her hair at all.

Her scrying efforts finally delivered a new response late in the afternoon of the day before the festival was scheduled to begin. The garnet still insisted on Richmond. But the divining rod had other ideas. When the wood wasn't yanked out of her hands to the northeast but pulled her gently south, Corwin gathered up her things.

She put Milo into the car coat pocket. She'd used some of her time, and the complimentary sewing kit from the bathroom, to reinforce the pocket. She clipped the glamearring onto her lobe and sang, "Emily." Then she wrapped her hair in a scarf and shifted her skin tone to Morgan's shade. It made her look different enough that Emily's men would not be a problem if they happened to see her.

I'll warn you if I hear anyone thinking about Emily.

Corwin took no comfort in the little voice's reassurance. She took the elevator down and dropped her key on the front desk. She moved quickly, in case the casino's enforcers were looking for her backpack. Outside in the Vegas heat, she regretted her clothing. The vest over an undershirt was a good choice, but Great-great-grandaunt Judith's maxi skirt left her sweaty thighs free to stick to each other.

She got strange looks as she pulled out the White Oak wood and followed it through the evening crowds. There was nowhere she could go to avoid the crowds so she put her head down and ignored the looks. Grandmother Misty's hat kept her face out of every tourist's pictures.

The rod wanted her to fly and morph through buildings. Since she could not do that, she had to backtrack a few times as she ran into dead ends. In the end, it took nearly two hours for the divining rod with Mother's hair tie still wrapped around the pointer to lead her, gently and confidently, to the Masquerade Hotel and Casino.

People watched her as she hurried through the casino to the check-in area. She knew wearing a sun hat indoors at night was odd, but she didn't want to take it off if it really was charmed to make her forgettable, as Emily had suggested. There was nothing she could do about her antique skirt and neon backpack.

You're no stranger than everyone else. Head up, the little voice pushed her.

So, strangers stared as neighbors had when she was a kid. She didn't let it bother her. She had a mission and she was so close. Her mother was here. She stood in the line at Hotel Check-in, keeping her eyes on the floor in front of her until a desk attendant called out, "Next."

"Hi." She forced herself to look up and meet the woman's eyes. "I'm here for the Consortium meeting. My boss forgot to give me our reservation number. His name is Mr. Charles."

The woman brushed an imaginary stray strand of hair off her face. Her name tag glinted in the lights as she moved. Alicia. She offered a polite smile and replied, "That is not a problem. Let me have your ID and credit card and I can look up your room that way."

"Actually," Corwin started to sweat. "I'm not staying here with them. I'm just delivering um, some paperwork. If you can just let me know what room Sita Corwin is staying in, I can run it up."

Alicia didn't type. She kept her hands folded on the dark smartglass screen. "Unfortunately, I cannot give out guest information. Perhaps you should give your boss a call and have him meet you here in the casino."

Alicia said here, but she gestured toward an area away from the desk. Corwin nodded her head and mumbled something appreciative. She tried to think of another angle, but nothing came to her before she started feeling really awkward and she stumbled away as the next guest stepped up.

The straightforward approach had failed. That was okay. Like she told Naomi, she couldn't play a song the first time she ever sat down at the spinet. She had to learn how to play the notes and learn which keys matched which little black dots on the paper. If the meeting was being held here, it was not being held in the casino, which meant it had to be on a different floor. Nobody used stairs. There might be escalators somewhere, but the only way up that was close to the check-in desks was a bank of five elevators.

Corwin would just blend in and watch the people getting on the elevators. Maybe she would recognize Jeremy or Carlos or Mr. Charles or Mr. Fivefivethree. She didn't even dare to hope she might see her mother. If her mother were some sort of prize Mr. Charles was going to show off, he wouldn't bring her in by the front door.

Corwin planted herself by a coin machine. She set her bags down and pretended to look through a brochure. In the first hour, more people piled on and off the elevators than lived in Salem. She actually read the brochure during the second hour, learning that there were magnificent, curving escalators flanking the permanent Masquerade parade float in the very center of the casino. Early in hour three, a guard tried to run her off.

"You have to have memorized that by now, miss." The peppering of freckles on the short guard's round face weakened the stern tone of his voice.

"Not quite," Corwin said honestly. "But would you like me to tell you how many crystals there are lining the canal bridges?"

The guard laughed at that and then reminded himself to be tough. "I'm going to have to ask you to move along."

Corwin didn't have any other plan. She knew she didn't fit in here. None was not nearly enough leg to be showing to fit in.

Be honest.

She tried what the voice said. "I'm looking for my mother and I have nowhere else to go."

Something in the way she said this caused a wrinkle in the guard's brow. He lowered his voice. "Do you need the police?"

She thought about it. Why had she never gone to the police? Because her father hadn't. Because how would she tell them about the fight between her mother and Kat Coogan? If she left out the magic, there wasn't really much to tell. Some long-locked-away memory from that day surfaced suddenly and Corwin murmured the remembered phrase, "a worthy daughter."

Had Kat Coogan called her an unworthy daughter? Her mind leapt from the memory as from a speeding train. She remembered Emily's warning about casinos sharing her picture around. Would they have given it to the police? She had made that slot machine give her money. That was stealing. She was a thief.

Corwin realized she'd failed to respond to the guard. "No," she whispered back. "Please, no."

He nodded as if he understood. "I will be making rounds. But mostly, I'll be right over there. If you need help when she gets here, you just whistle." He held a plastic whistle out to her. "I'm Keevan. Okay?"

"Okay, Keevan." Corwin didn't like the idea of being watched, but Keevan was kind. She pulled her penny whistle from her pocket and played a spell for happiness. "I've got a whistle. Thank you."

She watched him stroll back to his stand. When he spotted a drunk guy dropping chips in his wake, Keevan grabbed a plastic cup from a shelf inside the stand and rushed to gather the chips. He turned it down when the guy offered him a tip. The guy turned away from Keevan and nearly walked into a stranger with a dour expression on his face who was headed towards the ATM beside Corwin. Drunk guy handed Dour Fella the chip he'd wanted Keevan to take and stumbled off. That dour fella detoured from the cash machine and kicked an older woman's cane out from under her in his rush. He caught her and then offered his arm. After much blushing and patting of her white hair, the woman permitted him to escort her into the casino.

As they disappeared into the crowd, two familiar faces waded out of it. Jeremy from Richmond followed Mr. Charles right past Corwin to the elevator lobby. It took all her self-control to stay where she was as they got onto the rarely used fifth elevator. Jeremy, despite juggling three bags and an armful of folders, extracted a card from his pocket and tapped it on something before he hit the button for their floor. The doors closed and Corwin watched as the digital number over the door climbed to *13* and stopped.

She hadn't seen any of the other elevators stop on thirteen. She watched the others for a while and, sure enough, each of them skipped from twelve to fourteen.

She needed to take the fifth elevator to the thirteenth floor. She started to gather her things.

How do we get a keycard?

What was she thinking? The numbers over elevator five started counting down. A quiet bark drew her attention away from the elevator. She sniffed and listened for what had disturbed Milo.

A rough voice with a German accent stood out from the chatter, "Ugh, no more about the Montana Collective."

Carlos had said something about the Montana Collective when he was talking with Jeremy in the stairwell in Richmond. Two men emerged from the dance of people approaching the elevator lobby. The taller one, in a tan suit and carrying only a soft-sided briefcase, tapped the button beside the fifth elevator.

His companion shifted a suitcase and garment bag to access his armpadd. He shook his head and heaved a sigh at what he saw. "It's all madness."

"This is how Kathiris wants things, Phil." The German kept his eyes on the numbers over the elevator. "As long as we take the shots, we don't have to worry about catching anything from the masses."

Phil growled, "I'm not talking about Asher's viruses. I'm saying it's madness to gather all the leaders of the Consortium in one place, Miter. I think it's crazy to ever do it but especially not five months after one of *us* tried to kill the rest of us."

"That is why she wants to look us all in the eye." Miter tapped his keycard against the other man's chest.

Phil glared gently at the keycard and squeezed his lips together before answering, "To make sure we're sane. Yeah, I know. Look, I have to go check in. I'll see you tonight." Phil peeled off and trotted by Corwin and the cash machine. He didn't pay her any mind as she crouched on the floor in all black with her bright orange camping backpack.

The number over the elevator clicked to *L* and the bell dinged.

We need a distraction. The voice in Corwin's head was way ahead of her. Her plan had been to just follow Miter onto the elevator. Milo was on the side of the voice. He leapt from her pocket and dashed through the silver doors as they slid apart. Corwin had no choice but to follow. She pulled her whistle out to alert the guard and cause some kind of commotion, but as she raised it to her lips, she saw that Keevan wasn't there. Miter looked around the lobby, his gaze sliding right over her and then the doors were wide enough and he walked into the elevator and immediately noticed Milo.

"What the hell are you doing here?"

CHAPTER 28

Corwin sucked in a breath, ready to dive in to rescue Milo. Before she could move, Miter bent and scratched Milo's ears. Using the high-pitch common to people who like animals, Miter asked, "Are you Bulldog's mutt?"

Hide.

Corwin redirected her adrenaline into the order shouted in her head. She played an E-flat on the penny whistle and hummed one as well. While Miter was bent, his eyes on Milo, Corwin dashed past them and stashed herself in the back corner. Milo bounded to the corner under the floor numbers and rolled over to show his belly.

The man laughed. He didn't pet the proffered belly, though. He stood, swiped his card, and hit thirteen. He muttered, "What did he do to earn a gift from Asher?" Then he ignored Milo and turned his eyes to his armpadd, swiping and typing as everyone outside of Salem did instead of observing the world around them. Corwin wasn't sure she even needed to keep up the invisibility charm.

The elevator chimed and the doors slid open to reveal a plush lobby with more crystals than the canal bridges. A circular desk surrounded a prim, black-haired woman who superficially resembled Corwin's mother with her sharp face and stiff spine. The smile she turned up to the man was formal and no-nonsense. It put Corwin in mind of Mona Lisa, if Mona Lisa had secretly been a serial killer. Beyond Mona Lisa and her desk was another bank of elevators and a set of silver double doors that had been etched as dramatically as a 17th century lady's lap harp.

Two people stood near this door. The older man had a neat white beard and long hair pulled back into a queue—his cold, crisp suit did not blend well with his warm aura. The woman with him was very young, not much older than Corwin. She wore her red hair in a tight, low ponytail. Her suit was less crisp and lacked a jacket. For a moment, Corwin was gratified to see another woman in a vest. But this woman did not look kind. She snapped chewing gum and rubbed lotion on her hands, rolling her eyes. Despite being in the most fantastic place Corwin had ever seen, this woman made it clear she had better places to be.

Milo trotted off the elevator as if he had every right to be there. With his sparkling wampum collar, he certainly fit in with the crystal decor. And then Milo's tail froze. It tucked under and he shrank in on himself for the barest of instants.

The voice in her head whimpered, *Walter.*

Corwin's chest sank in with paralyzing grief. She stumbled forward to catch the closing doors. Her invisibility burned away in the anger that followed the inexplicable grief and fear.

"Hands up." Mona Lisa pulled a gun.

Miter spun around to see what she was pointing at and then wisely dropped below the level of the desk.

Corwin's heart and mind were too filled with unexpected fury for her to respond. Her eyes shot to the redhead as a cry escaped Milo and he tore across the lobby full of fierce fire, barking like a mad dog.

"Milo!" Corwin yelled.

"Hands up!" Mona Lisa insisted.

"Milo?" Hippy, high-powered Santa Claus looked with interest and no fear at the dog threatening his companion. "Laylea's Milo?"

Milo fell silent.

The flood of emotions overpowering Corwin swirled into confusion. She could conquer confusion with action. The elevator doors started to close. She slammed a hand against them to keep her escape available. Her voice held steady as she shouted, "I'm here to rescue Sita Corwin."

Mona Lisa didn't care. She held her gun steady. "You are not authorized to be on this floor. Put your hands up."

From his seat on the floor, Miter asked, "Do you mean Sita Ramamurthy? She doesn't need rescuing." He laughed at her.

"Who is Sita Ramamurthy?" she asked, the confusion ramping up to a full-body flush.

"Mr. Charles' protégé." The man said this at the same time Mona Lisa cocked her gun and said, "This is your last warning."

Corwin crumbled. Suddenly, the pack was too heavy, gravity was too much for her. She had totally misunderstood. She'd come to Vegas and wasted a week for nothing.

These people are evil. They are lying. The divining rod led us here.

That was true. If the divining rod had led her here, her mother had to be here.

The woman Milo wanted to rip to pieces slipped from her place by Santa Claus to Mona Lisa's desk ten feet away in the blink of an eye. It was like time had jumped. Milo whimpered. He spun to keep his bared teeth faced at her.

"Don't shoot the lady, Agent Carlsett." The gum chewer smiled, but the expression didn't reach her voice. "She's one of Walter's lost CF."

"I have no idea what that means, Ms. Delta. My job is to protect this floor."

"It means she's valuable to us." The redheaded Delta's tone was so cold, Corwin wouldn't have been surprised if the words had frozen Agent Mona Lisa where she stood.

The guard was convinced. She started to lower the weapon. And then one of the elevators in the bank behind Santa Claus chimed. He swore, and scooped Milo up, whispering into his fur as he ran towards Corwin.

Corwin didn't have time to take a step before the lights blinked and went out. The opening elevator doors froze. A click sounded behind Corwin and a door popped open from the smooth wall beside the lobby elevator. Agent Carlsett fired. Miter screamed.

Corwin reacted on instinct. The spell didn't even go through her mind before she sang out one clear, high note, sending the vibrations flying into the path of the bullet just as she had sent it countless times into the path of snapping harp strings. The bullet dropped.

"Sher?" Santa Claus looked at Corwin but shook his head and dropped Milo as if he had bitten the man. He mouthed the word, *Run*, and then spoke in a soothing tone. "You have nothing to fear. We'll take you home and fix you right up." He dropped his voice till it was so quiet she could barely hear him. His eyes blazed at Corwin. "You can't let them catch Milo."

Milo barked at Corwin from the doorway. It startled her out of her paralysis and she raced through the door. Behind them, she heard Miter say, "Don't worry. I've sent her picture to security. She won't get out of here alive."

Corwin tore the earring from her ear and dropped Grandmother Misty's hat in the stairwell as she and Milo flew down the stairs. The stairwell was narrow and had hand rails on either side. Corwin pulled her coat sleeves down over her hands and slid down them. They made it to the bottom in record time, but it wasn't fast enough. They burst out into the lobby, panting for breath, to find three soldiers in uniform black approaching Keevan's stand. She didn't bother trying to slow down and pretend to be just another guest. It would never have worked. They spotted her and her fourteen reflections in the mirrored walls and shouted freeze and other orders they couldn't really believe she would follow.

Milo took the lead. Corwin followed him into the casino. Their footsteps were muffled on the thick carpet and she didn't need to worry about how loud her gasping was because of the music overhead and the dinging, clanging, ringing of the slot machines. But the casino was too orderly, too calm for her and Milo to go unnoticed, especially with her neon orange backpack. She needed a distraction, like the voice had suggested just before Milo provided one to get them upstairs. Milo was too small to provide a distraction now. And he was running for his life as much as she was.

Chaos

That's what they needed. They needed more chaos to cover them.

The soldiers had looked fit and armed and she could see more of them running into the casino. She was not fit and was wearing thirty pounds on her back. Running wasn't going to work.

She barked, disturbing a couple of old ladies huddled at the edge of a bank of machines. She smiled at them and then veered between the machines when she saw she had Milo's attention. He grabbed the edge of her skirt in his teeth and she stumbled to a stop at the end of the row to let two black-clad soldiers race by. Milo dropped her skirt and bounded into the aisle. She was hot on his heels and spotted the answer to their problems at the same moment that he howled. He got to their destination first, bounding onto the padded seat and standing his front paws on the keys of a bright purple grand piano. It was even her color.

Corwin snagged a top hat from a frat boy hitting on a too-young girl at a machine and slung her bag from her shoulders. The back-pack slid under the piano bench and the Gladstone dropped beside it as Corwin leaped onto the bench and brought her fingers down on the keys, already sending the strings into a flurry of arpeggios with a glittering thought. For the first few moments, the crowds at the blackjack tables and the nearby lounge looked over in surprise. Then she caught them up in her song and they started dancing. People sang words to their favorite songs, no two of them the same. The pathways between tables and machines and bars filled with laughing, dancing, raucous people.

Chaos.

Corwin lost herself in the music, certain that the soldiers would lose her, too. They did. Ms. Delta did not. Corwin felt Milo growl and crawl into her lap before the woman slid onto the bench beside her. She faltered in her playing.

"Don't stop. Gandhi is arranging a distraction elsewhere, but it's not ready yet."

Corwin blinked at the woman's breath. She should have noticed her long before she sat down from the horrible combination of licorice and sandalwood that surrounded her. Milo bared his teeth. He was shivering. She purred, deep in her chest, trying to calm him.

She looked the woman in the eyes. "Who are you?"

The woman looked down at Milo when she answered, "I'm not Walter."

A whimper escaped through Milo's growl and tears leapt unbidden to Corwin's eyes. "Who is Walter?"

"Walter is Milo's father. He's evil. He hurt Milo and his brothers and sister. He is pure Consortium." She looked down at Milo again. "I'm pretending to be like him. I am not."

She's telling the truth.

Corwin dropped her eyes to Milo. "Does Walter have my mother?"

"Who is your mother?"

"Sita Corwin."

Ms. Delta shook her head slowly. "Walter was injured. He's not torturing anybody right now."

"But somebody in the Consortium is. I need to find her."

"We have other people on the inside, too. We can help you." Delta's face went blank and she twitched her gaze away from them. "Get ready. You take Milo and the cute little doctor's bag. I've got your backpack."

Corwin slowed the music. She transitioned to a sexy song, sending the romantic vibes out as far as she could reach, encircling all the lonely folks still dancing alone at their slot machines and dragging them out into the slowing chaos.

"Nice." Delta's grin was only in her voice. "Do you see the waterfall?"

Corwin scanned the room. When she found the waterfall descending from an upper floor into the canal, she nodded.

"There's a boat on the far side. Get in under the umbrella. When the gondolier docks, walk directly to the nearest elevator and take it up to room 2317. I'm sure you can handle the lock. We'll meet you there."

Corwin turned to see Delta's eyes. "Why should I trust you?"

Delta returned her gaze solidly, honestly. "Because Milo's brother is a friend of mine and I will kill anybody who tries to hurt him again."

Corwin's blood chilled at her declaration.

Milo barked. It was a sharp, doubtful sound.

Delta looked down at him, "Bayard. Your brother Bayard." She swung the Gladstone bag into Corwin's lap. "If you're going, go now."

Using the bag as a stool, Milo scrambled into her inner pocket.

Corwin swooped the song into a grand finish and made her way directly for the waterfall. She didn't look to see if Delta got her backpack or which way she went. She got her ass to the boat, got in, and held Milo tight against her beating heart. He had more secrets than she'd ever imagined. She felt shame burning on her cheeks as it occurred to her that she never had imagined anything.

CHAPTER 29

D ebussy's Clair de Lune did little to soften the stark whiteness of room 2317. The silver domes of room service didn't help either. Corwin charmed the door to open to no one who meant them harm. Then she lit the decorative candles with magic when she couldn't find any matches. She needed fire. She missed her hearth. She and Milo missed their books. They found a Complete Works of Shakespeare in the bedside table beside the Gideon Bible. Corwin opened it to *Julius Caesar*, the one with the "Let slip the dogs of war" line. But Milo tried flipping the pages with his nose until she turned back to the table of contents. He picked *The Two Gentlemen of Verona*.

There's a dog in Two Gents.

Corwin was too tired to argue with herself or with the voice that she could no longer pretend was just her deeper instincts. She was also too tired to read. She sat on the wide windowsill with Shakespeare and Milo in her lap. When he barked, she turned the page. Mostly, she looked down over the carnival parade marching through the casino and fought off waking dreams of Walter's cold, white and silver lab. Milo was a tiny dog. How much smaller and more helpless had he been as a puppy?

She alternated between wanting to search for her mother and wanting to never let Milo out of her arms. Walter had been after him all along, not her. Kat Coogan had warned them about Walter. Kat Coogan knew what Milo was.

The door clicked. Corwin sat up, but the voice in her head said, *It's just Gandhi.*

"Who's Gandhi?"

Santa Claus. He was broken by the Consortium. He infiltrated them to stop them from hurting other people.

The white-bearded old man who had called her Sher in the thirteenth-floor lobby walked through the door calling out, "It's a friend." When he saw Corwin, he said, "Hi. I'm Gandhi. We were not properly introduced."

Corwin stared at him. He had called her Sher, like the homeless woman in Salem. Had Corwin never seen her again because she had somehow jumped inside and was riding around in Corwin's mind?

No, Corwin.

She ignored the voice, focusing on this Gandhi. "Am I Sher?"

The man's smile disappeared in his white beard and he stumbled back a step. "No. No, dear. I was confused."

Corwin felt her forehead clenching. Her eyes heated, threatening forbidden tears. "Are you sure? Look closely."

"No." He said it gently. "Sher glamours herself sometimes, but she never forgets who she really is."

Corwin. It's me. You're not—

Corwin screamed in her head, *Shut up.* She put her hands on her ears as if that would help.

A second bearded man followed Gandhi into the room. Corwin jumped to her feet at the sight of him, letting the book fall to the carpet. She hugged Milo to her chest even as one hand went to her vest pocket. She still had the Milkbone the second man had given Milo in Richmond.

"FiveFiveThree." She didn't know whether to be afraid or not. He worked for Mr. Charles, who had threatened her mother, but he'd been nice to Milo.

He's the guy with the crowded head. The voice offered this information quietly, meekly.

"What?" Corwin's chest heaved. Gandhi and FiveFiveThree looked at her as if she were crazy, which was a reasonable and possibly correct assumption.

From the dreams about Mama and escaping the lab. He's. . . the voice went silent, flashing images and voices and smells through her head until she remembered. "Hardknock."

The craggy-faced man with black tattoos covering both hands nodded his head. Gandhi looked between them, confused. "Have you two met?"

There was a moment of silence while each of them waited for the other to speak. Corwin couldn't take it. "I saw him with Mr. Charles."

"Oh, yes, Hardknock pretends to be Mr. Charles' CF. He also pretends to be Director Asher, who assigned him to Mr. Charles' detail." Gandhi acknowledged her confusion with a sigh. "Yes, it is a lot to take in and we don't have time to explain everything."

Hardknock crossed to the walk-in closet. He dropped a compact hiking pack on the floor outside it and closed the door. The pack slumped. It was nearly empty.

Gandhi helped himself to a bottle of water from the tiny fridge. "The Consortium are experimenting with ways to kill the groups of people they find unacceptable. Large groups. Those who waste their brain cells gambling, for instance. Smaller departments within the Consortium do smaller evil things."

Corwin flashed on some of the worst images from her nightmares about Walter's lab. "Like experimenting on animals to see if they can be merged with humans?"

"Yes." Gandhi said it simply, then added, "and experimenting on humans to create super soldiers conditioned to follow orders." He lifted the king-sized bed off the floor with one hand and snaked a suitcase out with his foot. "Conditioned Force soldiers. CF."

Corwin put some pieces together. "Walter creates monsters and assigns them to other directors to help them create monsters?"

"Walter is not as successful as others. For a little while," Gandhi dropped his eyes to the high-tech contents of the suitcase, "they had a witch who was very successful at creating CF and then almost as successful at freeing us."

Hardknock came out of the closet. He had changed into an expensive suit. It fit so well that his muscles didn't ruin the lines. Gandhi tossed him three items in rapid succession. Hardknock caught each of them on his way to the bathroom. They heard the buzzing of an electric razor.

Gandhi fit some items into his tweed suit's various pockets, keeping his gaze averted as he asked, "I presume, based on your little trick with the bullet, that your mother is a witch?" He didn't wait for Corwin to respond. "We are not certain anyone in the Consortium knew that Sher was a witch." He shook his head. "Katherine, rather."

"Katherine Coogan?" Corwin asked, her mind reeling.

"Yes." He lifted the bed again to replace the suitcase. "If someone did know her secret, they would be eager to get a new witch into the ranks. But Mr. Charles is not one I would peg as keeping that kind of information close to the vest. He's a braggart. Delta sounded out his new protégé. Asked her if she used to be known as Sita Corwin, did she have a daughter? Nobody can ask a direct question like Delta. She's scary."

Corwin agreed that Delta was scary, but she didn't care about that very much. "What did she say?"

"I was there. This woman is scarier than Delta. She laughed in a way that made the hairs stand up on the back of my neck. Then she did a little spin and asked if that was a body that had ever given birth." He looked into Corwin's eyes finally. "I'm sorry."

Corwin was saved from responding as Hardknock came out of the bathroom. He'd tamed his long hair into a ponytail and trimmed his beard into submission. He'd also applied some makeup to his face that hid many of his scars. He looked like a completely different man. Milo barked.

Hardknock stopped on his way to the closet to rasp, "Thank you."

"We have to get to the dinner. We have a safe house for you and Milo to go to. After what Herr Miter saw, they will definitely be talking about you." Gandhi pulled a folded paper from his pocket and set it on the nightstand. "This is an open train ticket to Sacramento."

An open ticket means you can alter it. The voice supplied this information as Gandhi sipped his water.

Hardknock came out of the closet and threw a pile of women's clothes on the windowsill. He set a Milkbone on top of it and then held his hand out towards Milo. Corwin looked down at Milo. When he nodded, she moved closer. Milo sniffed the hand and licked one tattooed finger. Hardknock looked at both of his hands, growled, and disappeared into the bathroom again.

"You have a unique style. You might find it easier to go about incognito in something a bit more modern." He opened the coat closet and took a blue ball cap out. It advertised the Chicago Cubs. "Giving folks something to remember helps them forget the important details."

"Your face." Hardknock offered this from the doorway of the bathroom where he patted powder on his hands. His black tattoos were invisible.

"Quite."

Corwin took the cap.

"Your hair is rather memorable as well." When Corwin wrapped a hand around her braid protectively, Gandhi added, "And can be tucked into your jacket."

"A jacket with a strong inner pocket for Josh's brother." Hardknock extracted a light green windbreaker from the backpack on the floor. He dropped it beside the other clothes.

"Do be careful and wear a mask if you go out. Vegas is a filthy city. Who knows what kinds of diseases might be floating in the air." He set a black face mask on top of the train ticket.

Hardknock curled one of Milo's ears in his fingers. "Be a dog."

"In public," Gandhi added. "And Corwin, you might avoid doing anything witchy."

Hardknock shot his friend a twisted expression. "Witchy?" He left Milo and walked over to join Gandhi at the door. "Like what?"

Gandhi pulled a pair of glasses from his breast pocket and handed them to Hardknock. "I don't know. Don't get crushed by a farmhouse? Avoid cycling in a cyclone?" He fixed his hair in the mirror and offered Corwin a hopeful smile. "Delta will come by tomorrow afternoon to escort you to the station." His eyes dropped to the ticket. "Do take care of yourself. And Milo."

The door closed behind them with a click.

We're not supposed to wait for Delta.

Corwin set Milo on the windowsill and rifled through the clothes. They looked to be her size.

You're supposed to change so you don't stand out as much.

She picked up the jacket. There was an inner breast pocket with a wad of cash in it.

That's so no one can track us.

"Yes. I got it. But Milo's right in the middle of the play." She recovered the book from the floor and searched for the right page. Milo climbed into her lap and tapped his paw when she reached it.

She looked out the window but didn't see the parade. She chose to see her ancestor's handwriting. She chose to keep her mind filled. As she flipped through the pages of *Two Gents* on her lap, she flipped through the pages of the Corwin grimoire in her mind. She reviewed every protection spell, charm, and trick they'd written about. She had all that family. But, Milo. If her dreams were Milo's memories, then it meant that his father had tortured him and his mother had abandoned him.

Just like yours.

"My mother was taken from me."

She was banished, but she could have fought it. Pops Coogan is reasonable.

"All the Coogans are against us. They cursed our family."

Morgan Coogan isn't against us. Kat Coogan tried to warn us about Walter.

"Because she worked with him."

Oh, you just want to pout.

"And my father didn't torture me."

You dream about the times he made you stand on the stool because you kept falling asleep in the lab and you were small and so afraid that you would fall off the stool into the fire. He told you friends were a waste of time. He left you alone, scrubbing your mother's blood off the kitchen floor when you were just a scared little girl. How did you get those scars on your hand?

"Shut up. They are my family. They are all I have."

Milo sat up at her outburst. He climbed out of her lap and over the book, not looking at her. He hid himself behind the curtains.

"I'm sorry, Milo." Corwin felt awful. The voice was driving her insane, but Milo was the one getting hurt. "Let's scry for your mother."

He stayed behind the curtain. But he'd left enough fur on her lap that she didn't need his participation. Using oils from Great-great-granduncle Doctor Deacon's vials, Milo's fur, and her memories of the singing woman in her dreams, Corwin created a potion to evoke Milo's mother. She tried to remember if she'd heard the woman's name in her dreams and could only remember calling her Mama.

Rhea. Mama's name is Rhea. The voice sounded subdued, even littler than usual.

Corwin spread the map out on the pristine berber carpet and dipped the garnet crystal in the potion. Lyrics came into her head from one of her father's favorite songs: *Shower the people you love with love.* It made her sad and evoked his imperfect love.

Goodbye, Joe. Me gotta go.

"Me-o Milo," Corwin sang back, irrationally grateful to the voice for its support. Anything to help Milo.

The crystal pulled east. It tapped down on the dot labeled 'Chicago.' Rhea was in Chicago.

Corwin wiped the crystal clean with a washcloth from the bathroom as she considered whether she should try to scry for her mother again. The crystal insisted on Richmond. The rod simply pointed up. Her father was dead. Searching for Kat Coogan got them nothing. Corwin realized she didn't know Kat well enough to evoke her for the crystal.

An idea struck her. When she was cleaning the crystal in the bathroom, she'd shoved a bottle of lotion in a drawer because, even through the plastic, the smell made her want to vomit.

Milo peered around the curtain. He'd been watching her work. She offered him a weak smile. "We'll just try this and then get some room service."

She took the crystal into the bathroom and rubbed it with sandalwood lotion, holding Walter's most evil thoughts in her mind even though her skin crawled and her stomach rebelled. Milo was standing on Canada when she returned to the map. Corwin knelt beside him and dangled the garnet above the center of the country. It immediately pulled west. She lowered her hand when the crystal spun tightly over Northern California. The garnet brushed Sacramento. The train tickets were for Sacramento.

Milo leapt onto the map and smacked the crystal with his paw, sending it flying under the bed.

"They're sending us straight to Walter."

No. They don't know where he is.

Corwin lifted Milo onto the bed and curled up around him. She tried twirling one of his ears in her fingers like Hardknock had. It felt good. She fought the pressure and heat behind her eyes.

Stop playing the Rite of Spring, the little voice, which could hear inside her head, insisted.

"I can't. It's how I feel."

Milo licked her cheek.

You should not have put Walter in your mind.

"Gandhi and Hardknock confirmed it. Those things I imagined Walter doing to people, they're true. He messed with their DNA and made them into monsters."

Yes. That's why they're trying to stop him. Why are you thinking about that?

"You know why."

Yes. Because the divining rod keeps insisting that she is here.

"If my mother isn't here, why does the White Oak insist that she is?"

Why?

Milo crawled up to Corwin's chest. He laid his soft head on her neck.

Why?

Corwin pursed her lips to hold back her shameful tears. She wrapped her arms around Milo and held onto her own shoulders. Her voice, when it came, was as hoarse as Hardknock's. "Because Milo's father turned my mother into a monster."

And you're never going to get your family back.

"I am not worthy."

CHAPTER 30

Corwin and Milo slept as they were. They woke with the first rays of dawn and ordered room service again. While they waited for the food, Corwin changed into the clothes Hardknock dumped on the windowsill. The pants were more form-fitting than anything she had worn before. Both the pants and shirt and jacket were made of sturdy, easy-to-clean materials. The modern bra fit like nothing Corwin had pilfered from the Corwin House closets.

She transferred only essentials to the new backpack and the pockets in her pants and jacket. It was hard to leave the Gladstone bag behind. But that little voice in her head insisted the CF would take good care of it. They left the garnet under the bed.

She put a Morgan-like face on with the glamearring and ordered a taxi with Emily's credit card. At the station, they took the first leg of the ticket, a train to Barstow. At Barstow, they put the glamearring on the ticket and used it to get on a train to Chicago.

Running towards Milo's mama made Corwin feel less like she was running away from her own mother.

Despite her roiling thoughts, the rhythm of the train soothed her into a driving dream.

Mama wasn't singing. She circled the block and pulled to a stop.

Corwin climbed out of the box and leapt over the vast crevasse to Mama's lap. Mama helped her stand up against the door and look out the window.

A tiny girl, the smallest human she'd ever seen, sat on a block of stone in front of a gray house. Her faded black skirt spread around her folded legs like a gray sea. Gleaming black hair hung so long that it brushed against the stone as the girl braided it. She peered up into the gray sky, looking for the sun, and then stared down the street as if she were waiting for her Mama to bring her milk. The sun was low. Soon, Mama would drive to the parking lot by the loud water. She'd curl up in the back of the car with Corwin and dream of Laylea, Josh, Bayard, and Rhemy.

"She's sad." Mama held the broken heart charm on her necklace. "She needs a friend."

Corwin sang out her little song.

Mama smiled, even though there were tears in her eyes. "Yes, you could be her friend."

They both looked back out at the girl as she rolled to her knees, gathering all of the loose hair that had fallen around her as she worked. She looked up and down the street one more time, then leaned her whole body against the door to get it open. Corwin tilted her tiny head and barked when she imagined the girl had seen her in the car.

"Shhh."

The gray door closed on the gray girl. A thought floated from the door, over the lawn, across the street, and into Corwin's head. I will find my family. *The little girl did not believe herself. Corwin barked again. She loved that little girl.*

Mama held her up and kissed her tiny black nose. Her voice was wobbly and her thoughts felt like rain. "I guess it's time."

They didn't drive around the block again or go to the loud water. Mama curled up with her right there and told her stories all night long. She fell asleep to the music of Mama's voice and rain pattering on the roof of the car.

Corwin woke to find rain pattering on the window of the train. A peace fled her as her memories of the past week flooded into her conscious brain. She wanted to remember her dream, but it had abandoned her. Just like she had abandoned her mother.

Chicago was soggy. The precipitation wasn't what a Salem girl or dog would call rain. But the street outside Union Station was a sea of umbrellas. They walked along the river, thinking of Gary and Okuri-Inu. When they came to a bridge, the crowd surged east, over the water. Corwin turned west. In part to get away from the crowd. In part because crossing running water gave her the willies,f as it did any witch.

Milo stayed in her pocket, tucked in with the divining rod. The divining rod that had insisted her mother was in Las Vegas. The Consortium had been holding an international meeting in Las Vegas. Daddy said Mother had been captured by the Consortium. Mr. Charles was a member of the Consortium and he had threatened Mother when Corwin saw them in the mirror. Had mother disappointed Mr. Charles somehow?

In Richmond, Mr. Charles had been excited to show off his protégé, Sita. But then, in Vegas, Sita said she didn't have a daughter. Was she just protecting Corwin?

Was she still in danger and just pretending to work with the Consortium, like the CF were?

Corwin couldn't figure it all out. She tried to work the facts through in her mind as they walked farther and farther west, away from the crowds, away from the lights. She turned down an alley to avoid some kind of food vender.

A window flashed her reflection. It was boarded up from the inside. Corwin stopped, staring.

No.

The last time she had seen her mother had been in the mirror at Corwin House. The blood magic had worked.

No.

She would never hurt Milo again, but could she work the spell with her own blood?

No! Look out!

Corwin saw the shadow on the wall first and then the reflection of the baseball bat in the window, she flinched away and the bat missed her head by inches.

It slammed with full force into her chest. Milo yelped. The voice in her head screamed. And then both fell deadly silent.

"The fuck?" A male voice backed away from her.

Corwin spun around, wrapping her hands around her chest to protect Milo. Three young men cornered her in against one wall of the alley. She was almost in the exact middle. A dumpster blocked the view from the far street. The only thing between her and the street she'd come from was an overflowing rain barrel and the three thugs.

They all wore jeans and puffy coats. Two of them had ball caps pulled low over their eyes. The one who didn't have one dashed in and slapped the Cubs hat off her head. Corwin let him. She didn't care about anything except protecting Milo.

She had been thinking about cutting him when they were attacked.

"The fuck you got in your pocket, bitch?" The boy with the steel bat was genuinely curious.

His tall friend was more focused. He stood solid on his feet, holding one hand in his pocket as if he was about to pull a gun. A hunting knife was sheathed on his belt. "Drop the bag and give us everything you got or we gonna hurt you real bad."

The third one, a much younger kid, dashed in to grab her hat off the ground. The bat-wielder used his weapon to shove the kid back. "Don't be stupid, Tiny."

Corwin wrapped her hand around the solid, unmoving form of Milo and murmured the first spell that came to mind. It was just a little while after Mother had left. She'd ripped the scab off her hand trying to tie her shoes. Her father had covered her hand with his and said, "Flesh of thine, stitch up fine." He'd repeated it three times and never used it again.

The batter shook his weapon at her. "I asked you a question."

"And I gave her a fucking order, Park." The tall kid gestured with the hand in his pocket and Corwin decided to believe that he did have a gun in that hand. Otherwise, he'd just pull the knife.

She took her hands off of Milo one at a time to shrug out of the backpack. It fell to the ground. Then she unzipped her jacket.

"Slowly, bitch." The kid, Tiny, was too busy dragging the pack away to notice Park rolling his eyes at him.

Corwin lifted Milo from her pocket. The broken pieces of her divining rod fell to the alley floor. Milo didn't move. He didn't try to help her. He wasn't conscious. A sob escaped her. Pain shot through her chest that let her know Milo wasn't the only one who had been hurt. She just didn't care about her own pain. She pulled herself together and hugged him to her chest, chanting, "Flesh of thine, stitch up fine," over and over.

Tiny dug through her pack. He tore up her map and threw it like confetti over his head. He shoved her herbs and oils into his pockets. He ground her kalimba into the wet, broken cement under his foot. Emily's ID and credit card interested him and he pocketed them, along with the roll of cash the CF had given her.

Park and the tall guy just stared at Corwin as she bent over Milo, begging the universe to heal him.

"Bitch is cray." Park was right.

And at that moment, Corwin would have given anything to have that little voice in her head tell her what to do. But it had gone silent. She looked down at Milo's slack face. *Could it be?*

Then the gun came out of the tall one's pocket. He held it out to his side.

"Perfect. No one's gonna care if some crazy bitch gets popped. You want in, Tiny? You do her."

Park objected, "She's got a dog, Yo."

"Naw, man. She had a dog. You killed it." Tiny threw the pack behind him into the growing puddle around the water barrel. He danced between her and Park to snatch the gun from Yo. Then he spun and, without looking her in the eye, pulled the trigger.

Corwin screamed. Her left hand burned, but when she looked at her palm, it was just her old scars, glowing white and gold. No gunshot. Park and Yo laughed.

"Man, you so dumb. You got to turn the safety off. You moron."

The sound of sloshing must have been drowned out by their laughter and the rain because none of them turned to look. Only Corwin saw Kat Coogan climb out of the rain barrel.

CHAPTER 31

Corwin knew how to fight Kat Coogan. She'd beaten her before. She just had to heal Milo and survive these assholes first. The last time she'd defeated Kat, she'd simply shoved the witch outside the Corwin House protections. Corwin reached a hand into her pocket.

The boys didn't like this move. Yo grabbed the gun back from Tiny and flipped a switch on one side. He aimed, but he was too slow. Corwin got the penny whistle to her lips and played three notes. Her aura flamed into a bright purple shield around her and Milo. The gangster's bullet ricocheted off the shield and, at a simple flick of Kat's hand, shot into the dumpster. The clang echoed through the alley.

It scared the boys more than the sirens that wailed in the distance. They ran.

Corwin played a haunting tune on her whistle and focused all of her intention on Yo. He froze. The other two saw. Park slowed and for an instant, Corwin thought he'd stop to help his friend. Tiny just kept on running. Park quickly caught up.

They had hurt Milo. She had no qualms about using their blood to save him. He even had a knife she could use. She kept the shield up and hurried across the alley. Kat cut her off.

"What happened to Milo?"

"Get out of my way. I need his blood." Corwin held Milo tighter. "Why are you even here?"

Kat held her hands up in what was supposed to be a reassuring gesture. "I put a charm on you when you were in the hearth. I know when you're in danger."

It was just too blunt to be a lie. But Corwin didn't trust her. "I will heal him."

"Blood magic never ends well. I can heal him."

"Why would you want to help me?"

"For the same reasons I've been helping you since you were three. But right now, I want to help Milo because he is a good boy and my daughter's brother." Kat dropped all of her defenses. Her aura pulsed clear, inviting Corwin to see her fear and her certainty that she could heal Milo. "Please."

Corwin dropped her shield. She stepped forward and laid Milo's barely breathing body into Kat Coogan's arms. She started to step back, but the witch held onto her hand.

"He needs you close. Support his head." Kat ran a hand along Milo's fur, feeling for the injury and sending shots of golden magic into him. He stirred.

Corwin bent down and kissed the milk-drip mark on his muzzle. "Shh. Hold still now."

Kat adjusted her grip so that she could hold Milo's head straight on his neck with one hand while she pressed the other to his chest. The back of her hand brushed Corwin's ribs, making her gasp. Gold shot out into her own chest and she felt warmth as the pain changed. She could hear her ribs grinding and groaned.

"Why blood magic, Corwin?" Kat kept her eyes on Milo.

Corwin glanced around at the detritus in the alley. "What else do I have? They stole my crystals and herbs. They ripped up our map. They broke my divining rod."

"It's just a stick. You are Skilled. It's not in your tools."

Corwin gasped as the grinding of her ribs stopped and heat flared along her side. She growled, "It didn't even find my mother. She wasn't in Vegas."

"She was, though. She left early. But she was there." Kat looked up for an instant to catch Corwin's eyes. Her gaze slid to Corwin's ribs and then back to Milo before she went on. "Sita's maiden name is Rama-murthy. Walter didn't get to her. She is her own kind of monster."

Kat adjusted her hand, moving it away from Corwin. The heat faded to warmth and the pain faded completely. Milo's tiny body jerked under Kat's touch. Corwin kissed him again and softly began to sing, "Goodbye, Joe. Me gotta go."

Kat talked over her song. "Sita is a black magic widow. She hunts for powerful, vulnerable witches and enthralls them. She uses their Skill to get riches, power, new targets."

Corwin straightened. "That's not true. My father isn't rich or powerful. We lost the family's power when your coven took it from us."

The warmth in her ribs turned cold suddenly and she looked down to see lilac tendrils reaching out from her chest and blending with the gold suffusing Milo. His body relaxed so that Corwin and Kat had to adjust their grips on him.

"Corwin, the high priestess who hid Hobbomock's totem was Jonathan Corwin's mother." Kat spoke gently, but her gaze on Milo stayed intense. She moved her hand an inch and the golden-violet light moved with her. A hint of blue sparkled deep in the mix. "My family vowed to look after yours. It was my brother's duty to watch out for you. But then she killed him. That's why Morgan stayed so close to you."

It's not the only reason.

Milo's eyes blinked. Corwin felt hope lift her heart even as disappointment froze it.

Kat moved her hand farther up Milo's chest. "That's why I have kept an eye on you."

"Morgan was watching me?" All the moments they'd run into each other chased through her head.

No! She likes you.

Milo struggled in Kat's grip. She laid her hand over his eyes, pushing his head into Corwin's hand.

"I thought Morgan was my friend."

She is!

Milo turned his head and licked Corwin's hand. Kat leaned in to pile him into her arms. Milo immediately tried to climb up Corwin's chest.

You broke her heart when you tried blood magic on me. But then you tried to make it better and she thinks you're amazing for that.

Kat put her hands out to help Corwin get a better grip on the squirming dog. "Easy, Milo. You were mostly dead."

Milo ignored her. He kept his bright hazel eyes pinned on Corwin.

You remember what she said about blood magic?

Corwin whispered to the voice, "She said blood magic only works if you hurt someone you truly love." She dropped her head, burying her face against Milo's neck. "She said I didn't truly love anybody."

"Morgan said that?" Kat asked, but Corwin kept her attention on the voice.

But you do. You sacrificed your entire life for your parents. That's true love.

Kat tilted her head to get a better look at Corwin's face. "Corwin, who are you talking to?"

"No." Corwin turned away from Kat. "She was right. I found my mother and I abandoned her."

Then let's find her.

"How? I should never have left her in Las Vegas. I am unworthy."

Kat spat, "You are worthy. And whoever told you that you aren't is an idiot. If you need to find your mother to prove that to yourself, then find her. Just know that wading into the Consortium will put Milo in danger. Also, the cops are gonna be here any second."

Kat stomped through the alley to tap Yo on the breastbone. She took his gun, reengaged the safety, and stuck it in her waistband. She undid his belt, slipped the hunting knife and its sheath off, and dropped it into an insanely deep pocket on the side of her pants. She removed a wallet from his back pocket and looked at the ID before taking the cash out and returning the wallet. Then she pushed his sleeves up and grasped both of his bare wrists in her hands. In an unnaturally low voice, she said, "You will be kind to animals, Jeremy. Go."

The boy ran.

Kat scooped up the broken kalimba and crossed to Corwin. She handed her the cash, along with a spark of golden magic. "Take care of her, Milo. Corwin, be safe." Then she climbed onto the water barrel and dropped in.

Whoa.

An idea had sparked in Corwin's mind. But the siren chirped at the end of the alley, so she shelved it. She set Milo down and grabbed up the backpack, some pieces of the map, and the broken pointer of the divining rod. Milo raced down the alley, away from the siren.

Come on. There's a way into the building behind the dumpster.

The voice was right. It was a tight squeeze, but Corwin made it through the little window and dropped a shorter distance than she expected to a table that had been positioned right beneath it. Milo barreled through after her and she almost fell off the table with the momentum of his jump.

Go Go Go.

Corwin lifted Milo to the ground and followed him through the dusty halls of the old factory. He led her upstairs to a door that was as far from the alley as they could get. The drizzle had increased to actual rain. It was insulated in the old factory, so they climbed a few more floors and found an office with only one broken window and a torn-up couch. Tiny hadn't taken Milo's kibble or the energy bar that Corwin had stashed in her pocket. She thought while they feasted.

Corwin thought about her mother, about how she had isolated them on high holidays, covering the windows and keeping them all home to feast on their favorite foods. How Daddy would bathe Corwin in bubbles and then set her on Mother's lap in the rocking chair. Mother brushed her hair and whispered spells of strength into the strands. How she would sing at her nightstand while she brushed her own hair and then gather all the loose hair in the brush and burn it in a special mortor to keep them safe.

When they had finished their food, Corwin fished a bottle of Masquerade Hotel water from the bottom of the pack and poured some into her hand for Milo until he was sated. She took a few sips herself and then sat on the floor with Milo on the couch. She examined him from ears to tail and thought some more.

She thought about how her father had doted on Sita, bringing them flowers from his forest trips that Sita would weave into her hair. She thought about how Mother had held Corwin in her lap while Daddy coaxed the deer into their backyard. She thought about how Sita had leapt over the fire grate to protect her from Kat, and about how she couldn't exactly remember what happened after that. She thought that Kat was wrong.

She doesn't think she's wrong.

Corwin wrapped one of Milo's ears around her fingers. "You know that because you can read minds?" she asked her precious, tiny voice.

Kat looked into Sita after Archie told her he was worried about Daniel.

"I didn't know Morgan's father's name. I would have called him Morgan's dad, not Archie." She looked straight into Milo's eyes. "And I wouldn't call Daddy, Daniel."

Milo sat up. He leaned in until he touched Corwin's nose with his.

You're not crazy.

"I'm sorry I cut your tail."

I know.

"Do you think my mother loved me?"

I don't know. Let's find her so I can read her mind.

CHAPTER 32

C orwin woke on the filthy couch with the backpack under her head and Milo on her chest. He dropped his chin in a grin at her open eyes and then snapped his teeth shut as if he were holding something.

I found you a new divining rod.

Corwin blinked the sleep from her eyes. "Oh, good. I'm still not crazy."

Nope. I'm the little voice in your head.

"And you brought me a new stick." She wrapped a hand around Milo to keep him from falling as she sat up. "You must be exhausted, running all the way to Salem and back."

Pundu gave me a ride back.

Corwin pretended to take the imaginary stick from him. "Hope it works better than that." She looked down where they had tried to piece the map back together. Tiny had done a good job of destroying it. And he had taken all her crystals, in any case. Except the garnet they'd left at the Masquerade.

It doubles as a scrying crystal.

Corwin set the imaginary rod beside her on the bed. She picked up the pointer from the broken rod and rolled her mother's hair tie from the wood and onto her wrist. When she pretended to pick up the new rod, she already had memories of her mother in her mind.

Think of what she smelled like. Smell is important.

Her mother had smelled like jasmine and fresh-baked bread. The rod pulled north and west. Corwin looked at her hands, sure she would see an actual branch in them.

Believe!

Corwin nodded. She knelt in front of the disparate scraps of map. Milo sat beside her and rested a paw on her thigh.

She crushed the imaginary rod between her hands and slowly extended one finger. "Serve me well and please touch down where Sita Corwin can be found."

Something drew her forward, north and west of Chicago. Her knees scattered bits of Florida and Texas. Milo hopped forward, keeping in touch with her. Her finger touched down on a flimsy, barely matchbook-sized scrap of paper. Milo leapt forward to read it.

Delcampo, Montana.

Corwin focused her mind's eye, unconsciously adding a melody to her murmured words. "Serve me well and show me where Sita Corwin is brushing her hair."

I see it.

An image formed in her mind, coming into focus as if she were a bird, soaring closer to the metal archway that spanned a one-lane road weaving through a dark wood. The sign read 'Montana Collective.'

Mr. Charles ordered her to get the Montana Collective to swear allegiance to him.

"I guess we're going to Montana," she said.

Milo hopped up and down and spun around. *Yay! Montana.*

Corwin used Milo's divining rod for its original purpose and dowsed their way back to the river. From there, it was easy to follow suitcase-bearing tourists to Union Station. Yo's cash got them breakfast and a ticket to Bozeman, MT, that involved four busses, one train, and two days.

During a layover in Minneapolis, Minnesota, Corwin found a nearby park for Milo and leaned against a statue playing her penny whistle. Some people stopped to listen and dropped money in her backpack. They earned enough money to get a small bag of kibble for Milo and bread and cheese, also for Milo, according to him, as well as a small box of oatmeal.

On the train, their seat partner bought lunch and fed pieces of her sandwich to Milo inside Corwin's coat. Milo said that LaRhonda was returning home after meeting her first grandniece. She didn't travel much and had nobody at home to care about her adventures. Corwin was happy for the distraction. Milo helped her ask the questions that LaRhonda most wanted to answer. She was very understanding about Corwin's reticence to talk about herself. Milo said she had a secret. He was able to not hear the details and that fascinated Corwin, but she kept her focus on LaRhonda's stories and how they were going to get to the Montana Collective.

LaRhonda was not familiar with Delcampo, MT, but when Corwin told her where it was, the woman excitedly offered to drive them a little closer. She lived in Lewiston and her old Jeep had plenty of room for all of Corwin's luggage. Her laugh was infectious.

Milo's joy was also infectious as he hung his head out the window for nearly the entire drive. As they reached Lewiston, LaRhonda nearly sent him flying from the car when she jammed a hard left with no warning. She followed a series of colorful posterboard signs to a yard sale where she scooped up three fiestaware plates and a beautiful, old, broken Spanish Colonial bench she would repair and resell. Corwin found a bicycle with a wicker basket on the front.

LaRhonda slipped a box of energy bars, a water purifying thermos, and a collapsible bowl into Corwin's backpack before she let them go. Corwin pulled out her penny whistle and played "Luck be a Lady." She sent the spell out to LaRhonda and the kid who had sold her the bicycle for stupid cheap. Milo sang along in her head, his skill at harmonizing more impressive now that she knew it wasn't her own mind. Blue sparkles mixed with Corwin's purple magic and soared beyond the two, racing into the sky in spurts as Milo shouted *Luck* on the offbeats, sending the luck through the entire town of Lewiston.

Riding away to the sound of laughter and applause, Milo thought, *That's kind of a really sexist song, isn't it?*

"Yeah." Corwin agreed. "You're right. We should have played 'Rite of Spring'."

Fright of Spring, you mean!

"Ha!" Corwin tortured Milo for the first mile of their journey. Knowing he could read her mind let her accompany herself while she made up ridiculous lyrics.

Two days later, when Corwin was bent over the handlebars, pedaling as slowly as one could without falling off the bicycle, Milo paid her back with lyrics of his own. His were better.

The setting sun sparkled like magic through thick branches green with life when they finally crested a hill to find an archway carved of wrought steel like branches spanning the road from the glorious trees on either side. It read "Montana Collective."

Corwin's relief was physical. She slipped off the bike before she fell off it but rolled it along the dirt, one-lane road until she'd crossed under the sign. She was so close to her mother. It would be dumb to run in not knowing anything about the place, but it was hard to keep from jumping back on the bike and rolling right up to the door.

We need sleep. And information. We can use the invisibility spell and look around tomorrow.

That was a great idea. Corwin lifted Milo out of the basket. After taking care of business against the nearest tree, he ran a little ways into the woods and then returned to check the woods on the other side of the road.

This way. There's a creek.

Corwin rolled the bike off the road and found an easy path that led about twenty feet in to a small clearing beside a bubbling rill. It felt like home. She leaned the bike against a fir tree and knelt to fill LaRhonda's thermos at the stream. The water dripped through the filter as the sun dropped behind the horizon. Corwin stretched her legs and organized the twigs and branches Milo gathered into a tiny teepee. He dragged his paw through the dirt around the little campfire, humming the three notes of Corwin's protection shield spell.

She poured the first water into Milo's bowl and refilled the thermos for herself. While it dripped, she scooped kibble out of the bag and let Milo eat it from her hand. She liked the feel of his tongue rasping over the scars on her palm. It felt like a blessing somehow.

She had turned back to get the thermos when Milo barked a growling howl. It was such an unexpected sound, Corwin had her penny whistle in one hand, ready to fight faster than she could have imagined possible. There was nobody in sight except for Milo.

He stood at his bowl, splashing the water with a paw. The water sparkled with a familiar brown magic Corwin had thought she would never see again. She tripped in her haste and fell to her knees, nearly overturning the bowl. She lost her breath when she saw him. Her father's bruised and swollen face rippled in the water.

"Daddy!" The word was a squeak, a cry, a prayer.

His response was as brusque as always. "Where have you been, baby girl? I've been trying to reach you for days!"

"I'm here, Daddy. I'm—"

"Listen to me. They'll come take this washbasin away soon."

"Daddy, I thought you were dead. I thought they killed you." Joy surged in her, tunneling her vision to just the face that she had mourned. She felt Milo leaning against her leg and in her mind, supporting her.

"They didn't." Her father sucked in a rough breath. "But they did break me. I told them everything and now they're going to steal your mother's power. You need to come here to Montana and get your mother out."

"I'm here, Daddy," she said. "I'm in the woods just outside the collective."

"What? Don't come now. They have monsters guarding the place at night. Tomorrow, go around to the back. There is a break in the fence where students sneak out. You can get in that way." He reached forward as if he could reach through and touch her, but then he pulled his hand back, water splashing on his face. "One more minute, please." He stared away for a minute. When he looked out at her again, he spoke in a hurried whisper. "Head east till you find a clearing. That's where they plan to steal our power. They've built an altar. Come save us, baby girl, and we can be a family again."

"I'll be there. Before the sun sets tomor—"

But her father cut off the communication before she was done. The water sparkled red in the light of the campfire.

"So much for recon." Corwin spilled the water at the base of a tree, watering its roots as she scattered any chance of another witch tracking her father's communication.

He said students. It's a school?

"Maybe it's also a school." She refilled the bowl and filled the thermos again. "I don't like the idea of sneaking in through the fence."

Milo sent her the image of the deer trap in Betsy Chever's lawn back home.

"Exactly. How would Daddy know about it if they hadn't told him? I wish we knew more about the kind of school it is and what it has to do with the Consortium, and how many people live here and how many guns they have."

Milo barked. He took a breath and trotted over to the tree she had just watered. She thought he was going to water it, too, but he stood up, both paws on the bark.

Ask them.

Corwin tilted her head. She'd talked to the trees in Salem all the time. She'd talked to the tree in Richmond. Why hadn't she thought to talk to the trees all around her?

You're scared.

She didn't need to respond. Corwin imitated his deep breath and rested a hand on the tree. Her awareness was dragged down deep into the earth where she flowed into the roots of all the forest. At the same time, she shot up into the canopy of branches high overhead and soared through the collective being that was the forest. Her heart beat with the pulse of oxygen and carbon dioxide filtering in and out through the leaves. She felt the joy and comfort of being just one in many, nurturing the saplings and following the elders as they reached up and down into the world.

Many creatures lived in the woods. So very many tiny insects thrived as a part of their ecosystem. Birds, deer, squirrels, wolves, and countless other animals played among the trunks. Corwin's breath caught as she watched a hawk soar over a twelve-foot fence topped with barbed wire and land on a fallen trunk. The majestic creature shook from its crest to its tail feathers and suddenly a woman stood where the bird had been.

The forest, sensing her wonder, showed her memories of many different animals shedding their fur, feather, or scale-covered forms to stand as human children. For Milo, they showed a tiny, fawn-colored terrier with black paws shift into a naked teenage boy. Where all the others had been playing, this boy worked. He knelt by a box snuggled between the fence and a magnificent red pine. He used tools stashed nearby to take the front off the box and begin attaching something to the wires inside.

Corwin asked the forest to show her the human places inside the fence and the view tumbled her out of the thick woods to a collection of buildings hidden from a space cleared of trees by a long, tall hedge. One of the buildings had a sign over the grand entrance. This one read "Montana Shifter Collective." The Montana Collective was a school for shifter kids.

And they have a dog shifter. Milo's thought rang with excitement.

Corwin thought of her parents' faces but the trees couldn't tell one human from the next. It didn't matter. Once they got inside the fence, Corwin could find them. She wouldn't even need a map anymore.

With regret, she sent a pulse of love and appreciation and good will into the forest and then lifted her hand from the tree's bark. She found herself kneeling. Which was good, because she had to lay down for a little while. She rolled to her side and reached out to snag the backpack for a pillow. With a little bit of magic, her fingertips grasped the edge of Gary's blanket in the bottom of the pack.

Milo tripped over and curled up in the crook of her belly. Even as tired as she could sense he was, he turned three times clockwise and four times widdershins before he collapsed with his nose tucked against her neck. Corwin flicked the blanket out to cover the both of them.

We go in the front. You pretend you're my mother, he thought. *I wear Emily's glamearring.*

We make you a wolf, she thought back, *so you're a prospective student. You think they'll give us a tour of the school?*

If not, I can always run through it like a bad dog and make you have to chase me.

Corwin laughed. *Will they make you prove you're a shifter, though?*

Milo yawned, his warm breath on her neck sending a shiver down her spine. *Guess we need to practice our glamouring.*

We should shift to more comfortable ground before we fall asleep.

You are asleep. Milo snorted a laugh. *You're talking to me in your head.*

Corwin raised a hand and dug it into the thick fur at Milo's neck, massaging it. *I'm awake.*

Milo sat up and stared down at her face.

Corwin opened her eyes. *The dreams were just a tool, like my divining rod. It occurred to me that the trees are talking all the time. I only hear them when I listen.*

So, you're listening to me. Milo's jaw dropped in a doggy grin.

She shrugged, a little sheepishly. "Yeah."

Milo threw his head back and howled, "Arooooooooo."

In her head, he said, *finally.*

CHAPTER 33

Corwin rolled the bike the last few feet to lean it against a post of the wooden fence outside the front office of the Montana Collective. She checked the sun again to keep from staring at Milo in his wolf glamour. They'd waited until late afternoon in the hopes that the compound would be busy with dinner preparations.

There was no sign over the door. Nothing to indicate visitors were welcome. In fact, the *No Solicitors* and *You're Being Watched* signs made a very strong argument that visitors were not welcome.

She tried the knob. It turned and she ignored the adrenaline racing through her veins and stepped inside. She held the door for Milo and then smiled at the three husky humans watching her. The room looked like a ski lodge lounge, excepting the stack of guns resting on the South-western-colored cushions of a wooden couch. A man with biceps that looked to be winning a battle with his t-shirt lounged in one of the stiff, overstuffed chairs facing the couch. He shifted to display his body for her pleasure. A second man, whose facial hair had never even heard of the word grooming, stood from one of the two comfy leather chairs in front of the fireplace. His eyebrows attempted to become one over his glaring eyes. A fire crackled cheerily, but it was the only cheery thing in the room.

The most unhappy creature was the broad-shouldered woman polishing the enormous desk in a back corner of the room. The woman sniffed as she looked Corwin up and down. Her eyes slid away from the wolf that was Milo. Corwin couldn't read anything on her wrinkled face, but the poor woman's aura was black and heavy with grief. Something terrible had happened to her.

Corwin's heart pounded double-time. Now that she was here, she didn't know what to do.

Breathe out. Milo's familiar voice in her head calmed her just a little.

The men's auras pulsed with testosterone. The would-be Lothario stood, adjusting his privates, and both men approached her. She instinctively backed for the door. Luckily, a door opened near the desk and two new men came through. The testosterone men nearly bowed down to the Latino man who carried his intricately carved white ash cane like a weapon.

A man with native features and a cold smile followed this one over to Corwin. When he spotted Milo, his expression warmed. "Were we expecting a new student today, Grandpa?"

Grandpa's face remained an unreadable mask. He ignored Milo, preferring to rest his gaze on Corwin for far longer than made her comfortable. She held his gaze. She had the idea that if she looked away, bad things would happen.

Milo leaned against her legs. *He's a predator.*

After an interminable time, this old man with his young face and black streaked hair turned his icy gaze on his companion and answered, "No."

Everybody watched as he walked back across the room to the door he had come in through. He tapped the white ash cane on the carpet and then on the polished oak floor. The cane glittered.

Corwin blinked to clear her eyes. It wasn't a glitter she'd ever seen before. Her Sight didn't want to see it now. The dull black magic oozed along the ash and up into Grandpa's hand. A shiver surged up Corwin's spine and stayed there until the door closed on him and his cane.

"Impressive, isn't he?"

Corwin dragged her attention back to the man in front of her. It took effort.

236

He chuckled. "Yes, ma'am. That was *the* Grandpa Delcampo. An honor for you. Now, are you here to enroll this young cub?"

"H... Hi," she stuttered.

It's a school, not a prison! Milo's tone matched his wagging tail. *Say yes!*

Corwin struggled to keep focused while her mind flipped through contortions trying to understand what kind of place this was. Why would the Consortium be running a school for werewolves in the same place that they were gathering a militia? The possible answers terrified her.

Say yes! Milo barked and slammed his body into her ankles.

"Yes." Whatever Delta and Gandhi really were, their terror at Milo being captured by the Consortium was real. Why had Corwin brought him here?

Because I'm our only hope for getting in. Our story will still work. I'm Satchel, he prompted her. *And you're—*

"I'm Sienna. This is my brother, Satchel. Our parents died in a car accident last year and I've been trying to take care of us both, but he's..." She scowled at Milo, reinforcing his glamour with a gesture, "...being difficult."

Good girl. Milo sniffed and dropped his butt in a sideways sit.

It was too cute, especially with him looking like a wolf. Corwin controlled her features and went on with their story. "He has always wanted to go here. But. . ."

She trailed off. Milo assured her that primates hated a vacuum and would finish the sentence. Corwin was just now realizing that these apparent humans might not really be primates. But the kindly man came through and filled the vacuum, supplying a reason for her.

He nodded his understanding. "It is expensive. Has he sent in an application?"

Corwin shook her head. She glared at Milo.

"That's okay. I'm Ricardo. I can help you out." He nudged the sad woman out of his way to fish through a drawer of the desk and then brought a stack of papers over to Milo. "Even if you were thinking of coming as a presser, you'd need to fill out the application, cub."

"Can he fill it out here?" Corwin asked. She added, in a burst of inspiration, "We really don't have any money. I can do odd jobs, if you need somebody."

The testosterone brothers looked over. Their expressions called her an idiot. The old woman sniffed again and gathered up her cleaning supplies. She left through a side door that led outside, into the ranch.

Ricardo tilted his head in a question but recovered quickly. "The pressers handle all the odd jobs."

Corwin tried their original tactic. "Can we get a tour of the school?"

"No." Ricardo shook his head. "No, I'm afraid only students and faculty are allowed on campus. Cub, if you shift, you can sit out here as long as you need and fill out the application. A few essays are required."

Ricardo watched Milo for almost a minute before he raised an eyebrow and leaned in to Corwin to say, "I shouldn't have mentioned the essays."

She laughed.

Milo howled.

Corwin said, "He's better with music than with words."

Monobrow Testosterone asked, half-heartedly, "Any chance he can tune a piano?"

Corwin felt Milo perk up in her mind at the same time that hope sang in her heart.

Before she could find words, Ricardo explained, "Our music teacher says it needs tuning and the professor from Boston can do it, but she can't get out here until their winter break. Who knew it'd be so difficult to find a piano tuner?"

Milo howled and danced a little jig with his front paws. His tail thwapped the floor.

"If you have something to say, you'd best shift and say it." Ricardo's tone was more firm this time.

Corwin waited, maintaining a severe look herself until Ricardo gave up and asked, "Any idea what's got his fur matted?"

She let a humble grin flash and said, "I'm a musician. I specialize in building and repairing classic instruments."

"Really?" Monobrow tripped around the couch to approach her. "Think you could fix a piano?"

She shrugged. "Sure. It shouldn't be a problem. Any chance it might put Satchel's application at the top of the pile?"

"It might." Ricardo winked. "Any chance you have some time right now?"

Corwin didn't trust her voice. She nodded.

"Any chance you, sir, would care to shift and fill out this application?" Ricardo didn't give Milo as much time to answer this time. "Of course not. Well, you come with your sister and, if you change your mind, there are desks and writing utensils in the concert hall."

And then, that easily, Ricardo was leading them out of the front room and onto the Collective grounds.

Late day sunlight glinted off the water of a koi pond as they crossed a bridge over it. The creek that fed the pond wove away around about a dozen classic log buildings. Some of them were very big. Corwin didn't see many humans. Her heart jumped when a small pack of wolves raced across the grass in the distance, an ibex in their midst and an eagle overhead. Corwin did a double-take at the predator running alongside their prey.

It's not just wolves. Remember, we saw that kid shift into a dog.

Corwin looked at the koi again and saw a seal spinning through the water. *Are they all shifters?* She thought at Milo. Her world tilted.

Don't worry about that now. This place is huge. How many people... werewolves, live here? Milo was feeding Corwin. They'd agreed she should be the inquisitive type. She had forgotten.

"How many students do you have here?"

"At the moment, we've got about seventeen hundred students and eight hundred faculty and staff." Ricardo waved at a woman hurrying into a newer-looking building on the far side of an open quad. She didn't wave back. "And don't you worry, Satchel. You'll fit right in. About ninety percent of us are wolves."

The giddy feeling that had been bubbling through Corwin's body burst into a cold sweat. She shot a quick glance at Milo and murmured a rhyme to reinforce his glamour.

Ricardo looked over his shoulder. "What was that?"

"Oh, sorry, I just said, that's great," she replied with a wide, shaky smile. "We're surrounded by werewolves."

Yeah. Great. Or we are totally screwed.

CHAPTER 34

The concert hall was glorious. Ricardo led them through a series of doors and up a short set of steps onto a stage facing a two-thousand seat auditorium. Deep red velvet curtains draped the proscenium. Matching red velvet upholstered seats were interspersed with raised beds of velvet, tall brass poles holding horizontal bars, and enormous tanks of water with thick, clear pipes weaving over the seats and out through the walls of the theater.

Ricardo made them wait outside the curtain. He pushed between the heavy fabric and the wall. A moment later, a motor hummed and the curtains parted.

Corwin forgot all about the magnificent and unusual seating in the house.

The orchestra pit filled a moon-shaped wedge on the front of the stage that had been raised to fit snugly against the proscenium edge. The seating was even more varied here and was matched in variation by the instruments. Some small instruments had been left in their cases or on stands in the rows. The teacher in Corwin would like to hear a student explain how she practiced at home without an instrument. She'd also like to hear just how someone played the stringed instrument that lay parallel to the floor with pedals and tuning pegs on several edges.

New instruments. Corwin's rebellious, musical heart fluttered with joy at the discovery. She wanted to run to the percussion setup and play. With a shock, she realized that she did not have the right appendages to play the arrangement of pipes dangling over the tympani. Her fingers itched to examine them all, to see someone play these new wonders.

Stay cool. These might be common instruments here.

Corwin sent a mental nod and kept her focus on the glossy black grand piano. She ran the keys through an arpeggio from middle C and cringed. The piano was badly out of tune. The music teacher, whoever they were, should have been able to adjust it at least enough that it wasn't painful for non-musicians. She almost asked where they kept their tools but that would keep Ricardo with them and they weren't really there to fix the piano.

She turned to him. "I see why you're so anxious. Shall I just return to the fireplace building when I'm done?" He must think her so pitiful that she didn't negotiate a price first.

Ricardo didn't seem to be paying much attention to her at all. His eyes were on his armpadd as he replied, "Yes, thank you. Everyone will head to the start-of-year assembly after final classes, so you have the place to yourself."

"Just so long as it's quiet." She smiled and stood from the bench to raise the cover. At least the teacher had had the sense to muffle the off-key strings.

"If you need anything, just ring the buzzer by the door we came in. It will alert me in the office and the head of security, so don't be afraid when a very large wolf bursts in before me. He's a good man, but like many around here, he is dedicated to the safety of the school and Grandpa's vision. If there is real trouble, he has a hundred wolves who'll tear apart anyone threatening us."

Corwin's voice fled into her gut and froze there. She nodded, struggling to put an appreciative edge to the awe on her face. Milo growled and bounded at the door, lowering his front half and wagging his tail madly.

"Ahhh, so you're a fighter, are you, Satchel?" Ricardo laughed. His armpadd buzzed and he hustled for the steps. "I would arrange for an introduction, but the office is busy with the militia training consult—"

He cut himself off and laughed uncomfortably. "It's a busy day around here. Just stay in the theater and you should be fine." He leaned back in the door to wag a finger at Milo. "You be good, Satchel."

Corwin managed a strangled laugh and a wave of her hand. As she turned back to the piano, she thought hard at Milo, *Follow him. Make sure he's gone.*

She wasn't sure if he had heard her, but she heard Milo pad down the steps. Corwin took a multi-tool out of her hip sack and tuned the most egregiously warped strings.

He's gone. He shifted and ran away. That's super freaky. Let's find a back door.

Corwin shot one more glance over the new instruments and the massive audience. She wondered, what must it be like to have that many people listen to you play? And animals, she amended. And how bad could a place be that dedicated so much space to music? But those were questions for later. The only question that mattered now was, where was her mother?

She activated the feeling of the divining rod in her hands and followed Milo backstage and out a door behind some stairs leading up to the flies. The door led to a paved patio with chairs and then straight off into a field of grass crisscrossed with packed dirt pathways leading between artfully designed buildings.

Milo ignored the pathways and the buildings. He led her swiftly deeper into the property, stopping a couple of times and dashing on a detour to avoid the few people who were out and about.

The clouds were shaded pink by the time Corwin Found her mother. The sense was strong and her heart pulled her as relentlessly as the rod had when it flew out of her hands in Richmond. She took the lead. Milo followed close on her heels as they passed a farmed section and into the woods. Corwin could feel the trees all around her as if she were still a part of their ecosystem, as she had been last night. She ran her hands along their trunks as she passed, sending them health and sharing her joy as she rushed to finally reunite with her mother.

The images that shot through her as she touched each tree helped her weave an efficient route through the woods. As they drew close, the images the trees shared were unbelievable. Corwin, already panting for breath, gasped at the horror and Milo with his infinite energy bounded past her. She watched as he burst out of the forest into a ray of sunshine ahead. She felt his growl when he stumbled to a stop and knew, before she reached the clearing, that the trees had not lied.

Curved bleacher seats of wood showing the impressions of long use arched around a slight depression. Corwin's mind didn't have time to contemplate the paradox of a student werewolf militia compound having two theaters because the structures built in the depression, on the stage of this outdoor amphitheater, ignited ancient fear and anger in Corwin as a child of Salem.

A pair of stumps from recently cut trees stood together, a trough carved in the wood created a rectangle that drew the two into one. A clear sort of glittering disturbed the air around this altar. That was the feeling Corwin got from it. The canopy of leaves overhead rustled, despite the still air. They did not like the altar. They mourned the loss of their sister, cut down for this evil purpose. They mourned that one of their kin had been turned into a rough altar and two much more carefully constructed pyres on either side.

Two platforms had been raised over neat, well-formed stacks of logs, branches, and twigs, all taken from the same felled tree. Each pyre featured a rough, straight branch standing ten feet high at the edge of the platform. And each stake held one of Corwin's parents. Her father was alive!

The far platform held another figure, as well. Corwin growled deep in her throat, feeling more than hearing Milo echo her. The witch, Kat Coogan, stood with her back to them, securing the iron chains attaching Sita Corwin to the stake. This was why she told Corwin she'd be disappointed when she found her mother.

Because the Coogan was going to burn Corwin's mother and father at the stake.

The divining of Corwin's heart pulled her to her mother.

No, Milo dashed to the nearest pyre. *We need help. Free your dad.*

Corwin looked down for an instant and then ran with Milo to the near platform. She conjured heat into her right hand as she would when burning decorations onto the wood of her instruments. This heat had to be more intense, more like the heat needed to shape a harp's pedals. It would hurt. Corwin put that out of her mind. She started singing the familiar words and found new ones following.

Heat, flesh, to blue
To keep the string true
Love is the tune
And we're racing the moon.

She leapt the stairs in two bounds and spun around the post to see her father's broken face. One eye was swollen shut. The other eye widened in shock.

"Hi, Daddy." She reached over his head; for once, her height was a boon. Careful to avoid his skin, she wrapped her right hand around the chain and held it away so when it split, the white-hot links fell away from her father. She helped lower his arms slowly and held her sizzling hand to the manacles biting into his wrists.

"Oh, my baby girl," her father whispered, his voice a hoarse wreck.

Corwin put her left hand on his chest to be sure he could stand. "Let's go rescue Mother."

Her father nodded mutely.

"No!" A stronger voice screamed from the other side of the altar. Kat Coogan turned from the shackles she was sealing with golden magic. "Corwin, get out of here. The sun is about to set."

Sita's head fell forward. Her features were hidden by her prized hair and Corwin feared Kat Coogan had already hurt her as she had clearly beaten Daniel. But a strange wind blew from above and scattered the strands of auburn hair briefly. Sita was smiling.

Corwin turned back to her father. She dug the medicine bag from the zippered thigh pocket of her pants. "Here. It's all gonna be okay now. Let's go." She shoved the bag into his hands and then turned to leap from the platform straight onto the wide stumps of the altar. In mid-air, she cried a series of uncomfortable tones, gathered the confusion that had dominated her magical education, and shot that feeling at Kat Coogan. The witch stumbled back and tumbled off the platform. An inexplicably strong gust of wind, again from above, blew the witch away from the sharp logs and sticks of the pyre.

Milo ran down the steps of Daniel's platform and dashed to the altar, barking. *Pundu! It's Pundu!*

Wind that felt like a punch pushed Corwin back from the edge of the altar. Morgan Coogan's Impundulu landed where Corwin had been standing. The bird shrieked and thunder rolled overhead. Then the bird folded her great wings and blinked her red eyes. There was the slightest blip in reality and there, instead of the lightning bird, stood a Black human as tall as Corwin with deep black eyes that flashed with red in the very center.

The human-shaped impundulu shook her head as if settling crown feathers that weren't there. She reached out and placed a mitten-covered hand on Corwin's chest as Corwin had just done with her father. The eyes begged Corwin. It wasn't just a bird's gaze. The impundulu was being ridden.

Corwin asked, "Morgan?"

Milo barked. *She wants you to run away.*

"No, Morgan. I am not going anywhere without my mother."

"Baby girl." Her father stood at the base of the wide altar, reaching a hand up to her. Corwin jumped down, ready to race to her mother with her father at her side. Instead, her father swung her around and twisted a brown string of sparkles around her wrists, binding her with his magic. "Blood of my blood," he began chanting.

Corwin stared at her father. She didn't know what he was doing. Was this some spell to combine their powers? It wasn't necessary. She'd already knocked Kat Coogan down. All they had to do was release her mother's chains and get out of the Collective through the break in the fence he'd told her about.

"What do you need me to do, Daddy?" She tensed, her muscles preparing to fight for her mother's life.

Daniel didn't answer. Her father bent and lifted her as if she were a little girl. He swung her around. Corwin couldn't help but grin. It was the wrong time, the wrong place. But she had watched other daddies swing their kids around in the park and had dreamed of Daniel playing with her like that. She felt his magic lifting her up, raising her legs over the altar. And then her legs hit Pundu.

The bird's human figure fell from the stump, shifting as she did to catch herself with her wings. But her wings did not save her. The creature cried out, red magic surrounding her, and she fell to the ground.

Dust clouds rose around her as she struggled against the pain from an injury Corwin couldn't see.

Corwin sucked in a breath to cry out, to run to her, but her father was still swinging her around. Milo ran but could not get close to the bird. Thunder and lightning split the sky, striking so close, the electricity shooting through Corwin's senses. She fed from the energy and gathered her own magic into a hum. The hum burst from her in a cry as her father slammed her body onto the altar.

She writhed, trying to understand. "Daddy! What do you need me to do?"

He lifted a knife and there was pain in his eyes as he brought it to her throat, whispering, "I need you to die, baby girl."

CHAPTER 35

Corwin stared up at the evening sky. Lightning flashed from clouds as fluffy white as marshmallows. The impundulu's cries of pain battled with Milo's barking voice, though neither could drown out her father's chanting. Bright brown sparkles washed down her body with the tingle of magic. She couldn't move. She couldn't see anything but the sky, the leaves, and the knife her father brought down on her neck.

He chanted, "Blood of my blood, give me your power."

Lightning struck nearby at the same moment that a sharp, icy pain bit into her throat. Warm blood, her blood, burned against her skin. And then a golden sparkle shot across her vision and her father froze, paralyzed by Kat Coogan's magic.

Behind Corwin and getting closer, the witch yelled, "Release her!" Then she screamed a cry that was cut off. Sparks shot over Corwin from the wards holding her father still.

The ground shook. Corwin couldn't see what caused it from where she lay, trapped under her father's magic and his knife. Shadows on the edges of her sight poured in all around, and suddenly she could see dozens of wolves charging into the amphitheater from the school side of the forest. The altar beneath her was still connected to the trees and they showed Corwin what she couldn't see. Three of the wolves bowled Kat Coogan over into the dirt. Her shoulders hit hard because, rather than catch herself, she stayed curled around a bundle tucked tight against her chest. The wolves tumbled beyond her and leapt around, ready to take her down. They recoiled from the visible sparks shooting off of Kat's aura. She'd rolled to her feet and tried to raise a ward, but something was wrong with her magic. Fear flashed across her face to be replaced with a fierceness that would have burned them where they stood if looks could kill.

In her arms, Milo growled his own warning at the much bigger canines.

Most of the wolves stationed themselves around the perimeter of the stage, cringing away from the lightning strikes. A phalanx of them leapt to her mother's platform. Most of them tumbled off the small space but several shifted into men to release her from the chains. Kat Coogan's magic had failed there, as well. The men helped her down the steps and away from the stake. Half a dozen wolves bounded onto the lightning bird. A wash of red magic threw them from the impundulu's writhing form.

"Don't harm the witch, either, please. I need them alive to take their power." Sita strolled into Corwin's sightline. She ran a fingernail down Daniel's face, leaving a scratch that welled up with blood. "Sweet Daniel. And here I thought you were a total waste."

He raised the knife an inch, but then red glitters slithered from Sita's scratch, swirling in amongst the failing golden sparkles of Kat Coogan's Skill. He stilled again. Corwin's mother pried the medicine bag, the heart of Corwin House, from where her father held it against the knife's handle.

"What an ugly place to hide your family's power. Your ancestors must have been even more simple than you."

Corwin's brow struggled to wrinkle despite the magic holding her body still. The spell did nothing to hold back her magic, though. With barely a thought, she released her face from her father's charm. Confusion tightened every muscle. This was not what she had expected.

Her mother released her father then. He turned the knife so that the flat of it laid across Corwin's skin. His voice was as tight as her face as he asked, "What are you doing? We need her power to defeat the Consortium."

Her mother laughed. The thrill of it drove cold spikes into Corwin's skin, literally. It was like Sita released icy magic in a rain over her daughter. "Oh, my dear Daniel. A blood sacrifice of Daniella would give you very little power."

"She is my daughter. There can be no greater sacrifice, no greater offering to power." Her father quoted from Great-great-great-great-grandfather-Jonathan's grimoire. Corwin had completely misunderstood the passage.

Another laugh, more cold magical rain. "Ah, but she isn't," her mother said this gently and then went very still before she clarified. "Your daughter. Daniella isn't your daughter. Oh, ha ha, don't look like that. I didn't cheat on you."

Sita looked down at Corwin, examining her face, running her fingers through her hair. "She isn't my daughter, either. You wanted a child, and I still thought I could find the power hidden in your house. So, I stole a newborn during that horrid RV tour and made you remember our precious pregnancy, and a birth that never happened." She glanced up at Daniel with no reaction to the tears pouring down the sides of Corwin's face. "Yes, dear. I am that powerful. And soon, thanks to this changeling," she tapped Corwin's chest, "I'll have a great deal more."

"Do you want us to bind him?" A human-shaped werewolf kept his distance from Sita as he asked this.

Another cold laugh. "There is no need. Daniel could never hurt me. He loves me."

Corwin had to turn away from the possessive look Sita turned on her father, on Daniel. Her gaze fell on Pundu. The bird lay with her red head half hidden under one broken wing. Her aura pulsed with pain. Without thinking about it, Corwin sent a song she had sung to straighten a violin's neck through the wood at her back. It vibrated down to the forest's roots deep in the soil and over and up to the poor lightning bird. Her wing jerked and she gave a quiet squawk of surprise. Off in the distance, a bolt of lightning shot from one cloud to another in front of the lowering sun. Corwin hoped it brought Morgan some relief, too.

Beyond Pundu, wolves and burly humans surrounded Kat and Milo. Milo struggled in Kat Coogan's arms. Kat Coogan held him back, but Corwin could see her assessing the situation. Her bright eyes darted around the space, taking in everything.

Good wins. Kindness wins.

It wasn't so much a message to her as Milo trying to convince himself. But he was right. His instinct for kindness had always been right. Every time she did something nice for someone, something good happened for her. If she could do something kind enough, it might give her enough power and luck to stop Sita. She started searching the amphitheater, much as Kat did.

Meanwhile, the woman who was not her mother called to the heavens, holding the medicine bag, the token of the Corwin Curse, over Corwin's body. She chanted a complicated spell that didn't rhyme very well and did nothing creative with rhythm but nevertheless pooled power between her hands and soaked her aura with intense red need. Corwin sucked in a breath. She heard herself humming the little tune that protected her every time she walked through the flames at home. Fear paralyzed her thoughts. What good could she do here, trapped on this altar under her false mother's magic?

Sita brought her hands down and slammed them into Corwin's solar plexus. Hot, sharp pain spread through her body. It grabbed control of her muscles and tore at her mind, digging into her very cells. Corwin's body curled around her center and then every part of her was flung wide as Sita pulled her hands to her own chest. Pain wracked Corwin, and grief that tortured her worse than Sita's magic. But nothing left her when her mother pulled.

Sita repeated the last lines of the spell, ordering the power of the Corwin curse to release from the medicine bag and give her Corwin's magic.

"Come, curse of the Corwins that was broken,
by this girl in her innocence.
Come from the House's heart and hers.
Come to me."

A thought came to Corwin that was all her own. Not Milo in her head. She felt him crying to her at the edges of her pain but couldn't hear him. That she could think in the midst of the emotional and physical agony she was under brought her wonder. She wasn't a Corwin. Sita had said as much. So, why did the woman think she had assimilated the family's power just because she lifted the curse? And, come to that, how had finding the heart of the house lifted the curse? Did it? She wasn't even the one to find the bag.

She looked over at Milo as Sita brought her hands down again. Corwin heard her breast bone crack and she cried out. But again, her mind was too occupied with something else to be destroyed by mere physical pain. The wampum belt around Milo's neck glowed.

Corwin hadn't found the house's heart. She hadn't been the one to break the curse. It was Milo all along. And the power wasn't in the medicine bag. It was in the blue and white shell beads glowing and glittering in the most beautiful magical display Corwin had ever seen. Everything became clear. She had to give her power to Milo.

Hey Milo, she thought at him, using the pain as a conduit to a dream-like state. *Hey, Milo, my friend who never gave up on me,*

Hey Milo, my brother not by blood but by decree,

Hey Milo, take my power and set everybody free.

So mote it be.

She flung her left hand out, her scarred palm reaching for the dog.

Corwin finally understood what Morgan had meant when she said that blood spells didn't work unless you offered a true sacrifice. She used her power one final time and sent a string of purple light soaring through the sunlight into Milo. She bent her knees, reached up over her head with her right hand, and grabbed her father's hands, still grasping the knife. With all of her strength, she pulled it to her heart.

The spell worked. She felt her power leaving her. But her strength abandoned her, too. She found herself fighting her father for the knife. And losing.

He sang, low and sweet, in the voice she remembered from her cradle,

No more Corwin power shall be.

The Corwin line ends with me.

Take my power and turn it to Skill.
Rebuild our House by your kind will, my daughter.

And then he yanked with all his might and stabbed the knife into his own heart.

Sita screamed as if she had been the one stabbed. She turned her curse from Corwin to her father. His brown magic started twinkling along the connection into Sita's core, until Daniel tore his eyes from Corwin's and glared at his wife. "She may not have my blood," he hissed, "but she has my heart." And he placed one hand onto Corwin's forehead.

Power surged through her. The direction of flow reversed, drawing red magic from Sita to Daniel to Corwin and then across the theater to Milo.

The little dog she'd rejected a hundred times glowed with all the colors of the most dynamic magic. In a brilliant flash of sparkles, the dog transformed. Kat dropped him, but he didn't fall far. Human feet landed on the hard-packed dirt, sending a cloud of dust into the air. When it cleared, a boy stood in front of Kat Coogan. His messy hair was all the colors of Milo's belly. His hazel eyes sparkled with the many colors of magic that had just been poured into him. Freckles danced across his nose just as they did on Daniel's face. The boy held his head high revealing the wampum belt stretched across his neck.

He sang in a bright, clear falsetto, "Every good boy deserves fur!"

Corwin could see sparkling sine waves emitting from his mouth and all the resonating chambers in his face and neck and chest. She could feel the same waves in her mind, her chest, her face and neck. And she could see colorless magic flowing from every wolf in and around the altar and pyres. The deepest, most instinctual magic of their very beings poured out of them and into the song.

The Impundulu lay untouched, watching the invisible waves of magic over her head. She squawked and snapped at the flow as if she could capture a fish from it like from the sea in Salem.

Red and brown still flowed into Corwin from Sita and her father, though it was slowing as Daniel collapsed beside the altar. The clear magic of his soul danced into the flow of the sine wave. Sita's fought and failed and was subsumed as Sita herself shrieked. Her lush hair shriveled.

Her golden skin wrinkled and sank into her rapidly aging face. Her hands cramped into thick-knuckled claws and the medicine bag fell from her grasp. As light as it was, the tap against her shattered ribs drew a cry from Corwin which hurt nearly as much as the tap.

Slowly, with exquisite control, Milo released the final note. Silence fell. Sita fell to her knees.

Not one wolf stood in the amphitheater. Women and men lay unconscious all around. The impundulu struggled to her claws and shook the dirt from her feathers. One fell out and floated to the ground. She blinked at it, cried a heart-wrenching caw at it, and then picked it up with her beak. She flew to the altar and landed in her human form. The shift was so smooth, Corwin couldn't say how it happened.

Corwin coughed. Blood splattered her shirt. "Morgan?"

The impundulu tilted her head and slowly rolled it from side to side. She asked, "Pundu?"

The human-looking bird blinked rapidly. Then she opened her mouth and crowed. Corwin grinned and tried to imitate the sound.

Kat Coogan ran over, Milo, as a dog, in her arms. He howled, which said so much more than the word in Corwin's head. *Faster.*

Kat wasn't fast enough.

Sita stood, her joints creaking audibly. She didn't chant or gloat or savor the moment. She just took the knife, still dripping with Daniel's blood, and plunged it into Corwin's heart.

CHAPTER 36

Milo cried out one deafening bark that would have put a lion's roar to shame.

Sita flew back from the force of it. Her body slammed into the pyre of wood Daniel had been tied to. She slid to the ground and would have leapt to her feet, but a hairy mountain of a man ran from the woods faster than humanly possible and stuck a needle in her neck. Sita slumped over.

A slim, fawn-colored dog with black paws bounded out from under the stadium seating and dashed over to this man, whose terrifying, scarred face melted into a mask of love. Corwin knew the man. It was Hardknock, from Vegas and Richmond.

Corwin watched them cuddle with each other through the grace of the forest. Her own eyes watched Milo, in Kat Coogan's arms, getting closer as her vision shrank until his black nose was all she could see. And then the world faded into that black.

Corwin!

The voice in her head sounded so very sad.

A bird's cry echoed through the forest, blending with a howl and overpowering the cry of questions from new humans racing towards the altar. The forest picked her up and held her in the sunlight as a breeze added susurration and percussion to the symphony of voices below.

"Don't go, Corwin." This voice came to her ears. It was quiet and commanding. "I'm gonna need pressure here, Jay. You ready?"

"I'm ready." The new voice was quiet, muffled. It sounded very close to her ear and also very far away.

Please don't go.

She looked down. Kat Coogan stood poised over her body. She rubbed her palms together, but her magic only sputtered between them. A muscular, bald, shirtless stranger stood on the other side of the altar, his feet straddling her father's figure on the ground. He held his shirt in his hands, ready. Milo sat in the crook of Corwin's neck. He was a dog. She had seen him turn into a boy, but he was a dog again. She liked him as a dog. She liked him.

Her heart thumped, drawing her back a bit. She felt it in her body. The pain from the thump thundered through her bones, spiking where her ribs had been broken, sending blood spurting up around the knife. The bloody blade's red magic melted under the lilac Skill in Corwin's blood. Not only lilac. Corwin saw tendrils of glittering brown circling up the blade. She felt a smile brush her lips and it did not cause pain. Her father had not been her father. But he had loved her.

And she, too, loved. The realization sent a spark through her soul. It pulled her out of the trees. Though, her body hurt so much she fled again and was welcomed.

Come back. I picked you.

Him. She loved him.

She couldn't leave him. It didn't matter how unbearable the pain and fear and loss that stunned her body as Kat Coogan pulled the knife from her chest and the stranger, Jay, applied pressure, cracking more ribs. She loved Milo and she had spent her entire life fighting for people who weren't her family. What a waste it would be, what a shame, if she didn't fight for the dog who really was her family.

The forest heard her heart and cradled her a bit longer, not letting her go back entirely. The leaves and branches and grass rose up all around and within her as if taking a breath. The body she could feel and still see lying on the butchered tree trunk not so far below trembled.

Sprays of golden magic glittered around her, trying to fight through her wards. It was instinct. She'd spent her whole life defending herself from Kat Coogan. The woman who said she had been protecting her. The woman her mother had told her was trying to kill her.

Corwin felt as much as heard the witch's whispered plea, "Trust me, Corwin. Just this once."

A rough voice that sounded as scarred as the man it came from muttered, "Trust her. She can help you."

The black-pawed dog pushed his head into Hardknock's beard and howled.

The man holding pressure on her chest whispered, "Hi. I'm Jay. You don't know me. But trust her. She's got skills."

Let her help you.

Because Milo said so, Corwin focused on letting the witch past her wards. She stretched her aura out over the golden spittles of Kat's magic, over the deep black hands holding a shirt soaked in her blood to the hole in her chest, over all of Milo. The gold trickled around Jay's hands and his shirt and down into the stab wound. It burned. Corwin struggled to keep her wards down. She didn't want this pain.

Another dark figure moved in beside Kat. The impundulu in human form raised her dropped feather and crushed it between her palms, as Kat had summoned her magic earlier. But no glittering magic gathered. Instead, a soft, black dust fell through Corwin's aura. It soothed her, relaxed her mind. And where it fell, she came back to herself. A coolness drifted down through her skin, through her muscles, through veins and arteries and fascia and bone, healing as it went. Pain eased to ache, ratcheted up to itching, and calmed to relief.

The impundulu let go of the last of her feather and leapt into the air. Her wings spread wide over the altar, the humans, and Milo. A single beat and the forest released Corwin. She opened her eyes to see a feather floating down. She reached up and caught it.

Pundu soared off over the trees and out of sight. A happy howl drew Corwin's eyes to Milo. She grinned. *I'm alive,* she thought.

I know, he thought back, his jaw dropped in a grin. *I love you.*

I love you too, Milo.

He licked her nose. *I know.*

Their moment was interrupted by two naked boys who raced in and crowded Milo.

The smaller, scruffier one had a grin a mile wide, but a shadow crossed his joy as he turned to ask Kat, "Is she all better, Sher?"

Kat's idea of a smile glittered in her eyes. "I think so, Josh. Do we need to go?"

"Oh yeah, like super soon." He offered a hand to Milo. "Hi, Milo. I'm Josh."

"And I'm Bayard." The other boy, who wore shields on his wrists like Wonder Woman, slipped around to help Jay help Corwin sit up.

Milo set a paw in Josh's hand. He whispered in Corwin's mind, *These are my brothers.*

"I hope we get to spend some time together, soon. But you've got to go now." Josh shook Milo's paw. Then he turned to give Kat a filthy glass bottle that fit perfectly in her small palm. The top was sealed with black wax that glittered malevolently. Upon closer inspection, the glass glittered too with a slimy magic. It raised the hair on Corwin's arms.

"You need to destroy that," she said.

"We will," Kat assured her.

Jay, the man keeping Corwin upright, peered at it, getting closer than Corwin would have dared. "What is that in there?"

Josh hopped up on the altar to sit cross-legged between Milo and Kat. Milo's lip curled up and she felt a mental growl that didn't escape his teeth. Josh didn't notice. He said, "It looks like fur, hair, and half a dog tag in an oil solution."

Milo hopped over Josh's legs and sidled close to see the bottle. *My mama wore half a heart charm. It said 'friends.'*

Corwin ducked her head and murmured, "Milo's mother wore a charm like that."

Jay asked Milo, "Did it read 'friends'?"

Corwin and Milo both nodded. Corwin asked, "How did you know?"

"This one reads 'Best,'" he said and then stood straight up as his eyes went a little blank.

Milo tilted his head. As if in echo, Hardknock tilted his head, listening hard. He stood and crossed to join the crowd around the altar.

All Corwin could hear was birdsong. One bird, repeating the same sequence. The moment she realized it couldn't be a bird, a man dashed silently out of the woods leading to the school buildings. He wore camouflage clothing with a camouflage hood that covered his entire head excepting his brilliant blue eyes. He moved like Hardknock, faster and more quietly than possible. Kat sucked in a breath and headed for him. He slipped past her to Corwin's side. Kat's aura dimmed.

He nodded his head at Jay, and belatedly at Kat.

"How long do you need?" Josh asked, hopping to his feet on the altar. Corwin wished he would put some clothes on.

Jay answered, "Give us seven minutes to get through the fence."

The boy nodded and the air around him shimmered. Suddenly, where a skinny boy had been fidgeting, a fawn-colored dog with a face like Milo's stood hopping on his black paws. He turned to smack Milo with his butt, his tail wagging madly. Then he head-butted the fist offered by Hardknock and leapt from the tree stump, running hell-bent for leather in the direction of the school buildings.

Hardknock muttered, "I'll get the witch." He looked up at the raised eyebrow on Kat's face and then offered Corwin a softer nod. "The other witch."

There was an awkward moment with looks exchanged between Kat, Jay, and the new guy.

"Clark, you get Corwin." Jay looked down at Corwin. "This is Corwin." He nodded at the new guy, "That's Clark." Then he hustled around the altar to meet Kat.

Kat hopped up onto Jay's back and wrapped her legs around his waist, telling Corwin, "They can move faster than we can."

To prove it, Hardknock, with Sita slung over his shoulders like a sack of fish, disappeared into the trees heading away from the school before Corwin could blink.

Clark offered Corwin his back. He looked over at Milo. "Milo, I'll keep your friend safe. You go with Bayard."

A bark revealed a new dog standing on the far side of her father's body. The shields on his front legs told Corwin it had to be Bayard. Milo looked over the edge and then up at Corwin.

Do we trust them?

Corwin felt the torn and bloody fabric at her chest. She watched Jay lifting Daniel Corwin's broken body. Kat adjusted the dead man's lolling skull so that it rested against Jay's neck. Corwin rolled to her knees and climbed onto Clark's back. *We trust them more than we trust the werewolves.*

Milo barked his curt laugh and leapt off the trunk, racing his brother Bayard—an honest-to-goddess shapeshifter—to the trees. Jay followed with Kat and Daniel.

Clark jogged after them. "You ready?" he asked Corwin, a grin in his voice.

She nodded before finding her voice. She wasn't sure she was, but she said, "Yeah."

And they were off.

CHAPTER 37

Two days of traveling later, Corwin stuffed herself into the corner of the plush green couch in Kat Coogan's Oregon home. Or, rather, Sher Hillen's Oregon home. It turned out that the homeless woman who had warned them about Walter was Kat. Because she'd lost her powers, Corwin hadn't recognized the glamoured Coogan. She really had been trying to help Corwin all along.

Corwin ran her nails over the corduroy, wishing it were strings. Behind her, a fire crackled in the tiny fireplace she'd learned was common in newer homes. Rain painted the windows looking out over the front porch into the Foothills cul-de-sac. Out there, in the middle of the road, a half dozen rebel CF, conditioned force soldiers who had escaped from the Consortium, were moving in perfect sync through some martial arts routine. Or maybe it was Tai Chi. The rain didn't bother them at all.

Somewhere in the "rescue" of her mother, Corwin had left reality behind. Granted, she didn't have a wide experience of reality. She had come to understand that magic wasn't generally a part of most people's reality. She'd thought it was like Mr. Collins and Mrs. Cook's affair at Salem High. Everybody knew about it, but it just wasn't something you talked about.

Footsteps tapped across the dining room and over the carpet runner in the hallway. Jay leaned against the archway between the hall and the couch room. "I'm making a grilled cheese with tomatoes from Clark's garden. Want one?"

She shook her head.

"I mean, they're not up to his usual standards, but he's been traveling a lot and none of the rest of us are really gardeners."

Corwin brightened at the thought of being useful. "I have a green thumb. Can I help?"

"You have a connection with the earth?" Kat asked, coming around Jay to perch on the arm of a comfy chair.

"With the things that grow out of it," Corwin confirmed.

"Interesting. That's a Corwin trait."

Jay raised an eyebrow. "Why are you surprised, Sher? She is a Corwin."

"I'm not." Corwin shook her head and said it out loud for the first time. She felt tears tightening her eyes and tamped all feelings down. "Daniel and Sita weren't my parents. I'm not a Corwin."

"Not by birth." Kat stood. "Can you teach me how to cultivate the things that grow from the earth?"

Corwin dragged herself out of the couch's embrace. "Sure. It's simple, really."

The front door opened. The pattering sound of the rain increased for a moment. From where she stood, Corwin could see Clark come in, shaking his hat outside before he shut the door. Jay turned and gave him a nod.

Kat didn't notice. "Not for me. It's never been one of my interests and definitely isn't in my skill set."

Corwin asked, "Then why do you want to learn how to garden?"

"Because Clark has been traveling a lot and I think he's going to keep traveling and the garden means a lot to him." A glint of wetness rested in her eyes before it rolled down her cheek. "I'd like to be able to keep it alive."

"That's really nice of you, Katherine." Clark hung his jacket. Droplets of water glistened on the fabric. "Bailey used to help me, right? I must have taught him. I'm sure I can teach you."

Kat smiled with that nearly magical glitter in her face that she reserved for Clark. "Bailey only submitted because Laylea loved helping you and he liked Laylea."

"Laylea is their sister," Jay explained. Again.

The CF didn't have great short-term memories. It was actually quite helpful, since Corwin didn't have to remember every tidbit she was told. *Their sister* meant the dogs. Milo had three brothers and a sister.

"Oh, yeah. She was a good weeder." Clark looked around at floor height. "Where's Milo?"

Kat waited for Corwin to answer. When she didn't, Jay said, "Bayard is showing him Hardknock's monitor set up. I think they're hoping to catch a glimpse of Laylea."

"Shouldn't be too hard." Clark laughed. "Didn't Bailey trap her in the bar for her safety?"

"She lives in a bar?" Corwin did some math in her head. Milo was only 14 years old.

Clark took off his newsboy cap and ran a hand through his hair, mussing it. "There's a big rule in the Chicago shifter community. "

"I imagine it's big in any shifter community," Jay interrupted.

Clark conceded the point with a rude gesture. "No shifting in front of non-shifters."

"Like Milo did in front of all of us when he saved our asses from—" Jay cut himself off when Kat coughed loudly.

Kat and Clark stared at him.

He turned back to Corwin. "So, their kid, Laylea, did it in the middle of a huge party. And it wasn't the first time."

Clark ignored the dig. "She could be in big trouble. So, Bailey. . . "

"With the advice of their adult friends," Kat put in pointedly.

Jay added, just as pointedly, "Bailey is twenty years old. He is an adult."

"They're making her stay in the bar where they meet up," Clark continued. "It's a safe place and she's never alone."

"That sounds awful," Corwin murmured.

Clark offered a sad smile. "Yeah. She thinks so, too. And *she* is a social butterfly."

Corwin smiled. "Like Milo."

Clark smiled back at her. "Really?"

"Speaking of Milo," Kat dragged herself away from Clark. "I'd like to give you something for his collar."

Jay asked, "A tapper?"

Kat took Clark's hat and hung it on the coat rack. "Yeah."

Clark watched her. He ducked his head before she caught him. "I'm gonna get a sandwich and then hop on the HAM and check our arrangements. When the rain clears, meet me in the garden, Kat, and I'll show you how Jay killed the tomatoes."

Kat smiled a real, honest-to-goodness smile, and the two shared a look that made Corwin look away.

Jay punched Clark. "They are perfectly edible."

Clark rolled his eyes and headed through the dining room to the swinging kitchen door. "If you have no taste buds."

Jay followed him. "Well, that would be Sher's fault, wouldn't it?"

"Who?" Clark laughed, shooting Jay a look like he thought the man had lost his mind. He pushed through into the kitchen.

Jay stopped. His laughter died. He looked over at Kat. "I'm sorry. I keep forgetting. It's this Swiss cheese memory." He knocked on his head.

"Which is my fault." She sighed in return, hiding the grief that Corwin had seen pass over her at the name *Sher*. "Don't worry about it."

"Sure," he said, "like that's possible." And he followed Clark into the kitchen. "Hey, make a few sandwiches, would you?"

Kat led Corwin down the hall to a linen closet. She stepped inside, putting her back right up against the shelves, and invited Corwin to join her. When she shut the door, the darkness gave Corwin the courage to ask, "Why does Jay call you Sher when he knows who you really are?"

A sharp intake of breath made her glad she couldn't see the witch. She thought Kat wouldn't answer.

But, after a moment, she said, "It's a very long story. I took the name Sher Hillen to hide, after the Consortium thought I was killed. A few months ago, a man, who is dead now, made Clark forget Sher Hillen."

"He doesn't remember you at all?"

"At least he remembers the kids. We've got that."

"I'm so sorry, Kat."

She huffed a breath and the shelves with their towels and sheets and tablecloths suddenly cracked down the middle. "Don't be. Karma always wins out."

The shelves opened to reveal a metal-walled hallway. Kat strode to the end. The shelves closed behind Corwin once she passed through. She spun at the noise and turned back to see Kat walking through a solid wall.

Her voice carried through clearly. "Welcome to my lab."

Corwin took a breath, instinctively hummed her walk-through-fire tune, and followed. Her jaw literally dropped open. Kat's lab looked like the Corwin House lab would if it had been built by aliens on a space-ship from the future.

The hearth took up a third of the far wall. Corwin could imagine shiny silver robots walking, fully-formed, from the flames. She took a moment to orient herself and asked, "Is that the same fire as in the couch room?"

"Not exactly." Kat looked at it. "Same chimney, though. Come here."

Corwin joined her at the long, stainless-steel table running down the middle of the room. It was scattered with technical doohickeys, a Bunsen burner, and a set of scales. One end was dedicated to medical equipment. A few feet beyond that end was a surgical bed with a fancy light hung overhead on a track that allowed Kat to drag it anywhere over the table. Kat saw her looking at it.

"Oh, yeah. This is important. You are welcome here anytime." She touched Corwin's shoulder and where her fingers brushed bare skin, magic tingled. Despite Kat's casual tone, it was a formal invitation. "If you bring Milo or any of the dogs in, pull this curtain around the lamp." She demonstrated, pulling a white curtain that Corwin hadn't noticed around until it tapped the light's track. "It brings up bad memories for them."

Corwin flashed on the nightmares she'd had of being strapped down beneath a light like that. She could understand their fear. She brushed a hand against the tingle on her shoulder. "Your magic is getting stronger."

Kat looked down at her hands and made fists. Sparkles of gold glittered as she opened them. The magic spread across the worktable, landing on various bits of tech and tools she had laying here and there. "That was frightening. I felt like I wasn't me. How's yours?"

Corwin shrugged. "Hard to say. I thought I gave it all to Milo. But." She lit the Bunsen burner with a whistle.

Kat put the flame out with a snap. "You can't lose magic entirely. It's in the air. Look at you. You're not a born Corwin, but you're stronger than any of them I've ever known."

Corwin pretended to be looking over the tech on the table. Kat's kindness was nothing she'd ever expected from the witch. It shamed her. She'd spent twenty years living with lies. Lies her false parents had fed her and lies she had fed herself.

"These are tappers." Kat opened a box that looked like Corwin's tool kit dipped in titanium. "They are a way for us to communicate without being traced. You'll have to learn Morse code, but that shouldn't be hard for a pair of musicians." She picked out a metal clasp that looked just like the clasp on her rope bracelet. "I think this will work with Milo's collar. And you can have your choice of a medical bracelet, a ring, an earring, a necklace, or a lapel pin."

Corwin turned the clasp over in her hands. "What is this for?"

Kat looked at her in surprise. "So you can stay in touch with us. You don't have to get involved. We'd just like to keep an eye on Milo, in case Walter resurfaces."

"But," Corwin set the clasp back into the case. "Milo will be here."

Kat's face lit up. "Are you staying?"

"Isn't he? He found his family."

"Oh, Corwin. Family is like magic: it's easier if you're born to it, but it's not genetic." She took Corwin's hand and put two collar clasps in it. "Milo is your brother as much as Laylea is my daughter. Where you go, he'll go."

"I don't know about that."

"That's okay." Kat closed the kit. "I do. And he does. Come on, I've got something else for you."

CHAPTER 38

Corwin sat in the corner of the couch again. She wanted to fill her thoughts with music and crowd out everything else. Thanks to Kat Coogan's magic, she had a tool to help her with that. Kat had fixed her kalimba. It wasn't her harp, but she tried to make it suffice. She plucked out a song from a Noh drama that her Eastern Instruments professor had loved. It was enough of a challenge to distract her from her father's second death, but not quite enough to distract her from what might be going on down in the secret room below her.

Kat had run down to the basement to see if Sita was ready to talk. The basement Corwin hadn't even known was there. The basement that was only accessible by lifting a secret portion of the stairs going up to reveal the stairs leading down into darkness.

The woman who had stolen her. The woman who had cultivated her affection and devotion in an attempt to steal the Corwin family's lost power. The woman who had fought to join the Consortium because she was eager to help kill millions of people and reconfigure the world as a paradise for herself and the chosen few. She was down there.

Corwin did not want to know what the rebels had planned for her. And still, a traitorous part of her longed to go to her, to give Sita the chance to admit her errors and say she really loved Corwin. It offered little consolation that Corwin had enough self-control to stay on the couch.

A sour note twanged under her thumb.

Corwin had spent twenty years following the in-absentia decrees of a couple of people who weren't even her parents. She may as well have been enthralled to Sita like Daniel had been. Clark had suggested she might have been and Corwin had nodded like she agreed that was a possibility, but it wasn't. The fact that she could choose to stay here while that staircase doorway stood open proved that.

She was responsible for her own choices. All of them.

Corwin was wearing a floor-length sweater over form-fitting modern clothes. An old lady who lived in the neighborhood had sent a suitcase filled with clothes in her size. For the first time in her life, she had new shoes The faux-shearling lined boots left her room to wiggle her toes and didn't require an extra pair of socks or two. The clothes came with a piece of paper. One side of the paper listed what the clothes were called and the websites where she could buy them. The other side was filled edge to edge with a crayon masterpiece.

Corwin had always made do with the clothes in the house because it had felt right, like she was connecting with her ancestors and that would help her find the heart of Corwin House. But they weren't her ancestors. She was just a cuckoo bird, dressing up in other people's clothing.

The new clothes didn't feel like hers. She would have chosen different colors. She grimaced. She would have chosen black. Maybe it was good that Ms. Rucker had chosen for her. Thanks to her list, she could always go to the websites and choose different colors. Or black. She could choose.

She shivered. The rain had slowed to a drizzle and the sun had gone down. Kat kept a fire going when she was home, like a proper witch, but Corwin had chosen the couch facing the archway, where she could see the stairs. She pulled a blanket off the back of the couch. A pair of sweatpants fell into her lap. She tossed them back onto the couch facing the fireplace. There were pants hidden all over the place so Bayard could dress when he shifted. And he shifted a lot. He preferred being a dog, but he also had a lot to say.

Milo had family. In addition to Bayard and Josh, they had another brother who was still missing—Rhemy—and their sister, Laylea, who lived in a bar in Chicago for her safety. Milo's father was an evil bastard whose experimentation on Milo and his siblings was the reason their mama had hidden them.

He had a Mama, a real, true mother who loved him.

Corwin had nothing. Not even her name. She slapped the double board of her kalimba, playing all the notes at once. The sound heralded the arrival of a low figure pushing through the dog flap in the front door. Corwin sat up as a wolf trotted in and shook the rain from its fur. It loped over to the water bowl kept in the corner of the dining room.

Laughter floated out of the kitchen.

The wolf looked that way and sniffed. It padded over to the open stairs and perked up its ears. Then it looked at Corwin. Corwin reached for her penny whistle. She pulled it out of her sweater pocket. There were any number of charms she could conjure to protect herself. Although, if the wolf had gotten past Kat Coogan's wards, it must be welcome.

Its yellow eyes examined Corwin and its fat tail raised and floated back and forth in a gentle wag. Most of its fur would have fit in perfectly with Corwin's wardrobe. It was black and gray and matted with age. But its legs and the end of its tail popped with brown. A stripe of dark gray rose from its black nose up between its eyes, ending in a shape almost like an oval gem. Lighter gray along its brows accented this third eye marking. It gave the wolf a look of power and wisdom. Or perhaps it was age that gave it the look.

The wolf approached Corwin carefully. Its hips were stiff and it held its head carefully. Its yellow eyes stayed on Corwin, but it turned its head a bit as if to make its approach appear less aggressive. It worked.

Corwin forgot about her penny whistle. She forgot to be scared. She turned her head to the side to signal her own lack of aggression and the wolf blew air through its teeth in appreciation. It circled the coffee table to sit in front of Corwin. She offered her hand. The wolf sniffed it politely then shook again. Droplets of water rained on the coffee table and rug. It blew air through its nose in a way that gave Corwin the distinct impression she was being asked to explain herself.

"I'm Corwin." That didn't clear up why she was in this magically warded house, so she added, "I'm friends with Milo."

The wolf's shoulders lifted and its tail slapped the rug. It stood then and bumped its head against Corwin's knees before sitting again. Voices rose in the kitchen. The wolf looked over and then back and tilted its head at Corwin.

"I'm not in there," Corwin looked over and ducked her head, "because I'm not used to so many people."

The wolf blew air between its teeth. It seemed to be an agreement.

Corwin felt tears welling up in her sinuses and she added, so the wolf wouldn't think she was anti-social by nature, "I just found out that I'm an orphan. Or, well, that I was stolen, I guess." She paused. She'd searched so many times for her mother or father and failed. Or so it seemed. Was it possible the crystal had sent them to Richmond because her real mother was there?

Ooh, we should go back and see. Milo's mental voice preceded his tiny form launching over the couch arm and into her lap. The kitchen door flapped back and forth.

The wolf snapped a bark. Milo and Corwin both sat up. Milo tilted his head just as the wolf had been doing. *Who's that?* He looked up at Corwin.

She shrugged. "We just met."

The wolf pawed at Corwin's knee and pointed its snout at Milo.

"This is Milo."

The wolf clambered awkwardly up onto the couch and proceeded to examine Milo right there in Corwin's lap.

Cold nose! Cold nose!

The wolf's fur was cold, too. And still wet. When the wolf was satisfied with Milo, it gave Corwin a slightly less invasive examination, ending with a sigh and rolling to one side with its head on Corwin's leg.

That was weird. Milo stared at the big, wet head for a minute before he started licking rain drops from the wolf's ears. When the wolf didn't move, he started working more aggressively. *My sister lives in a bar. She used to live in an apartment with her human brother, but she did something bad.*

"Yeah," Corwin said aloud. "They said it's safer in the bar."

The world outside of Salem is strange.

Corwin nodded. Milo cleaned in silence for a while. Corwin snagged another blanket from the other end of the couch and arranged it over the wolf. She rubbed it on its fur to soak up the rain.

Bayard is really smart.

"So are you."

No, like he's really studied a lot. He fits in here.

Corwin laughed. She sent her thought to Milo without speaking it aloud. *Nobody here can remember what they ate for lunch. Even if they studied, they wouldn't remember it.*

Milo snorted. *I mean he's a fighter, just like them. He always was. He bit Walter's finger off once and then bit his nose, too. I remember that. They need him.*

"Are you happy for him?" Milo didn't sound happy. He sounded jealous and sad.

Yeah. He asked me to stay.

Corwin's heart fluttered. She brushed down the wolf's fur where Milo's licking had left it sticking up. "Would you like to stay?"

His answer was so quick, she knew he'd been expecting the question. *They don't have any instruments.*

She laughed. "I can build you anything you want."

Milo stopped cleaning the wolf and looked up at her. *Could you build an instrument that I could play, like that sideways harp we saw in the symphony hall?*

"You could play anything if you shift to human," she pointed out.

Milo tilted his head. His gaze went out of focus for a moment before he thought, *That felt weird.*

"You haven't tried it again?"

My brothers like shifting. I like being a dog. Can you build me an instrument?

It was a fabulous question. All the angst and self-doubt that had tensed up the muscles of Corwin's neck flitted into the aether, shoved out of her brain by the glorious idea of creating a new instrument.

Milo knew his scales. He could tap out basic melodies on the spinet if she held him up to the keys. She was sure he could pluck the harp strings if they were horizontal instead of vertical. She yearned to be home so they could build something.

You're already designing it, aren't you? Milo interrupted the pictures she was constructing in her head of how she could position strings around a sounding board for him.

"Bela?" Kat climbed out of the hidden stairwell. Her face brightened.

The wolf opened an eye and snuffled a reply.

Kat hurried over, sitting on the coffee table in front of the couch. "Bela, Josh found it."

The wolf, Bela, pushed itself up and leaned against Corwin. It pawed at Kat for her to go on.

Kat reached into a pocket and held up the old glass bottle that Milo's brother Josh had given her at the altar. Bela pawed at it and a choked sob started in its furry throat only to escape a moment later through human lips.

Where the wolf had leaned on her, now a woman did.

A scream escaped from Corwin, followed by a hysterical giggle as Milo leapt into the air.

CHAPTER 39

Feet pounded on the stairs to the basement and from the hallway. Kat yelled, "It's okay. It's okay. Bela just scared Corwin and Milo. We're okay."

The footsteps stopped and then retreated.

Corwin caught her breath. "I'm so sorry." She was horrified at herself. The ancient woman leaning on her wasn't dangerous. Certainly not more dangerous than the wolf that had just been lying on her. Bela, the human, looked like she might crumple into dust at any moment. And she looked cold, since the blanket had fallen off of her.

She's a good werewolf? Milo asked, his thoughts projecting images of the angry werewolves at the Montana Shifter Collective.

Corwin thought, *I think she literally couldn't hurt a fly.* Out loud, she asked, "Are you a good werewolf?"

"I don't know about that." Bela fixed the collar of her turtleneck sweater, which was twisted. "But, like other humans, werewolves can be kind or evil or lazy."

"Or deceptive," Kat added. Her voice was dry and she raised an eyebrow at the old woman.

Bela raised a hand to her heart and bowed her head to Kat. "I am sorry. I thought it necessary." She turned to take Milo and Corwin in her gaze. "And I am very sorry that I frightened you. You can call me Abuela."

A shiver wracked the old woman's body and Corwin hurried to pull the blanket up around her hunched shoulders. "It looked really painful when you shifted. Are you okay?"

The woman's crooked fingers looked more painful where they gripped Corwin's hand. "It has gotten worse in recent years. But it isn't that way for everyone. Just like not everyone gets to keep their clothes. It was more painful for me to see that charm." She tapped a gnarled finger against the bottle in Kat's hands. Her voice grew as tight as a bow string. "I am ashamed to admit I forgot about that necklace."

Corwin slipped a hand up to the ancient lady's bare neck and sent calm and peace into her with a quiet hum. Nobody should have noticed it. Kat and Abuela both looked over at her with gratitude written on their faces.

Then the werewolf patted Corwin's leg. "Life is meant to be felt. This sorrow is old. My cub tore the charm from my neck as his father tore him from my arms." Tears flowed unabated through the channels carved in her face. "I had to leave Cameron behind if I wanted to save my other cub. It was an impossible choice."

"Which infused the charm with more of your soul than it had before," Kat murmured.

"And it held a great deal of my soul before." Abuela reached over to caress Milo. "My best friend and I won the necklaces at the Topsfield Fair long before either of us even dreamed of being mothers."

Corwin felt Milo holding his breath. Whether he meant to or not, he was projecting an image to her. It was from one of the dreams she'd had on the road while they were searching for her mother. A woman held Milo close to her chest. He chewed at a half-heart charm while fat tears soaked his fur. He was too little to read it then, but the word on the charm was clear in his memory. It read "Friends."

"Was Rhea your best friend?" she blurted out.

Bela turned sad eyes filled with love on Corwin. It frightened her to be trusted with such painful honesty. Before she could shy away, the eyes turned down to Milo.

"Abuela means grandmother, though your mother told Josh that I was his godmother."

Corwin turned her head away, ashamed at how much it hurt to meet another one of Milo's growing family.

Milo felt a bit lost, too. He cuddled into her lap. *Why is the charm in that bottle?*

"It's a curse." Corwin twisted one of his long ears around her fingers and realized she hadn't brushed him since they'd escaped the Montana Collective. She looked up at Kat and Abuela. "Right? Someone put a curse on you."

Abuela nodded once. "My husband."

Kat asked, "How would you break the curse, Corwin?"

Corwin took in a deep breath. She shot Abuela an apologetic look as she answered, "You'll have to find the. . . the sounding board first, the totem it's connected with."

Kat looked confused, or at least uncertain of what Corwin meant.

Corwin took another deep breath. It was hard to talk about magic. Maybe it was easier for people who didn't learn it from books. "When you pluck a string, it'll let off a sound, right? But if you want other people to hear it, you really need a sounding board to increase the volume and depth of the note to send it in a certain direction. The way the magic in this bottle reaches out tells me it is connected to a. . . sounding board." Her mind took a detour from the practical to the theoretical and she followed. "You could spread a relatively weak curse or blessing by creating multiple complimentary or dissonant curse bottles like this one and connecting them all to a single totem acting as a sounding board. Does he have more bottles?"

She came out of her thinking place to see horror written across Kat's face.

Kat schooled her features and asked, "Let's say we don't know. How would you proceed?"

Corwin realized the witch was testing her. She sat up straighter and considered before answering, "Don't destroy the bottle, yet. It would stop stealing from you, but it wouldn't return anything the curse has taken. Also, the bottle will respond to the totem if they are brought near each other. Without the bottle, you wouldn't be able to identify the sounding board which must be destroyed to reverse the curse or curses. I couldn't say how to destroy it without seeing the totem first and how its magic interacts with the bottle."

"Very good." Kat nodded.

Corwin could hear a rattle in Abuela's chest as the woman asked, "How do we find the sounding board totem?"

Kat answered, "I'm not sure. But don't worry. We've got three witches on the case now. We'll figure it out."

"Three?" Corwin asked, wondering which of the many people she'd met was a witch.

"You, me, and Milo."

I'm a witch?

Corwin thought back to all their hours together in the lab and in the library. *Of course, you are.*

It made her feel a little less alone.

"I forgot!" Clark came jogging from the hall into the couch room holding up a driver's license and a couple other papers.

Kat hopped up from the coffee table and headed over to him. She didn't kiss him. It looked like she was going to, but she held off. "You got her ID?"

"Easy peasy. Rick was chuffed about making a fake ID with no fake information."

"Well," Corwin muttered, "the birthday isn't real."

Pick a different day, I'll call it my birthday, too.

Before she could respond to Milo, Clark announced, "You can officially sign any papers you need to. I got a social security card and birth certificate for you and a death certificate for your father. Would you like to take him home, now, Corwin?"

Milo whimpered and crawled from Corwin's lap to Abuela's. Corwin's heart shrank a little.

"You are welcome to stay." Jay spoke from the stairs. He reached over his head and pulled the up stairs down to hide the way to the basement and Sita. "We've got plenty of room."

Something relaxed in Corwin when the basement was cut off. And something jealous and joyful rose in her as the front door opened and Milo's brother Bayard tumbled in, pushed by the wind. He shook his jacket outside and tossed it onto the coat rack before lobbing an apple at Jay. "Catch. The OLR said you're hungry."

Jay snagged the apple before it hit him in the head. A wooden knife appeared in his hand as if it had always been there. He made several cuts in the apple and then speared the slices on the sharp tip of the knife and offered them to Bayard, who shook his head. The CF raised an eyebrow and pulled a face before eating the slices off the pale knife.

Something about the knife triggered a recent memory for Corwin. "Is that white ash?"

"Yeah." Jay swallowed and strolled over to the couch room archway. "You know how Clark can fly anything? I can make a weapon out of anything." Jay flipped the weapon in question and caught it by the blade. "The blade dulls quickly, but I can get the tip super sharp."

He raised it over his shoulder and flung it at the far wall. Everybody ducked. The knife vibrated where it stuck out of the wall. Chaos erupted with everyone yelling at Jay and Jay alternating between apologizing and laughing.

Corwin dragged her eyes from the white ash. She searched and found the curse bottle in Abuela's gnarled hands. "May I?"

Abuela nodded, taken away from the fight. Corwin lifted the bottle to the dim light coming in through the rising storm outside. A flash of lightning lit the room up and she could see the splinter of white ash floating in the bottle beside the *Friend* charm.

"That's the totem." Her words went unheard by all but Milo and the old woman. It was Abuela's gasp that grabbed everyone's attention.

Milo flashed her his memory of the scary man in the front office of the Montana Collective. *Grandpa*. Corwin nodded.

"What was that?" Clark asked.

Corwin turned away from all the eyes staring at her, waiting for her to speak. She gave the bottle back to Abuela. "There is a piece of white ash in the bottle."

Kat came over to look for herself.

Corwin said, "We met this creepy guy at the Collective who seemed too young to carry a cane."

Bayard murmured, "Grandpa Delcampo."

"Grandpa," Corwin repeated, looking at him. "Yes, they called him Grandpa. He carried a white ash cane that oozed black magic."

"His cane is the sounding board?" Abuela asked.

Corwin nodded. "I'd bet my triple harp on it."

Jay snorted. "I don't know if that means yes. Is this harp very important to you?"

Milo thought, *I don't know, are your balls important to you?*

Corwin blushed and covered her mouth with a hand. Bayard slid over the coffee table and leaned in too close to Corwin. He demanded, "What did Milo just say to you?"

Corwin pursed her lips and shook her head. She only answered, "Yes, the harp I built from scratch is very important to me."

Bayard started out skeptical and ended his question sounding impressed, "Wait, like, you bought all the pieces and strings and stuff and put it together, yourself?"

Milo blew air through his teeth in a scoff that was clear to everyone.

Corwin looked at her hands in his fur and let his pride encourage hers. "Like I found a downed tree, cured it, carved it, lacquered it." She wrinkled her nose. She should have done that outside. "I didn't hunt the deer. I got the gut for the strings from the butcher and the bone for the pins. I forged the levers from some old metal tools in our basement. And then, yes, I put it all together, myself."

Silence hung in the room so long, she finally looked up from Milo. Kat was the only one not staring at her in shock. The witch looked at the faces around her and started laughing. "I told you she was clever."

Abuela tapped her knee. "I would love to hear you play, mija."

Clark brought Corwin back down to Earth by handing her the papers and her ID. "Could I see your workshop when we take you home?"

"Sure." Corwin pushed herself up from the couch. "I'll get my things."

"Sit." Kat took a slice of apple from Jay and dropped into one of the comfy chairs facing the couch. "Nothing will be open. Let's go in the morning."

"You don't have to go with me," Corwin said.

"Yeah, I do." Kat crinkled up her face. "Bela is Milo's godmother.

She would do anything for him. I'm yours. So, ditto. And I've buried people in Salem, before."

Corwin sat. "Corwins don't bury their dead."

Kat caught her eye. "Coogans don't, either. It's a saying."

"Why don't you bury your dead?" Clark asked, squeezing himself into the same chair as Kat.

Kat leaned forward to let Clark put his arm around her, but he kept his hands to himself. She covered a sigh by saying, "We cremate our dead."

Jay laughed. "I thought they never burned witches in Salem."

Corwin murmured, "Only because they couldn't."

Kat said, "Our coven can't be burned while they're alive."

There was a moment of silence before Bayard exclaimed, "You burn your dead to be sure they're not still alive?!" He barely got the last word out before the world tilted around him and his clothes fell around his furry form.

"It can be hard to tell with a witch." Kat grinned a sly grin.

"How early can we leave tomorrow?" Corwin wanted to lay Daniel Corwin to rest. She wanted to lay that whole part of her life to rest and find a way to start over. She'd take the ID to take care of her father's and her mother's accounts. But then she had to find a birthdate. And a name. And a home that wasn't someone else's.

Clark said, "At first light. But I have a proposal for tonight." A grin as sly as Kat's revealed his dimples. "I happen to know Maggie left a guitar upstairs. I'll make a feast for dinner, if you'll give us a concert?"

"On a guitar?" Corwin didn't think the word concert applied.

Milo disagreed. He *pffd* at her and rolled his eyes.

"Her agent agrees!" Jay declared and led a parade to the kitchen. That was the end of the discussion.

Clark helped Kat from the chair. Bayard leapt onto Milo and wrestled him all the way through the swinging door. Corwin helped Abuela off the couch. The old woman's body was so bent, she barely came up to Corwin's chest.

She patted Corwin's hand and asked, "Would it bother you if I were the wolf again? She seems to be weathering the curse much better than I am."

"Not at all. I might just stay out here."

The woman laughed. "Oh, you can certainly try. But, mija, once Kat has declared you a part of the family, you don't really get a say in the matter."

Then she groaned through her shift and Corwin walked with her to Clark's feast, trying to forget that the woman she had thought was her family was trapped in the basement.

CHAPTER 40

"Again, I'm sorry for your loss, Ms. Corwin." The young lawyer didn't offer his hand. He stroked the thick file that he'd closed on many copies of her signature. "I promise we'll take good care of your funds. On a personal note, it means a lot to me that you're my first official client since I was made partner and given charge of the long-overdue Salem branch of Smythe, Touche, DeSantos, and Drakeson."

"Thank you for your help." Corwin stood.

Conner Drakeson stood as well. "I don't know if this is appropriate, but I wanted to tell you, my father helped your father set up the trust for you. Dad said his joy filled the office from first to last. Daniel's joy at being your father made my father step back from work and spend more time at home. It's why he never made partner. But that turned out to be a good thing. We lost him a few years ago."

"I'm sorry for your loss," Corwin said. She tried to think of what else to say but nothing came. Her head was too full.

Conner came around the desk and led her to the door. "He brought you with him, you know. You were an infant and he handed you to my father for a while. Dad said you were the brightest, happiest, most magical baby he'd ever seen." He offered his hand to her. "Dad wrote it in his grimoire."

Corwin looked into his eyes. She took his hand and sparks of sliver circled their grip with a hint of her lilac.

A broad grin crossed his face and he nodded before releasing her hand. "You do belong here, you know." He crossed back to his desk, murmuring, "I've always wanted to learn how to play guitar."

She knew he wanted to comfort her, but his words stabbed her, instead. She did not belong. She had never belonged in Salem. And knowing that Daniel Corwin had loved her only made it worse. She held her sadness deep inside, letting it churn into nausea in her gut rather than allowing any of it to show on her face.

Corwin left his office. She nodded politely to the receptionist, who offered an overly sympathetic head bob in return. Outside, she was surprised to see Morgan and a human-shaped Pundu sitting on a bench. The impundulu held yarn looped on her hands. She fed it to Morgan, who wove the yarn around an arrangement of sticks.

She kept working as she grinned up at Corwin. "Hi."

"Hi." Corwin examined Pundu. "Hi."

The bird in human form opened her mouth and cawed.

"She's good," Morgan said, taking the last of the yarn from her familiar and knotting it off. "Thanks for healing her wing. And coming home. I'm sorry about your dad."

"Thanks. He wasn't really my dad." Corwin saw questions and arguments in Morgan's face. She cut them off. "Are you okay?"

Morgan hopped up from the bench. "Yeah. Your mom hit us pretty hard. I knew I was safe in my room, but it felt like I was gonna die."

"I'm sorry." Corwin looked at her boots.

"Not your fault. I was more worried about Pundu. She's so brave." Morgan grinned at her familiar.

Pundu nodded, a self-satisfied expression on her masculine face.

Morgan turned to Corwin. "I lost connection when Milo did whatever he did. Where is Milo?"

Corwin started walking toward home. "He found his family. He's living with his brother in Oregon."

Morgan walked beside her. "Oh."

"And I'm not really home. I'm not a Corwin. They never even adopted me, so it's not right for me to stay in the house." She watched the toes of her boots as she walked, like she had when she was a kid.

Pundu ran off the sidewalk to kick a pile of leaves in the gutter. Morgan followed and kicked her feet high in the air, scattering colorful, crisp leaves everywhere. Corwin caught one on her boot and sang it back into the air. Morgan put a hand out and Corwin released the maple leaf on her palm. Morgan ran glittering green magic over it with her other hand and the leaf disintegrated, the pieces floating on the wind to land all over the town.

"Who will take care of Corwin House if you go away?" Morgan asked as Pundu raced ahead to ring the old ship's bell outside the Music Shoppe.

Corwin shrugged. She didn't have an answer. She stopped for a moment when she glanced in the Music Shoppe windows. Jack Jaga sat on a stool with one foot propped up. He was playing a classical piece. It was slow and his tempo was uneven, but his pressure on the neck was just right and the notes rang clear. He had been practicing.

He looked up and she ducked away from the window.

She would miss Salem. She knew everybody here and, unlike some, she liked the tourists. After only a short time on the road, she'd learned how very much she preferred having the outside world visit her to visiting the outside world.

Corwin House was a problem. She couldn't sell it. Aside from not really owning it, it would feel like a betrayal. The house was more than just her home, even if it wasn't her home anymore.

"Where would you go?" Morgan asked as they turned down a street that took them out of downtown. Pundu ran ahead and ducked between a row of trees and a house. A moment later, the beautiful bird hopped out and leaped into the sky. She soared overhead and then wandered down in lazy spirals.

Corwin shrugged again. "I think my birth parents are in Richmond. I might go look for them." She'd been wondering about that and thinking of scrying for them and Milo's Mama. Goddess knew there was enough of his fur in the house to use.

The sidewalk tilted. A need so fierce it tore her breath away tilted

Corwin's entire world. The cry was distant, yet it echoed inside her head at the same time. Morgan grabbed her arm to keep her from falling. The impundulu beat fresh air down on them.

Corwin gasped. "Did you. . . do you hear that?"

The cry came again, more focused this time. The voice in her head was too panicked for words. It was. . . Milo was sending her the chord changes from *Fright of Spring*. He hated that score. He'd always bury his head and cover his ears with his paws when she played it. Corwin let go of herself, trusting Morgan to keep her from falling. She opened her mind and her soul, her whole being, to Milo and saw through his eyes.

Rain poured down, pelting the rose bushes of the Foothills cul-de-sac. The world swam in the rain and she saw CF darting from the houses as her view bounced, scanning the whole neighborhood. A deep brown wash clouded her vision, as did the intense pain on her hackles. Her hackles were there for her mama to drag her to safety, to lift her to warm milk and away from tussling brothers. Her hackles weren't supposed to be gripped with knife-sharp nails digging into her flesh, tearing skin from muscle. Where was Corwin? She tucked her tail up and her ears back at the sight of weapons raised in nearly every CF hand. They closed in fast. Then she felt a cold, sharp edge settle on the front of her neck and yelped. She smelled her own blood.

Jay Doe, the only one approaching with no weapon, stopped in his tracks. He held his hands up as if in surrender. "Sita, don't."

"Touch me and he dies," Sita screamed.

The vision faded, but Milo's panicked *Fright of Spring* crescendoed over a memory Corwin had tucked away more carefully than the Corwin House curse had been hidden. She heard that voice, her mother's voice, so she'd been told, screaming those same words to Kat Coogan.

Corwin huddled behind the fire grate, protected from the splintered table and other detritus from the fight. Her mother was bloody, almost as bloody as the witch who had pushed her way into their home. Corwin wailed, scared for her mother. Then her mother was there, beside her, holding her close, and Corwin felt safe again.

The stranger, Kat Coogan, froze. Gold glittered prettily from her fingers, held still in the air. Her voice was distorted by missing teeth and a broken jaw, as well as the bruises around her neck. "Sita, don't."

Hearing it from the future, grown-up Corwin recognized Kat's vocal distortion as fear. She didn't want to remember anything more. And yet, the memory played on.

The grate stood in front of them, protecting Corwin and her mother from the witch. But the fire behind them licked at Corwin's back. It was very warm. She clung to her mother as Sita lifted her off her feet. The vibrations of her soothing voice cuddled Corwin and calmed her. "Touch me," her mother murmured, "and she dies."

Kat Coogan shook her head. "You wouldn't. She's a baby."

"You can stop me or save her. Which do you choose, godmother?"

Sita moved quickly. Corwin was lifted. She thought her mother was going to kiss her and hold her to her shoulder, letting Corwin bury her face in the precious mane of hair that sparked about her head in tangles. Instead, Corwin, dressed in her llamacorn shirt and fish-scale leggings, flew into the flames. As her body hit the burning stones, her left hand pressed into a glowing blue pentagram set in a triangle of sandstone. She screamed, her skin and clothes burning even as the fire died around her.

From there in the dying flames, grasping her bubbling palm to her chest, Corwin watched as Kat Coogan pulled her mother over the fire grate with magic alone. Then the pretty golden sparkles sputtered out and her mother fell to her knees. Kat grabbed the rod-backed chair that had sat by the kitchen door for centuries and tried to drag herself to her feet. She couldn't do it and collapsed to the floor. Sita snagged a knife that had been standing with the blade buried in the pantry door. She dove for Kat's back.

The broken stranger witch lay still, making no move to block the blow. Before Sita reached her, the ancient chair flung itself into the air and smashed Corwin's mother to the floor of the kitchen. Knives sucked themselves out of the cabinets and walls they'd been thrown into and flew to surround Sita in a circle, stabbing into the floor around her and the shattered chair.

Corwin screamed for her mother. But her mother didn't move. Instead, Kat Coogan twitched and then rolled over and dragged her broken body around Corwin's trapped mother. The fear in her eyes faded to golden relief as she peered through the iron grating that would not let her get closer to Corwin.

Breathing as though she'd forgotten how, the witch held onto the grate to keep from falling over. "You're okay?"

Corwin didn't respond. She wrapped her arms around her legs and cuddled back against the hearthstones, as far as she could get from Kat Coogan.

A trickle of blood threatened to drip into Kat's eye. She brushed it away and turned to release the last of her golden magic over Corwin's mother. "Go, Sita Corwin. You are banished from Salem."

Then the witch stood and struggled to the kitchen door where she turned back, her eyes hard. "Don't ever touch her again." Kat choked. She coughed up bloody phlegm, catching it in a fold of her shirt. Her grim smile, under eyes glowing with gold, frightened Corwin. But Kat kept her eyes on Sita as she coughed a bitter, bloody laugh. "I don't think Corwin House likes you very much."

The memory flooded back and away in the space of a breath. Milo's song, Milo's cry, Milo's need remained. Corwin took a breath, figured out gravity, and held on to Morgan's arms. She looked into her friend's green eyes and cried, "Milo needs me."

And then she ran. She ran through the streets of Salem to her yard. She ran up the walk and leapt over the cement doorstep, through the door as it opened for her. She ran through the front room into the kitchen. She and Milo had tamped the fire down to cold ashes before they left. Now, a fire burned fiercely against the cold stones. The grate slid aside for her and Corwin ran into the fire.

She ran through the Corwin House hearth and out of the Hillen's hearth into Kat Coogan's Foothills lab. She tripped with the surprise but caught herself and skirted around the worktable. She stumbled out of the linen closet but found her pace again and barreled out the front door to the porch. The CF in the cul-de-sac stood as if in tableau with Corwin's mother at the center, dangling Milo from his hackles and holding a knife to her best friend's throat.

CHAPTER 41

Corwin didn't stop. She kept running, down the stairs, through the CF, past Jay Doe and Hardknock. She stopped only when Sita shook Milo.

Corwin screamed from her soul, "Let him go."

Her mother laughed. She sounded as insane as her father had right before he left. Her face was sunken in and wrinkles weighed down the folds of her eyes. Her lush lips had withered and cracked and she was squinting as if she couldn't see so very well. Her fancy, expensive clothes draped limply off her boney limbs. Worst of all, her hair hung brittle and thin and gray. No glorious white locks like Pops Coogan's long hair, Sita's hair was ready to fall out.

Corwin cried, "Let him go, or…"

"Or what?" Sita asked. "Or what, little nothing? You gave all of your magic to the dog. You have nothing left."

"I have the dog."

"No, dear. *I* have the dog."

"You were my mother. I don't want to hurt you."

"I am your mother. I fed you from these breasts, nourished you with all the magic you so carelessly threw to your familiar. Where's the loyalty?"

"Loyalty? You left me."

"My daughter," Sita crooned. "I left so that Kat Coogan wouldn't kill you."

"You left so Corwin House wouldn't kill you. And you tried to kill me before you left."

"You're confused, Daniella. You were just a baby."

"Yes. I was. Just a baby that you threw into the fire."

Milo howled. He yelled into Corwin's mind, giving her a focus and a plan and distracting her from the pain of her mother's lies.

Sita shrugged, giving up trying to worm her way back into Corwin's heart. "It appears you survived just fine."

Corwin breathed. She breathed down the anger rising up her spine and breathed back the tears impeding her vision. She listened to *The Rite of Spring* and calmed her personal chaos. The CF couldn't hear Milo's plan and they moved in closer. Sita shook the dog.

Corwin spoke in a voice that should have frozen her mother in place. "Don't hurt him."

"He holds my magic." She shook him again. "I will get it back. I will get the magic you were supposed to give to me."

Corwin's heart skipped a beat as a few puzzling facts fell into place, "You were never a prisoner of the Consortium. You made my father lure me to you after. . ." Her eyes fell to the wampum belt nearly buried in Milo's fur. "After I broke the curse. You wanted the lost Corwin power. That was why you enthralled my father. That's why you supplied him with a child. Was I supposed to grow up and break the curse just so you could drain me?"

The false shock and offense on Sita's face denied the accusation and then Sita settled into an honest smile. She gazed at Corwin. "Yes."

"Why?"

"It's why we have children, to take their energy, their power. If you were truly worthy, you would have given me all that I wanted. That's what family does. Instead, you wasted it on your familiar, who will have to suffer a little to give it to me."

"He's not my familiar."

"This mutt is what, then, your pet?" she scoffed.

"No, Sita. He's my friend." Corwin wanted to give her another chance. She wanted her mother to hand Milo over and apologize and—

You want her to be someone else.

Corwin nodded. She picked a note out of the symphony in their minds and offered it. Milo didn't nod. He didn't dare, with the knife at his throat and the claws in his fur. He yelped in sympathy for the pain in Corwin's heart and then howled out the note she'd given him. Corwin sucked in a breath made rich from the trees' oxygen and sang out a dissonance that set her hair on end. She focused her tone with Milo's, focused the violent harmonics at her mother's hands, and on Milo's cue, they both pushed.

Sita screamed. Her voice didn't quite cover the sound of all the bones in her hands breaking. Milo and the knife fell, as Newton predicted, at the same speed. The knife landed in a rain puddle. Milo landed on his feet and barreled over to leap into Corwin's arms. Spots of blood trailed him.

The creature that had pretended to be her mother cackled. Holding her broken hands limply against her stomach, she doubled over, laughing. When the CF started moving in again, she stood straight, her face wiped of amusement. "Be careful." She turned her hands over to show a deep cut bleeding on one palm.

Corwin looked closely. The blood was glittering with speckles of blue. The blue reached for Milo. "What have you done?"

"I am worthy. I used what came to me." She smiled at someone beyond Corwin. "Thank you for the Orangina, Jay. It really hit the spot."

Jay looked confused for a moment and then said, "You heard us talking about the curse bottle."

Footsteps pounded on the pavement. Corwin glanced over to see Milo's brother Bayard running away.

"I did," Sita confirmed. "Thanks for the idea. I haven't made one of those in ages. All you need is something personal from the subject, like fur, and something personal to connect it to the recipient, like blood." She lifted her hands with a grimace and licked at the wound on her palm. "If you do anything to me, the dog will feel it."

Jay said the bit she hadn't said out loud. "And no matter what we do to you, you'll drain Milo's magic."

Sita laughed quietly. "You shouldn't talk so much in front of prisoners." Her smile dropped. "Back off. I'm going to leave now."

The CF backed away. But that was okay. They were never going to defeat Sita with brute force. It was always going to come down to magic. Sita thought Corwin had given all of her powers to Milo, and that was why he'd been able to shift and steal everyone else's.

Not everyone's. Just from the people with bad karma, Milo corrected.

I thought my blood sacrifice would transfer my power to you, she thought, questions swirling around the statement.

I don't like blood magic. Milo looked up at her, the blood staining his chest adding weight to his declaration.

Never again, she promised. *She believes you stole her magic. But if she has no magic, how did she create a curse jar?*

Magic is available to anyone. It can't be taken. He overran his own thought with another, *But she believes it can.*

She has no idea what she's doing, does she?

She should have hit the books more, Milo crowed, and then fear dominated his voice as he asked, *did she really curse me?*

I can see your energy in her blood.

That means yes? Milo asked.

It means that she successfully connected you to her. And her to you.

Corwin started walking toward Sita, who was backing away towards the entrance to the cul-de-sac. "You're bluffing," she said. "You can't have cursed him. You have no powers."

Doubt flickered in Sita's eyes before she covered it with a sneer, asking, "You believe magic isn't genetic, right? It's in the air for anyone who knows how to use it."

Corwin kept moving forward as she answered the woman who wasn't her mother. "But you don't know how. You never had to learn how to pull magic from the elements because you were born to it."

Milo wriggled in her arms. Corwin set him down. She walked with him, Sita retreating more quickly now. "We know how, though."

Milo trotted over to a little pool of water. He sat and then rolled in the puddle, soaking his fur.

"Magic isn't just in the air. It's in all the elements, like water."

Sita reached for her neck with one broken hand. Something gurgled in her chest. Milo hopped out of the puddle and Sita coughed up water. Her steps grew more unsteady.

"You connected with Milo's fur. Fur that had fallen off or been torn off anyway. It's not all that personal because he just grows more. And then sheds again, all over the house."

Getting a little off topic. Milo shook, sending droplets flying. He trotted over to the nearest lawn and dug into the dirt beneath a rosebush.

"Specifically, despite any intention you may have made, you connected his fur to your blood and it works both ways."

TMI! Milo shouted in her head as she thought the same thing.

Sita fell at the foot of the young trees standing sentinel over the entrance to the cul-de-sac. Her skin turned a shade darker and duller. She struggled to say, "Which means my magic worked. I have power."

The fingers on one hand straightened and she slashed at her own arm with sharp nails. Blood welled up along three superficial gashes. Sita swiped at the blood and then held her hand out. She spat one word, "Ignitus," and flame danced on her fingers.

Flame erupted on Milo at the same moment. He howled.

Corwin screamed. Without thinking, she threw her left hand out, palm open towards Milo. A coruscating white and purple glow shot out at him, quenching the glittering red flames.

Her mother shouted again, "Ignitus."

Milo's fur ignited.

Corwin ran at her mother with no rational thought in her brain. She'd gone two steps when a shadow flew overhead. It looked like a squat bottle of Orangina.

"Jay! Hit it!" Bayard's voice cut through the fog of fear and anger and then the tiniest of *plinks* vibrated her eardrums with an impossible glittering effect. Orange water rained on Sita. The flames on her fingertips were quenched by the liquid, but her flesh burned hotter, glittering red before it sluffed off. Cold-burning tumors opened wherever the orange liquid or golden fur landed on her. Blood dripped from the wounds, but more and more, it was dirt falling away with the ash that was her skin, her clothes, her precious hair.

Corwin fell to her knees on the street only feet away from the woman she'd called Mother, unable to tear her eyes away, unwilling to do anything to save her. She whispered to Milo, *this isn't you, is it?*

No. He pushed under her arm and leaned against Corwin's legs. She felt magic glittering through him as she buried her fingers in his cool fur. He asked her, *What color is the magic?*

Another dog, Bayard, sat himself on Milo's other side, only his tail touching Corwin's hand. The CF closed in, blocking the exit to the cul-de-sac, or maybe blocking anybody from coming in. Hardknock stood beside her and then crouched, just barely within arm's reach. Jay Doe sat and ran a hand through Bayard's fur, murmuring some reassurance.

"It's red," Corwin breathed through a sob. She didn't stop the tears that poured down her face as she lifted Milo into her arms. The magic eating away at the sad witch glittered red. Sita was dying from her own curse. It was right. Great-great-grandaunt Judith would say it was just. Sita had been offered love and she rejected it in favor of power.

They stayed like that until the curse had eaten away every organic bit that had been Sita Corwin. Then they stayed as the red remnants were soaked up by the dirt and the grass and washed down to the roots of the trees. The CF stayed with Corwin on the cold cement as she watched that tree transform the poisonous magic as it transformed carbon dioxide. She couldn't see what the tree transformed it into, but it felt good. It felt just.

Corwin kept Milo in her arms as she got up. She wasn't ready to let go of him yet. The others stood with her.

I like it here, he said.

You want to stay in Foothills? she asked.

No, doofus. He dropped his chin in a doggy laugh as his mental voice shook with amusement. *I like it here in your arms.*

Oh. She blushed and muted her smile as she turned to face Jay and Bayard.

Jay gestured towards Milo as if offering to take him. "Should we go treat your burns, Milo?"

Milo rested his muzzle against Corwin's neck. *Pff. Like I can't sing myself through fire.*

"He's good." She rubbed her cheek against his warm, soft, living head. "I think we'd like to go home now."

CHAPTER 42

After a feast, which Jay apologized for not being as gourmet as Clark would have provided, Corwin and Milo tried, individually and together, to get home to Corwin House through Kat's lab hearth. It didn't work. Instead, they made arrangements with Hardknock to drive back to Salem in his van.

Jay sent Milo off to the dog bed in the living room that was there to remind the universe that this was Laylea's home, no matter how far away she was. When Corwin headed for the couch, where she'd slept the night before, Jay led her upstairs to a room that featured two bunkbeds.

"The room is all yours for the night. We thought you might like the privacy." He opened a fresh toothbrush for her from under the sink and gave her clean sweatpants and a Foothills High t-shirt from the hall closet. He gestured to the guitar laying on one of the top bunks. "Maggie said you blessed it yesterday and now it's yours. She's not usually concerned with others, so it's kind of a big deal."

Corwin smiled and said thank you. She brushed her teeth and changed her clothes and sat on the floor with the guitar. Her fingers strummed an E chord. She twisted the pegs until the guitar was in tune. Then she struck a chord that set her teeth on edge. *Rite of Spring.*

She set the guitar aside and headed downstairs. She met Milo on the landing, took the bed from his teeth, and carried it the rest of the way up for him. She set it beside her chosen bunk and recovered the guitar. Corwin played for him. She ran through basic pedagogy, showing him what she did to create different notes. They chatted about chord changes and the Circle of Fifths and how it all wove in with magic for them but not for everyone.

Her fingers plucked the lullaby she'd heard over and over in her dreams. Milo sang the Mandarin lyrics in her head. He told her it was one of the songs that his Mama sang in the car while they were driving to Salem from New Orleans, just the two of them.

And when Corwin climbed into bed at last, she lifted Milo up and fluffed up a corner of the comforter for him. She spent a long time lying awake, feeling his warm, wet breath on her arm and wondering what they were going to do next.

In the morning, they got a hearty sendoff from the CFs and Old Lady Rucker. Hardknock grumbled at the edge of the crowd and Corwin was grateful when he insisted they had to get on the road. Traveling with Hardknock was much like traveling alone had been, except they had a place to sleep each night and never had to talk to strangers. Not that there was anyone stranger than this scarred old CF. Sometimes, Milo and Corwin agreed, when Hardknock was on the phone, strangers talked through him. They also agreed to never bother Hardknock when he was being someone else. Corwin didn't have a driver's license and Milo didn't have the height to drive. So, they let Hardknock's other personalities be.

They arrived in Salem around noon on the last day of Mabon. Hardknock drove them directly to the cemetery east of the animal shelter. He had been communicating with Kat through their tappers. Corwin had left their clasp tappers in her luggage, which was sitting in the front room of Corwin House. Kat had continued with the funeral arrangements and Daniel's service was to be held as soon as they arrived in Salem.

Hardknock had to slow as they turned onto Hobbomock Street. People swarmed the area, singing and dancing to a street band using antique and unusual instruments. Hardknock was directed to pull into the parking lot behind the animal shelter and, as they pulled by, Corwin saw locals dressed in old-timey clothes dancing in a circle around the White Oak. Children ran through the leaves, tossing them in the air and diving into piles raked by adults.

"Hi. I don't think you've been to a Salem funeral before, have you, Corwin?" Kat, wearing Sher's blond hair and brown eyes, opened the passenger door before Hardknock had put the van in park.

She shook her head and handed Milo off.

Kat set him down and unclipped his leash. "You don't need this today. No cop is going to interfere with a coven celebration."

Clark stepped up and offered Corwin a hand to help her down from the van. "I love that Daniel Corwin reintroduced local flora around town. The cemetery is beautiful. So is your yard. Jack Jaga says the deer came back because of your dad."

"Thanks." Corwin looked around at the revelers. "I didn't know that he did that."

"It was his Eagle Scout project," Kat said. She pulled Corwin close as she led the way over to the cemetery. "Nobody knows you weren't born to him and they believe he died of a stroke."

"Morgan knows," Corwin said.

"Morgan also knows that I've been around. She's a good one with secrets." Kat slowed as they approached an altar draped with brown and purple bunting. The altar featured two thick white candles with years of melt dripping down their sides. Between them sat a bronze urn.

Corwin grasped at Kat's arm and looked around their feet. Milo trotted between their legs to where she could see him. *I'm here. Look! Look up, over the water.*

Off in the clouds, a majestic bird with red feathers on her crown soared into the lowering sun. Her feathers glinted with all the colors of sunset. Corwin felt her breath come easier. But still, she whispered to Kat, "Do I have to say anything?"

"No."

She took a moment and looked around at the people gathering close. The butcher, Kali, and his family. Jack Jaga, playing a guitar with a tambourine strapped to its side. Kit Carrier came arm in arm with the owner of The Bookcellar amidst a gaggle of kids weaving around them with noisemakers. Naomi brought up the rear, playing a kazoo with Queen Katerina la Grosse trotting circles around her.

Kat said, "Back when witches were killed by people like your great-great-great-grandfather Jonathan and my super-not-great-uncle William, they tried to make us grateful for their deaths. We refused. We are grateful for every witch's life. We celebrate your father. For today, at least, all is forgiven and we join our magics together in joy that he was one of us."

"But he wasn't, really," Corwin said. "He rejected the covens and the whole community."

"Really?" Kat asked. "Then why didn't he move away when his parents died?"

"Hi." Morgan scooped Milo up and pulled a pair of mittens from her coat pocket. "Pundu wanted you to have these, just for today. She'll want them back when you don't need them."

It was cold. Corwin had forgotten how cold it could get near the waterfront. It felt like Kat was ready to let Corwin stand aside for as long as she wanted, but Morgan lifted a violin to her chin and pushed Corwin forward. She played a cheery ditty that was more fit to a fiddle, wrapping it up with a flourish as Corwin reached the altar.

"Daniel Corwin," Morgan began as people continued to gather. "Daniel Corwin tossed anonymous packets of herbs and leaves and bark over our back hedge when my dad got too sick to forage for us. Never took credit. And mom said we made sure never to catch him."

"Daniel Corwin," Betsy Chever, the neighbor who really hated deer, yelled from the far side of the altar, "made us a potion when our David seemed done for. He perked right up and was an even better mouser after that."

"Daniel Corwin occasionally over-tipped," a faceless voice yelled from the middle of the crowd.

"Daniel Corwin never met a plant he couldn't save."

"Daniel Corwin kept to himself, like many of you should." Old Mrs. Wenger set an orange-and-red maple leaf on the altar and retreated to the edges.

The compliments and memories kept coming. Corwin let it wash over her. It helped to have Milo in her head and Kat and Morgan on either side. She laughed and she learned about the man who'd never told her anything about himself. When the words from the crowd slowed, Pops Coogan stepped up to stand at the altar. Everyone hushed except for a bagpiper far off in the distance who might have been playing over someone else's grave.

"Daniel Corwin was a wizard. His greatest desire in life was to break the curse rightly set upon his family by his family so many generations ago. He went to his rest or his next life knowing that his beloved daughter succeeded."

There was a murmuring through the crowd and a shuffling as people she'd known all her life angled to get a better look at Corwin. She kept her eyes on the urn.

"Daniella Corwin, light of your father's life, we welcome your father's urn into the coven's crypt as the first Corwin to return to us whole and unencumbered by the sins of your forebears. We welcome you, as well. Tonight is the last night of Mabon, a time for honoring the gifts we work for and the gifts we are given. Five years ago, Daniella conquered her Samhain test—"

"It's Corwin," Kat whispered.

Pops' pupils widened as he looked over at his daughter. Corwin realized Kat wasn't wearing her blond glamour anymore. Then Pops was asking her, a twist in his voice, "Still?"

Corwin nodded.

He inclined his head to her. His gaze flashed to his daughter, but when he spoke to the crowd again, his voice had none of the emotion that flooded his eyes. "Corwin conquered her Samhain test with such Skill that she changed the town. Witness the tree her father didn't live to love." He gestured to the great White Oak across the street and the crowd turned as one to watch lights sparkling in the breeze all the way from the exposed roots to the thinnest branches a mile up.

"We should have celebrated Wizard Corwin's gifts then. But we didn't." He sighed gustily. "Now, she has given us the gift of lifting the curse and bringing House Corwin back into the fold. So, tonight!" He grew bigger, his cloak wafting in a breeze that sparkled with all colors of magic. "Tonight, we celebrate the life of our absent friend by welcoming his brilliant daughter into our coven! Let all witches be welcome! So Mote it Be!"

A cheer went up with fireworks of a very Salem nature. The doors of the crypt flung open wide behind Pops. People streamed past the altar, leaving leaves in all the colors of a New England fall around her father's urn. A dozen went through the doors and then a dozen more. They couldn't fit. The crypt wasn't nearly big enough, and yet they continued streaming in until only the Coogan clan remained, waiting at the entrance.

Morgan's grandmother, a proud woman with wild gray hair, piped a trill on a carved fife that could have been the twin to the one in the Corwin House library. She didn't speak, merely raised her eyebrows at her long-lost daughter.

Kat answered, "Save me a candy apple."

Her mother's aura gleamed though her lips barely formed a smile. She turned and herded everyone inside. The cacophony of their voices and noisemakers and instruments faded into distant echoes.

And then the cemetery was empty but for Pops, Corwin, the crew glued to her sides, and the distant bagpiper. She felt Kat tensing up as Pops stepped around the altar to join them. He looked at his long-lost daughter and took a breath.

Corwin cut him off. "Why the leaves?"

He looked to her and his face morphed. It softened and a parade of thoughts crossed through his eyes before he answered, "For most people, we would dress the altar with flowers. Your father would not have wanted flowers to be killed for him. The leaves were Jack Jaga's idea. He's of the mind that the entire forest was your father's familiar."

Corwin smiled. She wished she could have told her father about her connection with the trees and their world. She turned to Kat. "Thank you for arranging all this. What do I do with his ashes now?" She crossed to the altar and rested a hand on the urn.

"The urn goes onto the shelves in the crypt, like Pops said." Kat's voice turned sheepish. It was strange to hear from her. "Hi, Dad."

Pops wrapped his arms around her. "You are welcome home." He kissed her head and turned away so only Corwin saw the tears he blinked away.

She smiled at him. "There's no shame in crying."

Pops inclined his head to her and let his tears roll down his face as he squeezed Kat tighter before letting her go.

"Your father's ashes and the offerings from the trees he loved so well will rest in a spot of your choosing." Pops swirled his hand over the altar. The lid of the urn lifted away to the side as the leaves left by all the witches in town swirled in a sudden, unnatural gust and inserted themselves in the urn. "Go on. Take it."

The others hustled over as Pops headed into the crypt. Corwin picked the lid out of the air and replaced it on the urn over the ashes and leaves. She followed everyone inside the crypt.

It was empty. None of the hundred people who had crossed the threshold stood inside. She turned to ask Pops where they were, but he strode past her to the entrance. At the doors, he danced his hands in a fancy gesture that shrank the altar until it blinked into nothing. He stepped back. Another flair and the bronze gates of the crypt squeaked on their hinges and slammed shut.

With the evening light gone, Corwin saw that she and Pops were surrounded by magic, glittering in every color imaginable.

CHAPTER 43

"Come on!" Morgan danced past Corwin, carrying Milo away with her to the far end of the small crypt. Magic swirled in her wake.

The sparkles clung to Pops as he hurried past Corwin, an arm around Kat's shoulders as though he planned to never let her go again. The magic whirled like a wind blowing through as they stepped behind a statue of some old guy in a funny hat. Clark followed close on their heels with Morgan's encouragement. His laugh echoed back to them as the magic curled around his shoulders and pulled him behind the statue.

Morgan danced and spun toward the statue, grinning back at Corwin. Milo barked, *Not without Corwin!*

Corwin hurried over as Morgan stepped backwards and disappeared with Milo behind the statue. Milo's happy howl echoed off the walls. But, when Corwin reached the statue, she saw there was no space behind it. It butted up against the back wall of the crypt. She looked back at the closed doors and was blinded by glittering magic soaring toward her like a tidal wave. She took a breath and let it wash her through the statue of the old guy in a funny hat.

There, surrounded by stone that was more marble than slate, she found herself on the top step of a grand staircase curving down. The magic flowed past her, flitting around torches that burned along the walls like fireflies in the White Oak. A distant bass line echoed off the stone, calling Corwin to come closer, to hear it better. She hurried down the steps, turning widdershins once, twice the other way, Corwin could never remember the word for it.

Deosil, Milo supplied. His thought sparkled with laughter and she moved faster to catch up to him.

The second deosil turning led to a glorious set of doors carved from knotty alder wood. Kat and Pops stood before it, the only other people on the stairs. The door opened just as Corwin caught up to them. The scene beyond stopped her heart. It was a ball from a fairy story. The great hall went on forever. Roots twined along the walls and occasionally down through the center of the room like massive pillars. Spinning balls of light danced overhead, though when her gaze was drawn to them, Corwin saw that overhead wasn't the same for everyone. Stairs led up and down from the ceilings where witches in fabulous outfits dripping with jewels and joy danced. Shelves lined the walls of the massive octagonal hall. The shelves held many urns like the one in her arms.

"Where does he go?" Corwin asked.

Pops gestured grandly at the whole room. "Anywhere you want."

Morgan approached them. She held a hand out to Corwin. "Come with me."

Milo danced around Morgan's heels, barking and baying. His tail wagged furiously, flipping up the hem of Morgan's dress as the girl led Corwin to one side of the party. Morgan had changed. The sensible winter outfit she had been wearing in the graveyard was gone. Now, her hair was spun up into a fancy ponytail, pinned with a glittering tiara. There was something glittery about her whole outfit, from the impossibly high heels woven from crystal to the turtlenecked, sleeveless gown that hugged her chest and hips before cascading into a skirt of feathers. Her face was painted for Carnival. She would have stunned them in Vegas.

"I didn't know you had a tattoo." Corwin wanted to touch the deep black rendering of an impundulu wrapping Morgan's soft shoulder.

"Oh," Morgan blushed. "A whole crew of us did them after we passed our Samhain tests."

"I like it." Corwin rubbed her fingers tentatively on the tail feathers. She felt the sudden breath Morgan sucked in.

"Ah, a new Corwin wizard come to show us all how it's to be, eh?" Marjorie Betterman stood beside a tri-fold standing mirror. She had been wearing a carpetbag coat and galoshes when she dropped her handful of crushed leaves on Daniel's altar. Now, she stood on blocky platform shoes popular with women who didn't need to walk anywhere in the 1600s. Her dress dipped to show a great deal of the bosom her brocade corset pushed up. A bustle supported what may have been a literal ton of fabric dripping down her backside in a waterfall of grey and yellows.

"You look gorgeous, Ms. Betterman." Corwin blushed at saying something so forward. She hurried to cover her slip with the question she had wanted answered for a long time. "What even is the difference between a wizard and a witch? I know Corwins prefer wizard, but I thought it was kind of a superiority thing they did because the curse made them feel 'less than' in the community. The curse is over. Shouldn't I be called a witch now?"

Marjorie looked taken aback. She patted the tower of curls piled high on her head as if a strand could possibly be out of place and stammered, "Why, didn't your father teach you all of this?"

"I'm sure he meant to, ma'am." Corwin paused, considering.

You're legal now. What'll it hurt to be honest?

Corwin knelt to pet Milo, trying to hide her distress. *Would you tell? My father is still looking for me to torture me. I can't tell yet.*

Milo hopped onto her knees and she lifted him as she stood, rubbing his head with her cheek in sympathy.

"I'm sure he would have taught me a great deal more," she finally admitted. "But he left when I was eight to go find. . . his wife."

Marjorie Betterman's face went blank for a moment. Her aura dimmed as if she were blanching behind her white face paint. She fanned herself with an ostentatious pink ostrich feather fan. "Dear me. If you want to learn glamour Skill, dearie, you come find me. In fact, you should come see me in the back of Witchy Wicks. I'll get you into some proper clothes. I had no idea." This she murmured to herself, tapping her wand against her other hand. "A wizard is a more cerebral type of witch, to simplify things. They live in service to others and go in for psychology as much as magic. Used to be wizards on both sides of your coven. After Jonathan, no Coogan wanted to be called wizard, and in response, all the Corwins started taking the title. Some kind of defense of their worthiness."

Corwin shivered at the word. Milo scoffed in her head.

A pert voice spoke up from the floor. Sarah Ngundo lay sprawled on the floor, looking for all the world like an opium-enthralled goddess in an oil painting. "All those Corwins left Salem and the remaining Corwins kept isolating themselves until the families seemed like two separate covens."

Marjorie hmphed down at her and added, "Now I've heard you talking to my Piggy at his guitar lesson and I'd call you a wizard, and no insult meant."

Corwin turned to Morgan, though she was so beautiful, it was hard to think while looking at her. "We're in the same coven?"

"Yeah. That's one reason we're throwing you this party. We hope you'll rejoin us now that the curse is lifted." She grinned and took the urn from Corwin. "Now, answer Marjorie's questions and we'll find a place for your father."

Marjorie asked Corwin to name a pretty animal: Milo, to pick between seven colorful sketches: the blue-and-purple tree of life, and to describe her favorite body part: "It's ridiculous, but I kind of like how long my neck is."

Marjorie pondered a moment, then looked down at Sarah.

"Oh, I am ready," Sarah responded to the unspoken question. She waved a crystal wand in the air. "I have wanted to get this girl into some decent shoes for years. Let's do this."

Marjorie raised her wand and a parade of glittering mauve bubbles marched through the air to Corwin, encircling her and Milo from head to toe where royal blue streams of magic flowed around her feet from Sarah's wand. The bubbles burst and Corwin felt brightness rain into her from all sides. Milo giggled inside her head.

And then he was giggling beside her.

CHAPTER 44

Corwin had been half-dead when Milo shifted at the Montana Collective. She'd never tell him, but he was a very pretty fifteen-year-old.

I can still read your mind.

Corwin blushed. She didn't turn away. His multi-colored hair was slicked up into a mohawk of twists braided with wampum beads. The freckles across his nose glittered beneath a child's rendering of a dog face that had been painted on his human face. His tuxedo vest was very human and snazzy. The crisp blue shirt underneath fastened with wampum bead buttons and matched the voluminous skirts that hid his human legs.

Milo raised one hand to his neck, where his wampum belt collar had widened and lengthened to surround his neck. He reached to touch Corwin's neck and she tore her eyes from him to look in the mirror. Her long neck was draped with a matching wampum necklace. Her vest, like his when she looked closer, was embroidered with woven leaves and roots in the deepest blue thread.

Her skirt broke in the front, allowing her free range of motion and revealing her long, bare legs covered only by purple tap pants and tall, low-heeled boots embroidered with a White Oak and crystal leaves. She might have sat down right there and examined them if Marjorie and Sarah weren't losing their minds over Milo.

Marjorie stared at her wand in shock. "Ooh, I've never done that before."

"Have we ever had someone hold their familiar through the glamouring?" Sarah sat up and Corwin saw why she was laying on the ground. Her seaweed skirts parted to reveal a mermaid's tail.

"We have." Marjorie reached out to touch Milo's face. "Bry Cohn's rat came through in a marvelous little footman's outfit."

"That's right." Sarah sucked her teeth and examined her nails. "No surprise that Wizard Corwin's familiar is more magical than Witch Cohn's. Oh! Look at the girl's backside!"

Corwin had turned to help Milo remain upright on his new legs. She looked behind her and saw her own backside in the tri-fold mirror. Her long, fluffy dog's tail wagged her joy even while she kept her expression schooled. Tears welled in her eyes.

Ha! Can't hide your feelings now! Milo crowed.

Morgan slipped to Milo's other side and supported him as she pushed him and Corwin away. "Only till midnight, right?"

"The very stroke." Marjorie looked immensely proud of herself. She turned a bitter tone on her next victim. "Kat Coogan. What drags you back to our humble town?"

Kat encouraged the three away, rolling her eyes at Morgan, who laughed and fluttered the butterfly wings sprouting from her shoulder blades. "Marjorie, Sarah, I trust you to dress this prodigal as befits her shame. This is my husband, Clark. Ask him the questions and dress us to match, will you?"

Corwin wrapped an arm around Milo and talked him through the process of walking. He picked it up quickly, but still, they moved slowly through the swirling dancers. Morgan led them to an unpopulated landing at the base of one of the stairwells where she handed the urn back to Corwin.

She asked, "Any ideas where your father would like to spend eternity?"

Corwin spun around, dizzy at the options available on all eight wall/floor/ceilings of the hall. "Where is your dad?"

Her silence drew Corwin around to see a tear rolling down Morgan's cheek. She brushed it away with a laugh. "Thank goodness for magical makeup. Come on, I'll show you."

Corwin placed her father's urn beside Archie Coogan's. It didn't seem enough. Everyone outside had said nice things. Kat had said it was how the Salem witches behaved at funerals. If Corwin really was one of them now, she should think of something to say. But her mind stuck on how he had left her untrained and barely old enough to fend for herself. A loop started running of the many times he'd ordered her to behave like a Corwin or told her she was a disappointment or made it clear that Sita was the only thing that mattered to him.

He must have loved you, Cor, Milo thought. *He killed himself to save you.*

He shouldn't have had to.

Milo mentally shrugged at her. *He didn't have to.*

Corwin looked out over the revelers, at the magical tomb cum ballroom. Candles floated in the air, facing any which way as if gravity were only an option. Colleen Kelley leapt into the air with eagle wings and lifted Levi York with her by holding onto the curling ram horns growing out of his perpetually wild curls. Morgan's mother twirled above them, wearing crystals and gem-eyed snakes in her twists. She danced with Jack Jaga, who wore a traditional long-tailed tux in the parti-color of a jester. His white-blond hair floated from his head as a fluff of actual cotton candy that passing dancers snagged bites from.

If Daniel Corwin hadn't raised her as his daughter, she would never know about all of this. She wouldn't have been able to walk through fire to save a friend. She wouldn't know the evil that wanted to destroy the world, and she definitely wouldn't be in a position to help stop that evil. She turned and laid a hand on the brass urn. "Daniel Corwin, you gave me trees and a home and magic. Thank you. I wish you well." She said it and she meant it. Her heart felt lighter for the words.

The rest of the evening was a blur. Strangers who had scowled at her on the streets scowled a little more lightly beneath the earth. Corwin did her best to be friendly and chatty. Milo helped. He was very good with small talk. He didn't try speaking on his own but fed the words to Corwin. When they found Hardknock hiding in a raised seating area with piles of pillows and blankets, Milo dove into it, dragging everything around until he'd made a nest plush enough for his taste. After that, Corwin had no excuse to not join Morgan in a dance.

Morgan was a good teacher. When Corwin told her she didn't know how to dance, Morgan laughed at her. She taught Corwin the steps of a waltz and soon they were spinning through the other dancers. Then the music changed and Morgan dragged her to a group of kids they knew from school. Not that any of them were kids anymore. Some of them looked at her funny, but Milo cheered her dancing and that made her feel good. The movement shut her brain down in a way she had never experienced before. It was like becoming a part of the music with no responsibility for creating it.

She waltzed with Pops and Clark. Jack Jaga tried to teach her how to jitterbug with less success, but they had a good time anyway. She complimented his improved guitar skills. He assured her not many people in town knew about creatures like Milo and that Kat had asked him to support the idea that Milo's human form was all Marjorie's magic.

"How do you know what he is?" she had asked, shocked and doing an awful job of keeping Milo's secret.

Jack Jaga had spun her to a shadowy corner and twirled her around. When she faced him again, Jack was gone. A familiar, nine-foot-tall bear with puffball ears loomed where he had been. The universe shivered and Jack, in his parti-colored tails, stood before her again.

Until that moment, Corwin had forgotten about the dangers stalking them above in the real world. She made her excuses and worked her way over to Milo, who sat in companionable silence with Hardknock or, judging from the smile on the scarred CF's face, with one of Hardknock's alternative personalities. His bare chest displayed multiple glowing tattoos. As the pillows moved, she could see that his entire body was covered in the tattoos, even the soles of his bare feet.

"Hi." She rested on the edge of a tall chair.

Hi. You're beautiful.

Corwin grinned. It was safe to show Milo her true face. And Hardknock wasn't going to judge her. Plus, her tail thumped against the pillow stack, giving her away. "I won't miss this tail," she complained.

Yes, you will.

"Yes, you will," Hardknock echoed Milo.

"Think we have to wait till midnight to go home?" she asked, lifting her feet to rest the gorgeous boots against the back of a divan. "I'm exhausted."

"The tunnel should be open again now that the curse is broken." Kat peeked around the back of an overlarge loveseat. "I can lead you home, if you like."

Clark added, "I don't mind leaving before this all goes away. I want to remember this night as the wild rumpus it is right now." His face fell after he said this.

Milo rolled over and reached a human hand out to Clark. Laylea's father stretched out his own hand to take it. Milo sent a swirling image of the lights and stairs and fantastical dancers. *I'll remember for you, Clark.*

Clark's pupils blew wide and joy took over his entire aura. "Is that you, Milo?"

Milo nodded his human head and his mental touch. *You miss my sister?*

"Very much. My son, Bailey, too."

Milo released Clark's hand and crawled over the pillows with all the grace of a newborn puppy. *Tell me about them.*

Clark helped him off the seating platform and supported Milo as they followed Kat away from the dancers.

"Lean back," Hardknock called after them. Pillows cascaded around him as he stood. Marjorie had dressed the CF in nothing more than an Egyptian loin cloth and the tattoos that writhed around his thick muscles. "Josh had a shifting teacher. She said to lean back to walk."

Clark and Milo waited for Hardknock to join them.

"Are you going?"

Corwin spun around to see Morgan standing much closer than she had expected. "Yeah. It's been a long, um..." She couldn't think for how tired she was.

"Lifetime?" Morgan asked.

Corwin's tail flipped a yes. She searched for something to say and realized that Morgan was almost eye to eye with her. "I like those shoes."

Morgan's eyes flashed with mischief. "Me, too. I wished to be as tall as you."

"Me?"

"Yeah. You're very tall, you know. It's hard to reach you sometimes."

"That's not because I'm tall." Corwin picked at the fur on the end of her tail.

"Well, yeah, but I can handle that." Morgan brushed the tail and rested her hand on Corwin's.

She slid her other hand along the wampum necklace wrapping Corwin's neck until her fingers touched the bare skin just under her hair. She leaned in, only darting her eyes away when she was so close Corwin could feel her breath. "I hope you stay in Salem."

And then she pulled Corwin the final inch and kissed her. Her lips were warm and soft and made Corwin forget how to breathe.

CHAPTER 45

After an eternity that was far too short, Morgan brushed Corwin's hair and backed away. Her aura locked with Corwin's until she winked and spun away with a flutter of her butterfly wings. On the dance floor, Pops Coogan waited for her with his arms open. She jogged into them and the two swirled into the circling dancers. Pops waved a hand and, in a puff of smoke, he and Morgan were suddenly dancing on the air among the candles and globes and glittering, soaring baby dragons.

Corwin wished Milo could help her remember this moment.

Oh, I don't think you'll need my help.

She looked over her shoulder to see Milo looking back, waiting for her. She jogged over to join them, listening to Clark tell stories about his kids as they left the tomb behind and entered a low-ceilinged tunnel with offshoots leading who-knew-where. Kat led them confidently as she added to Clark's joyful stories about Laylea and Bailey, and how they had discovered Laylea was not just a dog.

Eventually, Kat took them down one last turning to an alcove reached through a wide wooden door. The stone of the walls was carved with runes Corwin didn't recognize. Shelves that looked as though they had been carved from solid tree trunks lined two walls of the room.

They were packed with old books. Thick, leather-wrapped manuscripts that were too tall lay on top of the bookshelves and on the obscenely clean worktable in the center of the room. A set of steep, thin, wooden stairs led up to the ceiling.

Kat sent Corwin up first and followed. The stairs needed some repair, but the few loose boards were easy to avoid as Corwin made her way up. She laid her palm on the stone overhead and it slid aside like a pocket door. The stairwell continued up, though it turned into the old library ladder that had been leaning against the wall in the Corwin House basement for Corwin's whole life. It was right beside the ladder that led up through the secret hatch in the floor of her lab behind the hearth. Corwin crossed through the basement instead and led everyone up the traditional staircase into the front room.

With prompting from Milo, she told Kat, Clark, and Hardknock, "You're welcome to stay. I have plenty of rooms."

Kat and Clark grimaced at each other. "Yeah, we've been staying in the gray room. The house let us in even after Morgan said you'd left, so we took that as an invitation."

"Of course it did. I don't know which one is the gray room." Corwin sat at the spinet, her tail wagging gently along the back of the bench. She ran her fingers through an old tune. "They're pretty much all gray. Sleep well. Hardknock?"

Hardknock sat on the couch. He looked around at the house as though it made him uncomfortable.

Milo tripped over and landed beside Corwin on the wide bench. He poked at the keys in a simple bass line to her tune. *Maybe being human isn't so bad.*

At that moment, the clock in the kitchen chimed.

Kat and Clark stopped at the top of the stairs. Kat did a spin, making her skirt flare into a bell. When she came back around, Clark grabbed her and pulled her into a kiss. Milo took Corwin's hand in his and laid his head on her shoulder as they each kept playing the spinet with their free hands. Hardknock stood and headed for the door. He ran a hand along the devil horns curling in his mass of blond hair.

In the kitchen, the muffled clapper hit the bell twelve times. A bubbling giggle rose through Corwin as she watched reality spin and whirl around the others until they all stood in their drab clothes from the funeral. Playing the spinet became much more difficult as Pundu's mittens reappeared on her hands. A thump drew her attention to her side, where Milo had slipped from the bench.

"Ahwooooooo!"

"Ahwooo, indeed," Kat agreed.

Hardknock pulled a tiny device from his pocket and tossed it to Corwin. She missed the catch and bent over to see Milo sniffing at a disc the size of her thumbnail.

"It does sound and video. Lick it and it'll stick anywhere." Hardknock opened the door. He started out and then growled and turned back. "Thank you for a lovely evening."

He closed the door gently behind himself.

Kat sighed from the top of the stairs. "It's a bug. He and Bayard will have access to its feed. And it's two-way audio, so you can keep in touch with your brother Milo and the rest of us. Put it somewhere safe."

Clark pushed her ahead of him through the doorway into the upper hall. "Good night."

"Sleep well." Kat's voice echoed down as Clark closed the door.

Milo licked the bug and stood up on the edge of the bench, thinking, *Somewhere safe.*

Corwin stood and lifted the padded lid of the bench. She set the mittens on Warren Coogan's music as Milo dropped the bug on a stack of scores. "Safe." She shut the lid.

"You know, I've been wondering, ever since Clark told us about Laylea's letter..."

She left the thought hanging as Milo trotted away, towards the coat rack. She followed him over to the wicker basket holding a blue blanket and a few stuffed toys. Milo dove on his impundulu and danced around with the stuffed animal for a minute before setting it to the side and helping Corwin dig through to the bottom. As they dug, they found the letter Pops Coogan had given her to open when she was ready.

She held the letter and considered so long that Milo asked her, *Are you ready?*

Corwin crawled over to the spinet bench and placed Pops' letter inside. She wasn't. *I'm ready for your letter.*

She crawled back and kept digging. Under the toys, under the blanket, lay a square, blue envelope. It was addressed in messy script to simply, *The Corwins.* Corwin settled against the wall, her legs stretched out in front of her. Milo climbed up and leaned against her belly while she slid a finger along the flap. The paper bit her and the blood was immediately soaked up by the envelope. Milo leaned forward, humming in his mind, and licked the cut. It healed.

Kat taught me a few things.

Useful, Corwin thought back. She unfolded the single sheet of hotel notepaper and held it low so they could both read.

Dear Corwins,

If Daniel Samuel is still around, you may recall a young Chinese exchange student who thought you were the sun and the moon. She didn't keep in touch because her parents forbade it. But she never forgot you. In part because I was born with your wide eyes and giraffe neck. [Ma said this with fondness.] She told me if I were ever in trouble, this house would keep me safe. I am in great trouble. There is an evil man who would do experiments on Milo and his littermates. I have given them all up to homes I pray will protect them. Milo is different. His compassion is limitless and I fear holds some of your family's Skills which would make him more of a target for this man and his bosses. Please take care of him. I have been watching the house and I've only seen one sad little girl coming and going, her eyes on her feet in shoes far too big for her.

I fear you need Milo as much as he needs you. This gives me the strength I need to let him go. This, and knowing that family will always be safe in Corwin House.

With Great Appreciation and Love for the family I've never known.

Rhea, Fan's daughter

Corwin and Milo reread the letter several times. Milo was the first one to find his voice.

We can stay!

"What?"

We belong here and we can stay.

Corwin realized what he was saying. "You can stay. It's your house."

The papers are all in your name. The house likes you.

A trill rang out from the spinet strings.

"But I'm not a Corwin."

I say you are. The house says you are. The coven says you are. He jumped out of her lap and danced around with his impundulu doll in his teeth. *I want to stay and I want to stay with you.*

"I don't know." Corwin loved this house and this town.

Milo dropped the stuffed bird in Corwin's lap and stood up on her chest, knocking the letter out of his way. *Morgan wants you to stay.* He dropped his jaw in a doggy grin and raised one eyebrow in a very human taunt.

Corwin remembered Morgan's warm lips on hers and how she'd ridden her impundulu all the way to Montana to help her and Milo. She smiled.

Milo took it as the yes that it clearly was and rolled onto his back, wriggling with joy. *We'll go find your birth parents and then come back and teach music lessons.*

A loud bang from upstairs drew them both to the stairwell. They were halfway up when Kat and Clark burst through the door, their bags in hand.

"We have to go." Kat continued tapping on her bracelet clasp as she hustled down the steps past them.

Clark went down sideways carrying both bags. Corwin and Milo hurried to get out of his way.

He explained, "Laylea is in trouble and we might have to get her out of Chicago."

"Did Walter find her?" Corwin asked. It was the first thought in Milo's mind, too.

"No," Kat and Clark exclaimed as one.

"No," Clark went on. "She shifted in front of humans again and the Chicago Council has scheduled a hearing to decide if she should be disenhanced."

What does that mean?

"What does that mean?"

Kat answered, "It means they'll make it so she can't ever shift again."

Milo's horror froze Corwin's heart. Her mind raced through possibilities as Kat raced for the door.

"How certain are they?" Corwin asked.

"What?"

"The people who saw her shift. How clearly did they see her?"

Kat stopped with her hand on the doorknob. "I don't know."

"It was at a party," Clark sighed. "A lot of people saw."

"But a party is chaotic," Corwin pointed out, having only just been to her first party. "They might not have seen her clearly. They might have been drunk or stoned or just high from dancing." She hadn't known that was a thing before tonight.

Kat's hand came off the knob. "What are you suggesting?"

OOH! Milo got her drift.

"You both said Milo has her face."

"He's a little smaller," Kat said.

"And fluffier," Clark added, "with more flounces on his ears and paws and tail."

PEOPLE DON'T LOOK AT DOGS!

"People don't really look that closely at dogs. It won't matter." Corwin looked down at Milo. *You want to go to Chicago?*

His tail started wagging before his thought reached her. *But what about your family?*

Corwin knelt. Milo padded over to her and put one paw on her knee. She thought, *We can find my birth parents anytime. Your sister is in trouble. Your mama said I needed you and she was right. Now, your sister needs us.*

But you've been looking for your family for so long.

Yeah, she thought. *Silly me. You were right here all along.*

THE END

AFTERWORD

Thank you for reading my book. I hope you enjoyed it. If you had a good time with this story please take a moment and leave a review on Amazon. I'd love to hear what you think and it helps me figure out what you want to read next.

Sign up at Wyrdos.net to be the first to know all the latest on my books and audiobooks. I promise I won't inundate you with mail and I will not share your email with anyone. Just ask my sisters. I don't share.

You can also connect with me on Facebook, and on Twitter I'm @gwendolyndruyor.

SHIFTER SCHOOL

BY GWENDOLYN DRUYOR

CHAPTER 1

Normal fourteen-year-olds don't wake up thinking about death. But Laylea wasn't anything close to normal. She woke up composing a letter to her adopted parents telling them all the things she'd never get the chance to say in person. Sometimes she thought of writing a letter to her brother, Bailey. Some mornings she imagined leaving a letter for her birth mother too, in case they ever found her. Laylea had been composing the morning letters ever since she'd gone to a veterinarian's office on a case last summer. Waiting in the lobby for the tech she was following, she'd read every pamphlet the clinic had. Including one that said the average lifespan for a twelve-pound terrier was thirteen to fifteen years.

She'd been fourteen for eight weeks now.

"Lee!" Bailey's voice sliced through her morbid thoughts.

They lived in a basement studio apartment. He didn't need to yell.

Laylea whined back at him and stretched all four paws against the bedsheets. She rolled to her side and tucked her nose under her tail. She loved her tail. She'd probably spend more time in her human shape if she could keep her tail. Not that she really had a choice in the matter, as Bailey constantly reminded her.

"Laylea Hillen." Bailey could sound an awful lot like their mother when he wanted to.

Laylea missed Sher and all her rules. She missed Clark even more, if she were honest. After three years apart, the aching loss had dulled a bit, but now, with fifteen looming on the horizon, Laylea found herself getting a little desperate to see her parents again before she died.

An uncommon scent drifted over the bed. Her tail, with no permission, popped out and thumped against the mattress. Laylea poked just the tip of her pale muzzle between folds of the tangled sheets and sniffed the air. The familiar, soapy musk of her brother and the tang of his computers were muted by the joyful smell of a peanut butter oatmeal tuna muffin. Laylea barked. She wriggled out of the sheets, stupid tail throwing her balance all over the place.

She was thrown even more off balance by Bailey's shout. "Lee Woodford! The solar panels are blocked and Madame Hu's grow lamps are dimming."

She stared at him for another moment. He'd used her alias. Though unusual, that wasn't so terribly surprising. After three years in hiding, she was used to answering to the name, just not used to him using it. But she stared at him because he looked like his natural self. His hair lay in black curls over his light-brown face.

When they ran to Chicago, Laylea and Bailey needed to hide as best they could from the Consortium. It was easy for Laylea to live under the radar. But Bailey had been accepted to DePaul as Bailey Hillen. There were public records pointing straight to him. He couldn't change his name. So he changed his face.

He changed his entire appearance, actually, to look like Laylea's blood-brother. It was the only magic he did these days, and since he never changed back, Laylea had almost forgotten how different he really looked. Where she was tiny as a human, he was big. He had wide shoulders, a preternaturally muscled torso, and perfectly monstrous thighs. Where she was pale as a Swedish shut-in, he could have won a tanning contest in Belize.

He leaned out of their galley kitchen, holding onto the post with one thick forearm, blue eyes sparking and sharp features setting off the cleft chin, which was one of the few innocuous genetic traits he'd inherited from Clark. One hand held the walkie-talkie their landlady had given them when she offered to lower their rent in exchange for handyman help. His other large hand held a plate with her adoptionversary muffin.

He lifted the muffin to his lips. "If you don't get out of bed and up to the roof, I'm going to eat your breakfast."

Laylea wriggled out of the sheets and leaped to the cushioned barstool Bailey used as a bedside table. She used the back of the stool to help her spring up to the empty shelf on the brick and 2x4 bookshelf they used as a headboard. The window was open a crack, which made it easy for Laylea to push it with her head and paws until it was wide enough for her to squeeze out into the little wooden crawlspace under the front porch.

"Don't forget your—" Bailey's admonition was lost as the dust under the porch tickled Laylea's nose.

She gave one sharp sneeze, blowing the dirt around and dusting the stash of emergency sundresses she kept piled in the corner. She never wore them for long anyway. She took a peek through the latticework to check for witnesses before pushing through the loose slat on one side of the crawlspace and out to the front steps.

Laylea shook the last of her sleepiness away and took a breath of the crisp air. The low sun was awfully bright for May in Chicago but clouds warned of rain later. She hopped up the stairs and ran out to relieve herself by her favorite tree on the devil strip. Out of habit she grabbed a quick sniff at the base of the tree for any new dogs in the neighborhood. Smelled like Nemo was still on prednisone, poor Shepherd.

Laylea pushed her dog instincts to the side and head-butted her way through the rarely latched gate to their side alley. Near the back of the house, she trotted up the ramp on an old shoe-shine stand Madame Hu used as a table for the food she put out for area strays. Lee jumped from the base up to the faded and torn bench seat and from there to the fence between Madame Hu's backyard and the apartment building next door. She tight-rope walked along the fence for three feet before she could leap up to the back porch of the second-floor west apartment. A nice lady named Sue lived there.

Laylea took the rickety wooden porch steps up to the third floor.

This was the tricky maneuver. She backed up the entire length of the porch the top two units shared and raced like an airplane down a runway. She leaped to the railing at the last second and vaulted into the sky, aiming for the slightly higher rooftop of Madame Hu's house.

Halfway through her death-defying leap, Laylea remembered to retract her claws. This distracted her just enough that she twisted as she landed on the slick, tilted solar panels. Her little body slammed sideways into the smart-glass surface and she tumbled down, hurtling toward a thirty-foot drop.

Even as her heart clawed its way up to choke her, Laylea diagnosed the problem with Madame Hu's power. The neighbors had erected a projection screen on their roof that was blocking two-thirds of the solar panels.

The edge of the solar panels slid past and Laylea tensed. She prepped her dad-like reflexes. By the time she hit the wide gutter surrounding the roof, instead of bouncing off and falling thirty feet to her demise, she was ready to launch herself back over the divide to the apartment roof. Her normally sharp internal sensors were kind of dizzy by the time her paws hit the gravelly tar paper of the apartment building's unfinished roof deck. If she fought her momentum, she might just tumble backwards off the roof, so she just tried to keep on her feet as she barreled forward on all fours.

The makeshift movie screen was just a white sheet hung from a hastily-erected PVC frame, and Laylea's trajectory sent her smack into the base. The entire structure collapsed.

When the tumbling and crashing quieted and the sheet finished billowing down over her, Laylea gave herself a moment to breathe.

Bailey could have gotten to the rooftop, too. And he could have opened doors and climbed the inside stairs to get there safely. Why had he sent her instead? Was there some reason he needed to get her out of the apartment on this very special day? Were Clark and Sher hiding around the corner just waiting for her to leave so they could sneak in?

No. They could have snuck in while she was sleeping and woken her up with Bailey like they did back home.

Was he kicking her out like he'd threatened to if she couldn't control her shifting between human and dog? She really was trying. She just didn't have anyone to help her. The only other shapeshifter she knew was Captain Morioka, and the dragon-lady's advice hadn't been particularly helpful since she'd learned how to shapeshift literally eons ago. Laylea might as well ask her to explain how she blinked.

Laylea tried to not blink, but the white sheet didn't really block much sun, so she gave up.

Sher said that certain people, most people, were wired to respond. If you said blink, they would blink. It was a basic principle of operant conditioning. Maybe she could condition herself; think *shift* or ring a bell like Pavlov every time she changed shape.

She felt a pressure deep in her mouth, right back where it turned into throat. The birth of a yawn. As soon as she thought the word, the pressure rolled forward, up through her face bones and down along her lower jaw. The pressure rolled her long, pink tongue right out of her mouth and squeezed a squeak from her. Yawns happened naturally. But she could also make herself yawn. Just thinking the word again did it. She yawned.

Maybe shifting was like that.

She tried to feel the tingling burn that started in her stomach when she shifted naturally. But all she dredged up was a gurgle of hunger and a memory of the delicious muffin waiting for her downstairs.

Today was her adoptionversary!

She scrabbled her way out of the sheet and scattered frame. Right on time, someone on the third-floor porch pulled down the hatch with hidden stairs. Laylea scampered over behind the trash-barrel keg on the far side of the roof. Anyone coming up would be drawn to the disaster that used to be a cool private movie theater. They'd be looking away from the keg.

"Is someone up here?" The guy's eyes were so quickly drawn to the mess that he almost fell up the last couple of steps. "What the hell?"

Laylea didn't wait. She raced out from behind the barrel and glided as silently as she could down the skinny steps. Once on the porch, she gave up all caution and galloped to the ground level. Jumping the fence would be faster, but she was done with fantastic leaps for a few hours at least. She scrambled through the neighbors' out-of-control azalea bush and wiggled through the tunnel she'd dug under the fence a year ago. It came up behind Madame Hu's tomato plot. She ran back along the alley and then down the stairs, into the crawlspace, and smack into a closed window.

CHAPTER 2

Laylea fell back into the dirt under the porch. Bailey had closed the window. She stuck her nose beside the frame and pushed. It didn't budge. She tried to use her paws and had no better luck. He'd locked the window, too.

She pawed at the glass and whimpered. She could see her brother, sitting at his desk, facing the three giant ultra-private monitors attached to his computer. She couldn't tell if he was working on some class report or his own personal research. But what did it matter? She'd been gone ten minutes and he'd locked the window and gone back to work.

Maybe he really was kicking her out. Maybe he'd finally decided her shifting issues were too likely to get them discovered. But she really was trying. She bit back another whimper.

Bailey never did anything but study. Every day he drowned himself a little more in learning everything his teachers and the vast interwebs could teach him about biology. He never spent time any more practicing magic. He knew how hard it was to get magic right and how much he'd learned during those few years when the mom was giving him lessons. So why was he so hard on Laylea for not figuring out her own magic when she'd never had anyone but a Pre-Cambrian Era dragon-demon to teach her? He had to see what a double standard that was.

Plus, if he kicked her out, Sher and Clark would kill him. Wouldn't they?

Laylea spotted her peanut butter oatmeal tuna muffin sitting on the desk beside him. He hadn't eaten it. Why would he have even made it if he was kicking her out?

She barked.

Bailey swept his screens blank as he spun around. He pointed at the door and raised his eyebrows. She raised her eyebrows and lifted one thumb-less paw. He held up the muffin. She showed her teeth.

Was he trying to force her to shift? A shift-or-you-don't-get-the-muffin kind of thing?

Laylea tried again to think of the burning spark in her belly. Then she realized she was in a three-foot-tall crawlspace with a half-foot-wide exit and stopped.

Inside, Bailey was holding something up in his other hand. She pressed her nose against the glass to see better.

It was a standard brass door key with a green sleeve over the head: her house key. Even if she could shift, she still couldn't get inside.

Don't forget your key.

That's what he'd said. That's what he said pretty much every time she left the apartment. Like he never forgot his key when he was a kid. Even if she did forget to take her key now and then, their landlady, Madame Hu, always buzzed her in. Madame Hu would invite her upstairs for tea or her grand-niece would run down to sit on the porch and pet Laylea's belly for hours. That kind of reinforcement didn't really help her remember her key. One time, when she'd *had* her key, she'd scratched at the door anyway just for the belly rubs.

Laylea backed away from the window and slipped out to their door under the stairs. She made one more half-hearted attempt to shift before she started straight-up howling. She heard Bailey's chair smash into the desk inside. Bailey tripped once getting to the door and nearly ripped it off its hinges when he got there.

Laylea quietly trotted past him and hopped right back into bed.

"You have to remember your key. You can't count on Madame Hu or Fan to buzz you in. We need to be more invisible." Bailey paused for a breath. "Do you get it? Do you know what the Consortium would do to you if they found you? If they found me?"

Laylea dropped her head. She pasted her ears back against her head and sunk so far into herself that she felt like she was being swallowed up in the comforter. Today was her adoptionversary, her special day. It was the day her bio-mom saved her life by finding her the best dad and mom and big brothers in the whole world. Fourteen years ago today, six-year-old Bailey had found her on the front porch; a tiny fawn-colored puppy with a white triangle over her eyes, tucked in an old Easter basket.

Today was supposed to be the best day of the whole year.

"Happy Adoptionversary, Lee." Bailey said it with a sigh in his voice. He didn't mean it. She wasn't his beloved puppy or sister anymore. She was just a burden.

He sat on the edge of the bed. "It's just that they're counting on me, you know? To keep you safe."

Laylea looked up. He took the muffin off the plate and held it out. As he reached toward her, the hair on his hand turned blue. He made the blue wash up his arm to his elbow.

Laylea dropped her jaw in a grin. He was doing magic. She barked through a mouthful of muffin and her brother smiled.

He scratched her ears for a bit as she ate. Then his mind went back to his own day. "I've got a meeting with Dr. Palmer after class, so I don't think I'm gonna make it to your barbecue at The Office."

She pouted up at him.

He wiped a chunk of tuna off her nose. "Oh, you won't miss me. Every time I meet you at The Office, you and your Team Wyrdos run off to save the world or rescue a nest of fledgling imps or something."

Laylea stopped licking her paws to stare at him like he was crazy.

He glared back. "Every time."

He stood and Laylea leapt up to lick the last bits of muffin from his blue hand. He took the plate to the kitchen while she stuck her butt up in the air in her first good, long, morning Downward Dog.

Laylea spun around at a sudden clank from the ancient claw-foot radiator. She felt that spark in her belly that she'd been trying to ignite. If she could tamp it down and stop the change, that would be something. But she couldn't. She barely had time to think the thought before the spark blazed up into her chest and filled her whole body with electric pain. She shifted. In a flash she went from cuddly fuzzbucket stretching on the side of the bed to awkward, stick-shaped girl losing a wrestling match with the sheets. Laylea yelped as she tumbled off the bed. She landed on her left hip and yelled, her human vocal chords unable to imitate the canine cry she heard in her head.

Bailey swept all the dishes into the sink with a clatter. His sigh could have been heard in outer space. "You're hopeless, Laylea."

Even though she agreed, she coughed out an objection. "Be nice. It's my adoptionversary."

Talking was always difficult right after she shifted. Her stubby tongue felt awkward and fat. She loved the thumbs that came with being human. But speech was overrated.

"Hey!" Laylea hustled to grab her short green robe from its hook over the bed. She had a whole list of things she needed to do while she had thumbs, and she couldn't be sure how long she'd have them. First on the list, a request Bailey was guaranteed to deny. "Could you make my hair purple? As my gift. I saw a girl at the library with purple streaks and she looked so cool."

Bailey did not deny the request. He ignored it. From the doorway to the bathroom he asked, "Your hip okay?"

It was nice to hear his concern. Most of the time he was too preoccupied with his studies to worry about his little sister.

"Yeah. It never bothers me as a human." She grabbed her water bowl from its spot on the floor by the radiator and hustled over to the kitchen to rinse it and refill it with cool water. "Not since Mom woogied it."

Bailey had invented the word *woogie* to describe magic. The bathroom door clicked shut. Apparently he was done talking about it for the day. Laylea sighed. She worried about him. Sher had said if he didn't practice, he'd be dangerous. Bailey was her son so he got half his genetic makeup from her crazy-powerful witch family. But he was also Clark's son, and Sher had genetically modified Clark for the Consortium. Sure, they knew Bailey was strong. He had heightened hearing and pattern recognition skills rivaling a computer's. But what else had he inherited from Clark? And how was that affected by his magical side? They had no answers and the mom and dad had only just begun testing him when the Consortium found the family and they all had to run.

Laylea took a deep breath and tilted the bowl up for a drink as she crossed back to replace it on the floor.

She'd covered their cement floor with layers of rugs other, more discerning, Chicagoans had thrown out. One of the more recent acquisitions still smelled a little like the explosion that had left its former owner not needing rugs anymore. She couldn't even cajole Bailey into woogiing the gas smell away, as easy as that would be.

She knee-walked her way over the rugs to one of the six packed bookshelves that insulated their walls. Her hardcover copy of *The Call of the Wild* was tucked in behind a row of must-reads Bailey would never voluntarily pick up. Plus, it was on the bottom shelf, which was, historically, her domain. Listening to the shower start up, Laylea opened Jack London's illustrated classic to reveal a hollow center filled with cash.

Laylea didn't exist as far as the United States government was concerned. This meant she couldn't open a bank account. The whole hiding-from-a-team-of-evil-scientists also precluded leaving a money trail. But since she couldn't go to school, Laylea worked.

Laylea solved problems. Mostly she hired herself out as a Private Investigator specializing in Paranormal Mysteries. She couldn't call herself that, though, for two reasons. First, her cop friends wouldn't let her call herself a PI because she wasn't licensed. Detective Kyle Nellwin had said she could call herself a PUPPI, a Preternatural Underage Person Pursuing Information. Though, mostly she didn't, since her clients wouldn't get the joke. Second, most of her clients didn't realize their mysteries were paranormal. Most of her clients were thumpers, natural humans, and most thumpers had no clue about the supernatural world all around them. Laylea had only ever known of one thumper in the know, and Kyle wasn't a thumper anymore. All her friends knew he was dead, but that wasn't the whole truth.

When Laylea did spend money, it was usually on clothing. She wasn't a fashionista or anything, she just lost a lot of clothes. She only wished there were more size one homeless girls in Chicago to benefit. Well, she didn't really wish there were more homeless at all. But she did keep caches of clothing all over the north side for shifting emergencies.

Their friend Amal's grandson ran a clothing warehouse and provided her with size one sweats, t-shirts, and sundresses in bulk.

Amal and his brownie friends Orin and Lucio had worked with a Renn Faire artisan to create a wide fabric collar for Laylea. The yellow polka dotted collar featured several zippered pockets and elastic all around so it would fit both her dog and human neck. The tag read *Lee* since that was the name the boys knew her by. It was Laylea's most prized possession. The only other thing she'd ever really owned was the stuffed lizard Sher had made for her out of a patchwork of fabrics. Laylea'd had to leave the lizard behind when they ran away. She still missed it on sad nights.

She unzipped one of the pockets on her collar and wrestled out a folded wad of bills. She smoothed them on one knee and added the cash to the hidden stash in her book. Laylea didn't hold on to much money herself. She mostly ate kibble since she couldn't count on turning human at meal times, and Amal got her a killer discount on the bulk clothing orders. She didn't have an El pass since there was nowhere to hide on a public train or bus and lots of loud, surprising noises that might make her shift. She couldn't fit a cell phone in her collar and couldn't risk carrying around a GPS tracker anyway. So her costs were pretty minimal.

But there was the rent. Bailey's full-ride scholarship had included room and board, but they'd had to find a new place to live after Bailey had been kicked out of the dorms for hiding a pet.

Clark and Sher sent cash when they could, but they'd not sent any money or letters in months. And as sparsely as the Hillen kids lived, Laylea worried that Bailey wouldn't be able to survive on his own after she died. So she hid most of what she earned in Jack London's masterpiece. She'd have to mention it in her letter to Bailey, when she finally got around to writing it.

The back door slammed outside. Laylea pulled a few bills out of the book and then slipped it back onto the shelf behind the novels their parents sent for them to use as ciphers. Laylea had read all of them. Bailey never read anything but textbooks and scientific journals.

Laylea headed over to the desk and reached up to twitch aside the heavy brocade curtain on the window. Madame Hu was rolling a wheelbarrow along the path between patches of her vegetable garden. Madame Hu's garden was her pride and joy. She spent hours working over it in all weather. She even had a small herb garden inside her apartment for deep winter, and she loaded Laylea down with herbs each time she succumbed to the old woman's entreaties to join her for tea.

Madame Hu was a dream landlady. She'd bought the converted three-flat just days after Bailey and Laylea had applied for the apartment. She lived on the top floor with her grand-niece, Fan, who always carried liver treats in her pocket.

Laylea took Bailey's wallet from his backpack and slipped the bills inside. Then she grabbed the envelope sitting in the empty ashtray designated to hold *her* things and hollered to Bailey, "I'm running out to pay the rent. Think about the purple. I'd look so cute!"

The door was already closing behind her when she realized what Bailey had yelled back, "Don't forget your house key!"

She spun, but the door latched behind her.

"Shit."

To be continued . . .

I HOPE you enjoyed this little teaser for *Shifter School*. You can pick up the full story on Amazon HERE.

ALSO BY GWENDOLYN DRUYOR

Wyrdos urban fantasy series

WereHuman 1: The Witch's Daughter

WereHuman 2: The Warrior's Son

WereHuman 3: The Hunter's Heir

WereHuman 4: The Wizard's Mutt

Voices of Reason(AVAILABLE FREE TO NEWSLETTER SUBSCRIBERS)

Shifter School

Shifter Ghost

Shifter Witch

Dee

Laylea

Junior

Doug vs. The Boogeyman(AVAILABLE EXCLUSIVELY TO NEWSLETTER SUBSCRIBERS)

Mobious' Quest fantasy series

Geoffrey's Queen

Hardt's Tale

Callie's Crown (COMING SOON)

Killer on Call thriller series

Ecstasy

Gin

Morphine

Valium

Pot

Absinthe

Justice (AVAILABLE EXCLUSIVELY TO NEWSLETTER SUBSCRIBERS)

First Edition, October 2022
Library of Congress Control Number: 2022907629
ISBN 978-1-948421-21-8(ebook)| ISBN 978-1-948421-24-9(print) | ISBN 978-1-948421-22-5(audiobook)

Cover design by Logan Prather
Editing by Leslie Schipa
Proofreading by Shenoa Carroll-Bradd

Published in the United States of America.

Wyrdos.net

www.ingramcontent.com/pod-product-compliance
Lightning Source LLC
Chambersburg PA
CBHW071048250626
47159CB00002B/401